I0732744

An Armenian Affair

A Novel

By

James Christian

WORKBOOK PRESS LLC
187 E Warm Springs Rd,
Suite B285, Las Vegas, NV 89119, USA

Website:	https://workbookpress.com/
Hotline:	1-888-818-4856
Email:	admin@workbookpress.com

Ordering Information:
Quantity sales. Special discounts are available on quantity purchases by corporations, associations, and others. For details, contact the publisher at the address above.

ISBN-13:	978-1-952754-43-2 (Paperback Version)
	978-1-952754-44-9 (Digital Version)

REV. DATE: (03/09/2020)

To the lady of my life for more than half a century;
together we've traveled the deep valleys,
the high mountains and
everything in between.

TABLE OF CONTENTS

CHAPTER ONE

Granite Shoals, Texas, 1995

When Oma's call came, he'd been sitting on the porch of the lake house, his boots propped on the railing, drinking Shiner beer and watching a bass boat bobbing around the opposite shore. The phone's ring shattered the serenity of the afternoon and set the train of his thoughts down a dark track. His father had been in a car accident in London and he'd been badly hurt--concussion, a collapsed lung and some broken bones.

His father was no role model unless it were the model of somebody he didn't want to be. Always walking the tight wire toward some get-rich scheme, full of lies and grand ambitions that never came true. He was   seldom home for the large moments of Tom's life--birthdays, confirmation, football games, graduations. Their relationship was one of broken promises and absences. His father's character flaws made a single parent of his mom. Yet there remained, even now, some longing, some wished-for attachment. For his mother's sake, he'd tried to find it. He spent a year with his father in Europe trying to get to know him, to find his redeeming features. That was how Tom had come to know Andre Petrossian and how he almost got himself killed.

After Europe, Tom called his effort to find a relationship with his father a failure and tried to put him out of his life. What did he owe his father, after all? As for Oma, he owed her a great deal and since she asked him, he would see about his father in London.

Later that day, Mariah Carroll called.

"Been a long time," she said.

"Couple of years. Are you calling from Indonesia? The connection
is really good."

"No. I finished my contract out there two months ago. I bought into Peter Karekin's firm. Do you know him?"

"Not personally. Just by reputation as somebody with heavy-duty connections. Congratulations."

"Thanks, but listen," she said. "Guess whose name came up on a special, high-priority deal? Yours. We need you to go to Armenia to clean up a proposal for a big World Bank loan. AID will get the technical assistance on the program and Peter and I want to be in on the ground floor on that. I need you out there pretty much right away."

Tom laughed. "I'm not in the game just now, Mariah. All I do is play golf and fish, ride a little, drink single-malt Scotch and the best wine I can find and eat my grandma's cooking whenever she'll have me. Life is good. Sorry about the job, but I'm just not interested."

"I don't think you understand, Tom. The Armenian government asked for you by name. You know how rare that is."

"I'll put it in my memoirs. Look, Mariah, it's wonderful to hear from you, but I'm just not working these days. Now tell me how you're doing. Did the Indons treat you right?"

"We can talk about that when I get down there. I'm coming to get you."

"Well, I'd love to see you--really. But as for the job, what part of 'no' don't you understand?"

"I'm told there's an airstrip at Granite Shoals.I'll be there tomorrow afternoon."

She disconnected and Tom took a long pull on the bottle of Shiner. Mariah. Smart, sexy Mariah. Special memories he wasn't entirely sure he was ready to revisit. Anyway, he'd grill a rib-eye for her, bake a potato. Open a bottle of good St. Emilion. Ought to have a salad, but he didn't have any fresh greens. He'd have to run into Marble Falls to the grocery store.

* * * * * * * * * * *

He'd been basking in the midday sun beside the packed clay runway for half an hour when he heard the distinctive harmony of a twin engine aircraft descending on final approach. He scanned the treetops to the west, spotted it bearing down the lake and watched it bank gently on the port wing to line up with the runway, props flashing in the sunlight. He couldn't see her yet, but he imagined Mariah behind the controls and, the job in Armenia notwithstanding, he was excited by the prospect of seeing her again.

She chopped the throttles the moment the Piper Seneca crossed the threshold and an instant later puffs of dust from the landing gear marked the plane's return to earth. With brakes smoking as she screamed toward the end of the short runway, he held his breath to make sure she was under control. Throttles back, the plane stopped its forward momentum, came about and taxied toward a parking spot on the grass near where he waited. He strained to see her face, but all he could make out was a figure in the left seat. She parked the plane tail to the road and cut the engines, the props whirring in dying circles, finally fluttering to rest. He could see her arms and head moving in the shadow of the cockpit and imagined she was flipping switches, going through her check list. At last, the cockpit door opened, she emerged, tiptoed down the wing root and dropped to the ground. A baseball cap and aviator sunglasses disguised her face, but the blue coveralls were cut for a man and it was impossible not to see the way her hips and breasts stretched the material. She pocketed the sunglasses, stripped off the baseball cap and shook out her hair--still cut short with sun-streaked shades of amber.

She stood beside the plane waiting while he came toward her, arms outstretched for a hug. "Tommy," she said, her voice the throaty contralto he now remembered so fondly.

"You're looking good enough," he replied, reaching out and pulling her to him. He gave her an abrazo, welcoming the feel of her body heat through the flight suit.

She leaned back in his arms and smiled up at him. "You're hard to find, compañero."

He let her slip out of his grasp and pointed his chin toward the Seneca. "Plane buttoned up? Can we go?"

"I need to check in," she said, looking carefully at his face. His dark brown hair was shot through with gray and the scars of time and care that people call 'character lines' were deeper. To her eye, he'd dropped twenty pounds and looked lean and fit. She guessed it was the Texas sun that had scrubbed him clean and given him that leathery, cowboy look. With a hat and a horse he could have been the Marlboro Man.

"Over there, then. A friend of mine owns the place," he said, pointing to the one and only hanger across the runway.

He looked down at her, a head shorter, appreciating the soft, angular lines of her face and her impertinent nose. She looked fresh and scarcely changed from the last time he'd seen her in Tunisia. "Do you ride?" he asked, grinning like a kid with a new pony.

She raised her eyebrows. "As in horses? You have horses?"

"No. Too much bother. I rent from a local stables. I'll show you around tomorrow. Take you over to Saddleback Mountain. Put you up close and personal with the Hill Country."

"Wouldn't I love to," she said. "But we have to be out of here tomorrow."

He drew his mouth into a scowl. "You know you're wasting your time with me. Might as well forget about it and enjoy a few days of Texas sunshine."

"Can't do it, Tom. We need this job and we need you to do it." Two furrows creased Tom's brow as he registered the determination in her voice, her tight-lipped intensity and the use of the plural pronoun, 'we.' Being a principal in Karekin's firm now, she had a stake in the bottom line and, as a newbie in the firm, he guessed she had a compelling felt-need to prove she could contribute.

A middle-aged man in well-worn boots, faded Levis and a checked shirt came out of the shadows of the hanger, wiping his hands on a red rag.

"Hey, George," Tom called to him. "Want you to meet a friend of mine. This is Mariah Carroll. Mariah, George Smalley."

George nodded to her and said, "Saw you come in. Nice touch. A little tight here for a Seneca. We only have two-thousand feet of runway."

"Tell me about it," Mariah said with a grin. "But I grew up with tight spaces. My daddy was a crop duster."

"He teach you to fly?" George asked.

"I was sitting on his lap in a Piper Pawnee when I was five." She looked back at the plane. "OK to leave her there?"

"No problem. How long you staying?"

"Just overnight. I'll be out of your way before noon tomorrow," she said with a quick look at Tom.

"No hurry," George said. He swung his arm around the little

facility and added, "We ain't exactly crowded this time of year."

"Thanks. Can you top off the tanks? I'll pay you when I leave tomorrow if that's OK."

George nodded. "I'll tie her down. Y'all just go on."

"Great. Thanks again," she said and turned to Tom. "My bag's in the plane. Where's your car?"

"Over there," he replied, pointing toward a dark green Ford Explorer parked on the shoulder of the road. "The house isn't far."

Mariah trotted off across the runway toward the Seneca, the midday sunlight glinting in her hair. The two men stood shoulder to shoulder and watched her go, admiring her lines the way a horse breeder appraises a promising filly at morning exercise. When she disappeared inside the plane, Tom winked at George, tossed him a two-fingered salute and headed for the Explorer. Mariah threw her briefcase and small nylon duffel into the back seat and climbed in front beside Tom. In two minutes, they were pulling into the driveway of the lake house. She bounded down from the Explorer, taking in the rustic limestone house and what could be seen of the cove, its waters lapping gently at the dock and the retaining wall. Tom retrieved her bag and briefcase and followed her around the gravel pathway beside the house.

Standing on the deck beneath two giant cypress trees, squinting at the sun's twinkling reflections on the water, she whispered, "So this is where you've disappeared to."

"Come on," he said. "I'll show you the rest of it."

He took her up a wide flight of stairs onto a deep verandah that spanned the width of the upper story and wrapped around the sides. From there, she could see the expanse of the cove and the lake beyond its mouth. Entering the house scarcely changed the feeling of openness, because three walls of glass surrounded the beamed-ceiling, lodge-like room which combined a sitting area with a large stone fireplace, a modern kitchen and a small dining area.

"This is pretty much it," he said, standing in the center of the big room. "My office is on the ground floor. The bath and bedrooms are back there." He pointed down a short hall. "Bathroom's on the left. You can throw your stuff in the guest room on the other side."

While Mariah settled in, Tom made ham and cheese

sandwiches, put them on a tray with a pair of Shiner Black Lagers, olives, pickle slices and potato chips and brought them to a glass-topped octagonal table in the sitting area. Under the glass, lying on dark green baize, the copper, bronze and silver of an extensive coin collection gleamed like a pasha's treasure trove.

"That looks serious," Mariah exclaimed, staring at the collection.

"Mostly stuff from places I've been. Just sentimental value. I lucked into a few good pieces. I keep them at the bank," he said, sinking into the leather couch. He pointed to the tray of sandwiches. "Dig in. You look hungry." He'd always admired her appetite and, watching her attack the sandwich, he thought back on what he knew of her from their candid conversations over the years of their acquaintance.

He saw a five-year old tomboy being brought up in a double-wide without a mother. Crop dusting paid well enough in season, but her father wasn't that enterprising and there were more lean months than fat ones. In the end, the only thing her father had willed her was an exceptional ability to fly an airplane and an inquisitive and capable mind. It wasn't a whole lot to go on.

They'd been attracted to each other long before Seline left him and in that miserable twilight of hurt and confusion, he'd let Mariah into the aching, vacant space Seline had left. They both knew that his pain over losing Seline was no basis for a long-term commitment, so Mariah took herself to the other side of the world with a two-year assignment in Indonesia. Tom retreated to his grandmother's bosom and the lake house. Now their lives had intersected again. Seeing Mariah again brought back the barbed wire fences he'd put up to keep away serious relationships with women. Seline had inflicted on him the feeling that they weren't loyal or trustworthy. The lake had helped him push that away and he felt almost whole again.

After only two months, she couldn't have made her bones with Peter Karekin's outfit but she was "all in" with her savings from the Indonesia job. Pulling off the Armenia assignment would establish her as a player. Did he owe her that? Was any of it his responsibility?

If he turned her down on this Armenia thing, he'd probably never see her again. What difference would it make if he took it? It was just another job. If he hated it, he could always come back to the lake house and do what he'd been doing for months--playing golf, fishing, watching the sun set, drinking Scotch in front of the fire in the winter. What did he have to lose? Impulsively, he made a quick decision.

"Let's get this Armenia thing out of the way so we can enjoy the rest of the day," he said, grinning.

She took another bite of her sandwich and chewed appreciatively, eyes wide, surprised he had given in without a fight. She swallowed, took a big sip of Shiner Black.

"You'll go?"

"Maybe. But on my terms," he said.

"Armenia needs you for three weeks and right away."

"Can't do it right away. I have to stop in London and see my father. He's in the hospital."

"Oh. I'm so sorry. Serious?"

"Oma--my grandmother--says it was a hit-and-run and that he's pretty busted up. I'll know when I get there."

"How long will you need?"

"A day, two at the outside. It's all up to the docs anyway. Nothing I can do. But let's not change the subject. Armenia's the old Soviet Union, isn't it?"

She nodded, watching him closely to read his reaction.

"On top of an economic collapse, they had a major earthquake just before the breakup of the Soviet Union and the Turks and the Georgians have blockaded them because of their little war with Azerbaijan over a province both Armenia and Azerbaijan claim. It's a little war, but a big problem. The World Bank is offering a loan, but they want reforms--as they always do--and the Armenians are having trouble complying. The AID Mission has agreed to give them some help moving the loan request along. There's a deadline for resubmission. A really tight one. Like four weeks from now." Mariah paused, catching her breath before she continued. "As I told you, the Armenians asked specifically for you--Tom Yeager. Somebody from the Armenian Embassy's even standing by to meet you at Washington Dulles to give you a visa. When's the last time you got that kind of treatment? And if you should turn them down . . . well the loan just might crash and burn. There would at least be a long delay getting it back into the queue."

Mariah leaned forward, gripped her hands in front of her and tried not show white knuckles, her eyes fixed on him, watching him digest what she'd just told him.

"Why didn't AID just call me?"

"You wouldn't have come for a phone call, would you? Art Lewis knows you and I have--or had--a relationship and you've turned down the last three or four assignments . . ."

"My wife left me," Tom protested, bristling. "And AID doesn't own me. I don't have to work for them, now or ever."

Mariah held up her hands. "I'm sure that's not it, Tom. It's just that they want you to do this job because the Armenians want you. The State Department wants an ally in the region--Azerbaijan and Georgia are still close to Russia. Turkey's always problematic and we have all these Armenians in the US. . . . Anyway, I guess they thought I'd be better at persuading you than some AID weenie calling you from Washington. I wasn't going to say 'no' when they asked Karekin to send me down."

"Well, that's fair enough," he said, not yet able to grin though he wanted to, so he grunted and shook his head. "Doctoring up loan requests isn't my special thing."

Mariah raised her eyebrows. "And that's a mystery, isn't it? Sure you don't know the answer?"

He got off the couch and walked to the window. "One of my last jobs was a macro survey of Jordan and I worked with a guy out there named Raz Melikian. The family's Armenian even though they've lived in Jordan for a couple of generations. Raz and I got along, so maybe he recommended me. He could have done it himself, though. Let me have a look at the Terms of Reference. At least I can see what the job is."

"While you do that, I'm going to shower," Mariah said, breaking into a smile.

Mariah changed into Levis and a faded blue turtleneck and

unloaded her briefcase on the big octagonal table. Together they scanned the background material on Armenia, read the Terms of Reference and mused over the possible surprises the assignment might present--there were always surprises. Tom demanded a layover in London for a day--two if necessary--to see his father. Finally, as the sun began to fill the room with copper-colored light, he signed the Consultant Agreement.

"I'll have to change your tickets," Mariah said, as if she'd known all the time that she could persuade him.

"Pretty damn sure of yourself, booking flights."

Mariah tucked the copies away and said, "There's a big-time travel advance." She pulled a large manila envelope from the pile of papers and held it out to him. "There's five thousand US in cash. The Armenians have restricted banking relationships right now--no credit cards and no traveler's checks. Not even in the hotel."

"Really?"

"It's a cash economy. One bank's operating internationally, but nobody trusts it enough to use it for short-term people."

Tom shook his head and withdrew a stack of crisp $50 and $100 bills and riffled them with his thumb. Any other surprises for me?"

"Just the usual that nobody can predict," she said, smiling the sparkling, self-satisfied gleam of victory, leaning back against the couch and stretching her arms above her head. The leather creaked as she relaxed from her stretch and fell back into the couch.

"Then it's time for a drink," he said, feeling like the generous pushover he knew himself to be.

"And some air," she added, rising and turning toward the cove. "Good grief," she exclaimed. "Look at that gorgeous light."

Tom took his feet off the table and came to stand beside her. "The sun sets behind us, so my side of the cove gets the kind of reflected light that makes you think of the Dutch Masters--Vermeer and van Ruisdael and those guys. Throw on a coat, I'll pour us a drink and we'll go outside. It's even better out there."

Tom slipped on an old sheepskin coat from the closet, took a bottle of Cardhu single-malt scotch from the bar and splashed generous portions into two tumblers. He handed one to Mariah as she emerged from the guest bedroom, running her arms into a soft leather jacket. The chill air refreshed them immediately and Tom led her down the stairs and out to the boat dock, where the slap of the waves was throwing up a fine spray. The evening breeze off the lake sharpened their senses as the golden glow of the setting sun deepened around them.

"I can see why you like it here," Mariah said in quiet wonder, coming to stand beside him, drawing herself to him with an arm around his waist. Reflexively, he put his arm around her shoulders, welcoming her warmth, inhaling the subtle fragrance of sandalwood she'd brought from the shower.

They stood that way, sipping scotch, watching the color of the sky change from copper to gold with traces of chartreuse, then to orange and pale purple as the sun sank behind them. Finally, he said, "Why don't you go on in and warm up. I'll crank up the grill out here and cook you a steak."

He detailed her to pour another drink while he took from the fridge two well-marbled rib-eye steaks, lettuce, onions, tomatoes, olives and a chunky bleu cheese dressing he'd made himself. He brought baking potatoes from a bin below the sink and by the time Mariah had fresh drinks in hand, dinner was underway.

Watching him move around the kitchen, Mariah shook her head and said, "You actually know what you're doing. I'm impressed."

"I've been cooking for myself awhile. Aside from bacon and eggs, I do lamb chops with Montrachet cheese and catfish in a mango sauce. Jaegerschnitzel with a white wine cream sauce and mushrooms. The way my grandmother makes it. And sauerbraten with red cabbage and potato dumplings. Baked apples on the side, of course. I don't neglect the French. I make crème brulee and with the proper encouragement, a passable chocolate soufflé."

"Wooo. I wish I could stay for that. All of that," she said. "Jaegerschnitzel--is that your version of weiner schnitzel?"

"Jaeger is 'hunter' in German. That's my name, with an Anglicized spelling. It's pork. Weinerschnitzel is veal."

"I've had sauerbraten and I remember it being pretty heavy."

"Not on a cold winter's day. I use venison and pork for mine.

Marinate it for four days in vinegar and about a dozen different spices. Serve it with some dark bread and a big red wine in front of a roaring fire . . . Pretty good stuff."

"You share that with anybody special?" Mariah asked.

"Sure. Not a lot of people up here in the winter, but I've got some good friends. Golfers mostly."

It was an answer, but not the information Mariah was trying to elicit. She wanted to know if there was a woman in his life.

"Do me a favor, will you?" Tom said while he scrubbed the potatoes. "There's some Camembert in the fridge that needs to come out. We'll have it after. And there's a good bottle of St. Emilion I've been saving. Under the bar. Pull the cork and let it breathe awhile. The steaks won't take long once I slap 'em on the grill. While you're dealing with the wine and the cheese, I'll get a fire going in the fireplace, knock the chill off this room."

****

After dinner, they took what was left of the St. Emilion and sank into the couch in front of the fire. Tom put on a tape of Tchaikovsky's "Pathetique", carved off some Camembert and a slice of apple, put it on a small plate and handed it to Mariah. With the aroma of burning oak scenting the air and the afterglow of the wine smoothing out the wrinkles, they settled into companionable silence. Mariah pulled her legs up under her and Tom propped his feet on the octagonal table. Over dinner, they'd caught up on mutual acquaintances and gossip from the international consultant community but they knew they were going through the social motions, speaking one thing, thinking about where the evening might be going.

She wanted to touch him. That one hug at the air strip had been enough to bring back memories and standing beside him on the boat dock, his arm thrown casually around her, had made her long for more. But she sensed he wasn't ready, that the ghost of Seline still stood between them and she took the conversation away from it.

"What do you do down here?" she asked.

"I play golf. Ride a little. A couple of people on the cove have sail boats and we go out when the tourists leave. Some friends enjoy my cooking, which has become something of a hobby."

"And your wine selection," she said, saluting him with her wine glass.

"And my wine selection," he nodded with a smile.

"Keeping the wine cabinet well-stocked gives me an excuse to run into Austin once in awhile."

"What about the boat down by the water?"

"I use it for fishing. Bass for sport, catfish to eat."

"And that's it? That's why you've been turning down jobs?"

He didn't answer right away. "I needed a change of place to heal after Seline. And think about what went wrong. Come to terms with what was my fault and what was hers. Oma took me in for awhile and got me over the worst of it."

"Oma?"

"My grandmother. Very German. When she thought I could stand on my own again, she threw me out, but I stayed close enough to see her once in awhile. She's over in Fredericksburg." For an instant, he saw Oma's round face, her brown eyes beneath a snowy cap of white hair. And her kitchen, always smelling so wonderful. Apples cooking or bread baking. Gleaming copper pots and pans hanging over the butcher block island where he sat and listened and watched.

"So how's it going with the healing, if you don't mind my asking."

"Good, I guess. It's been almost three years. No 'significant other' in my life. I've got friends here who let me be who I am." He paused. "I guess you understand that I'm not looking forward to lacing up my boots for Armenia. You'll owe me one. Now, enough about me. What's been going on with you?"

Mariah shifted in her seat and looked down for a moment. "You know about my time in Indonesia. I was teaching linear programming and optimizing investment decisions at ITB up in Bandung. Bandung was nicer than Jakarta--cooler, not so crowded. I had a few friends, Europeans and some Aussies, but it was basically an ex-pat experience. The Indons are strange people. Hard to know or feel comfortable with. I was glad to leave."

"Engagement completely off?" She nodded.

"Yeah. Too big a gap to bridge. He wanted . . . oh, I don't

know. It would be unfair, but not entirely inaccurate, to say he wanted a stay-at-home mom."

"And you didn't want to be one?"

"I might have for about fifteen minutes. Then I just sort of gagged on the whole idea. My 'world view' is larger than that."

"So you partnered up with Peter Karekin?"

"It seemed like a good place to invest my savings from Indonesia. Peter's getting long in the tooth and about all that's left of the firm is his reputation. He wanted some new blood in the firm and made me an offer I couldn't refuse. If I play my cards right, I could wind up running the show."

Tom looked at his watch and got up. "I need to pack and you're probably tired," he said. "You can have the bathroom first. Holler if there's anything you need."

From the guest bedroom, she could hear the sounds of his packing--drawers opening and closing, clothes hangers rattling in the closet, his footsteps back and forth, collecting items that would go in his bag. She undressed, put on pajamas and lay back, staring up at the ceiling. She wondered if he would look in on her before he went to sleep. Probably not.

"Why, she wondered, had she not been in touch with him while she was in Indonesia? She heard about Seline on the grapevine. She could have written her condolences. It had just felt wrong, somehow opportunistic. She felt sure he knew where she was. He could have been in touch as well as she. And now, chance had thrown them together for a couple of days. She'd felt the old attraction they'd once had. Had he? He hadn't shown any signs of it, but maybe the ice had been broken, maybe they could be friends again."

****

They had cereal for breakfast, drank the last of the milk. Tom bagged the perishables in the fridge to take to George, locked the door and went down the stairs to the deck. Charlie, the great blue heron who patrolled the cove, startled Mariah when she went down to the boat dock to have a last look at the lake before they left. The big bird launched with a sudden, raucous squawk and a rumble of his heavy wings. When Mariah recovered from her fright, they stood together on the boat dock, laughing, watching Charlie slowly cross the cove on powerful wings and head out over the lake, long legs dangling out behind him.

Going over to Houston, Tom sat in the right hand seat, read background material on Armenia, dozed a little and let her fly the airplane. They didn't say much until they were settled in the first class cabin of the United flight to Washington. Then they got into reminiscing about Tunisia, the last time they'd been in the field together. It had been just the two of them for a job that deserved a four-man team and they'd only had one weekend free of the mission. In the spirit of adventure, Tom hired a car and they drove south from Tunis.

"Remember that old Roman coliseum at El Djem?" Mariah said.

"A perfect miniature of the one in Rome. And we had it to ourselves. But it's not what I remember best about that trip. Do you know?" he asked.

"Maybe," she said, smiling.

"After El Djem, we went on down to Sfax to see the spongers. Sponges hanging all over the boats and spilling out of those little tumble-down drying sheds. You hardly ever see real sponges anymore. They're all made of recycled something or other."

Mariah's eyes widened and she feigned dismay. "You thought that was the high point of the trip? What about that little town up the coast?"

"I was coming to that. Monastir, wasn't it?"

"We went down to the harbor and walked out to the end of the pier to that pavilion."

Tom nodded. "With the stucco flaking and just that one old guy serving."

"The Mediterranean was blue, blue, blue and the most marvelous breeze was blowing."

"It wasn't much of a lunch," Tom said, laughing, remembering how the wind had fluttered her hair. "But the beer was cold."

For a moment then, something sad and wistful came into her eyes. "That's where I fell in love with you all over again," she said.

He'd never known that. She'd been engaged at the time. What was he supposed to say? On impulse, he played it light. "Left your heart in Monastir?" he teased, wondering if he'd been responsible in some way for the breakup. That would make two-- hers and his own.

She gave him a half-hearted smile. He sensed that she was about to lie. "The sun was in my eyes. I thought you were Robert Redford." She turned serious again and said, "You're not going to say you didn't feel something for me that day, are you?"

"I felt a lot for you," he said and left it there.

That was as close as they came to opening a window on feelings that might have gone beyond friendship. They'd had a chance in Tunisia to talk about it, but they hadn't. They'd been out of touch while Mariah was in Indonesia. A chasm opened between them and there seemed to be no going back. They'd let it slide at the lake house, on the flight from Houston and yet again sitting in the Red Carpet club at Dulles International, waiting for his flight to Amsterdam. When the club attendant came to tell him his flight was boarding, Mariah went with him into the concourse to his departure gate.

"Look out for yourself over there in the Wild, Wild East," she said.

"I will."

She checked her watch and said, "Gotta go!" For just a moment, there was something tender but unspoken in her eyes. Then she kissed him quickly on the mouth, turned and walked away before he quite realized what she'd done. He watched her merge into the bobbing flow of passengers moving down the concourse. She waved once without turning around, her hand disembodied above the heads of the crowd. And then she was gone.

CHAPTER TWO

London, 1995

Jet-lagged and weary, Tom fell into the back seat of a black, boxy London taxi at Heathrow and told the cabbie to take him to the Royal London Hospital, where his grandmother said his father had been taken. The cost of the cab would be daunting, but he was more than flush with the stash of fifties and hundreds Mariah had given him for Armenia.

The Royal London was a melding of ancient and state-of-the-art. The Intensive Care Unit where Gunter Yeager lay beneath crisp sheets connected to an array of monitors was decidedly state-of-the-art and, as a close relative, Tom was allowed to see him there.

Every one of Gunter's sixty-two years showed in his face-- hair still full, but dull gray and lifeless, the skin of his hands above the sheet wrinkled, the sclera of his brown eyes red-veined and cloudy. They stared dispassionately at Tom as he approached the bed. Beard stubble sprang from his father's ashen cheeks. Tom should have felt something--guilt, pity, remorse, even anger--but he didn't. Whether Gunter lived or died today or this year or next, Tom knew it would be the last time he'd see his father and it wouldn't matter.

He approached the bedside slowly, reluctantly. Gunter's fingers curled around Tom's hand and his eyes searched his son's for some connection.

"Sonny," he whispered in a rasping voice.

"Hello, Dad."

Gunter managed a weak smile. "Glad you came. Hoped you would. One last time. Listen. Andre," he wheezed. "Something for me. Yours now. Trust Andre. Your debt to him almost paid. He'll honor that."

"Don't try to talk, Dad."

Gunter straightened in the bed, drawing on his meager reserves of strength. "Do what I tell you, Sonny. Tell Andre . . ." Gunter faded and slipped back against the pillow and closed his eyes. "Ëzkoosh. Watch out."

For a moment, Gunter opened his eyes again and stared at Tom. "Sorry, Sonny. Could have been a better father. Will you come back?"

"I'm on a job, Dad. I'll be in Armenia for three weeks. I'll see you before I go back to the States," Tom lied. Gunter might not last the night, certainly not three weeks. *What debt?* Tom wondered. *Surely he'd paid in blood for the fiasco in Vienna so long ago. Didn't Andre simply count that as part of the cost of doing business? But Gunter paid it?*

A nurse in starched whites had been observing the exchange from the doorway and came forward to take Tom's elbow. "Sorry, Mr. Yeager. That's enough for now. He needs to rest."

Tom took one last look at his father and followed her into the hallway. "What happened to him?" Tom asked.

"Struck by a lorry. You Americans can never remember to look the proper way when crossing the road."

"My dad's lived here for years. I don't think that was it."

"Be that as it may," she said. "He's been crushed rather badly. Mild concussion, a broken arm and several broken ribs. A rib pierced his right lung. We barely saved him two nights ago. Pulmonary embolism moving toward his brain. It could happen again at any moment."

"Will he recover?"

"Ask God. He's in charge now."

Gunter seemed to be sleeping, so Tom went to the canteen for a cup of tea. When he came back, there was a crowd of white coats around Gunter and they were declaring him dead, began stripping away the tubing and disconnecting the monitors. He hadn't been moved, no more than if he'd witnessed the passing of a stranger. They'd scarcely spoken in ten years. He wasn't in London because of any special feelings for the man. He was there because his grandmother, his oma, had asked and because Mariah had given him the opportunity.

CHAPTER THREE

Amsterdam, 1995

Tom pretended to relax in one of the plastic chairs in the glassed-in waiting room of Gate D-22. From the corner of one eye, he watched the middle-aged ticket agent. Armenian, Tom guessed. He wore a baggy blue blazer, had a shaggy haircut and a heavy, three-day old beard. Tom's other eye and his rapt attention were focused on the hallway beyond the glass walls. If the Dutch police showed up, he was trapped.

Finally, the agent took up the microphone and announced the flight, first in Armenian, then in Russian and finally in English. An immediate crush of people and carryon baggage pressed toward the door to the jet bridge. Most of the passengers wore heavy, misshapen suits and the baggage was an eclectic mixture of cardboard boxes and bulging, strapped-closed suitcases. Tom buried himself in the crowd, presented his ticket and squeezed past the agent's kiosk into the jet bridge.

The sleek modernity of Amsterdam's Schiphol Airport disappeared in the cluttered chaos of the cabin of the Armenian Airlines jetliner. The carpet down the center aisle of the old Tupolev had come up and stretched out in a damp tangle beneath the shuffling feet of the boarding passengers. Without seat assignments, they jostled each other and pushed their vast amounts of carry-on baggage down the aisle, crammed it into open overhead racks and under seats whose upholstery was soiled and worn. This, he supposed, was the new Armenian entrepreneurial class, hauling Western European goods back to a threadbare motherland. The cabin lighting cast a decrepit yellow haze over the tattered scene.

He found a window seat and wondered if this were a sample of what awaited him in the rubble of the Soviet Union. He'd spent time in Budapest right after the fall of the Berlin Wall and thought the city wasn't too much the worse for wear from forty years of communism. The trolleys ran on time, the Hungarians were reasonably well-dressed, cars were everywhere, the plumbing worked and the food was good. Better than Cairo and only a cut or two below Vienna, its cultivated sister city across the Danube. Budapest was chock-a-block with tourists, too, mostly Germans. On that same trip, he'd flown up to Prague on Malev, the Hungarian national airline. They were flying Tupolevs like this one, but the Hungarian plane was clean, in good repair and the service was comparable to American carriers. To Tom, that part of the Second World looked a lot like the First World. It just had better exchange rates.

Through the Plexiglas, he stared out at a purple sky pierced helter-skelter by the lights of Schiphol Airport. He suspended his thoughts about where he was heading and concentrated on the movement of the plane. The whine of the jet engines increased and the plane began to taxi, rocking forward on its landing gear, flexing its wings and stretching its tired skin for one more over-loaded flight. The pilot made the final turn onto the threshold, ran up the engines, released the brakes and sent the plane rattling down the runway, gathering speed to struggle into the air. Airborne, Tom exhaled his relief and hoped not too many rivets had popped loose. He took a last look at the lights of Amsterdam and drew his coat around him against the cold.

He closed his eyes and tried to sleep, but he couldn't shut out the babbling of the passengers and the bustle of the stewardesses up and down the aisle. The dull yellow glow of the cabin lights reminded him of the permanent nicotine stain on Andre's fingers and teeth. He replayed the scene against the screen of his eyelids.

****

Walking up Egelantiersgracht, nothing had changed. In the cold blue light of morning, wispy tendrils of fog rose from the still water and boats of a dozen descriptions lay snugged against the banks of the tree-lined canal. A pair of cyclists swept past on their way to work, tires hissing on the herringbone weave of gray brick. Otherwise, the neighborhood was quiet, almost deserted. The Jordaan was heavily populated by artists and intellectuals--not the sort to be out and about this early unless they were on their way home. Approaching Petrossian's townhouse, he saw the milk and the morning paper, probably De Volksrant, still on the landing. What could be more normal? Vermeer could have painted the scene.

But the door was ajar. Not normal. By the time he reached the steps, he saw why. The heavy lock was shattered. Nothing less than a charge of C4 would have done that. A small charge probably, but powerful. The base of his spine tingled and a hollow space yawned in his gut.

Tom took the last two steps, eased the door open and looked in. Petrossian slumped against the far wall of the foyer, his gaunt, sunken cheeks illuminated by the wedge of pale sunlight streaming through the partly open door. His deep-set, coal black eyes stared vacantly into space. The shock of coarse black hair had turned to gray since Tom had seen him last and the bony, nicotine-stained fingers of his right hand were curled into a claw, one finger pointing toward the narrow, antique table in the shadows.

Tom slipped through the door and knelt beside the body, removed a glove and pressed his fingers to Petrossian's wrist. He knew it was a futile exercise. Andre had been shot in the throat. And not long ago. His body was still warm and the pool of blood in which the right side of his head lay had barely coagulated on the parquet floor. The skin around the bullet hole was purpling and pitted with black powder. Shot at close range. Because he'd seen it done in the movies, Tom closed Petrossian's eyes with a gentle touch of thumb and middle finger. Now the old man seemed asleep except for the ugly hole in his throat.

Just one shot. Blood splatter on the plaster and a smear down the wall traced his collapse to the floor. With his throat destroyed, he couldn't have called out and he probably hadn't died instantly.

As Tom's eyes adjusted to the dim light of the foyer, he saw a Persian cat on the stairs perched on its haunches, green eyes cold and dispassionate against dark gray fur, an indifferent witness to his master's murder. While Tom stared at him, the cat licked a paw and calmly washed its face.

He stood up. The cat sprang from the stairs and bounded through the partly open door, down the steps and into the street. Tom's eyes followed it for a moment, then turned back to Petrossian.

The dull shock of finding Andre dead battled with the adrenaline sizzling through his veins. The house was quiet--no creak of a floorboard, no rasp of shuffling papers. That didn't mean the killer might not still be there, but this wasn't a robbery. This was Petrossian's house, not his place of business. His neighbors thought he was a poet, not an out-of-the-System diamond dealer/smuggler. Without quite knowing how he knew, Tom understood this was an assassination, retribution for a deal gone sour or some perceived betrayal.

He considered going upstairs, then noticed the small package wrapped in brown paper, almost out of sight beneath the foyer table, his name scrawled across it with a black marker pen. He took it, made room for it in his briefcase and decided it was time to go. He could call the Dutch police from the airport. Just before he boarded. Or not. Either way, it wouldn't make any difference to Andre.

He eased the door back to the way he'd found it and skipped down the steps, faintly marking them with traces of Andre's blood from his shoes. A man and a woman on bicycles sped past, bells jingling bells to warn him of their passage. The woman wore a black pea coat, pale hair pulled back in a pony tail. She caught his eyes for one penetrating moment and he felt exposed and memorized. He turned up the collar of his leather coat, pressed his face into it, wished for a hat to hide beneath and walked quickly away, his eyes alert for someone suddenly appearing on a boat deck. He hurried past the coffee house on the corner by the stone bridge. Through the panes of the windows he could see an early morning crowd clustered around the warmth of its hearth, finishing the evening or starting the day--it was hard to tell which. At the corner, he turned to see if there were anyone behind him. No one. Breath steaming, he walked briskly along Tichel Straat until he reached the Prinsen Canal and crossed over at the Westerkerk. He found a Mercedes taxi, fell into the back seat and told the driver, "Schipol, please."

He tried to control his breathing, to push down the adrenaline surge by focusing on the first blush of spring. Trees were budding in Holland's distinctive light. Early tulips and daffodils touched the city with daubs of red and yellow. Had Andre liked flowers or if, after spending most of his life in Amsterdam, he no longer noticed them?

The flowers and the sunlight didn't correlate with death. For an instant he imagined Andre's dead body lying in a bed of tulips--something out of an Italian movie--instead of being sprawled out in the blood-smeared half-light of his foyer.

The woman on the bicycle might identify him, but he probably had twelve hours before news reports of Petrossian's murder surfaced. By then, he could be on a plane to any point on the globe, out of the reach of the Dutch police. Was he, himself, at risk? He knew he could be even if he didn't quite know why.

As the Mercedes worked its way through the morning traffic toward Schipol Airport, he fought against the direction events were taking him. Tear up the ticket on Armenian Airlines and fly back to Granite Shoals on the first flight he could get on? His life in the Texas Hill Country was peaceful. He didn't need the job in Armenia and wouldn't have taken it if Mariah hadn't come to ask. It wasn't too late to back out. He wouldn't have gone to see Andre if he hadn't had a 12-hour layover in Amsterdam or if his father hadn't more or less made it his last wish.

He had no great affection for Andre. He'd always found him cold and morose, but Andre and his father were business partners. Tom had helped them on a few occasions--his old man trying to teach him a trade, disparaging Tom's academic degrees as irrelevant egocentricities.

He'd done his duty to Oma; he hadn't needed to stop in London for his own sake and the layover in Amsterdam was a duty to his father. As Andre's body was fresh in his memory, so was the face of a father he scarcely knew, swathed in bandages, punctured by plastic tubes and dangling IV drips, patched into green-screen monitors.

He'd paid the hospital, which included a charge for a phone call to Amsterdam on the day Tom had come. And he made arrangements with a mortuary, stayed the night at the Portman and flew to Amsterdam the next morning. That was when he found Andre and the package.

Should he have done more for Andre? He'd left him lying in his own blood. Even the cat had fled. Shouldn't he at least feel something more? Did he owe Andre anything beyond the two million dollars worth of diamonds--at 1974 prices--he'd been stripped of in

Vienna? What would they be worth now? He wasn't sure, but there had been about three hundred uncut Russian stones. Their weight was palpable in the briefcase he'd carried chained to his wrist. How had Gunter repaid all that? It was touching and unnecessary as far as Tom was concerned.

What he remembered now was that Andre hadn't visited him in the hospital. Why should he have? Obviously, the Russians had followed the stones through the pipeline from Siberia to Vienna and tagged him as soon as he picked them up from the Aeroflot stewardess who'd brought them across. He'd never known, but he assumed it was a straight heist--the stones were being diverted to some Russian's Swiss account. After all, the hard work of getting the diamonds into Europe was already done and the stones were at their least secure in the courier's hands. The shot was intended to kill him, not just take the diamonds. It seemed senseless, excessive, unless there was something more to it. All Andre would have accomplished by visiting him was to get himself killed. So, turn about. What would Tom have accomplished by staying with Andre's dead body? It would have put him at risk of indictment in a Dutch court. Days of interrogation at the very least. Maybe Andre had thought down the same lines when Tom was shot.

Stirring the cold ashes of these memories did nothing to resolve his practical problems and neither did the damned airplane. What a piece of scrap. The old Tupolev shuddered every time they hit turbulence and Tom imagined he could hear rivets popping. He hoped it would hold together for six hours or however long it took to get to Armenia.

CHAPTER FOUR

Yerevan, Armenia

He woke as the Tupolev began its approach into Yerevan's Zvartnots International Airport. The plane was letting down steadily into total blackness. Suddenly, his teeth were jarred by the wheels slamming into the runway. A few widely-spaced runway lights flashed past the window. The pilot tapped the brakes on the corrugated runway, reversed engines and finally slowed to a taxi roll.

Deplaning, the gaggle of passengers entered a semi-dark tunnel that led into the passport control area--two wooden kiosks lit by a 25-watt bulb. It was Dracula's cave and Tom thought he should be able to find Vampire bats hanging from the rafters. He pressed into a line and eventually came face to face with a gaunt immigration official wearing a soiled shirt and a three-day growth of beard. His breath was as foul as his rotting teeth, but he stamped Tom's passport without comment and allowed him to pass on into another tunnel that led to the baggage claim area and customs. Outside the last set of double doors, he found a young American with an unruly shock of dark red hair waiting for him.

"Dr. Yeager?" the young man asked. Tom nodded.

"Yep. You from AID?"

"Sam Rhodes," he said, grabbing the handle of Tom's hardcase and steering him toward the outside doors. "Sorry you didn't get the VIP treatment here. It's hard to roll out the red carpet for these middle-of-the-night flights. Both Paris and Amsterdam are bummers. Only Moscow has a decent schedule," Sam said as they emerged into the freezing air of the Caucasus mountains.

Too weary to make conversation, Tom trudged along in Rhodes' wake until they came to a Jeep Cherokee.

"Here we are," Rhodes said, opening the rear hatch and loading Tom's baggage. Rhodes slammed the hatch and they got in. "Rough trip?" he asked, maneuvering out of the parking area onto the airport road.

"It's a long hike," Tom muttered, thinking it wasn't just the miles. In less than twenty-four hours there had been his father, dying peacefully, and Andre lying in his own blood.

"At least you're here on the weekend. You can rest up a little. The brass want to see you at the Mission, but not until Monday morning."

"I didn't see any lights coming in. How far are we from town?" Tom asked.

"Actually not far, but the city doesn't waste juice on street lights. Electricity's in very short supply--courtesy of the war with Azerbaijan and the Turkish blockade. Not much oil or gasoline coming through. As soon as the passengers from this flight clear, the airport will go pretty dark again. The hotel's got power from its own generators, but most everybody else goes without. Even the government's rationed."

When they reached the city, it seemed abandoned and surreal, even allowing for the fact that it was almost two o'clock in the morning. It sure as hell wasn't Budapest. That impression was heightened by the black basalt stone of Yerevan's buildings and the eerie shadows cast by the headlights of the Jeep. They bounced along the cobblestones and broken pavement, twisting and turning through the deserted streets until they entered a parkway and began a gentle climb. Tom noticed a slight lifting of the inky blackness that shrouded the city. It proved to be the lights of the Hotel Armenia.

The doorman and an elderly porter ambled out of the main entrance to take Tom's luggage. He and Rhodes mounted the shallow flight of steps and followed them to the reception desk, where a sleepy, dark-haired young woman awaited them. Rhodes spoke to her in Russian, telling her Tom's name, that he was with the US Embassy and was booked for three weeks. Marta nodded and laid blank registration forms in front of him.

"Pay the full three weeks in advance," Rhodes said. "You won't have to carry all that cash around. And there's a big delegation coming in toward the end of your stay. They're electing a new Supreme Catholicos of the Armenian church--he's like the Pope. It's a very big deal and if you're not paid up, they might throw you out to make room for some delegate who didn't book in advance. One more thing. The hot water's only on from seven to nine, morning and evening, so you've missed it. I know you're bushed right now, but what if I meet you for breakfast in the morning? I could show you around a little."

"I won't like getting up," Tom said. "But I'm not going to go without a hot shower and breakfast. Come on by."

****

Large double doors opened into a grand hall that was the hotel's main dining room. Crisp white linen was laid out on every table, but the waiters, lounging around the doors to the kitchen, easily outnumbered the diners. Tom thought they must be early, that the other guests would start showing up in due course.

A long buffet was set in front of towering, two-story windows facing Republic Square. The other side of the room featured murals extolling the honest toil of the working class, incongruously accented by salmon colored marble fit for a Roman emperor's palace.

Breakfast didn't measure up to the lavish room--a cold buffet, fried eggs burned on the bottom and sausage swimming in grease. Rhodes drank tea and lectured nonstop on the woes that had befallen Armenia after the earthquake, the war with Azerbaijan that prompted the fuel shortage and the Turkish blockade that compounded all the economy's difficulties. Tom ate with a will, listening to Rhodes with only half an ear, watching the door for new arrivals who never came.

There was virtually no one in the square below, either. You could tell a lot about a place quickly just by looking at the people, how they dressed, if they were lively and laughing. The national income accounts were dead numbers without a human context. Tom assumed without giving it any thought that Armenia would be like every other country he'd ever worked in, but even writing off his late arrival last night and the fact that it was Sunday morning, he was getting the lowest reading on his human activity monitor of any place he'd ever been. So far, Yerevan looked like a city that had been hit by a neutron bomb--buildings still there, but the people all vaporized.

When they emerged from the hotel, Rhodes said, "This is called Republic Square now. It used to be Lenin Square. They had a

26

big statue of him over there." He pointed to the right where a black granite pedestal stood empty--like the rest of the square.

"I guess there was a big celebration when that came down," Tom offered.

"Actually not," Rhodes said. "Lenin went very quietly one night after independence was declared in 1991. He was there one afternoon and gone the next morning. It was like a political correctness thing. You need to understand that the Armenians weren't looking for independence. They cheered when Gorbachev laid on glasnost and perestroika. That's when the big celebrations were, back in the '80s. I'm told it was quite a scene up around Opera Square. Of course, the Sovs got nervous and sent tanks and troops to keep a lid on it. Classic example of Soviet paranoia."

"Huh," Tom said, suddenly feeling like an unwelcome guest and continuing to look for people--people walking, people sitting on a park bench, a car or two, anything. "I thought it would have been like the wall coming down in Berlin."

"Not really. Armenia was a Soviet republic back in the 1920s, not occupied territory like Poland or Czechoslovakia, much less Germany," Rhodes said. "The Russians were the Armenians' allies against the Turks, so the alliance was voluntary, even welcome. Ultimately, the Armenians had a problem with the Soviet system but for the most part, they wanted to reform it, not destroy it. You need to understand that they're coming to a market system now because they've got nowhere else to go."

Rhodes pointed to a dominating five-story building constructed of pink stone set in a Moorish, checkerboard pattern. "That's Government House. You'll be spending a lot of time there." The building's main entrance was a graceful concavity lined with lacy arches capped by a colonnade tier. The wing of the building fronting the square featured a clock tower with the colonnade tier repeated. It was an impressive, unique piece of architecture.

Government House was the principal structure on the square, but the Post and Communications Building and Trade Union House were in the same pink stone and architectural style. The Hotel Armenia followed the design, though its concavity was less pronounced because the building was considerably smaller than any of the other three.

"What's that white building across the square?" Tom asked. "The one that doesn't look like the others?"

"That's the History Museum," Rhodes replied. "Bit of a puzzle why they didn't use the same architectural style."

Crossing the narrow street beside the hotel, Rhodes called Tom's attention to the park that ran downhill for at least two blocks from Lenin's empty pedestal.

"This is Anniversary Park," he said. "Hard to tell now because it's still winter and there's no water in it, but there's a cascade of two-thousand-seven-hundred and fifty little fountains running down the center of the park, one for each year of Yerevan's existence up to nineteen-sixty-eight. It's mind-boggling, but Yerevan was founded in seven-eighty-two BC, about the same time as Rome. Can you believe that?"

The reference to Rome made Tom think of what Rhodes had said about the election of an Armenian Pope.

"You said there was going to be a big delegation here in a couple of weeks to elect a new Pope for the Armenian Church. What are they, cardinals and such?"

"I'm not thoroughly familiar with it," Rhodes replied. "But both clergy and lay people are involved. They come from all over the world for this because, like the Pope in Rome, this only happens when the sitting Pope dies. I don't know how many will be coming, but a fair number."

Approaching the Post Office, the fifth building on the square, Rhodes stopped in front of a tall arch. "On a clear day, Mt. Ararat is perfectly framed right here. It's a fantastic sight. The mountain used to be in Armenia, but now it's in Turkey. The Armenians still claim it, of course. They even have it on their new national currency."

"Ararat," Tom said, moving on past the arch and away from the square. "That's where Noah's Ark is supposed to have landed after the flood, isn't it?"

"It's debatable, of course, but that's the legend." As they went down the hill, the ponderous, black basalt that gave Yerevan its medieval look replaced the pink stone of Republic Square. They passed a cinema with an outdoor café attached, dead leaves from the sycamore trees swirling among the empty tables. Tom looked at it carefully, imagining it could come alive quickly enough if there were patrons.

There had been no traffic around Republic Square, but farther down the hill, Tom now saw a streetcar making its turn through a major intersection.

"The market's just beyond the Rossya Kino. Not much farther."

"What's the Rossya Kino?" Tom asked.

"That big building that looks like a coliseum. It's a movie house. Rossya--Russian. Kino--cine or cinema. The Russian movie house. There's a Metro station there, too," Rhodes added. "The whole Soviet Union was pretty big on public transportation--see the trolley tracks running along here? It's a Godsend now. Armenia has the largest number of automobiles per capita of any of the Soviet Republics, but you don't see them now because of the gasoline shortage. Gives you an idea of how far the country's fallen. It was a prosperous republic during the Soviet period, not like what you're seeing now."

"Were there any people here then?" Tom asked.

Rhodes laughed. "Yeah, sure. At least I guess so. I've seen pictures, but I didn't come until after independence and it's been quiet like this except for places like the open air market we're going to and the Saturday flea market over by the Mamikonyan monument. Certain occasions bring out the people, too. It'll be time for celebration of the Last Bell in another month or so. That's graduation for the high school. Last Bell, no more school bells, get it? That'll go on all day and half the night, with all the kids drunk on champagne and vodka. The fountains will have water in them by then and kids will be splashing in every one of them. They make it a blast."

The open air market was a jumble of improvised stands with canvas covers, the aisles between them crowded with people browsing through an eclectic assortment of goods--fresh fruit, hard candies, vodka and brandy, shoes and socks, chocolate bars, children's toys, cigarettes, even housewares, lots of candles--utilitarian, not decorative. There was a shortage of electricity. People had to have light.

The market gave Tom the first opportunity to examine Armenians. Most of the men were grizzled with two or three days' growth of heavy, dark beard. The women bulky and heavy featured, many in leather coats and boots. Except for the children, they were a somber, unsmiling lot.

Tom took his time strolling the aisles, getting his first idea of what was available in a blockaded economy.

"We could go on to the Central Market down the street, but going back will be all uphill," Rhodes said.

"Another time. I've got a sample at least. Let's get some lunch. Any place to eat around here?"

"Our best bet is back at the hotel. We passed a restaurant on the way down, but the selection would be pretty limited there. Not that it won't be at the hotel."

****

As Tom and Rhodes returned to the main lobby after leaving the hotel's ground-floor café, the woman behind the registration desk spoke to them in Russian.

Rhodes turned to Tom. "There's a message for you," he said.

Olga Nercessian held out an embossed envelope to Tom, using it to indicate a striking, dark-haired woman standing beside the desk. Tom accepted the envelope absently, his eyes riveted on Ana Stepanian.

He was taken first by her dark brown eyes, almond shaped beneath full lashes, and thick, gracefully arched eyebrows. Her hair was parted in the middle and framed her face--glossy black, heavy, cut shoulder length and brushed to a sheen. Her mouth was full, her nose straight and strong. A white silk blouse peeked out from the collar of a gray suit of some hard-finish material. Her knee-high boots left her no more than five feet, three or four inches, but her slender frame made her look slightly taller.

She'd heard him talking to Rhodes as they came down the hall from the café, saw him walk into the lobby with the fluid movements of a natural athlete. He was tall and lean and his voice was pleasant. She couldn't make out what he was saying because his back was turned to her, but his words were clearly formed and his tone was crisp. That he wasn't old and bald and fat made up for the fact that he was an American. That also made him more dangerous to her. She didn't want to like him. The Americans were as bad as the Russians who had betrayed them, making them pawns--not even as consequential as pawns--in some global chess match that had brought them to ruin.

When he turned around and came back to the reception desk, Ana took in the lines and angles of his face, noticed the flecks of gray in his hair and saw warm brown eyes. She sucked in her breath and spoke to him for the first time.

"Dr. Yeager," she said in a silky voice, almost a whisper. "I am Ana Stepanian. Minister of Finance Manoukian tells me to make myself known to you. I am to interpret you." She shook her head. 'No, no. That is not right.' She blushed and corrected herself. "I am to interpret for you."

Tom had been frankly appraising her until he realized he was making her uncomfortable. Finally, he noticed her hand extended to him. He took it and held it.

She made it into a handshake, smiling in spite of herself, vowing not to let her political resentment get in the way of doing her job. His mission was to help Armenia. Alienating him would serve no purpose.

"I'm pleased to meet you," he said.

"Hello," Rhodes said. "I'm Sam Rhodes, with the AID Mission here in Yerevan." Ana smiled her 'hello' to Rhodes.

"Sorry, Sam," Tom said, shaking his head. To Ana, he added, "I'm forgetting my manners. I only arrived a few hours ago. I'm still jet-lagged."

"Please," Ana said. "I came only to deliver greetings of the Minister of Finance." She pointed to the envelope, which Tom had forgotten.

He slipped a forefinger under the flap, ripped it open and withdrew a folded sheet of heavy stationery, embossed with an official seal. He couldn't read the Armenian script, but he assumed it was the seal of the Ministry of Finance. He scanned the message quickly. The first paragraph invited him to lunch and the second introduced Ana

Stepanian as his assigned interpreter and the personal representative of the Minister. It was signed with a scrawl which he presumed belonged to the Minister. Tom looked up to find Ana Stepanian's eyes on him, appraising him almost as frankly as he had appraised her a few moments before. For the first time, he noticed the hardness in her eyes and felt chilled and uncertain about his welcome.

"Lunch tomorrow," he said. "I'm honored."

The frozen smile still in place, she nodded and said, "I must go now. May we meet here tomorrow five minutes before midday? I will take you to Minister's office."

He nodded and watched her turn away, crossing the lobby with sure steps and a graceful swaying of hips that she had difficulty concealing. She passed through the double doors and was briefly framed by the white stone of the History Museum on the other side of the square. Then she was gone, but a certain electricity hung in the air.

Rhodes took his leave and Tom was left alone, staring at an empty lobby. He considered going to his room and sleeping, but he let the afternoon's bright, winter sunlight draw him out of the hotel into Republic Square.

He filled his lungs with fresh mountain air and walked over to the empty pedestal where Lenin once surveyed this remote corner of the far-flung Soviet empire. On his walk with Sam that morning, he'd scarcely had time to notice the park that ran down the hill. Now he decided to explore it on his own.

He wondered how it looked with the fountains working. Did they just gurgle and send the water rippling down the long cascade or did they launch an exuberant spray into the air? There was no way to tell.

Still no people. It was Sunday afternoon, a time for park strolling, bench sitting, sun taking. This park, however, was all but deserted. Near the pedestal, an unsmiling photographer with an antique bellows camera mounted on a wooden tripod bargained earnestly with a young mother tending a pram. Down the incline of the park, the benches waited silently, except for one small knot of men watching a chess match.

His mind tried to get a grip on this strange country. It was a weird place, even in the daylight. The old Tupolev had flown him through a time tunnel to a Dracula's cave of an airport. Sam Rhodes had driven him through the inky blackness of the city to a tiny island of light that was the Hotel Armenia. And this morning, the somber, deserted streets had scarcely lifted the pall of abandonment. The open air market was the only place he'd actually seen any significant sign of normal life.

For all that, Yerevan clearly had once been prosperous and alive. From his hotel window, he could see monolithic Soviet statues on the ridge above the city, probably commemorating the victory over the Germans in the Great Patriotic War or worker solidarity. Just below lay the denuded greenbelt that had once been a forest. Rhodes had explained that the trees had been cut down for fuel during the past two bitter winters. Many people had frozen to death in their apartments for lack of heat because there was no fuel to run the central facility.

Some of those people would once have filled the tables of that sidewalk café they passed on their walk down the hill to the market. Today, the café was shuttered, the tables empty and the terrace ankle-deep in fallen leaves.

At least the children at the market hadn't seemed beaten down. There was delight in their eyes as they took a cup of ice cream or a hard candy wrapped in colored paper. But their parents' eyes had seemed dull and sad.

Not like the woman who was to be his translator. Ana Stepanian. Her eyes were bright and glossy even if they did seem hard. That forced smile wasn't becoming, either. Maybe if he'd asked her to stay and talk, even for a little while, she might have warmed up a little. They ought to be on better terms if he was going to rely on her to learn what he needed to know and to communicate with his counterparts. She hadn't given him much of an opportunity to invite her to stay, but what he'd seen today made the job more difficult than he expected. He hadn't begun and already he felt behind.

The contrast to all of Tom's international experience made Yerevan a major mystery. He granted that this was the Second World and his experience was mainly Third World, where the problems were unmistakable--overpopulation, poverty, ridiculously unequal distributions of income, official corruption, shortages of schools, clinics, safe water and every kind of infrastructure. But there was no shortage of vitality. The cities were colorful and overflowing. The people spilled out of doorways and into intersections, hawkers pushed their wares from broken sidewalks and crowded squares, car horns honked incessantly, the exotic aromas of spicy foods warred with the fetid smell of open sewers and unwashed bodies. The languages and the architecture changed from one hemisphere to the next, but the problems were as similar as they were intractable. But not like this. Armenia felt defeated and hopeless.

He continued down the hill, leaving Anniversary Park and its cascade of rusting fountains behind and finding another vacant park. He marked his surroundings to make sure he would know what to look for when he headed back to the hotel. It wasn't just that he didn't speak the language--even if he had, there was no one around to ask.

He entered the park and, following the curving walks, found abandoned rides for children, a silent, vacant open-air theater, statues of the famous and the forgotten. But it was all overgrown, rusting and cracking. It felt like an archaeological site in the making, a corpus no longer delicti, the flesh long-since scavenged but not yet bleached to bones. Unlike ruins he'd visited in other parts of the world, he could feel the fading warmth of the men who built this park, planted the trees and the grass and poured the fountains, who came on Sunday to turn the carousels and push the swings to the squeals and laughter of their children. Would they ever come back? Would they breathe life into this place again?

CHAPTER FIVE

The Ministry of Finance

As Ana walked away from the Hotel Armenia toward her apartment, she felt the exhilaration of the beginning of a new project, but a certain confusion as well. He wasn't what she'd expected. He wasn't some old man with fat hands and a superior attitude.

It had begun only two days ago--her meeting with Minister Manoukin.

****

"Ana," Katya called softly to avoid disturbing the others in the library. "There's a message for you at the desk. Important, they said."

Ana Stepanian nodded and pushed herself away from the long table. The sunlight was almost gone and without electricity, the library would soon be dark and cold. She swept her heavy, dark hair back from her face and took a moment to appreciate her soft brown leather gloves. They were lined with silk and came from a little shop near the castle in Budapest, as did the leather coat she wore. Since the collapse of the Soviet Union, her days with Intourist were over, but she remembered her postings in Russia and Hungary with great fondness.

Beyond the memories of better days her clothes evoked, she was grateful her wardrobe reflected few of the economic horrors of the years since Armenian independence. The foreigners who used her as a translator depended on her fluency in six languages, but she also understood that they preferred to be escorted by an attractive young woman who wore acceptably stylish clothes. On both counts, she was at the top of the list of the staff of the Hotel Armenia. She did not stand in such repute with the new Armenian government, where she remained under a cloud because her father had been a prominent Communist and because she had held a position with Intourist, long a handmaiden of the KGB. For reasons she didn't entirely understand, that cloud seemed to be lifting a little. The government was now calling her from time to time to translate for foreign dignitaries. Since such visitors chose more agreeable times of the year than late winter to visit Armenia, she expected that the message at the desk was from the hotel and that some Englishman or Frenchman was looking for a license to export Armenian cognac.

But that wasn't the case. The message said: "Please come to the Office of the Minister of Finance at 0900, 17 March." It was signed "Krikor Manoukian, Minister." Tomorrow. Her heart fluttered. She'd met Krikor Manoukian the previous autumn when she had interpreted for an official French delegation. Notwithstanding the weather, perhaps they were coming for another visit and had asked for her.

She folded the note carefully and tucked it into her glove. She'd have to show it to the guard at the door of Government House to be admitted. She left the library by the main entrance and found herself on the sidewalk not quite ready to go to her own cold and lonely apartment. She really couldn't afford to eat at the Hotel Armenia, but if Marta or Olga were on duty at the desk, she could get a key to one of the vacant rooms and have a hot shower before her appointment with the Minister tomorrow. She might also be able to find out who was coming so she'd know what language she'd be working in. Then a small cognac with her friends to celebrate the job would be perfect.

Two cars that might have been taxis and a white UNHCR jeep were parked in front of the hotel entrance. Across the square, a Russian-built International Harvester Scout in faded camouflage paint was stationed in front of the Museum fountain. It was the solemn duty of the policemen inside the Scout to direct traffic in the square. There being so little, they spent their watch smoking, talking and drinking vodka.

Ana skipped up the steps of the hotel entrance where the old doorman welcomed her with a broken-toothed smile. Through the second set of doors, she looked to her right and saw no one behind the registration desk.

To her left, Marina Vartanian was serving in the lobby bar. Two tables were occupied, but each had only one man. Both Russians,

Ana thought, but one a peasant and the other an aristocrat. She looked up to the mezzanine, where her old Intourist office sat dark and vacant, like all the other spaces except Vahram Abeghian's souvenir shop. Vahram himself was bent over one of the glass counters, smoking and reading a newspaper. Ana walked up the short flight of black marble steps and stood at the door of the shop. Vahram sensed someone there and looked up to see her wide smile.

"Ana," he greeted her, tossing the paper aside. "What a long time since I've seen you. Come in, come in. You look wonderful. A little too thin, perhaps," he added, standing back to look her up and down.

Ana smiled and replied, "You sound like my mother. And you, old friend. Do you think you're going to make any money tonight or are you just getting away from your wife?"

Vahram ran the palm of his hand over the gray and black stubble of beard on his chin and cheek. "I came over to shave and then I saw those Russians downstairs. They have money to spend. So . . . Why not see what happens? I have nothing else to do."

"Who's on duty at the desk?" she asked.

"Marta's working tonight."

"She wasn't there when I came in. I'll see if I can find her. Take care." She waved gaily to Vahram, feeling awake and alive for the first time in days.

As she reached the door of the shop she stopped cold. Below, Aleksandr Avakian swept in with his Russian pilot. She'd heard his name was Deshnikov. The plane must have just come in from Turkey. She was relieved Aleksandr didn't look up. He might have seen her.

She watched him cross the cold marble floor of the lobby toward the bar, moving with purpose and only a slight limp, one of his souvenirs from Afghanistan. She was glad she couldn't see the scar that ran down his left cheek and marred his handsome face.

Ana knew Aleksandr. Once, she had even loved him.

The memory of the day she first met him flashed before her eyes. She had just left her desk at Intourist and was standing almost exactly where she was now. He had just walked into the Hotel Armenia wearing major's insignia on blue, KGB shoulder boards. He had seen her at the same moment, making a drab Intourist uniform look almost stylish. She fought the memories but they came in a flurry--glittering winter evenings at the ballet, passionate nights in the steamy tangle of sheets, summer afternoons on the grassy slopes around Lake Sevan watching his lovely eyes and his bright smile, pretending to listen to him expound Soviet socialist principles.

Then, as Aleksandr crossed the lobby, he and Marina Vartanian appeared in the frame of Ana's vision and she saw them together in her mind again, damp and naked, in Aleksandr's bed, Marina's eyes wide with surprise. She shrank against the marble column and shook her head to clear it. The past. All in the past.

Aleksandr and Deshnikov disappeared into the bar and Ana slipped down the stairs into the office behind the registration desk.

"Ana. How marvelous. Where have you been?" Marta squealed, rising to give her a hug, her round face lit by a wide smile.

"Just home and the library," Ana replied. "Nowhere to go. No money, no job." She shrugged. "But I think I have work coming," she said, brightening. "So I decided to celebrate by seeing my friends."

"Too bad Olga isn't here," Marta said. "She won't be in tonight. I have it all to myself. No problem. Only the regulars and the staff."

"Who's coming in over the next few days? Any business groups or trade missions?"

"One American," Marta replied. "He must be an official. The American AID mission made his reservation."

"Perhaps that's it. English. How long is he staying?"

"Three weeks."

"Marta," Ana said, holding her friend's arm, thinking how welcome three weeks work would be. "I'd so love to have a hot shower before I go to see about the job. Could you give me a key--something on a quiet floor?"

Marta found a vacant room in the north wing and turned to Ana. "See Sofia on the fourth floor. Tell her to give you four-twenty-six. Come down and talk afterward."

Ana inserted the key Sofia gave her in the lock, turned it and drew the heavy bolt. She pressed gently against the door and it swung open noiselessly. She flipped the switch and felt a small thrill when the lights came on. Putting her head into the bathroom, she saw fluffy white towels racked on the hot water pipes. Tentatively, she touched the polished steel. It was deliciously hot.

She turned the taps and slipped out of her clothes. The bathroom soon filled with steamy clouds of humidity. She relished it on her skin briefly before she stepped into the tub, pulled the curtain and adjusted the shower head. She let the hot water strike her full in the face, course down the separation between her breasts and splash about her feet. She lathered her hands with soap and began to bathe.

****

The next morning, Ana withdrew the Minister's note from her soft Hungarian glove and presented it to the guard inside the main entrance of Government House. She wore a light gray suit and a white silk blouse under her leather coat. She had used her dwindling supply of cosmetics sparingly and the look she achieved was modesty and crisp efficiency.

The guard on duty and his several cohorts certainly seemed to approve. They compared the picture in her blue Republic of Armenia passport with her person much longer than necessary to determine that she was who she claimed to be. Smiling, they finally allowed her to pass. As her boots clicked across the spacious lobby, she felt their eyes follow her all the way into the ground floor corridor and was reassured.

She opened the door to the Minister's waiting room at five minutes before nine o'clock and was greeted by Manoukian's gruff senior secretary, a bulky woman with a perpetual scowl under heavy brows and a dark, downy mustache. The two young secretaries who typed and filed and fetched for the Minister had not yet reported for work.

"Good morning," Ana said. "I am Ana Stepanian. The Minister asked me to come at nine o'clock."

"You're early," the secretary said, not quite growling. "But I'll tell him you're here."

Ana retreated to a wall of the cramped ante room to give the secretary room to pass through the padded red-leather door into Manoukian's inner sanctum. When she returned seconds later, she forced a smile and held the door open. "The Minister will see you now."

As Ana entered, the Minister rose from his desk and came around to greet her. "Miss Stepanian," he said, smiling and holding out his hand. "How nice to see you again. Please sit down."

She shook the Minister's bony hand, smiled and seated herself demurely, crossing her legs at the ankle and tucking them under the seat of the chair. Tucking her feet under, she knew, would throw her forward slightly, indicate her rapt attention to the words the man across from her might speak and force her to straighten her back to produce the ladylike posture her mother taught her so long ago. "Thank you, Mr. Minister," she replied. "I'm flattered you remembered me."

"I hope you are free to accept a three-week assignment," the Minister said, coming directly to the point.

Three weeks! It must be the American Marta told her about. At her usual daily fee, it would be her largest payday in a long time. She contained her enthusiasm and replied, "Yes, Mr. Minister, I am."

"This is an important assignment. You have no competing commitments during this time? You will be able to devote yourself to the task fully?"

She smiled and inclined her head to indicate the affirmative.

"Good," Manoukian said, allowing himself a grim smile. "Well, then," he went on, pulling several pieces of paper toward him. "In light of the long hours we anticipate, I am going to authorize Administration to pay double your daily fee and to provide a one week advance. Will that be satisfactory?" He looked over the tops of his glasses at her, holding a pen poised over one of the documents, awaiting her answer to sign it.

"Of course, Mr. Minister, but your offer is so generous, I hope you don't mind if I ask the nature of the work?"

Manoukian laughed softly. "Forgive me. We are not asking you to assassinate anyone. I need an English interpreter. But not just speaking. There will be written material to translate from Armenian to English and later, a report in English to translate into Armenian. And you'll be involved with one of our high-level committees--ten self-important, difficult people who take pleasure in fighting with each other." He smiled and then continued. "Your client is an American who's never been to Armenia, probably knows nothing at all about us, but a great deal depends on his help. No matter how difficult or disagreeable he may be, you must make him understand our problems and help him with the Committee. You may be sure that even your talents will be challenged." Manoukian paused to give her time to absorb what he had said. "Does that answer your question?" he said at last.

"Yes, but may I know what this American and the Committee will be doing?"

Manoukian nodded. "We have a loan pending from the World Bank for a hundred million US dollars. This is the first tranche of a line of credit that might ultimately reach five hundred million. We need this money to build the infrastructure of a new market economy. Our first request was rejected. We must not fail this time." Manoukian fell silent for a few moments and then offered Ana a cigarette.

"No thank you," she said.

Manoukian lit the Russian Marlboro and drew deeply from it. "In any event, it is of paramount importance that this American--Dr. Yeager--give us a strategy the World Bank will approve. I remembered your excellent work with the French delegation last fall and knew you were the person I needed. So . . . I can count on you?"

"Of course," Ana replied, her elation over the money the job would bring her now soured by its purpose. 'A foreigner who knows nothing about us or our country must come to rescue us? Is it our destiny to hold out our begging bowl?' she thought, even as she presented a smile to Manoukian. "Thank you for the opportunity to be of service," she said. "I will do my very best."

"I am sure you will," Manoukian said, signing one of the papers with a flourish and passing it across to Ana for her to sign.

"Now," Manoukian said. "Only one or two more things. Dr. Yeager is scheduled to arrive tomorrow on the midnight flight from Amsterdam. The Americans will bring him to the Hotel Armenia. His people will want to see him first, but I want him working with the Committee as soon as possible. I'll let the Americans have him Monday morning, but no longer. You'll have to see to that."

He opened a drawer of his desk and rummaged around in it for a few moments, finally withdrawing a sheaf of heavy stationery with the ministry's letterhead . Then he dictated an invitation to lunch and told Ana to transcribe it in English. "Now, Miss Stepanian, if you deliver this message to Dr. Yeager on Sunday--in person--I do not think he will refuse." The Minister smiled and winked at her. "Bring him to this office. He can meet the Committee after lunch." Then he looked gravely into her eyes. "You are doing Armenia a great service."

'Yes,' she thought. 'I am helping deliver my country into bondage again.'

Chapter Six

The USAID Mission in Yerevan

Tom struggled out of bed, showered and shaved, dusted his shoes with a dirty sock, put on a coat and tie and looked around for his briefcase. He had nothing to put in it, but it was part of the uniform and there might be papers to bring back from the AID Mission. He popped the locks and immediately saw the package he'd brought from Andre's. He'd forgotten about it.

The brown paper was taped around a hard case about the size of his hand. With a penknife he used to clean his fingernails, he cut through the tape and peeled away the paper. Inside the case was a watch resting in a red velvet cocoon. Not just any watch. A Rolex with a gold case and bracelet. A cobalt blue face and bezel with gold numerals. Luminescent hands and dial markers. A window for the date, but none for the day of the week. The fine print on the case said 'submariner.' A very elegant piece of functional jewelry, not so gaudy as to attract unwanted attention, but impressive to anyone with an eye for such things. This Rolex had to have cost somewhere in the neighborhood of $25,000, even if it wasn't much different from the black-faced Seiko he'd paid $80 for and which kept excellent time.

In addition to the watch, there was a note from his father.

Sonny,

This is yours now. It's all I have of value. Your debt to Andre will be paid in full if you do one last pickup. I told Andre to send the goods to Armenia. Wear the watch. A brush pass. Sorry I couldn't have been a better father.

Dad

Tom knew the meaning of the note, understood that a courier would find him in Armenia, identify him by the Rolex and slip a handful of diamonds into his coat pocket. Then all he had to do was take the diamonds back to Andre and that would be that. Except there was no Andre anymore. Moreover, the diamonds would be his if he chose to take them. Owning them and selling them were, of course, two different things and he'd have a large bullseye on his back if he tried to walk around Antwerp or Tel Aviv looking for a buyer.

At a minimum, whatever debt he owed Andre was now cancelled whether he picked up the diamonds or not. His last pickup for Andre was 1974 and two million dollars worth of cut stones were stolen from him, but he'd never felt he owed Andre anything. A guy like Andre was sure to lose a shipment once in awhile. Just part of the business. But what was it with Gunter? Honor among thieves?

His thoughts swirling, Tom felt a stab of guilt. Paying Andre off and leaving a hideously expensive watch for him proved that his father had cared for him, just not in the way Tom wanted. Maybe Gunter had felt incapable, awkward, relating to a kid. Paying Tom's debt by continuing to smuggle diamonds for Andre was all he knew how to do.

Did he owe Gunter anything? Maybe. Finish what he started, no matter how meaningless it now was. He could put on the watch and wait for a packet of diamonds smuggled out of Russia or West Africa or he could not put on the watch, forget about Vienna as he had managed to do for so long, just do his job here and go back to the lake. Trying to sell the diamonds would be risky in the extreme. Yet, in some mysterious way, he felt Gunter's hand reaching toward him from the grave. He held his father's last wish and his legacy in his hands. Should he honor Gunter and give him a final rest or turn and walk away? The choice was his.

But what to do with the watch? His briefcase hadn't been disturbed. The hotel safe might offer adequate protection. Then again, it might not. He snapped the case closed and put it back in his briefcase. He'd see it there often enough to remind him that he had a decision to make.

****

Bob Lange, the tall, sandy-haired Deputy Director of the AID

Mission in Armenia, rose from his chair and stretched out his hand. Lange's blue eyes were level with Tom's and were alert and intelligent. Their handshake was without bravado, too. It was firm and conveyed a mutual respect that Tom took immediately as a good omen. "Have a seat," Lange said. "Did you get squared away at the hotel?"

"No problem. Sam met me at the airport, set me up at the hotel and even showed me a little bit of Yerevan yesterday. Jet lag's still a bitch, but otherwise I'm ready to get after it."

"Good," Lange said. "The Armenians are eager. And they do need that loan approved post haste. Our Mission Director is George Marcos. He's been up in Georgia and was supposed to be back today. Anyway, since he's not and we haven't heard from him, we assume he went on over to Baku and will be back later tonight. We cover three countries, you know. He'll want to see you soon, but I wrote your Terms of Reference, so I can brief you and answer any questions you may have about what we're up to."

"Sounds great. I'm ready to get going."

"Well, that's a bit of a problem," Lange said, shuffling papers on his desk as if he were searching for something. "I have a couple of meetings this morning," he said and looked up to meet Tom's eyes. "Why don't we meet for lunch and do your briefing this afternoon? There's a good little shashlik place around the corner. I'll introduce you to the local cuisine. You can see the Director tomorrow and start with the Armenians in the afternoon or the day after. How about that?"

Tom shook his head. "That's not going to work. I'm having lunch with the Minister of Finance today. I have a notion he wants me to get busy."

"You're having lunch with the Minister of Finance?" Lange exclaimed, a frown furrowing the space between his eyebrows.

"That's what the invitation says. It was delivered to me yesterday at the hotel. Sam was there," Tom said, looking to Rhodes for confirmation.

"That's right," Rhodes said, grinning at Lange's surprise.

Recognition clouded Lange's face and a sarcastic note appeared in his voice. "Oh, yeah. I forgot. You're some kind of friend of the Minister. He asked for you by name."

"Sorry," Tom replied, deadpan. "I'm not his buddy. I never

heard of him until yesterday. And all I know about Armenia is what I've read in the last couple of days. I even had to look it up on the map."

"Then I'm mystified," Lange said, the resentment in his expression fading. "Krikor Manoukian is the second or third most powerful man in Armenia. He does not meet with consultants, much less have lunch with them. For all I know, the American ambassador has never had lunch with him. I met him once--at an official function with a hundred other people--and I wasn't even allowed in his office the other day when he called the Director in to tell him to bring you out here. Notice I said 'tell,' not 'ask'."

"Sorry. I still haven't got a clue," Tom lied with wide-eyed innocence. "From what you say, though, I don't think I want to start by asking the second most powerful man in Armenia to postpone."

"You sure as hell don't," Lange agreed, taking a deep breath and letting it go. "OK, then. Sam, ask Mary to come in."

A trim, middle-aged brunette in a wool skirt and white silk blouse appeared in the doorway and arched her eyebrows.

"Mary," Lange said. "Reschedule Fulton for after lunch. He wants to talk about next year's program submission. Cavendish is on my calendar for this morning, too. Reschedule him for later in the week. And ask Vartan to stand by."

"Got it," Mary replied crisply and disappeared.

"Let's get to it, then. Did you say you had to be at the Ministry at noon?"

"Right," Tom replied. "The interpreter's picking me up at the hotel, so I need to be there a bit before."

"What interpreter?" Lange asked.

"The one the Ministry's providing," Tom said.

"She's the one who delivered the invitation," Rhodes added, grinning even more broadly. "She's very dishy, too."

Bob Lange scowled at Rhodes for being a smart ass, but the way this was playing gave him a sharper understanding of why Krikor Manoukian was so close to the top of the power structure in Armenia. Marcos would have given Tom the chief AID interpreter, Vartan Karapetyan, figuring Vartan would provide regular progress reports on what was going on. Now Manoukian had cut that maneuver off at the pass by assigning his own interpreter.

"OK," Lange said at last. "The Armenians have 'one-upped' us. I imagine the Director wanted to take you over and 'present' you to the Minister. You wouldn't have had to jump out of a cake, but I'm sure he would've liked to take some credit for getting you out here. I'd take you, but I'm not invited for lunch and I think we'd better leave it that way."

"Fine by me," Tom said. "But I don't have much time to deliver and no time at all to play games."

"You're absolutely right," Lange replied. "Let's ring the school bell. You're about to get a crash course on the Armenian economy. Sam, would you mind calling down and laying on a driver to take Dr. Yeager over to the hotel about quarter to twelve?" Lange paused and stared at Tom. "Manoukian didn't assign you a car, too, did he?"

Tom grinned and shook his head. "Not yet."

CHAPTER SEVEN

Government House

She was standing to one side of the reception desk, where they'd met the day before, the long leather coat slung over her shoulders. Her cheeks were flushed from the cold outside and her eyes seemed more lively and exotic than the first time he'd seen her. He still sensed some reserve, some stiffness.

Crossing the lobby he held her eyes and tried to visualize the sort of man her husband was. He was certainly a fortunate one, but cursed as well because he had to know that every time she left the house, other men would stare at her and imagine things about her, just as Tom was doing now. Perhaps she was difficult to live with. You never knew about those things. He thought about Seline for a moment. She had hidden her resentment from him for months, probably years, and then one day just went away, leaving him with the barest of justification or explanation.

When he was in speaking range, he stopped and, for a moment, neither of them spoke.

"Hello," he said at last.

"Hello," she replied, offering him a polite smile.

"Should we go?" he asked.

"Yes, if you like."

Standing close to her, her scent floated up to him--something fresh, earthy. Still tantalized by the unanswered questions of who she was and what her life was like, he followed her across the lobby, through the two sets of doors, down the steps and into the square. It was another chilly day, but pleasant in the bright sun. Tom allowed her to lead the way.

Just beyond Lenin's empty pedestal, a crowd was gathered at the Post Office building, a striking contrast to the emptiness of the Square on Sunday. "What's going on there?" Tom asked.

"They wait to telephone friend or relative in another country--Russia or France, even America."

"Do all international calls have to be made this way?" Tom asked.

"Yes," she said.

"Even in the hotel?"

"Oh. No, there is telephone for international calls in hotel. I can show you where."

As they came even with the main arch of the Post Office building, they saw Mt. Ararat, perfectly framed, just as Rhodes had said it would be.

Ana stopped and pointed toward the mountain. "Look," she said.

"Good grief," Tom exclaimed. "That's fantastic."

"Yes," she said. "Sometimes in morning. Not at this hour."

"It's huge. But it's in Turkey, isn't it? I didn't realize we were so close to the border."

"It is tall mountain--we call it Masis. More than five thousand meters. We see it so large because on flat earth it is alone, not like one mountain with other mountains. Do you understand?"

Tom nodded, still staring at the mountain.

She was silently angry with herself. Where were the English words she needed to explain? She had practiced the night before and was sure she would be better today than she had been the day before at the hotel. They would be with the Minister in only a few minutes. She had to concentrate.

Reluctantly, Tom allowed her to draw him away from the vision of Mt. Ararat. They crossed Prospekt Tigran Metz and entered Government House. Tom showed his US passport and Ana explained to the guard that he was expected by the Minister of Finance. The guard remembered Ana from Friday, but nevertheless required her to show her passport. He also telephoned the Minister's office to confirm that he was expecting Thomas K. Yeager.

"Are you called Thomas?" Ana asked when the guard had cleared them and they were walking down the corridor toward the central staircase. "The guard said 'Thomas Yeager'."

"I go by Tom," he said. "Thomas seems a little formal and Tommy is what my family called me when I was a child. Tom's a grown-up name without sounding . . . you know, pretentious." He paused a moment. "And you're 'Ana'?"

"My name is Anahit," she said. "It means 'Mother of Earth,' but I am called Ana."

As they climbed the stairs, Tom admired the enormous carpet, the colors faded and worn, but the quality of the weave unmistakable. When they reached the corridor he let her lead, shamelessly watching the roll of her slender hips and the way her skirt tightened against one leg and then the other as she walked. Too quickly, he thought, they arrived at the Minister's office.

Manoukian's crusty assistant ushered them directly into the Minister's office. They found Manoukian on his feet, smiling, moving forward to greet them.

"Dr. Yeager. Welcome to Armenia," he said in heavily accented English.

"Thank you, Mr. Minister," Tom replied, taking Manoukian's outstretched hand. It was firm and bony, like the man himself. Tom's initial impression of him was of a man who had been ill. His cheeks were sunken and the parchment of his skin was stretched across his skull as tight as a death mask. His eyes were set deep in their sockets, but they put the lie to his unhealthy appearance--they were alive with quick intelligence, energy and drive.

"Please," the Minister said, motioning them to three overstuffed chairs set against the wall facing the windows and arranged around a low coffee table. Manoukian rattled off something to Ana and then motioned again for them to sit.

"Minister Manoukian says he has now exhausted his English and that it is time for me to work."

"The Minister has me at a disadvantage," Tom said. "I know no Armenian at all. Nor Russian, which I understand is the second language here." Manoukian smiled too quickly, before Ana's translation could have registered with him. The Minister's English was better than he pretended.

"I have asked that lunch be served to us here. We can speak in confidence and comfort," Manoukian said, waiting for Ana to translate, but giving Tom no opportunity to reply.

Ana was translating almost simultaneously, speaking softly, leaning toward Tom, close enough that he could feel her breath on his cheek from time to time. He continued looking at Manoukian, listening to his intonations and the rhythms of his speech, watching his body language and trying to take a more complete measure of the man, but Ana was a powerful distraction, so close to him, the fragrance of anise on her breath as she whispered the Minister's words. He seldom worked with translators and he'd never had one like Ana so close to him.

"Our situation is this, Dr. Yeager," Manoukian said through Ana's translation. "We remained tied to the Russian ruble in the first days of independence. When the ruble exchange rate collapsed, the Russian inflation infected us like a virus and made what little capital we had worthless. It would not have been enough in any case. So we are now desperate."

Manoukian cleared his throat and went on. "After the earthquake, we had help from everywhere in the Soviet Union. You have probably seen the cranes and you will see the domiks--the shelters--in the suburbs. But when the Soviet Union broke apart, everyone went back to their own republics. Since then we have had assistance from international agencies in repairing the damage and they have helped us with the refugees from Karabagh, but that assistance cannot take us forward. It cannot even take us back to where we were."

The door opened and three waiters trooped in to serve lunch. Two of the three needed a shave and their appearance fell short of the elegance their white jackets was meant to convey. One of the waiters set plates, flatware, napkins and glasses before them and poured mineral water. Dishes of sliced cucumbers and fresh tomatoes were laid out. Levash--the thin Armenian bread--was placed in the center of the table. Then a plate of ground meat mixed with grain and spinach was served.

Manoukian gestured toward the food laid out on the table. "Please," he said in English and began filling his plate. "I do not like to speak of problems when I am hungry." The Minister gave Ana a chance to eat by continuing in English, asking Tom about his journey and his accommodations, his impressions of Yerevan, what he knew about Armenia and Armenians. Each time Tom stopped talking, the Minister asked another question.

As they finished eating, the Minister spoke to Ana. She

listened and then translated for Tom. "The Minister says I am to teach you about Armenia and give you good thoughts about us." She hated having to say this. It was part of the begging.

"Tell him I think you've made a fine beginning."

The Minister nodded, smiling, and pressed a button on the console beside his chair. The waiters came, took away the dishes and brought tea. Manoukian offered Tom a Marlboro, which Tom declined. The Minister lit a cigarette with a slender gold lighter and exhaled a great plume of smoke. He picked up where he'd left off before lunch. Ana again leaned in toward Tom and began her murmured translation.

Manoukian took him through the steps they'd taken to privatize the economy and prepare the legal groundwork for private investment, but capital was needed to retool the economy's industries and repair and upgrade the physical infrastructure. Manoukian paused at the end of his discourse and fixed Tom with his piercing eyes.

"If we do not win this loan . . . You understand that many of our people have left the country, particularly the young people." He held out his hands, palms upward. "Who can blame them? There is so little for them here. We must give them a reason to believe they have a future here. You must make the World Bank give us the money. If they do not, a country that has existed from the time of the Great Flood will die."

"I didn't fully appreciate the stakes involved, but I do now, Mr. Minister," Tom began. He balanced on the edge of the question he wanted to ask, but wasn't sure he dared. Curiosity about what Manoukian would say won the battle and Tom plunged ahead. "I'd like to understand why you asked for me. My specialty is development finance, not planning or loan structuring."

Manoukian waited for Ana's translation and smiled when she finished.

"A man who is a special friend of Armenia gave us your name."

"Would you mind telling me who that is?"

Manoukin smiled. "His name is Petros Karekin. Perhaps you have heard of him."

The name rang a faint bell. Didn't Mariah say she was with Karekin Associates? That would explain the extraordinary treatment- -Mariah flying into Granite Shoals, an Armenian consular officer waiting at the airport to put a visa in his passport, first class on United.

"Is he an American?" Tom asked.

"He lives in America, but Armenians live everywhere," Manoukian said. "In America, in Russia, in France and England, in Israel, even South Africa, South America and India. The Turks scattered us to the wind a hundred years ago." He grunted a laugh. "What you see here is all that is left of our ancestral homeland--from the time of Noah's Ark. We are losing it now because our economy is falling apart. Without this loan, all that will be left of Armenia will be the mountains and the rocks, the sheep and the vineyards. How much brandy can the world drink?"

Manoukian's speech had come in a rush, not the measured explanation he had given Tom earlier. He paused for breath and then said, "There's no mistake is there? You can help us?" Manoukian blinked rapidly again, waiting for Tom's answer.

"It'll work out," Tom said with greater confidence than he felt. Manoukian visibly relaxed and Tom went on, his own tension rising with the burden of higher stakes than he'd expected. "I understand you have a committee developing the loan request."

"Yes," Manoukian said. "You will meet them this afternoon. Each ministry of the government is represented. The Chairman is the Minister of Economy but I answer to the President for its work. I have already told the members that they are to cooperate with you in all things and that whatever you want you are to have without delay."

****

They met the Committee in a small conference room a few doors away from the office Manoukian had set aside for Tom. When they arrived, the room was already filled with people, spirited conversation and cigarette smoke. The Chairman, Petros Zadigian, Minister of Economy, went around the table introducing each of the ministers. Altogether, there must have been twenty-five in the room counting the ministers' senior staff.

Manoukian made a short speech that was received with smiles and a few laughs, then squeezed Tom's shoulder and sat down. The atmosphere in the room was relaxed, but Tom couldn't avoid his awareness that this was the cabinet of the government of Armenia. And unless Manoukian was putting him on, they were counting on him to save a country that had existed for almost three thousand years.

Tom cleared his throat. "Thank you, Mr. Minister," he began, relieved that his voice didn't break, that it lied for him admirably, projecting a confidence he didn't feel. "I appreciate the opportunity to help you prepare this loan request. I'm going to need to review what you submitted to the World Bank before I make any suggestions, but I hope that won't take long. Would it be possible for a member of the Committee staff to work with me on that?"

Minister Zadigian replied eagerly, "Our Committee Chief of Staff, Levon Abovyan, has been assigned to you."

Tom nodded and smiled at the young man Zadigian indicated. Abovyan wore thick glasses and had a heavy mass of dark, untamed curly hair. His eyes were bright and quick but he was strung as tight as piano wire.

"In the broadest terms," Tom continued, making the obvious sound profound and pausing often to allow Ana time to translate his words. "The World Bank will want a strong statement of your long-term strategy--what kind of economy you want to have in five or ten years--and how you plan to get there. They'll want to see in detail the collection of projects you're proposing and a rational implementation schedule for those projects. You'll have to show how the projects and the implementation schedule will produce the end results you're after. These are the critical elements of the loan request and if we get them right, the rest of it won't matter much. Do you have any questions?"

Zadigian launched into a long monologue that seemed to be in the nature of a pep talk. Tom wasn't sure, but he thought Ana translated only the high points. By the time he stopped for breath, no one had any desire to prolong the meeting. When the room finally cleared, Tom, Ana and Levon Abovyan were standing alone. It was three o'clock in the afternoon.

"Would you like to see the documents now?" Levon asked and Ana translated. "Yes,"

Tom said. "Very much."

Abovyan led them to a narrow office with a high ceiling and a hardwood floor that sang a soft welcome as they crossed it. A dozen bulging file folders were stacked on a table beside a bank of file cabinets. Levon patted them and spoke briefly with Ana.

"Levon says these are the files of the loan request. He wants to know if you would like to take them to your office?"

Tom opened one of the folders on the table and found to his delight that it was in English. "Is all this in English?" he asked.

"Yes, he says. It is what they sent to the World Bank."

"And this is the whole submission?"

Ana asked Levon, he replied and she said, "Yes, everything."

"Terrific," Tom said, smiling broadly. Even before Ana translated, he could see Levon, who had been standing stiff as a board, relax a little. "Tell Levon I'm looking forward to working with him. Since the first thing on my agenda is reading the submission, let's carry it to the other office and I'll get started. You're coming along, aren't you?" he asked Ana.

"Of course," she replied. "I am to be with you at all times," she added with an uncertain smile.

CHAPTER EIGHT

Hotel Armenia

Two Russians arrived that afternoon and Marina now appraised them carefully as they sat at separate tables in her bar. The only thing they could have had in common was that they'd come in on the Moscow flight. One was a beefy sort whose expensive suit could never conceal his peasant origins. The other was an aristocrat by comparison, as refined and elegant as the other one was coarse and crude. The peasant ordered Stolichnaya and displayed a robust and rowdy thirst. The elegant one asked for tea.

Some of the mystery evaporated when Aleksandr Avakian and Ivan Deshnikov came through the front door and went directly across the lobby to the beefy Russian's table. As Marina's eyes followed Aleksandr, she noted with affection and a certain pride that his limp was barely noticeable and that the ruddy tint his skin had taken on in the Caribbean last month obscured the scar that ran down his cheek. He looked in Marina's direction and caught her eye, giving her a silent, solemn greeting.

"Aleks," boomed the burly Russian. "About time."

"Hello, Boris," Aleksandr said without changing expression. After a moment's inspection of Boris to gauge his stage of drunkenness, his eyes shifted to the Russian drinking tea.

"Sit down and have a drink," Boris rumbled.

"What's your room number? Go there. I'll come up later."

Boris frowned, but snatched the key with its bulbous fob from the table. He looked at the bottom of the fob. "Five-oh-five," he said, slurring the words.

Aleksandr turned to Deshnikov. "Go with him. Keep him away from the vodka bottle. Don't let him pass out before I get there."

Deshnikov helped Boris to his feet and steered him toward the elevator. Aleksandr watched them go and then gave his full attention to the only other occupant of the bar.

Aleksandr knew Nikolai Danilov only slightly. They had

been in different directorates of the KGB and their paths seldom crossed. Until he'd been transferred to a different sort of duty in Afghanistan, Aleksandr had run agents into the United States from Mexico, supporting them on station and recovering them when their missions were accomplished or their cover blown. He'd done similar duty in Armenia after his successful tour in Mexico. From Yerevan, he guarded the Philby Gate, handling agents who were too sensitive to use the normal European routes. Kim Philby, the British spy, had passed that way before Aleksandr's time and given his name to the route that snaked its way through Lebanon to Syria and across Eastern Turkey to the Soviet Socialist Republic of Armenia. Many of the same Turkish contacts who helped Aleksandr then now constituted the network he used to deliver poppy paste to the morphine and heroin labs in Russia, the Ukraine and Belorus.

Danilov had been part of the less glamorous counterespionage directorate, rooting out counter-revolutionaries who spied for the West and those miscreants who undermined the Soviet system in other ways. It was rumored that Danilov was a top assassin in Yuri Glazunov's black ops group.

Had he come to Yerevan on such an assignment?

"Nikolai Danilov," Aleksandr said, a statement of fact, not a greeting.

"Hello, Sasha."

"Don't call me Sasha."

Danilov shrugged, his dark eyes cold and steady, fixed on Aleksandr, waiting.

"What brings you to Yerevan?" Aleksandr asked.

"I came to see you."

"To buy drugs or to kill me?"

"Neither, actually," Nikolai said. "But I'd prefer not to tell the world. Why not join me?"

Aleksandr crossed the short distance, pulled back a chair and sat down.

"Drink?" Nikolai asked.

Aleksandr shook his head. "What do you want here, Russian? Do you still work for Yuri Glazunov?"

Danilov shook his head slowly. "Glazunov is, what should we say?--retired. I watch over our interests these days, Sasha. Yuri became careless in his old age. I'm handling some unfinished business and diversifying."

"Diversifying?"

"It's the capitalist thing to do these days."

"So you want to buy drugs?"

Danilov snorted. "No, Sasha. No drugs for me."

"You think it's a dirty business," Aleksandr bristled.

"I didn't say that, my friend. I don't want to be in the drug business because there are already too many competitors. The new capitalists of Russia are buying real estate in the south of France, yachts, Mercedes, fine art and jewelry. I've always been a jewelry man. You know that."

"I didn't," Aleksandr said. "I thought you were just one of Glazunov's assassins."

"Are you insulting me, Sasha? A drug dealer looking down on an assassin? You should tell your cow to be silent if someone else's is mooing."

Aleksandr's eyes flashed anger. "Don't try me, Russian. You never did frighten me and you don't now. I'm tired. If you have a proposition, speak it and we'll find out if there's any point to this conversation."

"Oh, Sasha. Were you always this difficult?" Danilov said, removing his rimless glasses and polishing them with a handkerchief. He put them back on carefully, then steepled his hands, only the fingertips touching, and leaned toward Aleksandr.

"I'm looking for antique jewelry--pieces with provenance and history. Perhaps a cross carried by an early Patriarch of the Armenian Church. Something of value to a collector."

A thin smile spread over Aleksandr's face and he shook his head. "I'm a drug dealer, Russian. Armenian crosses aren't in my inventory."

"Forgive me," the Russian persisted. "But I understood you were the source of some interesting pieces that recently appeared on the market in Europe."

Aleksandr stared at Danilov for a long moment. "What makes you think I can get anything a collector of fine arts would be interested in?"

"I've seen some new additions to private collections that once were in the catalog of the History Museum here. What I saw wasn't very impressive--minor pieces. But they were Armenian and I was told you'd be a good person to talk to."

"Who told you that?" Aleksandr asked, his head cocked to one side.

Danilov didn't care what happened to his source if Avakian took offense so he had no reluctance about naming him. "A man called Bandini," he said. "I met him on Martinique. He said you come to the island once or twice a year. That you fish together."

Aleksandr nodded, recalling the time Bandini came to his hotel room unexpectedly and saw three pieces of antique jewelry Aleksandr was delivering to a French collector. Bandini asked him about it later and, in the exuberance of three Planters' Punches, Aleksandr foolishly bragged to Bandini about his pipeline to the vaults of the History Museum.

Aleksandr stared at the Russian with new interest. A long time ago, Glazunov had made his name exposing a nest of thieves in the trade mission who were stealing diamonds from the Aikhal mines in Siberia and smuggling them to the West. It had all been very secret, but inside the KGB, it was known that the thieves had been spared the embarrassment of a trial. The rumors went on to name Nikolai Danilov as their executioner. Now the Russian sat here, cold as a cobra, either spinning a cover story or making an interesting business proposition. Aleksandr wasn't sure which.

"So . . . you and Bandini," Aleksandr said.

Danilov nodded. "I'm interested in museum quality. Nothing that would bring less than fifty thousand US in the European market."

"I don't take orders," Aleksandr said. "I won't procure this or that because you want it. If I find something I think might interest you, I'll contact you."

Danilov gave Aleksandr a sideways nod of his head to signify his agreement, put a finger and thumb into the breast pocket of his suit coat and withdrew a card. "That's a fax number in St. Petersburg. If you find two pieces, send a message that says 'two lambs are ready for shearing.' If you have three pieces, 'three lambs,' and so on. That's all you need to say, except where to reply."

Aleksandr nodded. "Fax the business center here at the Hotel Armenia for 'The Shepherd.' Say nothing except when you will arrive."

The Russian nodded.

"If we agree on price--and after my bank in Zurich confirms your deposit--you take delivery here. I'll guarantee clearance at the airport in Yerevan. Understood?"

Danilov nodded again.

"Goodbye, Russian," Aleksandr said and got up. Boris was

waiting.

"There's one other thing," Danilov said. "You might be of some help."

"Oh?"

"I'm consolidating our diamond trade. Stopping leaks, you might say. Glazunov was careless with the pipes. They rusted out here and there."

Aleksandr stood silently, looking down at Danilov, waiting for him to go on.

"A small package of stones may be coming this way. If you hear of anything, I will pay for the information."

Aleksandr grunted and walked away. "Dasvidaniya, Russian," he said.

CHAPTER NINE

Anniversary Park

Dusk had already fallen when Sarkis Melikian locked the doors of the Armenian History Museum. As he did so often these days, he'd lost track of time. With the power shortage, no street lights burned in Yerevan and the afterglow was barely sufficient to light his way. Republic Square was already dark and the fading light touched only the higher ground above it. He walked briskly up the hill, almost keeping pace with the last rays of the sun. His apartment was in one of the buildings built in the Stalin era. It had been largely undamaged by the earthquake, but the quake had made a shambles of Sarkis' life. That was why he often worked late.

Even before he turned the key in the Museum's lock, he began to think of what he would find when he reached home. Setta, his sister-in-law, the only surviving member of Karine's family, lay paralyzed in the second bedroom, always on the verge of excruciating pain, rapidly descending deeper into the abyss of drug addiction.

A year. A year that seemed like forever. That was when the doctors had given up hope of repairing the spinal damage the collapsing building had inflicted on Setta. Sarkis couldn't think of it without grinding his teeth. They'd kept her on drugs so long, trying one thing and another. Then they washed their hands of her. Send her to the state asylum, they'd said, as if she were a piece of defective equipment.

He remembered Karine's face when she returned from visiting that place. She was ashen and near hysteria. They had no drugs to make Setta's pain bearable. She would have died in that bedlam, not peacefully, but painfully. Karine hadn't been able to do that to her sister and Sarkis hadn't even thought of asking her to.

That was when the nightmare began. The only drugs available were illegal ones and he was forced to go to Aleksandr Avakian to supply them. It was a deal with the devil. Avakian wanted payment in the only currency Sarkis could provide--jewelry from the Historical

Museum. Setta's need was so great by then that Sarkis had no choice. He'd put his foot on the slippery slope and begun to steal from the Museum.

In despair, he'd decided to end what little was left of Setta's life to save his and Karine's. A drug overdose would have been the simplest, but Karine kept jealous guard over Setta's injections. Finally, he'd decided that he would put a pillow over her face and smother her, quickly, painlessly. But every time he got out of bed, no matter the time of night, Karine awoke, as if she knew his plan and was determined to thwart it.

Then two weeks ago, his thoughts of desperate measures had given way to hope and now he was doing an anxious dance along a high wire.

His cousin from Jordan, Razmik Melikian, one he scarcely knew, appeared in the doorway of his work room at the Museum. Thinking of him now, Sarkis imagined he had seen a halo around his head, so much like an angel his arrival had been.

When he learned about Setta, Razmik had been ready to bring them to Jordan, pay for Setta's treatment and help them begin a new life. Karine had almost collapsed with relief and was ready to begin packing immediately, but Sarkis' pride rose up and he'd held back. He rebelled at the thought of building a new life in a foreign land on the charity of distant relatives.

Hope had sprung from an idea he'd had months ago for expanding the Museum's holdings of heirloom jewelry. He'd seized on Razmik's offer to help as a chance to turn that idea to his own purposes and Razmik had agreed to back his play.

At first, Karine had screamed at him, beaten her fists against his chest and finally fallen to the floor, sobbing. He'd been merciless in forcing her to recognize that he was risking not only his career, but disgrace and prison, to feed Setta's need for drugs and he'd made her accept his conditions for leaving, and in the days after Razmik's return to Jordan, she spoke only the most essential words to him. The light went out of her eyes and she slept in their bed without touching him.

Sarkis was high-wire walking now, waiting for the money to come from Jordan, continuing to pay Avakian the only way he knew how and holding Karine at bay with the promise of leaving if his venture with Razmik failed.

His time for reflection came abruptly to an end when he reached the street corner opposite his building and made out the chalk mark on the curbstone in the last luminous glow of twilight. Avakian had summoned him.

He considered going directly to Anniversary Park, but his door was only a few steps away. Perhaps the news would make a difference to Karine. Meeting Avakian would mean a new supply for Setta. If Karine would only understand . . .

He found the apartment dark, not even a candle burning.

"Karine?" he called, his voice a hollow echo.

"Here," she said softly, from only a few feet away.

Turning toward her voice, he made her out in the gloom, sitting on the sofa with a blanket around her shoulders.

"Why are you sitting in the dark?" he asked, feeling his way to a side table and lighting a candle.

She didn't answer.

"How is Setta?" he asked.

She didn't respond. Even in the candlelight, her eyes were cold and lifeless. She drew in her breath, as if speaking required an effort. "I have just given her the last of it. Tonight--or tomorrow--she will be screaming in agony."

"I'm meeting him tonight," Sarkis said. "Don't worry. I'll make him give me a new supply."

"You know what we are doing only prolongs this curse. She could be helped in the West. I know she could. If we had only gone with Razmik . . ." She stopped in mid-sentence.

****

Lighting the way with his flashlight, Sarkis trudged back down the hill to Republic Square and walked around it, past the Trade Union House and the Hotel Armenia. The hotel's lights filtered into the street, eerie, dreamy beacons of a bygone world. He stopped and stared at them for a moment. The hotel might as well have been a spaceship come to earth. He turned off the flashlight to save the batteries and crossed the street to Anniversary Park.

The cascade of fountains that graced its center aisle was dry and cracked and the tall sycamore trees, dark sentinels rising on either side of the park, stood barren of their leaves. During the day, old men sat on the benches and smoked and talked. After sundown, it was deserted. But tonight Aleksandr would be waiting.

Sarkis was halfway to the Shahumyan Monument at the foot of the park when a voice echoed from the silence. "I'm here," Aleksandr said softly. Sarkis had walked past him in the dark.

"My God, you scared me," Sarkis whispered.

"I have new requirements for you," Avakian said.

"Please, I must have something for Setta," Sarkis said.

Aleksandr took Sarkis' elbow and placed a package in his hand.

Sarkis started at Aleksandr's touch, but grasped the package in both hands and tucked it into his coat pocket.

"Now to the new requirements," Aleksandr said and described what the Russian was looking for--museum quality artifacts on which Sarkis would write a provenance and sign his own good name to validate it.

"I can't," Sarkis protested, feeling his footing slip on the high wire. "Such pieces would be missed."

"You have no choice, Sarkis."

The thought of a pillow over Setta's face flashed briefly in Sarkis' mind, but he said nothing.

After a long moment of silence, Aleksandr asked, "You do remember that I was once in the KGB, don't you?"

"I remember," Sarkis said, his voice quavering.

"Then you know why you have no choice. If you fail me . . . I will take you and your wife to a place where you can scream as loud as you like and no one will hear. I won't hurt you, Sarkis. I'll let you watch me do such things to your wife that you cannot imagine. She will teeter on a razor's edge between unendurable pain and unconsciousness. Because of you, Sarkis. Because of you." Aleksandr could feel vibrations of fear emanating from Sarkis as he whispered the words.

"We could make her last a very long time. And you would watch it all. Do I make myself clear?"

"Yes," Sarkis croaked.

"Good," Aleksandr said and melted into the night.

Sarkis was left standing alone, shivering, his heart racing. He swallowed hard and hurried out of the park, almost running back up the hill to his home, to Karine and Setta.

65

CHAPTER TEN

The Museum

On Monday, Sarkis came early to the Museum and went directly to the vault area to select something to appease Aleksandr. He found an obscure gold brooch with fine filigree work that he thought would polish well and took it back to the work table in his office. He was so totally absorbed in cleaning it that he didn't hear the Museum director, Robert Hajiniyan, come up behind him.

"Interesting piece," the director said over Sarkis' shoulder.

Startled, he dropped the brooch as if it were on fire. He whirled around to see the director staring at him with a puzzled frown.

"My God, you scared me," Sarkis said, nerves still ajangle.

"Sorry," the director said. "I tapped on the door. What are you doing with the brooch?"

Sarkis shook his head to clear it, his heart now pounding as he searched frantically for an explanation. "Ah, just cleaning it. I came across a drawer of them. Now that the Coins of the Kings have been on display for some weeks, something like this might serve . . ."

The director nodded, seeming to lose interest. "Yes, yes," he said. "Good idea."

"Was there something I could do for you, Comrade Director?" Sarkis said, flattering him with the old form of address, hoping to avoid any further discussion of brooches.

The director held an envelope in one hand and tapped it against his fist. "Brother Arteshesh has made another grand 'discovery' out at Geghard. I responded to his last flight of fancy. It's your turn to go this time. Who knows? Perhaps it will be something other than his imagination," the director added, holding the envelope out to Sarkis.

He opened the flap as the director turned and left. Sarkis kept his head bowed, but his eyes rose above the tops of his glasses and watched the director pass through the door and disappear down the hall. His legs almost buckled then and he placed both hands on the workbench to steady himself. It was some moments before his heart stopped pounding. Would the director remember the brooch? It was bad enough that he noticed something out of the ordinary. As he went back over the scene in his mind, he was grateful that it was Brother Arteshesh's note that had brought the director, not one of his idle walk-arounds. If he'd just been bored sitting at his desk, it would have been a close run thing. Killing time, the director would have wanted to know about Sarkis' plans to display the museum's brooch collection.

He sat down heavily in his chair, Arteshesh's note crumpled in his right hand. He tried to force himself to believe he was over-reacting. He was a senior curator, above reproach, at least in the old days. Now, hard times had made the director suspicious of all the staff. Only last week, the guards had made a surprise search of coats, briefcases and packages. It wouldn't be the last time. Now the director had seen the brooch. If Sarkis were caught taking it out of the museum, that would be the end of it all.

This wasn't getting easier. He needed Razmik's money by the end of the week when the vernesazsh would be held. If the money didn't come by then, Setta's supplies would soon be exhausted and he would have to go to Aleksandr again. And what if he were wrong about the jewelry? No, he couldn't be. It was there. He just had to find out who had it and strike a bargain.

Not for the first time, the heightened threat of Aleksandr himself loomed in his consciousness. When they'd met last in Anniversary Park, Aleksandr had talked about what he would do if Sarkis didn't deliver. Now, even if he did deliver, would Aleksandr let him leave? Sarkis tried to banish his fear with belligerence--how could Aleksandr stop him? As long as Aleksandr didn't know . . .

Remembering the note from Brother Arteshesh, he smoothed the wrinkles from the paper, laid it on his desk and scanned it quickly. He skipped over the hyperbole, picking out the meat of the message. Workmen had found a previously unknown cell--that was hardly news. The site of the monastery was riddled with caves and no one knew exactly how long it had been used by monks and hermits and pagan sects before Armenia became a Christian nation. As Sarkis read more carefully, Arteshesh explained that this wasn't a cave used as a monk's cell, but a room hewn from the rock and later sealed deliberately and quite thoroughly. A few fragments of documents were found, ready to disintegrate into dust, and a stone box that Arteshesh had had the good sense not to open. Sarkis sat back for a moment, contemplating the note. Not the Dead Sea scrolls, he was sure, but his curiosity was nevertheless piqued by what the documents might say. Well, they'd lain there for centuries already. A few more days wouldn't matter. He turned his attention back to the brooch.

It was fine filigree work. Appraising it, he turned it one way and then another, letting the sun and shadow alter the delicate gold engravings of tiny birds and beasts and the inlays of small emeralds and rubies. It was one of several owned by a distant cousin of King Tridat III and its provenance was straightforward. The piece showed some Celtic influence and was a good example of 3rd century artistry. The Hermitage in St. Petersburg had an extensive collection of such brooches and so did his own History Museum. Since it was under Sarkis' direct charge, the principal risk of it being missed was the director's memory of seeing Sarkis with it and asking to see it again. Sarkis wrapped the brooch in a square of black velvet he would use to display it to Aleksandr and tucked it into his overcoat pocket. He prayed the director hadn't laid on another surprise inspection. That was less likely at noon, when it was his custom to walk the few blocks up the hill to take lunch with Karine.

****

Aleksandr was pleased to see the diagonal line on the light pole on Abovyan Street, across from the Museum. It meant that Sarkis had something to launch this new business with the Russian. He passed through the archway of Trade Union House and crossed the courtyard into Restoran Ararat. He was meeting his 'mule' to discuss a shipment of poppy paste from Turkey. The mule and his pilot, Deshnikov, were waiting for him. They were making a pickup that night at a primitive airfield near Patnos, Turkey, a hundred flying miles from Yerevan.

Deshnikov and Aleksandr had been friends since the Afghan War, where Deshnikov was an Air Force pilot. A casualty of military cutbacks after the collapse of the Soviet Union, Aleksandr had brought him into the drug smuggling enterprise. All Deshnikov had to do was fly the aging, twin engine Cessna 310 he'd purchased, ironically, from US government surplus. Until recently, the plane had belonged to the US AID Mission. The new Mission director had replaced it with a Piper Cheyenne and offered the Cessna at auction as part of the American privatization program. Aleksandr, using Deshnikov as a dummy buyer, had won the bid over Felix Zakarian, the godfather of the Armenian Mafia. They were the only two rich enough to satisfy the reserve price.

Aleksandr sat down at the small table, put the briefcase between his chair and the mule's and wasted no time coming to the point.

"Ivan, you're expected at Patnos after midnight. Don't arrive before." Deshnikov nodded. "The money is here," Aleksandr told the mule, patting the briefcase. "Don't let the Turk bargain with you. The price is set. The shipment is five hundred kilos of first quality. Check it carefully. The Turk seemed nervous when I talked to him. I don't know why. Understand?"

The mule nodded and pulled the briefcase next to his leg so he could feel it beside him.

Aleksandr rose and said to Deshnikov. "Call me when you return to Zvartnots. I want to know how it went."

Aleksandr had arrived at Restoran Ararat, conducted his business and was back on the street in less than five minutes. Next, he would walk to Bagramyan Prospekt and leave a chalk mark for Sarkis. He slanted the mark to indicate Akhtanak Park at noon the following day. Perhaps he would take along a treat for Sarkis' lunch, something to reward his effort. Beluga and a little vodka.

CHAPTER ELEVEN

Akhtanak Park

When Sarkis arrived in Akhtanak Park, a few mothers were trundling their toddlers around the Mother Armenia Monument in prams, so bundled against the chill it was almost impossible to see them. Aleksandr was late and Sarkis thought it was just another way of intimidating him--making him wait, letting him know who was in control. Sarkis refused to let it bother him. Instead, he watched the young mothers and thought wistfully how it would be when he and Karine had children. The waiting must be so much worse for Karine, he thought. She seldom went out any more. She was as much a prisoner of Setta's dark affliction as Setta herself.

He pushed these gloomy thoughts aside, looked out across the city and gave his imagination free rein. He swept away the clouds from Mt. Ararat and draped a snowy shawl around its shoulders, splashed green over the grass and attached new leaves to the trees. He breathed life into the old stones of the city with bright dots of red geraniums in window boxes and added people and traffic. Piece by piece, in his imagination, he restored life and color to the city. He wondered how long it would be before it looked that way again.

Into this reverie came Aleksandr Avakian, carrying a picnic basket. A long black overcoat and slouch hat was a vain attempt at concealing his identity. His characteristic limp gave him away. Sarkis sucked in his breath and tensed. He prayed no one who knew him was in the park to see him meeting with Avakian. Why would a curator of the History Museum be spending time with a KGB Major who was now known to be Armenia's principal drug dealer? The answer was too obvious.

He deliberately exhaled to relax. Aleksandr was difficult enough when one felt strong. He dared not show fear--weakness stimulated Aleksandr's lust for intimidation. Chance would have to protect him from curious eyes. Sarkis squeezed the brooch in his coat pocket to make sure it was still there. He wanted to give it to

Aleksandr and go as quickly as he could.

"Well, Sarkis," Aleksandr said with an inquiring smile when he was a few steps away from where Sarkis was standing. "It's pleasant here, isn't it?" When Sarkis made no reply, Aleksandr went on. "Sunlight like this inspires artists to create beautiful things, don't you think?" He looked piercingly into Sarkis' eyes, challenging him. "This statue of Mother Armenia, for example."

Sarkis looked at the Soviet-style statue reflexively, but said nothing. Aleksandr's presence reminded him that an enormous statue of Stalin--history's cruelest and most blood-thirsty dictator--once stood nearby. It was an ugly contradiction that he couldn't reconcile with the Armenia he loved.

Aleksandr held up the picnic basket. "We have something to celebrate, I think. Is that not so?"

"Perhaps you do."

"Now, Sarkis," Aleksandr cooed, taking him by the elbow and leading him toward a vacant bench away from the walkways. "Remember that you came to me. And remember that if it were not for me, your sister-in-law would be in a raging torment. And your lovely wife--what about her, Sarkis? She doesn't want to see her sister so, does she? Come, Sarkis. Be friendly," he said, sitting down and opening the basket. "I have Russian vodka to warm your heart and Beluga caviar to nourish your soul. Come. Eat."

Sarkis could not keep his mouth from salivating. He wanted to give Aleksandr the brooch, collect the narcotics for Setta and leave the park, but he found himself sitting down beside the picnic basket. He watched Aleksandr dip into the dish and bring up a spoonful of glistening, black caviar and put it into his mouth.

"Mmmmmm," Aleksandr rhapsodized. He opened the bottle of vodka, poured the clear liquid into an elegant crystal flute and dashed it down. "That's the best there is. Beluga and vodka. Let me give you some, Sarkis." Aleksandr didn't wait for a reply. From the basket he drew the open tin of caviar, the slippery black eggs glistening in their juices. He spread a generous portion on a scrap of levash and held it out to Sarkis.

For a long moment, Sarkis stared at the caviar waiting in its nest of levash, then took it from Aleksandr, closed his eyes and put it into his mouth. He let the flavors caress his taste buds, chewed slowly and finally swallowed. Aleksandr watched him, smiling, then handed him a crystal flute of vodka. Sarkis took it down swiftly, feeling its fire course down his throat and begin to warm the blood in his veins.

"Another?" Aleksandr asked.

Sarkis nodded dumbly.

They each had several more flutes of vodka and finished the Beluga. At last, Aleksandr looked around to make sure they weren't being observed and asked, "Show me what you have now."

His head buzzing with vodka, Sarkis took the brooch from his overcoat pocket. He placed it in the palm of his hand and peeled back the corners of the black velvet, allowing the stones to catch a little of the sunlight.

"Ah," Aleksandr sighed, unable to contain his pleasure. "Yes. That should do nicely. What can you tell me about it?"

Sarkis took a folded sheet of paper on Museum letterhead from his coat pocket and opened it for Aleksandr to read. In Russian, it described the history of the brooch and its chain of possession. Beneath the text, Sarkis Melikian, Senior Curator, had signed his name. Aleksandr inspected the letter quickly, finding it difficult to take his eyes off the brooch. "Yes," he said at last. "Well done, Sarkis. Be on the lookout for another one."

"No, Aleksandr," Sarkis said. "This is not just another piece of old jewelry. There are records, catalogs, inventories. This is an obscure brooch so it may not be missed right away. But please do not ask for ever more grander things. The risk is too great." Sarkis stood up and faced Aleksandr, his anger tempered by fear.

Aleksandr looked up at him with a condescending smile, then said, "Oh, yes. Setta. I almost forgot." He passed the picnic basket to Sarkis. "In the bottom."

****

Karine held the letter in her hand, turning it over, holding it to the sunlight streaming through the front windows, examining its foreign postage stamps. She laid it carefully on the brass tray in the foyer and returned to the kitchen, her head spinning. It was from

Razmik, but what did it mean? She feared another disappointment, but she could not stem a rising tide of hope that the letter brought some kind of news for their salvation.

An hour later, as night was falling, she heard the door open and hurried to the foyer, drying her hands on a cup towel.

"Sarkis," she said. "A letter came from Razmik. There on the tray."

His large dark eyes focused first on Karine, not quite able to make out her expression in the gloom, then fell to the brass tray where Razmik's letter reposed. He forced himself to turn away and finish hanging his coat and hat on the pegs by the door.

At last he picked up the letter and took it into the parlor to read it by the candlelight. It was double-sealed--one envelope inside the other. Sarkis loosened the flaps methodically, extracted the letter and began to read. Karine stood by anxiously, studying his expression for some clue as to what it said.

The writing covered both sides of the single sheet and Sarkis read it slowly, struggling to make out Razmik's written Armenian script. At last, he turned to Karine.

"What does he say?" she asked, holding her breath.

"He has spoken to his brother. They have sent ten thousand dollars to our bank here. It should be there already. The letter was mailed many days ago. Raz will come again when I have enough jewelry to send out. When he has seen the sample, we will decide what to do next."

"Is this good?" Karine asked anxiously. "Will we be able to leave now?"

Still smiling, Sarkis sat down in his chair, holding the letter. "Bring us a glass of brandy and let me explain. I've been thinking about this for a long time," he said. Karine went to the cabinet to fetch glasses and a bottle of brandy. Trembling, she poured two drinks and handed one to Sarkis. He took a sip and waited for her to sit beside him.

"We must be very careful," he said. "I'm sure Aleksandr has spies everywhere. I don't want to think what he might do if he found out we were planning to leave."

"Then how can we go?" Karine asked, her eyes bright.

"Quickly," Sarkis said, laughing, pleased to see that he'd banished the worry lines from her face, that she'd caught a little of his exuberant mood. "When Razmik has sold the jewelry and we receive our share, I'll ask my friend, Stepan, to buy blank airline tickets for us. We won't write our names on them until the night we leave."

"What about our papers? Won't we need papers to leave?"

"Razmik will help us with the papers we will need to enter Jordan. And he's already looking into treatment for Setta. But listen, Karine," Sarkis said, suddenly grave. "You must act as if nothing has changed. Don't pack a bag or do anything that might suggest to any of our friends or neighbors that we're preparing to leave. Do you understand?" Sarkis had turned quite serious and almost barked at Karine. "I don't know who to trust. If word came to Aleksandr . . ."

"Yes," she answered and the relief she'd felt when Sarkis laughed evaporated. What he said now frightened her.

Chapter Twelve

Hotel Armenia

The heavy lock closed on the door and Tom threw the bolt, impressed by the quality of the fittings. He dropped his briefcase on the chair, loosened his tie and hung up his coat. He toed off his shoes and stripped off his socks, shirt, pants, shorts and tee-shirt. Only fifteen minutes of hot water remained and he wanted a shower before dinner.

He ate alone in the café downstairs--borsht with delicious French fries as slender as strings--and took a brandy in the bar.

****

He propped pillows against the back of the narrow bed and pulled the heavy blanket up over his knees. He brought the heavy case that contained the Rolex to his side, but didn't look at the watch. Instead, he focused on reading the loan request documents he'd brought from Government House. He wanted to begin outlining a new strategy statement sometime tomorrow--Wednesday.

An hour later, he closed the folder, tossed the folder on the other twin bed, set the Rolex case on the bedside table and turned out the light. He rearranged the pillows and closed his eyes, expecting sleep to fall on him like a hammer. Instead, a flurry of snapshots of Ana Stepanian raced through his head.

It had taken awhile that afternoon for the three of them to get comfortable. Tom was aware of their watching him while he read, eager to help, to answer any question. To put them at ease, he'd concocted questions for the first half hour to keep them busy. It had also given him an opportunity to watch Ana. He'd been taken by her eyes from the beginning, but that afternoon he came to notice her hands, long slender fingers with close-cut, rounded nails. As she conferred with Levon over a question Tom had asked, her hands fluttered gracefully in tune with her words, like a prima ballerina in harmony with the music of the dance.

Her heavy dark hair often spilled across her face and she would pull it back with one of those exquisite hands. Then the eyes again, bright and excited when she believed she had extracted an answer from Levon.

As the light faded, he'd let them go. Working with him, bearing the heavy burden of responsibility they both so obviously felt, had been a strain and he saw how fatigued they had become. Levon disappeared down the hall and Ana walked him across the square to the hotel, helping him carry the files he intended to read that night.

In the cold, crisp air of evening, he realized that the experience he was sharing with Ana and Levon--Ana in particular--filled a void he hadn't recognized for a long time. He was lonely. Maybe it was Seline's rude and unexpected departure and his long process of healing that had left this emptiness. Whatever, Ana was now filling it.

He held the last snapshot against the back of his closed eyelids. She stood at the steps of the hotel offering to stay and help, a mountain breeze teasing the strands of her hair, her eyes dark and glossy. As much as he would have liked her to stay, he assured her he'd be fine, that he didn't intend to work long. He did invite her to have breakfast with him the next morning. He thought about that as sleep took him.

****

Tom was seated by one of the massive windows in the main restaurant. He'd just ordered eggs and bacon when Ana appeared in the door, her cheeks flushed by the cold.

"Sorry to be late," she said, a little out of breath. "My mother came this morning to say she was going to Moscow. I was very surprised."

"That's all right," Tom said. He'd begun to worry that she wouldn't come. He knew the way to Government House and was sure he could find his office and the files, but he wanted the time with her, apart from work.

A waiter hurried to the table to take her order. There was a chattering of Armenian that Tom didn't understand, but he imagined the waiter was trying to persuade her to have something more than she'd asked for. She shook her head and then made that fascinating move with her fingers to arrange her hair.

Tom smiled, watching her. "Your mother's going for a visit?"

"It is a medical conference, with many people. She is physician. After, she goes to my aunt in St. Petersburg. She leaves tomorrow, so we will eat dinner together tonight."

"Will she be gone long?" Tom asked.

"Perhaps a month," Ana replied. "The hospital is not demanding now so they do not mind if she is away."

"I've never been to Moscow," Tom said. "What's it like?" he asked, anything to keep her lips moving. They were full, but not pouty, and her mouth was generous and strong. In forming the words, the corners of her mouth turned up in a charming twitch.

Ana had been describing Moscow for several minutes when the waiter returned bringing her a glass of steaming tea, a small plate with a single blini and two dishes, one with jam and the other with sugar. The waiter spoke to her again, with grave solicitousness. Compared to the way the same waiter treated Tom, Ana could have been the Queen of Armenia. She gave the waiter the briefest of royal smiles and then looked at Tom.

"I am sorry. I do not remember what I was saying." She paused for a moment. "But I do not think you were listening."

Tom laughed in spite of himself. "I wasn't, but I was enjoying watching you."

She lowered her eyes for a moment, then looked up as if she hadn't heard his compliment. "Did you finish your work last night?" she asked.

He nodded. "From what I saw yesterday, I think the project design and documentation are in good shape. I want Levon to sit with me today to go through the rest of the package. OK?"

"Of course. Whatever you wish."

"If we can finish the project files this morning, we can start drafting a strategy statement this afternoon."

CHAPTER THIRTEEN

Government House

With Levon looking on, Tom began going through the projects, occasionally asking for clarification. Six general areas of supporting infrastructure had been carved out--power generation, transportation, health, housing and municipal services, communications and finance. Armenia's dependence on an unreliable source of energy made the power generation projects obvious--another nuclear plant and two small hydroelectric projects.

They needed airport improvements, too. The odds were that Armenia was going to be connected to the rest of the world mainly by air for the foreseeable future. Even if the Turkish and Azerbaijan borders opened, there were still problems in Georgia, which was the main overland route to Russia and the Ukraine and to Georgia's Black Sea port at Bat'umi.

Armenia was seriously behind in telecommunications technology, too. At least as much as airport improvements, more telephone trunk lines, modern switching equipment and an expansion of the cellular system were needed.

Tom was particularly sensitive to the lack of financial infrastructure. They needed to estimate the seed capital and technical assistance requirements to develop financial market institutions--banks and a stock exchange--to support a market system. Otherwise, the meat-and-potatoes of the program the Armenians had proposed was hard to argue with.

"Levon," Tom said when he'd finished reading the project files. "We've got to integrate these projects into a program. And we've got to have a statement of development thrategy to rationalize it. In the cover letter for the submission to the World Bank, you recognize this need in a general way, but I don't see a detailed strategy statement anywhere. Have I missed it?"

"It is difficult to get the Committee to agree on such things," Levon replied. "Each ministry feels strongly about its own projects."

"Yeah, sure," Tom said. "But we've still got to have a strategy statement." And they needed a way to handle the 'prima donna' problem of several ministries vying for limited resources.

"Let's see what we've got," Tom said at last. "First, Armenia has no significant natural resources to exploit--in particular, it's almost entirely energy dependent. The border's still open into Iran, but you can't reach much of the global economy through that hole--Iran's a pariah state. For all intents and purposes, the only reliable way in or out for people and cargo is by air." Tom stopped long enough for Ana to catch up and for Levon to absorb what he was saying. "What we have going for us is a well-educated, highly-trained labor force, so let's think manufacturing and high technology. Electrical machinery was an important industry before independence, wasn't it? Electric motors and such?"

Levon agreed. "Yes, and the factories are still here. We have the dies and the tools to make motors and machine tools."

Tom thought for a moment. "Armenia is supposed to have a strong scientific community--research and development. Is that right?"

"Yes," Levon said. "Several institutes employed scientists for the development of military technology. There is no need for that now. But there were also scientists supporting technology for the chemical industry. We have strong chemical science."

"These institutes are probably having a hard time getting funding now, huh?"

Levon nodded.

"Then we'd better bring them into the program. Do you know how many key people have migrated to other countries?"

"Many have gone, but I do not know about their skills or occupations."

"How about market studies, trade missions, promotional efforts?"

Ana translated what Tom had said, but both she and Levon were unsure what the question meant.

"You've got to find markets for Armenian production," Tom explained. "Before the World Bank lends money for roads and telephone systems, it has to believe Armenia will earn enough foreign exchange revenue to repay the loan. The Bank also has to know what's being done outside the framework of the projects it's financing to make the economy successful. I guess it used to be that you'd get orders for goods from central planning. It doesn't work that way in a market economy. You have to go find the markets and assess the competition."

Nothing was said for a few minutes while Tom's explanation sank in. Finally, Levon said, "The Ministry of Industry is responsible for providing producers with information on world markets, but I do not think they have sent anyone to Europe or America to learn what Armenia might sell there."

"We can ask Manoukian about that," Tom said. "Ana, see if we can meet with him tomorrow afternoon. Tell him we may want to call the Committee together again on Thursday or Friday."

CHAPTER FOURTEEN

Hotel Armenia

A cold wind was cutting through Republic Square when Tom and Ana emerged from Government House late that afternoon.

"That was a full day," Tom said. "Can I offer you a drink?" Ana smiled and said, "Yes. Thank you. I go to my mother's at seven o'clock but there is time. We can go to the café. It is best for talking."

They took a small table on the balcony overlooking the main floor, one surrounded on three sides by walls--private, but offering a view of the street through the wrought iron railing. He did not fail to notice that upstairs, but not downstairs, there were red candles on the tables. They were mounted in old brandy bottles, rivulets of melted wax running down their necks. He wondered why the candles were only on the balcony. Was it meant to be romantic? He asked for mineral water and a bottle of Armenian brandy. Whatever was left, he'd take to his room. When it came, he poured a small tumbler for each of them, raised his glass and offered a toast.

"To Armenia," he said. "May she thrive and prosper."

"Yes. Thank you." Ana thought to herself as she raised her glass, 'and at what price?'

Tom drank the rest of the brandy in his small glass and poured another for them both.

"How do you think we're doing so far?" Tom asked, relaxing a little, feeling the warmth of the brandy flow into his veins.

"Perhaps you should say."

"It feels pretty good," he said. "I'll work on a strategy statement tonight. We can go over it with Levon tomorrow, then run it by the Minister. My guess is that if we make Manoukian happy, the Committee will go along."

Ana didn't answer for a minute, wondering if she should. Finally, she decided it was appropriate for her to speak. That was what the Minister had encouraged her to do.

"The Committee has many important officials," she began.

"Minister Manoukian may be able to say what the Committee will not accept, but I do not think he can say what they will accept."

"Oh?" Tom asked. "Well, that may be, but we don't have a lot of time for them to debate it. I'll put together what I think the World Bank will buy and try to explain it to Manoukian. Then it'll be up to the Committee to run with it--or not."

"I see," Ana said. "But how will you persuade them that what you suggest is what they should do?"

"I hadn't really thought of persuading them. There aren't many different ways to do this. In fact, if they want the money, the World Bank way is the only way. Isn't that why they brought me over here? To give them the answer?"

Ana lowered her eyes to hide the anger his arrogance aroused. What he said was true. What this one man--this American--thought and said meant more to Armenia's future than what the committee thought. Even if he were right, his presence in Yerevan put a lie to Armenian 'independence.' Armenia was not independent. It had not been independent for a very long time. Would it ever be? She wanted to tell him this. Instead, she changed the subject. "Would you like to see some of our country this weekend?"

"That'd be great," he said. "What've you got in mind?"

"We could drive to Garni and Geghard on Saturday. Garni was our Armenian king's summer palace. It is ruins now, but one building is restored and they have an important mosaic. Not far from Garni is Geghard. It is very old monastery with caves built into the mountains. It began before Christ, but it has been a Christian monastery for almost two thousand years. You should see Echmiadzin, too, which is for Armenian Church like Vatican is for your Roman Church. Our Supreme Catholicos is also like your Pope. He has died and now people will come to Echmiadzin from all over the world--even America--to elect a new Supreme Catholicos. So I do not think we can go there at this moment, while they are preparing. But on Sunday, we could drive to Lake Sevan if we have good weather. It is farther from Yerevan than Geghard and we could take our food. You say 'picnic', yes?"

"Picnic. Exactly," Tom replied. "Will I get to meet your husband?"

"I do not have husband," she said, not knowing exactly what

his question meant. Did he want to talk with other men to understand about Armenia? Should she invite Levon? Or was he asking . . . she didn't know, but she had her first indication when his eyes softened and a slow smile spread across his lips. She realized then, that he'd been asking about her status. That frightened her.

"I would like to make a party for you, to let you meet other Armenians," she said. "But so few speak English. It is difficult for you, I think. You are meeting only government people. How can you work well if you do not know the people?"

"What I do isn't affected very much by whether I know the people or not."

"Really? Do you prefer it so?"

"It's not that," he said. "You can't learn much about a country's culture or its people in a few weeks. Your eyes give you educated impressions and you meet a few people who have an enormous impact on you because they're all you have. But sometimes they're misleading and it's better if you don't let them influence your work beyond what you can see with your eyes and what your experience tells you." Tom shook his head. "There really aren't any hard and fast rules. Sometimes knowing how a country's culture and its institutions work is important. Other times, none of it matters."

"Do you mean you do not know if what you do will help?"

"It's not quite that. Something unexpected can always happen to make your best plan impossible. Sometimes--not nearly as often--you get lucky."

"You make it sound almost like a thing of chance. Even if you do your work well, you do not know if it will succeed. Not like science."

"Even pure science has its happy accidents. They're part of the game. What's really essential is finding the right people in-country to fight for the program. As I see it here, Manoukian is the key player. If he's on board and we can get the World Bank to go along, it might work. Even so, you can't always make things turn out the way you'd like them to. That used to bother me a lot more when I was younger."

'So,' she thought. 'That does not sound so arrogant. At least he gives the minister an important role. And he treats Levon with respect. Am I wrong to resent him?'

She stared out over the railing into the street for a long moment. "When glasnost came, it was like a great stone had been lifted from us. We sat in the cafés and walked in the streets, talking and dreaming all through the night how things would be. And our leaders were with us. But then . . . Well, now you see us sad and discouraged. Things have not turned out as we wanted them to. I would like to have those days of excitement again, when we were dreaming so many things for our Armenia."

Her large almond eyes fixed on him and, looking into them, he could think of nothing to say.

CHAPTER FIFTEEN

Government House

Ana was waiting in the lobby when Tom came down the central staircase.

"How was dinner with your mother?" he asked.

"Very nice, thank you. We are good friends."

In the expanse of Republic Square, the ever-present Russian-built Scout car sat in front of the Museum fountain, concealing the two policemen who waited patiently inside it for traffic to direct. The Scout was the only car in sight. A pair of pedestrians began to walk across the square and both policemen got out of the Scout and blew their whistles.

"It is not safe to cross on foot," Ana explained. "Because of the traffic, you see." Then she smiled.

"Right," he said. "So I noticed. I actually feel sorry for the cops, having so little to do. Why don't we cut across, too? It'll make their morning."

Ana sternly shook her head. "It is not good to be involved with police, even in a small matter."

Levon was waiting for them in Tom's office when they arrived. Tom waved a good morning to him, stripped off his overcoat and threw it over the back of a straight chair, finishing in time to watch Ana remove her own long coat. She was dressed more comfortably this morning--a white turtleneck sweater over a rust-colored wool skirt. She draped her coat on another chair and sat down on the edge of a straight chair beside Tom.

"I've been thinking about a strategy and we need to go over it today," he said. "Can we see the Minister?"

"Yes," Ana said. "At midday. He will come to this office and lunch will be brought to us as before."

"Then let's get cracking so we've got something to talk to him about," Tom said. "We decided yesterday that Armenia's strongest point was its high-quality labor force, so we need data to describe

85

it. We want to demonstrate an existing capability to produce certain types of goods and services." Tom paused while Ana translated for Levon, who began taking notes. Tom continued talking, crafting a strategy featuring scientific research and manufacturing tied to chemicals, electronic components and machine tools under contract to companies already well-established in global markets. Much of the export component of the strategy was keyed to high-value-per-unit-of-weight products that could easily be air-lifted.

Levon's enthusiasm for the approach was evident. "This is good," he said. "But how will we get companies in America and Europe to make contracts with us?"

"Maybe the Armenian diaspora can help," Tom said. "I doubt you have a list of Armenians living in other countries, much less a list of what they do and what kind of influence they have over company policies, but we need a notion of how to get the word out. If we knew who the prominent Armenians were in, say, electronics, it would help. No matter what the textbooks tell you about markets and market behavior, there's no substitute for being 'connected'. You might even get some really useful technical assistance from them--productivity shortcuts and ways to raise quality to world standards. If this started to build, private investment would follow. You can't live on World Bank loans, I promise you that."

Levon was nodding and Ana brightened. Tom could feel the enthusiasm mounting in the little office. He hoped the Minister would be half as taken with the approach as Levon and Ana seemed to be.

****

Manoukian rose to leave at four in the afternoon. He'd been a charming host during lunch, an attentive listener while Tom went through the draft strategy and a productive participant for the remainder of the afternoon. He'd been particularly useful in pulling together the proposal for sending trade missions to Europe and the US.

"Now I see why the World Bank was unhappy with our proposal," Manoukian said as he prepared to leave. "I will have Minister Zadigian call a meeting of the Committee for ten o'clock tomorrow. Will that give you time to prepare a written outline for them?" Manoukian asked, looking at Tom.

"I think so," Tom said, nodding. "I guess you're going to want this laid out in Armenian, too."

The Minister spoke a few words to Ana, who nodded confidently, though she had no idea how much Tom would write. "How many copies should there be?" she asked Manoukian.

"Ten. Committee members only," Manoukian said, holding out his hand to Tom and switching to English. "Thank you."

When the door closed behind him, Tom, Levon and Ana stood looking at one another. Slowly, the smiles began to appear. The doubt and confusion Ana felt the night before had disappeared.

"I hope you're able to work tonight," Tom said to Ana.

"Of course. It is my duty."

Levon left and Tom and Ana were alone in the little office, late sun streaming through the window, bathing the room in a soft glow. "Where are we going to get an Armenian typewriter and a photocopy machine?" Tom asked.

"The Minister would authorize us to work here this evening, but we would need passes and it is already late. The Business Center at the hotel has an Armenian computer and a copy machine. And it is open throughout the night."

"Then let's get over there now and get our ducks in a row," he said.

"Ducks in a row?" Ana asked, puzzled.

"Sorry," he said, smiling. "One of those expressions. I just meant make the necessary arrangements."

"I see," Ana said, reaching for her coat. Tom grabbed it first and helped her on with it, catching the earthy fragrance of her hair and letting his hands linger briefly on her shoulders.

****

The young man on duty in the Business Center showed Ana the computer with the Armenian keyboard and the copy machine. Tom tagged along, not following the conversation, but understanding that the necessary arrangements were being made.

"Now we have our ducks in a line. Is that correct?" she asked him.

"Close enough," he replied, smiling. "It's 'ducks in a row.' But you've got the idea. And now we'd better get the English version down. I'm all set up in my room. Will it destroy your reputation if you come up there?"

"I do not think it is a problem," Ana said, smiling. "In this hotel, everyone knows me. They know we are working together and they will not think bad things about me if we work in your room. They would also know if we did not work," she added pointedly. "A hotel has many eyes."

Sofia, the woman in charge of the northwest wing of the fourth floor, was watching television in her room when Tom and Ana got off the elevator. The door was open and Sofia got up to give Tom his key. She and Ana greeted each other and Tom thought Ana probably did know everyone in the hotel.

"Can this lady bring tea?" Tom asked Ana.

"Of course. And some cakes?"

"Sure. Cakes, too."

Sofia followed the conversation between Tom and Ana with great interest, not understanding what they were saying, but watching the way they looked at one another. She would have something to tell the other floor ladies later that evening because Ana Stepanian was to the hotel staff what a film star was to the tabloid press.

Tom unlocked the door and allowed Ana to precede him into the room. She knew that rooms this size were identical in almost all respects, but she was anxious to see the mark he'd made on it. One of the twin beds was neatly made and uncluttered but the other was littered with books and papers. Small squares of yellow paper with notes scribbled on them were pasted to the wall over the writing table, which was taken up with a black laptop computer and a portable printer. Clothing lay in disarray on the room's one overstuffed chair.

Tom scooped up the laundry and dumped it in the wardrobe. "Sit here. Or better, let's move it so I won't have my back to you while I'm writing."

Sofia came and went and for the next two hours, Tom hammered away at the outline, asking Ana from time to time how she remembered a particular point that Levon had made or something the Minister had said. At seven o'clock, he thought he was finished. "Let's print this out. You look at it, see if it's what we agreed on this afternoon." He set up the portable printer and tediously fed the five pages through it, one page at a time.

Ana read them as they came from the printer and began translating them into Armenian. He wrote clearly and she had been present the whole time, so in her mind, the translation was already done.

While Ana was reading, Tom brought out the bottle of brandy from yesterday afternoon. There was only one glass in the room, so he took their tea glasses to the bathroom and rinsed them out. As Ana put the last page down, he opened the brandy.

"A toast?" he asked, pouring a shot in Ana's tea glass and another in his own.

"All right," she said. "To what?"

"To good luck," he said and they drank it down.

Pointing to the outline, he asked, "How long will it take?"

"I have translated it once already today," she said, smiling.

"I guess you have. So what do you think--an hour, two hours? I'm getting hungry and I thought it would be nice if you had dinner with me. Would you?"

"Yes," she said. He saw her smile, but not the flutter of anticipation that rippled through her.

"Great," Tom said. "I'll give you a little privacy, go downstairs and have a drink in the bar. When you're finished, come and get me. I'll shower while you type up the Armenian version. Then we'll go to dinner. How's that sound?"

She smiled and nodded.

"I ate in the café where we had drinks last night," he said. "If you know a better place, I'm wide open to suggestions."

"Have you been to Maran?" she asked.

"No. What's Maran?"

"Maran means 'wine cellar.' It is the restaurant under this hotel. They have chicken and there is music. The other restaurants are very quiet, do you think so?"

"Yes, I do think so," Tom said. "In an hour?" he asked, checking his watch.

****

Ana quickly translated the outline and went to bathe. As she undressed, she couldn't help noticing Tom's shaving things, his toothbrush and toothpaste. She removed the top of his deodorant stick. 'Ah,' she thought. 'This is his fresh smell.'

She decided on the tub instead of the shower, stoppered the drain and turned on the taps. She removed her clothes slowly, letting the room fill with steam. It had been a long time since she'd been as conscious of her body as she was today. This morning she'd felt naked before Tom's gaze and had welcomed it. Now she cupped her breasts in her hands and tested their firmness. She was proud they were still strong and that she was still appealing.

At first, the water was almost too hot to bear, but she adjusted to it and slowly sank into its embrace, letting it flood up to her neck. She took his soap and tested it. It was creamier than the kind she used and it lathered wonderfully.

****

Her attention was on the computer screen, typing her translation of the outline, but she saw him from the corner of her eye as he entered the Business Center. Reflexively, she looked up, straight into the cold dark eyes of Aleksandr Avakian. He met her surprised, wide-eyed stare without expression, then passed beyond her view into the main Business Center office.

He removed the fax that had been placed in his box and scanned it quickly. A date, a time, an Aeroflot flight number and a typed signature--'Danilov'. He folded it, put it in his coat pocket and walked back to the doorway of the room where he'd seen Ana.

"Well," he said, his voice flat, without feeling. "Anahit." It was a statement, not a greeting.

"Aleksandr?" she replied, her chest tightening.

"You work for Americans these days, I am told."

"I work for Armenia," she answered, holding her chin up, but quavering inside.

"Yes, of course. Manoukian. He was always a radish--red on the outside but white through and through. He has what he wants now, I suppose."

They held each others' eyes for a time, neither speaking. She couldn't imagine what his thoughts were. They might have been sweet, distant memories of her, though his expression revealed only what he had become, something menacing and malignant. He stood in the doorway, only a few feet from her. He read her thoughts--she knew he did--and her primal fear of him rose.

Ana swallowed hard as he moved toward her. Her heart began to hammer in her chest before he reached her side and pressed himself against her shoulder. So close to her, his body touching her so intimately, he slipped his hand beneath her hair. With his fingers gently stroking the tense cords of her neck, her loins awoke, betraying her, and a long-forgotten lust for him returned.

"Aleksandr . . ." she croaked, fixing her eyes on the computer screen.

He bent down to her and whispered, "You remember, don't you? So do I, my dear Anahit. It's time you came back."

She couldn't speak.

He waited for her to respond, his breath warm against her cheek. When she said nothing, he took it as a rejection and straightened up, taking his hand away from her neck. "Whore," he spat at her. "In the American's room. Have you sold yourself for so little?"

Her face flushed with anger and she pushed away from the computer. "How dare you say such a thing to me?" she hissed at him. "You put filth in people's bodies and flaunt your money like the corrupt bourgeoisie you have become. How dare you call yourself a citizen of the Soviet Union? How dare you call yourself an Armenian? You aren't fit to be Armenian!"

Tom appeared in the doorway just as Aleksandr drew back his hand to slap her. He lunged and caught Aleksandr's wrist in a steel grip, twisting his arm up and back between his shoulder blades.

Aleksandr grunted with pain and bent forward to break Tom's hold, kicking back with his good leg, but Tom had anticipated the move. Aleksandr's kick passed harmlessly between Tom's legs and threw

Aleksandr further off balance. Tom exerted a little more pressure and Aleksandr went to his knees.

"Don't even think about moving," Tom growled. "I'll take your arm out of its socket and feed you the bloody stump." With Aleksandr immobilized and grunting with pain, Tom looked at Ana. "What's going on here?"

Ana's mouth was open in astonishment. It had all happened so quickly. Aleksandr, no longer menacing, was on his knees at her feet, his breath coming in short, strained gasps. Tom Yeager stood over him, legs spread, a gladiator. Wide-eyed, she found her voice at last.

"Tom, please. Do not break his arms. Let him stand up. He . . . it is . . . I cannot explain. Please, just let him go."

"And then what?" Tom asked, his voice stern and heavy with the hostility that seized him when he thought Ana was at risk. "Why don't I just frog-walk his ass out of here and pitch him in the street?"

Ana's eyes widened further. "No! No, please, Tom. No one has seen this. If you humiliate him, he . . . I will tell him to walk away now. Please. It will be all right." She knelt beside Aleksandr and spoke to him softly in Armenian.

When Tom saw Aleksandr nod his head, he eased his grip and put his other hand on Aleksandr's elbow to help him stand. When he sensed that Aleksandr was subdued, he released his wrist and stood back, coiled in case Ana's words hadn't put an end to it.

Aleksandr turned slowly to face Tom, cradling the arm that had been twisted behind him. The fury in his eyes went beyond loathing. Through clenched teeth, he spat an incomprehensible sentence at Tom. Tom didn't understand the words, but there was no doubt about the menace in their meaning.

Ana understood what Aleksandr said and she understood what he whispered to her as he left. "It isn't over, Anahit," he said. Then he was gone, leaving her drained and trembling.

CHAPTER SIXTEEN

Maran

The delicious aroma of roasting chicken wafted up to them as they made their way down two narrow flights of stairs to Maran. The restaurant was a two room affair decorated in wine-cellar motif with six rustic tables in the main room pushed against the walls to make space for a small dance floor. At one end of the room stood a Yamaha keyboard and a pair of serious amps and speakers.

There were eight other diners in the room--two young couples, laughing and enjoying themselves, and four men, drinking vodka and talking earnestly. Only one vacant table remained after Tom and Ana took theirs.

The waitress spoke to Ana for a few minutes as though she were an old friend. When she left, Tom said. "I need a drink."

Still shaken, Ana said. "I have already told Raya to bring vodka."

Raya returned shortly with a half bottle of Stolichnaya. She poured two small glasses to the rim and left without another word.

Ana's mouth was so dry she could barely swallow. With a trembling hand, she tossed down the vodka and held out her glass for another. Tom filled hers and his own. She drained the little glass but the vodka failed to fill the void of fear yawning in her stomach.

"Are you all right?" Tom asked.

She turned a grim face to him. "I am sorry for what has happened."

"No need for you to be sorry," Tom said quickly. "Who was that guy anyway?"

"You do not understand. He is dangerous man. And he is now your enemy. I am afraid for you and it is my fault. I spoke strong words to him and made him angry."

Tom shrugged. "Not much I can do about that now. I didn't think about it. I just reacted. I wasn't going to let him hit you."

She put her hand on his forearm and her expression softened a little. "Thank you for what you did. You appeared from nowhere. If I had known . . . I would not have said those words to him."

Tom shook his head. "Well, whatever. But maybe you'd better tell me who this guy is and what your argument was about."

Ana held out her glass again and Tom filled it. She drank it quickly and faced him. "His name is Aleksandr Avakian. He was a major in the KGB. Not now, of course, but he . . . he is not a pleasant man."

"He used to be in the KGB? But not now. Is that right?"

She nodded.

"So what makes him so dangerous now?"

"He brings narcotics from Turkey for people in Russia--and here, too, I think. I do not know exactly. He does not care any more about honorable things. He is only for himself. He would know how to hurt you and nothing would stop him."

"I'll watch my back, then," Tom said. "I see a keyboard and some big amps," he said to change the subject. "Does that mean we're going to have some music tonight?"

"Yes," she said, looking behind the bar. "Armen and Tigran are here tonight. I think you will like their music. But listen to me. You must believe what I am telling you about Aleksandr."

"I believe you," he said. "And I'll be careful. But you're the one he was going to hit. If he's so dangerous, isn't he likely to look for an opportunity to smack you again?"

"I do not think so," she said, holding out her glass. He poured for her and another for himself.

"Why not?"

She drank the vodka in one motion before she spoke. "We were lovers once. He might slap me, but he would not hurt me. It is different for you. You are American and he does not like Americans." She paused, forcing him to meet her eyes before she added, "He said he will kill you."

"Shouldn't we order some food now?" he asked, lightheaded from the vodka and the sizzle of after-action adrenaline. "That chicken smells fantastic."

"Yes," Ana said. "I will tell Raya."

The two musicians emerged from behind the bar while Ana was talking to Raya. They began the set with something from Santana that Tom recognized from the late '60s or early '70s. The young man playing the keyboard--Armen--worked out a few more numbers as Tom and Ana devoured the food Raya brought--broiled chicken, golden brown, hot and flavorful, crisp French fries and chilled, fresh vegetables.

Tom was aware that Ana had been watching him from the corner of her eye while they ate. He had come down from the confrontation with Aleksandr, but he was still working on what Ana had told him about the man.

He made putting himself in harm's way in foreign countries a personal cardinal sin, but it had all happened too fast. Anyway, there was no way he could have stood there and watched that guy hit Ana. So what was done was done. He still had a job to do and he wasn't going to head for the airport to catch the first plane out of Dodge.

She said they had been lovers. That shouldn't have bothered him, but somehow it did. He wasn't keen on Avakian saying he intended to kill him, either.

Armen and Tigran finished their set and the room was given over again to the clatter of silverware and the conversation of the diners.

"That was fantastic," Tom said. "Can't be the same cook who works at breakfast."

"No, this is Raya's place. She does these few things very well and does not try to do more."

The four men left. The two couples remained, still chatting and laughing amiably, but more subdued now that they'd eaten.

"Another?" Tom asked, holding up the vodka bottle. She gave him a sideways half nod of her head and her hair brushed his cheek as he leaned toward her to pour. He filled his own glass and they drank.

"Any trouble with the outline?" Tom asked.

"No. It is finished. The copies are being made now."

"Tired?" he asked.

"Yes. And a little too much vodka."

"But you're all right?"

"Yes," she replied. "But I am afraid for you. You are very

brave or very stupid. I do not know which one. Are there children who will suffer if a bad thing happens to you?"

He laughed softly and shook his head. "No one would miss me, I'm afraid. My wife and I had no children and we no longer live together."

For a moment, she saw a wistful sadness in his eyes, but it disappeared as quickly as it had come. "And so you are like gypsy, belonging to no one and no place?"

"It's not quite like that," he said. "I have a house on a lake in Texas and an apartment in Washington. When I'm not traveling, I'm in one of those places. I have friends. I have a life."

She put her elbow on the table and rested her head on her hand, smiling at him a little drunkenly, her guilty dread dulled by the vodka. "A house on a lake? Tell me about that," she said.

"It's a small house. Two stories, with a veranda around the top floor. My office is downstairs and on the top floor, there are two bedrooms. There's an open space for the kitchen and the living room. Glass pretty much all the way around so that you can see the lake. It's not grand, but it's comfortable."

"It sounds like dacha."

"I guess. Something like that."

"And the lake. Is it a big one?"

"It's long and narrow. What we get when we dam up a river. It's big enough, I suppose, but not like a regular lake," he said, making a circle with his forefinger.

Ana nodded, accepting, but not understanding. "And what do you do there?"

"I ride horses and read books. I have a boat and sometimes I take it down the river or up the river to fish. I go out with friends who have sailboats. I play golf," he added, then paused. "What else? I drink scotch and . . . "

"Tell me about riding the horse. I have not done that."

"It's a strange partnership. The horse is bigger than you are. But he'll go where you want him to if you can make him respect you. My favorite is an old mare named Rachel. She knows the hills better than I do and she's good company any day. Doesn't matter if you're up or down, old Rachel's there for you."

Ana's distress over the incident with Aleksandr faded as she listened to Tom and watched him. With Aleksandr, she had seen him quick and sure, strong and unafraid. But here, he seemed a gentle man. She was not sure what that meant, but being with him made her less afraid.

The musicians returned and began the set with a haunting piece. The melody came slowly, softly against an assertive bass beat. Then, from the keyboard's electronic magic, muted French horns blended plaintively with violins, organ and an abstract chorus from some distant echo chamber. A pan flute chimed in high register to accent the melody. Tom's arm turned over, his hand opened upward and Ana's slipped into it. He knew her hand had come into his--he'd wanted it to--but the music held him captive. He thought it Continental--French or Italian--yet in some abstract way, it perfectly suited Armenia's melancholy.

The music spoke more clearly to Ana--wildflowers struggling through rocky soil, lonely breezes in tattered sails on Lake Sevan, the youth of Armenia lost to the morning flight to Paris, a distant echo across the barren high plains. It spoke to her past with sadness--and warmth--and affection. They sat quietly when the music stopped, absorbed in the resonance of the feelings it evoked. The spell was broken when the two couples called for dancing music and the violin joined the keyboard to render a rousing piece from Zorba the Greek. They watched the two couples' exuberance through several of these before Armen and Tigran took another break. Watching the dancers expend so much energy made Tom realize how exhausted he was. Tomorrow, they'd be up against the Committee. He looked at Ana.

"Are you ready to leave?" he asked.

"Yes," she said. "I am tired."

"How will you get home?" he asked.

"I live quite near. I walk."

"Shall I see you home? To make sure that guy isn't waiting for you out there in the dark."

She frowned, remembering the threat. How she wished Tom hadn't come into the Business Center, that she hadn't provoked Aleks. She could imagine him waiting outside in the dark at that very moment. He knew how to kill quickly and silently and he wouldn't be caught off guard this time. She couldn't lead Tom into such a trap. "It would be more dangerous for you," she said, forcing a small laugh. "You could become lost. I know the way and I have my flashlight."

"Well, OK," he said. "It's your turf, so maybe you know what you're talking about."

"Thank you for this evening," she said, holding his arm as they climbed the stairs. "Food and music, everything. All very nice."

"My pleasure, I assure you."

He walked her to the front doors. "You sure you're OK?"

"I am sure. I will meet you here in the morning?"

"Would you like to come early and have breakfast?"

"No," Ana said. "Thank you. I will come at nine o'clock."

CHAPTER SEVENTEEN

Government House

The Committee room was crowded and filled with smoke when Tom, Ana and Levon arrived. Lively conversations were in progress in every corner. Tom took that as a good sign. It was easier to steer a group in motion than one standing still. Zadigian, the voluble Minister of Economy, came rushing over, all smiles, hands outstretched. Ana translated his gush of greeting, to which Tom uncomfortably tried to reply in kind.

Krikor Manoukian came briskly into the room and the hubbub of conversation died, replaced by an air of anticipation. Manoukian smiled at Tom and placed a hand on his shoulder. The significance of the gesture was not lost on the room.

Ana leaned toward Tom, her hand resting lightly on his arm as she began translating. He still wasn't used to having her that close to him, her scented breath against his face, her soft voice in his ear. She took him through Zadigian's and Manoukian's opening remarks and told him when it was time for him to speak.

"Thank you, Minister Manoukian," he began, speaking through Ana. "First, I want to compliment the Committee and the staff of the ministries responsible for the documentation of the individual projects in the loan request. They're complete and carefully presented and I'm sure the World Bank will have no problem moving quickly to feasibility assessments. However, as you know, the Bank was not satisfied with the strategy statement. Consequently, other elements of the loan request were also unacceptable. In particular, the implementation schedule you gave them was vague at best. So this is where we must begin. With the considerable assistance of Levon Abovyan, I've prepared a discussion outline on these issues."

Levon distributed the ten copies to the ministerial principals and they read it with their staff looking over their shoulders. Tom then presented the Strategy Statement formally, explaining the reasoning behind its elements, much as he'd done with Manoukian the day before, except this version had the benefit of Manoukian's refinements. The discussion went on for another hour after Tom finished, but by the time they broke for lunch, they had Committee agreement. Manoukian cornered Tom and said in serviceable English, "A good beginning. Next you talk about implementation sequence? Be careful. We have trouble, I think."

"Anything we can we do about it?" Tom asked.

"Be patient," Manoukian answered, again putting his hand on Tom's shoulder in that gesture of support, and moved away to speak to one of the other ministers.

The afternoon session opened at two o'clock--explosively. Zadigian had scarcely cleared his throat when the Minister of Transportation, a giant of a man with a full beard and coal-black eyes, seized the floor and began making an aggressive case for according first priority to the transportation projects. The Minister of Energy leaped to his feet, shouting that it was absurd to put airport improvements ahead of the nuclear power plants they desperately needed to achieve energy-independence.

Tom watched in dismay as the sweet harmony of the morning degenerated into a clanging medieval duel--mace and chain, broadsword and ax. The Minister of Communications weighed in, arguing that telecommunications had to come first because you couldn't do business in a global economy without a world class communications system. Not even Manoukian could maintain order for more than a few minutes at a time. Ana tried to keep Tom abreast of the battle, but the best she could do was track its general drift. After an hour of acrimony, Manoukian shouted them all down and declared a recess. He met Tom's eyes and jerked his head, summoning him, Ana and Levon Abovyan to join him in a corner of the room. The Committee members pushed back from the table with a raucous scrape of chairs and began to stretch and mill about. A tea service had been delivered to the conference room and several poured fresh glasses of tea. Others left for the toilet or smoked and talked in solemn tones. The mood was dark. Manoukian spoke first to Tom through Ana. "Can you suggest how to break this impasse?"

"They all have legitimate arguments," Tom replied with a shrug. "Actually, I like the Transport Minister's idea of doing a tanker airlift to relieve the gasoline shortage. I don't know if it's cost effective, though. The Americans and the Brits weren't counting costs when they ran the Berlin Airlift. Using cargo planes to get manufactured goods out is probably a sound idea, too, even from the cost standpoint. Whether it is or not depends on the mix of production and how far you have to fly the stuff. If you produce goods that have a high ratio of value to weight, it makes excellent sense."

"So you are saying that we should support the top priority for Transportation projects?"

"No," Tom said, shaking his head. "Let me finish. The Energy guy has a case, too. It takes years to bring a nuclear plant on line. But if you don't have electricity, you're not going to produce much to sell at home or abroad. The Communications guy is on target with the need to upgrade telecommunications, too. Setting the priorities isn't going to be easy, even on the merits."

"Of course. You're quite right. Worse, the Transportation Minister is not well-liked among his colleagues. And look." Manoukian nodded toward a clump of people in another corner of the room. "The Construction Minister is talking to the Energy Minister and the Labor Minister. They do not even like each other."

"We need a substantive agreement, not a cosmetic one," Tom persisted. "It's not in Armenia's interest to paper over basic differences here. The Bank would smell it out and you'll get turned down again if the implementation schedule is weak."

Tom turned to Levon. "Levon, is there somebody in the University or the government who does mathematical programming?" When Levon looked blank after Ana had translated, Tom tried to explain. "It's a technique for making investment decisions." Tom briefly described the concept, but Levon only shook his head. Ana might not be getting the translation right, but Tom thought if Levon knew the technique, he'd see the need for it even if the language weren't precise.

Tom turned back to Manoukian. "This is your Committee and I know you're in a hurry, but I wouldn't let them make a decision today. It would be best if we had an Armenian team here to optimize this program, but since we don't, I know somebody in the US who's a wizard at it. She's available just now. If you can keep the decision open for a while, I think I can get her over here to run the numbers and then the Committee can set the implementation schedule on objective criteria. Maybe it'll defuse the situation."

Manoukian was frowning. "Yes, I agree," he said. "They should not make a decision this afternoon. But we must discuss bringing someone else. That may be complicated."

Tom nodded toward the group standing in smoky knots around the conference table. "That's not complicated?" he asked.

****

They followed Manoukian into his office. Without breaking stride, Manoukian said something to his assistant that Tom assumed was the Armenian equivalent of 'hold all calls.' The four of them sat in straight chairs at Manoukian's conference table. "Who is this other American you want to bring?" Manoukian barked at Tom.

"She's a specialist in mathematical techniques for dealing with the kind of problem we ran into this afternoon." Tom tried to keep the explanation simple, but Manoukian had no patience for it.

"All right, all right," he said, raising his hands in surrender. "Enough. So you can find a way through this if your mathematical person comes here?"

"Yes. I think so."

"I have another problem you may not know about," Manoukian said. "If this person is an American, I will have to ask the American AID to pay for him. Is that not correct? I'm reluctant to do that."

"You played hard ball with them to get me over here."

"Excuse me. Hard ball?" Ana asked.

"I just mean aggressive, tough," he replied and she finished the translation for Manoukian.

"The person I want to bring over is Mariah Carroll," Tom continued. "She's one of the best in the world. And incidentally, she's one of Peter Karekin's partners."

"A woman?" Manoukian exclaimed.

Ana looked quickly at Tom, afraid she'd made a mistake. "You said 'she' did you not?"

"Yeah," Tom said, looking from one to the other. "Is that a problem?"

Manoukian shook his head and Tom went on. "Look, it's in AID's interest to bring her out here if I think I need her--and I do. And it's in Armenia's interest to get the World Bank's OK on the loan. I can go back to my hotel room and write up an implementation schedule--quite independent of the Committee. I can do it before the sun goes down. I can make it defensible on economic grounds and odds are the Bank would approve the loan, but if the Committee doesn't support it, the loan won't disburse on schedule and you'll have all kinds of trouble. If we bring Mariah out for a week or ten days we'll produce an implementation schedule that I think the Committee will support and the Bank will approve."

"At what cost?" Manoukian asked.

"Twenty-thousand dollars, give or take a little. If having her here is going to get you a loan for a hundred million, I'd say it's a pretty high rate of return, wouldn't you?" Tom didn't give Manoukian time to answer before he went on. "You tell me you're at war with AID. That'll make trouble down the line, too. So suppose I ask AID to finance Mariah as an amendment to my contract? You won't have to ask them yourself. AID might want to say 'no' but if you stand ready to fund her yourself, I may be able to make this come out right, save face for everybody. AID won't forget that you pushed them around to get me out here, but if they bring Mariah out to save my bacon, they'll take credit for getting the loan approved. You'll have to be gracious about that, but maybe they'll be a lot more supportive in the future."

"Excuse me," Ana said. "What is 'save the bacon'? I do not understand."

Tom rolled his eyes. He'd gotten excited and drifted into a slang term she didn't understand. "It means . . . rescue me. Finish the job I couldn't finish. It makes me look bad, but right now, the thing is to get the job done."

Ana nodded and finished the translation for Manoukian.

"You need my guarantee that the Government of Armenia will pay for this person if AID will not?"

"Exactly. Or if the Government of Armenia can't pay for her, you could ask Karekin."

"Very well," Manoukian said. "I will make the necessary arrangements. You will speak to the AID people about bringing her here? Please do this today. Tell me what the AID says tomorrow. I plan to go to my dacha this weekend and it is difficult to contact me there."

here? Please do this today. Tell me what the AID says tomorrow. I plan to go to my dacha this weekend and it is difficult to contact me there."

Chapter Eighteen

The USAID Mission

"So, how's it going?" Lange asked.

"Some plus and some minus," Tom said, taking a sip of the coffee Mary Patterson brought him. "Mmmmm," Tom said. "This tastes like the real stuff."

"We try to have a few of the comforts of home."

"The Committee signed off on the strategy statement," Tom said. "But they got into a knock-down, drag-out when they tried to deal with the implementation schedule. All the big dogs want the first bite. I'd like them to decide for themselves, but they need some tools to do that and they're just not extant in the country."

"What do you mean?"

"The way to do this is with optimal investment programming. I won't get into the technicalities, but the trick is to get them to agree on criteria to judge the projects--employment creation, export earnings, whatever. Then you crank it through a program that scores the projects you've fed it and it gives you a critical path. You have a rational basis for deciding which projects come first. There's a hell of a lot more to it than that, but it helps get you past the wrangling."

"I see," Lange said, without seeing. "So what do you need?"

"The right kind of help," Tom said. "I know the concept, but unless I'm going to stay out here for six months flailing away at it, I need an expert to knock out the analysis. I know who I need and I think I can get her out here in a few days. A long, hard week or ten days of her time should get us through the analysis and wrap up the package for the Armenians. It'll cost about twenty thousand. You don't need a new contract. Just amend mine."

"What's her name?"

"Mariah Carroll. She's just back from two years in Indonesia teaching this stuff, so she's up to speed. And she's got fifteen years experience in the Third World. She's world class."

"And when do you need her out here?"

"Yesterday," Tom said. "If we could get her on a plane this afternoon, it'd be great. That's why a simple contract amendment would expedite things."

"What do you figure the chances are the Armenians will get the loan without this slick implementation schedule?" Lange asked.

"The major hang-up was the strategic rationale. They seem to be past that now. I could probably get Manoukian to impose an implementation schedule and get it through the Bank. But if we did it that way, there'd be trouble down the road. Really--twenty thousand to do it right when the loan package is a hundred million? It'd be crazy to cut corners like that."

"Yeah," Lange said. "I agree. But we have to sell it to the Director."

"What's the problem?" Tom asked.

"The Director and Minister Manoukian are not exactly bosom buddies, for reasons I won't get into just now."

"I heard something about that," Tom said. "I might as well tell you, though, that Manoukian is prepared to finance the additional technical assistance I need out of Armenian coffers or from private offshore sources. If there's a rift between AID and the Armenian government, turning Manoukian down on Mariah Carroll is going to make it worse. Saying 'yes' to a few thousand bucks to finish the job right might heal some wounds. And if you want to be cold-blooded about it, just imagine how it'll go when the Armenians get the loan. That's a fair-sized chunk of capital and they'll need technical assistance of all kinds to put it on the ground. Part of AID's deal out here is technical assistance, right? And the more technical assistance coming the Mission's way, the more important the post, yada, yada, yada. Right? The Armenians will have something to say about that though, won't they? If the AID Mission isn't on good terms with the Armenians and the technical assistance contracts start going to the Brits and the French, somebody at AID/Washington--or worse, somebody in Congress--is going to wonder what you people are doing out here. Why not patch it up with Manoukian now and put it behind you?"

"Hey," Lange said. "Great talking points. I buy every one of them. But I'm not the guy who has to sign off. The Director is." Lange looked at his watch and continued. "We're supposed to see him in ten minutes. Maybe we can move it up."

Lange was back in thirty seconds.

"Let's go," he said, and Tom followed him into the Director's office.

"Mr. Yeager," Marcos said, extending a soft, pudgy hand. "How nice to meet you." The greeting satisfied the minimum requirements of cordiality and neglected the courtesy of addressing Tom as 'Dr.' "Tell me how you're progressing."

Tom went through a more succinct version of the progress report he'd given Lange. Marcos scowled when Tom told him he needed Mariah for optimal investment analysis, but Tom didn't mention Manoukian's willingness to bring her out independently. He'd play that card if Marcos turned him down. He went through the arguments for funding her for the ten days he thought it would take, watching Marcos clench and unclench his teeth. When he finished, Tom held his breath. "Mr. Yeager," Marcos began. "I'm pleased your work is going so well. I'm sure Mr. Lange will be able to deal with the complications. I'm sorry, but you'll have to excuse me now. I have some other matters to attend to." Lange got up and Tom knew the meeting was over.

Back in Lange's office, Tom asked, "Did that mean the decision is yours?"

"Let's say the blame is mine if this project goes to shit city. Sit tight. I'll be right back." Lange went to Mary Patterson's desk and dictated a fax message to AID/Washington, then returned to Tom. "I just told AID/Washington that this Mission is authorizing ten days of Mariah Carroll's time. If you've got her phone number in the States, you can call her from here and give her a heads up. You're sure she's available?"

"She was a few days ago," Tom replied, digging in his briefcase for his address book. "What time is it in Washington?"

"A little before three in the morning."

****

After five rings, Mariah's answering machine kicked in and Tom had to talk through it to wake her up. Finally, her sleepy voice came on the line.

"Tom?" she mumbled. "It's the middle of the night."

"Sorry about that," he said. "But you gotta wake up. Don't go back to sleep and forget we had this conversation. Are you awake?"

"Yeah, kinda," she replied, sounding slightly more alert.

"OK, now listen up," he said. "I need you out here for ten days--right away. Did you get that?"

"I heard you," she said. "But Tom . . ."

"I didn't just cook this up," he said, relieved that she sounded normal, awake. "I really do need you here, as fast as you can come." He hit the high points of the problem and his solution to it. Then he was stunned by her answer.

"Tom," she said. "I'm working on a major project in Morocco. Rittiman was going to do the investment analysis, but he picked up a case of dengue fever in Sri Lanka. He's not going anywhere for awhile. I'm supposed to leave on Sunday. I was going to call you in the morning to see what you thought."

He let the news sink in slowly.

"Well, let me tell you, your big boss--Karekin--is the one who got me out here. His family's Armenian. I need a world-class numbers cruncher out here and you're it. Who's leading the Morocco team?"

"Jean-Paul Laurent. Do you know him?"

Tom snorted. "No wonder it's a probem. Laurent won't find the toilet for two weeks. You can clean up Morocco after we finish here and no harm done. Look, I'm going to grease the skids for your visa and get AID's paperwork moving. In the last hour, the mission has approved a contract amendment that gives you ten days. I'll turn you loose when this job is done and not before."

There was silence on the other end of the line and Tom held his breath, wondering if he might have overplayed his hand. He cast a worried eye toward Bob Lange, who'd been listening to Tom's side of the conversation.

"I can't make it by Monday," Mariah said at last, firmly enough to discourage Tom from arguing. "It'll be Tuesday or Wednesday. What's the weather like?"

"About like Washington this time of year. Still chilly. Listen, make sure you bring a heavy-duty computer with everything you need to do the job. They don't know what I'm talking about out here, so you need to be self-contained." He took a breath and added, "It'll be good to see you, kid."

"Never a dull moment with you, Yeager. You're going to owe me big time for this if I lose this contract in Morocco."

"You're going to lose an even bigger one if you don't get your ass out here and help me. Remember that you're the one who told me how important Armenia was to your future with Karekin," he said and rang off before she could change her mind.

****

Ana was waiting for him downstairs.

"The deal's set," Tom told her as they went through the front door of the Mission.

"Now you will have the help you need?"

"Yeah. But I wish these guys would do their own negotiating. Will you call Manoukian and let him know?"

"Yes, of course. What am I to say?"

"Tell him AID's going to fund ten days of Mariah Carroll's time and that she'll be here early next week. Ask Manoukian to contact the Armenian embassy in Washington and tell them to expedite her visa." Tom scribbled on the back of one of his business cards and handed it to her. "There are Mariah's phone numbers in Washington--home and office. Tell your embassy to call her and set things up. OK?"

"Yes. I understand," Ana said.

****

When Ana returned home, she went to the parking area behind her apartment complex to make sure her white Zhiguli sedan would start. The seven-year old car was her prize possession and she kept it in pristine condition. The gasoline shortage had curtailed her visits to her mother's dacha and all but eliminated weekend jaunts to Lake Sevan, but she bought enough gas to start it every few days to circulate the oil and keep the charge in the battery.

The engine turned over briskly, burst into life and settled down to a steady idle, bringing a smile to her face. She wrapped her coat around her, rested her gloved hands on the wheel and indulged her thoughts about the weekend. She could scarcely believe that only a week had passed since she met Manoukian in his office to receive the assignment that brought the American, Thomas Yeager, to Armenia. She was confused by him. He was not what she expected and she couldn't deny that her own body was responding to him. How would it be to spend the next two days with him?

CHAPTER NINETEEN

The Vernesazsh

Sarkis was reluctant to leave the warmth of their bed, but Karine had already risen to tend to Setta and prepare their breakfast. Now, without her beside him, that special place at the edge of slumber lost its luxury. In any event, today was the vernesazsh at the Mamikonian Monument, the day he would use all his expertise and Razmik's American dollars to buy the jewelry he hoped would be the first step on their road to salvation.

He threw back the covers and padded into the toilet where he relieved himself, brushed his teeth and splashed cold water on his face. He dressed hurriedly in a heavy sweater and thick socks and followed the rich aroma of the coffee Karine was brewing. She was in front of the stove, stirring porridge. He put his arms around her waist from behind and gave her a gentle hug.

"Good morning, my love," he said, burying his face in her neck. "The coffee smells delicious. How is Setta today?"

"She slept," Karine replied. "But I think she's growing weaker day by day. I don't know what to do."

Sarkis nodded. "Yes," he said. "But today we make a beginning--at the vernesazsh."

Karine nodded and began scooping porridge into two bowls. Yesterday's optimism hadn't survived the night. Dawn brought her familiar despair.

Sarkis had his own waking nightmares. He was never far from fear--the fear of discovery that would end his career and plunge him into the unimaginable horrors of prison that would truly be the end of all their lives--and the fear of the acts of terror Aleksandr had promised if he refused to continue stealing from the Museum. But thanks to Razmik, he was now a moving target, no longer a hopeless hostage at the mercy of events beyond his control.

Sarkis placed his bowl beside the sink, took the last sip of his coffee and walked into the bedroom to remove the money from the niche in the wall behind the wardrobe. The niche was a happy legacy of the earthquake--a crack in the wall that had loosened one of the building blocks. It made a perfect place for Sarkis to hide his coin collection and Karine's jewelry.

He counted out two thousand of the ten thousand dollars Razmik had sent--hundred dollar denominations and fifties. The leathery smell of the ink and the velvet texture of the paper imposed on him an uncomfortable, alien power. He did not rejoice in their possession and wanted to exchange them quickly for treasures he understood. With a sigh, he distributed the bills around his pockets and went into the hall to collect his coat and scarf. He called to Karine as he pulled them on. "I'm going now," he said. "I won't be back until afternoon."

Karine came out of the kitchen, wiping her hands on her apron. She stopped a few feet away from him, looking tired and forlorn.

"Don't worry, my love," he said, his hands on her shoulders. "Everything's going to work out." He hugged her, gave her a quick kiss and left.

****

The day had dawned sunny with a damp promise of spring. Sarkis walked down his hill and crossed into the park above Mamikonian Monument. It was early, but the crowd was already arriving. Near the base of the monument, at the foot of the hill, he found working men with rough hands and high quality tools on display. Sarkis wasn't mechanical, but he admired the oily sheen of the tools in their trays. Those on offer that were well-used and well-cared for were emblems of despair. The others, new ones displayed by workers who still had access to factory tool sheds and warehouses, bespoke the desperation that cracked a worker's moral code. The men sized up Sarkis quickly and ignored him as a buyer--they knew instinctively that his gloves covered soft hands and that he'd never set foot on a factory floor or a construction site.

A few women hovered beside the low walls surrounding the paved areas of the park. For the same reasons the craftsmen selling their tools had scarcely glanced at him, the women eyed him hopefully. Several of them had the defeated look of refugees from Karabagh and he moved toward them first. Necklaces dangled from their outstretched fingers and their sad eyes pleaded with him to buy. His heart turned over at the sight of their ragged clothing and the rough, weathered skin of their faces. But the jewelry they had to offer was worthless--scarcely more than colored glass. He was tempted to give them a few drams and had to stiffen his resolve. He was here for Karine and Setta and himself.

He went past the Karabagh women, up the hill, looking for a certain kind of face, one that showed the blood lines of an old family, one like his own perhaps, that had long ago fled from Eastern Armenia before the Turkish onslaught.

A few women hung quilts and embroidered table cloths from lines strung between the trees. Some brought small tables to display their wares, but most simply spread a cloth or heavy paper over one of the low walls. He saw no face like the one he was seeking among them.

Sarkis had come to the vernesazsh before, but he hadn't noticed the variety of things for sale. Heirloom silver gleamed on a few tables--ewers and serving trays, silver napkin rings, flatware. Oriental and Caucasian carpets added faded color to the brown patches of the park's late-winter lawn. New production of emerging cottage industries was appearing--needlework, wood carvings and decorative boxes. Here and there an artist's easel held a fresh canvas.

He was drawn to an area where coins and medals were on display. Most of the medals were Soviet awards for productivity, but a few recognized valor in The Great Patriotic War. Sarkis wondered how a veteran of the Battle of Stalingrad reconciled his sacrifices and hardships with the wreckage of the Soviet Union. The gray men--the apparatchiks--had lost all they'd won on the battlefield. Perhaps it didn't matter. The soldiers had suffered and survived and that fact alone made them victorious.

The coins were of greater interest to Sarkis, but nothing caught his eye until he spied a copper three-kopek piece minted in 1891. This particular coin wasn't rare, but Sarkis sensed its presence among a handful of undistinguished Soviet coins meant something more. A middle-aged man detached himself from a clutch of other sellers and turned his attention to Sarkis. He had a heavy shock of dark hair and his wrinkled face wore a thick coat of gray stubble, but his blue eyes were lively. He was dressed in a well-worn suit and a soggy white shirt without a tie, but he was not beaten down. His dignity remained intact.

"Interested in coins?" he asked.

"Just a hobby," Sarkis replied and picked up the 3-kopek piece. "Anymore like this?"

"Not like that one. Is there a particular period you're interested in?"

Sarkis wished now he hadn't stopped. Perhaps if he named coins the man would be unlikely to have, he could get back to the purpose of his trip to the vernesazsh.

"Russian. Early 18th Century?" Sarkis ventured, thinking about the first rubles minted by Peter the Great.

"Oh, of course," the man replied sarcastically. "A full set of the first screw press coins of the St. Petersburg mint or only selected denominations?" He cocked his head and looked at Sarkis suspiciously.

"I'm sorry," Sarkis replied. "I couldn't afford Peter's rubles even if you had them. Forgive me." Sarkis began to move away.

"Wait," the man said. "Did I say I didn't have Peter's rubles?"

Sarkis, already a few steps away, stopped and looked back at the man, who was grinning at him. Now that he had Sarkis' attention again, he said, "Actually, I don't have any of Peter's. But what about Catherine's five-kopek coins?"

Sarkis' resolve melted and he turned back.

The man reached into his coat pocket and removed several coins wrapped in a soft cloth. He peeled back the corners and, in the palm of his hand, displayed three large five-kopek copper coins. Sarkis recognized them instantly. Two were minted with the imperial eagle, the more common coin. The third was the Siberian equivalent with two ermines holding a tablet beneath the imperial crown. They weren't in mint condition, but Sarkis thought they'd probably grade Very Fine.

He didn't pick up the Siberian coin, but removed his glove and used his fingernail to turn it over in the man's hand. Yes, he thought, it would grade Very Fine. He didn't think either of Catherine's coins were investment grade, but they were still impressive coins and any collector would appreciate them.

"How much do you want for the Siberian?" Sarkis asked.

"Why not take all three?"

"How much for all three then?"

"They've been in my family for four generations. I hate to part with them. Let's say ten thousand drams."

Sarkis countered at five thousand drams and they agreed on sixty-five hundred--about fourteen US dollars. The man had other coins he wanted to sell, but Sarkis renewed his resolve and moved on. He'd come for jewelry, not coins.

He made his way up the hill, but saw nothing that suggested any valuable pieces were for sale today at the vernesazsh. Yet he'd seen it there before. When he reached the large fountain, cracked and dry like all the others in the city, he looked back down the hill at the sea of people and decided to tour the other side of the park.

He was scarcely halfway to the monument when a chess set caught his eye. The oversized wooden board was hinged in the center and folded into a carrying case. The case was olive wood, polished by the natural oils of players' hands through the years, but otherwise unremarkable The chessmen, however, were extraordinary. The white pieces were carved in Oriental alabaster with veins of red and rust. The black pieces were of lapis lazuli--dark blue, flecked with pyrite gold. The kings and queens were possibly five inches high and an inch and a half at the base. Faces appeared beneath their crowns. The kings were the tallest, of course, and were further distinguished by square-cut beards. The powerful queens featured prominent breasts jutting proudly from floor-length cloaks. Elongated crosses were carved in the miters of the bishops and the armored knights were mounted on rearing horses. The castles were taller than conventional pieces and though austere, were deftly rendered. The pawns were two-thirds the size of the major pieces-- an inch in diameter at the base and two inches tall. The carver had spared them their customary anonymity by rendering them in the most colorfully veined alabaster and the most spectacularly flecked lapis lazuli. Arrayed in preparation for battle, the two armies were as gaily decked out as if they were on parade.

The man standing nearest the chess set had a face like a hawk, sharp and angular with a prominent, hooked nose. His eyes were jet black and his beard dark and heavy. His trousers bagged at the knees and the heavy green sweater he wore had a number of snags.

Sarkis nodded to him and asked, "Yours?"

"Please," the man said, inviting Sarkis to inspect the set.

Sarkis picked up one of the white pieces. Yes. Oriental alabaster. Twice as hard as true alabaster and twice as difficult to carve. The lapis was an even greater challenge because it was harder still. Hand-carved, the workmanship was truly superior. The man had been a master of his craft. In all his museum days, Sarkis had never seen anything like it.

"What can you tell me about it?"

The man smiled, displaying decaying teeth stained by tobacco smoke. He sensed Sarkis' appreciation by the way he handled the pieces. "We think the chessmen came from Persia," the man said. "Quite a long time ago, though I don't know exactly. My great-grandfather brought the set here from Syria in the 1890s. My grandfather made the case."

"Do you know how he came by it?"

"My great-grandfather kept a caravanserai in Aleppo. We suppose he took it in payment from a passing merchant. Are you interested?"

"I wish I knew more about its history," Sarkis said, rubbing his jaw.

"If that's important, give me a few minutes and I'll make up one for you," the man said.

Sarkis laughed. "How much are you asking?"

The man looked Sarkis in the eye and said, "A hundred thousand drams."

Sarkis' heart sank. The starting price was much too high. He looked again at the venerable carvings. If he could get it for seventy thousand . . .

Sarkis offered fifty thousand and had to make a 'final' offer twice and walk away before the owner accepted seventy thousand, provided Sarkis paid in US dollars.

"I hope you'll give it a better home than I did," the man said.

"I'll take good care of it," Sarkis said and moved on down the hill.

It was then, flushed with the success of his bargain on the chess set, that he saw the kind of woman he was looking for. In her sixties, her face fleshy but still handsome, she carried herself with dignity, sitting quietly on a low wall among tattered refugees from Karabagh and grizzled factory workers, her back straight, her legs crossed at the ankles. Her iron-gray hair was carefully coifed and her navy blue wool coat fit her too well not to have been tailored. Sarkis stopped some distance from her and strained to see what she had laid out on the small table beside her. A single bracelet weighted down a scarf that covered other objects, hiding them from casual view.

Sarkis approached her and found in her large dark eyes the embers of her youth. They were warm and expressive and danced quietly when she smiled, as she did when he spoke to her. "Good morning," he said.

"Good morning," she replied.

"That's a nice bracelet," he said, not looking at it or touching it, but rather watching her eyes as he spoke. "Do you have any other pieces?"

"Bracelets?" she replied, returning his gaze, inviting him, actually.

She must have been a man-killer in her day, he thought.

"Not necessarily. But something with gem stones."

"I see," she said, still looking at him intently, judging him as a mother might appraise a suitor for her only daughter. "Could you be more specific?" she asked.

"Emeralds?" he ventured.

"Ah," she replied and turned over a corner of the scarf beneath the silver bracelet. "Something like this, perhaps?"

Shielded from casual passersby, but open to Sarkis' eyes was an emerald ring. The gold mounting displayed a one-carat square-cut stone. The design of the ring was simple and well-executed. Sarkis reckoned it to be no more than 100 years old. Not the antique he was seeking.

He started to pick it up to examine it more closely. She put out her hand to restrain him.

"Please," she said. "Don't show the world."

"Of course," he replied, squatting down so that he brought his eye to the ring. He slipped off the glove on his right hand and lifted the ring an inch or so from the little table. Without a loupe, he couldn't examine the inclusions or estimate the grade. The light was lively in the stone, though, so he judged it to be of high quality. "It's a good stone," he said at length. "But I'm looking for something older than this, an antique, an heirloom."

The woman inspected him again. She noted his sensitive features, his slender fingers and, although she was no expert herself, she thought the way he handled the ring suggested that he was. That put her at a disadvantage in the bargaining. "For a gift?" she asked finally.

"No," he said before thinking. He started to explain, but caught himself. For a long moment, they looked into each others eyes, reaching an understanding without words.

"I might have the sort of thing you're looking for," she said slowly, her eyes still fixed on him. "But not here."

****

It was late afternoon when Sarkis left her flat, walked down two flights and emerged onto the sidewalk. The five-kopek coins of Catherine the Great rested in their soft cloth in his pocket. But the two thousand American dollars he'd brought with him were gone. Instead, four pieces of antique jewelry shared the olive-wood box with the alabaster and lapis lazuli chessmen. The first was a small Armenian cross set with five, faceted, oval-cut emeralds of approximately one carat each set in a gold mounting lovingly worn and polished by prayerful fingers through several hundred years. He also had a gold bracelet which might be a genuine Celtic torque dating from the first century BC when Celts lived in Galatia. Quite apart from its historic and artistic value, the gold alone was probably worth what he'd paid the woman, whose name he still didn't know. The other two pieces were rings, one mounted a lively ruby on delicate gold filigree and the other a handsome, wide gold band with filigreed crossings inset with a faded, blue material he couldn't immediately identify.

Sarkis' money had run out long before her cache of jewelry. She hinted that several of her friends might also be willing to part with some of their heirlooms and they agreed that Sarkis would return to her flat the following afternoon.

CHAPTER TWENTY

Garni and Geghard

Tom dressed comfortably in sturdy khakis, threw a lightweight windbreaker over a button-down Oxford shirt and a sweater and pondered what to do with the Rolex while he was out touring with Ana. The back of the drawer of his bedside table came free with a few intricate twists and he judged that there was enough room between the outer shell of the table and the back of the drawer to accommodate the Rolex case. From his shaving kit, he took a roll of adhesive tape and spared none of it in affixing the case to the back of the drawer. He'd return it to his briefcase on Monday.

He took breakfast and went downstairs early to enjoy the crisp morning air. After half an hour a small, two-door sedan came down the street from his left and nosed into the curb. It looked like one of those boxy Fiats he remembered from the '70s. Through the windshield, he saw Ana Stepanian behind the wheel.

"Good morning," he said, getting in the car.

Ana smiled her greeting and asked, "Are you ready to know Armenia?"

"You bet," he said. "Where'd you get the car?"

"It is my car," she replied proudly.

"Fiat?"

"No. Zhiguli. Russian Zhiguli. A fine car."

The tailored, gabardine slacks and soft brown leather jacket she wore over a white turtleneck sweater gave her a casual freshness he found hugely appealing. She let him settle into his seat and then backed away from the curb, drove around the square into Abovyan Street and ascended one side of the bowl in which central Yerevan sits. They were still climbing when Ana exclaimed, "Ah, there," She pulled to the side of the road to stop at a makeshift gas station.

A tanker truck stood in a side street and several cars and their drivers were parked around a kiosk of odd-sized boards, painted bright yellow. 'Shell' was emblazoned along the side in black, stenciled letters. The attendant was filling an assortment of plastic buckets and supplying funnels for a self-service operation. Tom and Ana got out to wait their turn.

"Is this gas from Iran?" Tom asked.

"Yes," Ana replied. "Our border with Iran is still open, though the Azeris can close it when they want."

Their turn came and before Ana could speak to the attendant, Tom said, "Get two of these. The gas is on me." He pointed to a five-gallon jerry can sitting beside the kiosk and held up two fingers.

"No, no," she said. "It is not necessary. I can pay."

"I'm sure you can," he said. "But it's your car, you're driving and I expect you to tell me fantastic things about the places we're going to see, so I'm going to contribute something to the day."

She laughed at his blitzkrieg of words and said, "How wonderful. It will fill the tank."

They pulled away from the gas station and continued climbing along a major thoroughfare.

"Where are we now?" Tom asked.

"It is Miasnikian Avenue. We are passing by the zoo." She pointed to the right. "You say 'zoo'? Place for wild animals?"

"Exactly," he said.

They turned again at an interchange and drove through another area of grim, Soviet-style apartment buildings, their concrete walls stark and gray, their balconies enclosed with makeshift materials to extend the living space.

As they drove on, the road stretched out behind them and houses gave way to a rocky, rural plain. Ana checked her mirror often but there was no sign of anyone following them. Presently, they came upon a community of two-story stone houses, clustered up a barren mountainside, many still under construction and no two of them alike. "Do you see?" Ana asked, pointing to the houses. "That is *dacha*."

"Those are dachas, huh? Looks like an American suburb."

"Would you like to see my family's *dacha*?" Ana asked brightly. "We pass by it on the road to Garni. We could go there as we return."

"That'd be great. Sure are a lot of them unfinished. Do people work on them little by little or what?"

"That is how we build dacha, some each season until it is finished. Many *dachas* began here in 1980s, but now people have no money to build."

"I don't see any people," Tom said. "Doesn't anybody live here?"

"*Dacha* is for weekend and summer. We live in city or village, not in dacha."

"Why is that? These places look like they could really be nice."

"Dachas are outside the city and busses do not come here. Also the city does not give water or heat or electricity or telephone. We must make electricity with our own generators. Some dachas have wells for water but most buy water from a truck. And the roads are difficult in snow. So we do not use dacha very much in winter. In summer, though, people come to plant gardens and tend fruit trees. It is good for children, too, so if there is a house, mother and children can stay all summer and father comes on weekends."

They soon reached open country with expanses of rolling mountain pastures. Around a curve in the road, they almost ran into a young shepherd in a Russian camouflage jacket and his flock of sheep. Ana had to stand on the brakes to keep from hitting them. Undisturbed, the sheep flowed around the car. The shepherd smiled and waved as he waded among them. When the last of the flock passed the car, they drove on.

A little farther down the road, a huddle of houses appeared. "This is Garni village," Ana said as they turned into a narrow street running between stone houses. "Soon we will see Garni Fortress and Sun Temple."

They rounded a corner and saw before them part of a wall and a gray stone gate. Ana parked beside the wall and turned off the engine. There were no other cars or vehicles. The sudden stillness inside the car made them acutely aware of their heat and aroma. Surprised, they turned to each other and exchanged a long confused look. Ana caught her breath and recovered first. "Would you like to get out and see?"

"Lead on," he replied and got out of the car.

The chill air braced them as they walked up a stone ramp onto a flagstone path lined with still leafless trees. At the end of the path stood a small temple in the Grecian style.

Built of blue-gray stone and surrounded by graceful Ionic columns, six in front and seven more down each side, the Sun Temple was small compared with Greek and Roman ruins Tom had seen around the Mediterranean. The entrance was almost as high as the capitals of the columns, but there were no windows or other openings. The frieze and shallow-sloped roof line were simple and more graceful for their lack of elaborate decoration. A jumble of stones and the outline of a foundation gave evidence of another building that once stood beside the temple.

"Come," Ana said. "You should see the valley." She led him to the far side of the temple and stood at the edge of a sheer cliff. Far below, he saw the ribbon of a river curling through a steep cleft in the mountains, white water spewing through the rapids of the stream. The narrow floor of the valley was tilled and planted for a new season. Cultivated terraces marched up the slope to the edge of the village.

He didn't know how long he stood there, but he felt Ana's hand come into his and his heart leaped at her touch. She led him across the open ground a little way, to the other side of the temple, where another vista opened up. The river wound on between mountains whose slopes spread the legs of the valley. Still holding his hand, Ana sat down on the grass and drew him down with her.

"Tell me what you think," she said.

"It's fabulous," he said. "Are those the king's vineyards going up the slope over there?" he asked, waving his arm toward the terraces.

"Yes. But they are the people's vineyards now. No more kings in Armenia. No more Armenian empire."

"Empire?" Tom asked.

"Once, Armenia was most of Turkey and part of Syria. That makes our land here more important because it is what remains. Our main root. Do you say 'tap' root?"

"Yes, tap root."

"It was to this place that King Tigranes came after Roman army defeated him at our grand capital, Tigranocerta. It would be a difficult place to attack. The Romans took our empire, all but what we have now. Even when the Turks killed us and scattered our people to the wind, we held this land and kept it safe for Armenians everywhere."

"Armenia was part of the Soviet Union," Tom said.

She shrugged. "Only for a little while. Seventy years is nothing in our history." She opened her mouth to go on, thought better of it, because she felt her frustration rising and knew she shouldn't offend the American.

Tom studied her as he listened, his eyes tracing the graceful lines of her face and the soft curve of her throat.

They were silent for a while. "A good place," he said at last. "You can feel . . . I don't know . . . sanctuary maybe." He was quiet again, looking out across the valley. Finally, he turned to her. "Thanks for the history lesson," he said.

"You are good listener. Later, perhaps I will tell you how we were Christians before the Romans."

Ana sat down where the slope became steep, pulled her legs up and wrapped her arms around them. Tom joined her. Their faces were only inches apart, so close they seemed to occupy the same space. A vagrant breeze caught a strand of her hair and laid it across her forehead. He lifted it with his fingertips and laid it back into its place, letting the palm of his hand slide away and rest against her neck. Her eyes searched his for a moment and then closed, the lashes dark and heavy against her cheek. Without willing it, he leaned toward her and tasted the velvet softness of her lips. She let him kiss her, then felt the heat and lay back against the slope, taking him with her, her mouth melting, meeting his kiss fully.

"Please," she said, pulling away. She sat up to catch her breath and turned to look at him over her shoulder. Her eyes were pleading. "We must not . . ."

He put a finger to her lips. "Sorry," he said. "It was just . . ."

"There is no need to be sorry," she said, brushing dry grass from her slacks. "But we should go. Geghard Monastery is not far. After, we will have lunch."

A gaggle of children in tattered clothes were playing around the Zhiguli when they came through the gate. Ana shooed them away. They danced down the dusty street, jeering happily as they fled.

****

Geghard Monastery lay at the base of a narrow box canyon five or six kilometers from Garni. Its principal steeple could be seen from the road, rising like a castle turret--its peak a stumpy cone without eaves, not a slender spire. Several other cars, all Zhigulis, were parked beside an imposing stone wall. To their left, a cobblestone ramp rose toward the monastery and half a dozen peddlers offered candy and Armenian crosses from spindly folding tables. Midway, the ramp reversed direction and led them upward toward a massive archway framing two tall wooden doors. They passed through the tunnel of the gate into a courtyard beside the main church.

"Where the stone rises--cliffs, you say?--you will see many caves and carvings. Once this place was called Ayrivank, which means Monastery of Caves. Did I say why this place is now called 'Geghard'? It means 'lance' or 'spear'. Do you remember that a Roman soldier put his lance in the side of Christ when he was dying on the cross?"

Tom nodded.

"This lance was brought to Armenia by Jude Thaddeus, one of the Apostles. St. Jude is the saint of hopeless causes. Perfect for Armenia, yes?"

Tom nodded again, charmed by Ana, but not quite understanding the reference to hopeless causes.

"The lance was kept here for many years, in the Chapel of the Upper Tier. Now it is at Echmiadzin Cathedral."

They walked the length of the courtyard to the main entrance. The sun's rays lit the entry, where they bought long, orange tapers. Beyond the portal, they entered a small chapel with a raised altar and passed through an archway into a large sanctuary, lit mainly by the blaze of candles set in sand tables and by slits of sunlight streaming through several narrow windows.

"This is main chapel," Ana said. "It has two altars, you see, where candles are. Three other rooms are here also, cut from the mountain. Two of them are extraordinary and we are here at the right time. The sun comes in directly through the windows in the cupola at midday." Ana led him into a darker room where tapers also burned in sand tables.

"Be careful not to fall. There is spring and water is on floor. This is where people came in pagan times to hear oracle speak to them, as at Delphi. Sound can come into this room from another place. The oracle was a person, but the people could not see her, so they thought she spoke from the world of spirits. I cannot think how to say what that must have been like."

"Eerie," Tom offered. "Like the voices of ghosts."

"Eerie. Yes, something like that. But it is different when people sing from the place where she stood. Then it seems that angels are here."

She led him to another sand table forested with burning tapers. "We still have candles," she said. "What shall we pray for?"

"Truth and love."

Ana looked at him for a long moment, the features of his face wavering in the shadows cast by the candlelight. "Truth and love," she repeated. Together they touched the wicks of their tapers to candles already ablaze and pressed them into the sand side by side. They turned away and missed seeing the candles shift in the loose sand. One leaned toward the other, their flames touched and the tips of the two candles melted together.

"Many young people come here to marry," Ana said as they emerged into the courtyard. "They make parade when they leave the church. Bride and groom go down the road and everyone is dancing and singing and playing music. They dance from here to Restoran Geghard to eat and drink and celebrate. We can go there for lunch."

"Lunch," Tom said. "Great idea. Is there more to see here?"

"I would like to show you the Upper Tier Chapel, where the lance was kept, but repairs are being made and it is closed now."

****

The Restoran Geghard was cantilevered over a cliff on the opposite side of the road from the monastery. They walked beside the building into a small courtyard on the side of the precipice and went in. Tom wasn't surprised that the proprietress greeted Ana by name or that the two women chatted like old friends before they were taken to a table with a view of the crevasse created by the stream that roared out of Geghard's canyon.

As they sat down, Ana said, "The dish today has long name.

In Armenian, we say sembook yev mesovghorovatz. I hope you like it."

"I'm hungry enough to eat anything, but just out of curiosity, what is it?"

"It is only lamb and eggplant," she said, laughing.

When they had tasted the wine, Tom reminded her that she'd promised him another story, one about how Armenia had become a Christian nation.

Over lunch, she told him of the beautiful Christian maiden, Rhipsime, the Roman Emperor Diocletian and the Armenian king, Tridat.

"Before Diocletian had thought her the most beautiful woman in the world and wanted to marry her, but she ran away to Armenia because Diocletian was a pagan. Diocletian asked King Tridat to send her back, but Tridat, too, thought she was the most beautiful woman in the world and wanted her for himself. When Rhipsime refused him also, Tridat had her stoned to death, but then he was so filled with remorse, he became ill and could not be healed by any of his doctors.

The king's sister, Princess Khosrov, had heard of a holy man who worked miracles. His name was Grigor. He was a Christian and he was being held in the king's dungeons at that very time. The princess promised to release Grigor if he would heal the king. Grigor prayed over the king and he was healed. King Tridat was so grateful to God he became Christian and decreed that all Armenia would be Christian, too. And that is how Armenia became first Christian nation, ten years before Romans were permitted to worship Jesus," she concluded.

Tom got up and went onto the balcony of the restaurant, where he could see the valley. He put his elbows on the railing and stared into the afternoon haze that was beginning to soften the sharp edges of the mountains. Petrossian's bloodied face came to him unbidden, an ancient warrior protecting his homeland against invading barbarians. But Petrossian was no patriotic warrior. He had never known Andre to be interested in anyone except himself and never spoke about this dramatic homeland tucked away in the mountains. To Tom's knowledge, he had never even mentioned it. In that moment, he resented Andre more than ever. Andre was putting his life at risk for a handful of diamonds and Andre was already dead. Screw the diamonds. He owed Petrossian nothing. There was no contact, no rendezvous, no reason other than a few thousand dollars for him to put his life at risk. Casting off the diamonds freed him.

The door opened behind him and Ana came to join him.

Ana stood beside him, her elbows also on the railing. "Do you still want to see my dacha?" she asked.

"I hoped you hadn't forgotten."

****

She turned off the main highway onto a dirt road, badly rutted from the winter thaw. "Our roads are not smooth in winter. Soon they will be repaired for people to come to make gardens."

"Manoukian said he was going to his dacha this weekend. Is he ahead of time or what?"

"Some people come early. Whatever pleases them. I have not seen his dacha, but when my father was a minister we had comforts others did not. Now it is the same for Minister Manoukian."

The Zhiguli bottomed out on its springs so often that it was difficult to talk and Tom asked no more questions so that Ana could concentrate on driving. Her dacha was among many built on the slope of an old mountain and the road was made more difficult by the grade and the frequent switch-backs they had to traverse. Finally, they reached a level section where every plot was taken and the *dachas* were built close together. Ana parked the Zhiguli on the shoulder of the road in front of a high wall.

"This is our *dacha*." She got out and turned a key in the padlock that held the chain securing two large steel doors in the wall. Tom followed her into an open carport and up a flight of metal stairs. They emerged onto a second story balcony that offered a panoramic view of the countryside and the snow-covered mountaintops.

"You see?" Ana said to him, waving her hand in short strokes back and forth between two fence lines. "This is dacha. We have garden, three trees for cherries and two for apricots. Not a grand thing like Europe or America. But air is clean in summer and soon, when spring comes, blossoms in our garden will smell very pleasant."

Ana turned away from the balcony and unlocked a door to the

house. "Come," she said. "I will show you inside. Mother has had the shutters taken down and we have a little sunlight. We could start our generator to make electricity, but perhaps there is no gasoline."

The *dacha* was austere, almost utilitarian--a sparsely furnished living room, a narrow kitchen with an electric stove, a refrigerator and a sink. Ana tried one of the taps and water gushed forth. "At least there is water," she said and led him into a narrow hall. An open door revealed a small bathroom with a basin, commode and shower. Farther down the hall she stopped in a doorway. "This is my room," she said. "Where I have slept since I was a girl." She lit a candle and the room came to life in soft light. Like the rest of the dacha it was sparsely furnished. Her bed was similar to his at the hotel, with two important differences. Like his, it was near to the floor. Unlike his, it was wider and the mattress didn't sag like a hammock. A collection of framed photographs on top of the chest of drawers caught his attention.

"Let me guess," he said, picking up one of them. "The gorgeous little girl is you at about nine or ten years old and the woman is your mother. She's quite beautiful." They were posed in front of a tall, trimmed hedge in a park. "Is this your father?" Tom asked, pointing to a generously-proportioned dark-haired man with a heavy mustache.

"Yes," Ana said. She looked at the photograph with him for a few moments, then took it from him and placed it back on the chest. "You have seen dacha now. Would you like to take some wine and watch the sun go down?" she asked.

"Yes, very much."

She took him back to the kitchen, retrieved a bottle of red wine from a cabinet, handed him a corkscrew and two stemmed glasses. "Will you open this? I will see if there is food." Tom pulled the cork, sniffed the wine's aroma and set the bottle on the counter to breathe. Ana was rummaging in one of the cabinets.

"We have only these olives," she said, holding up a can. "Shall I open it?"

"Let's just have the wine. I'm still stuffed from lunch."

"Oh, look!" Ana exclaimed. "Come quickly." She pulled him out onto the balcony.

"That's awesome," Tom said, taking in the colossus of Mt. Ararat jutting out of the plain, its base bathed in the mauve and purple shades of dusk, its snowy peaks and upper reaches still dazzling white in the last rays of the sun.

"Do you see the mountain beside Ararat? We call it 'Little Ararat'," Ana said. "It is fortunate to see them both this way."

Tom leaned forward, rested his elbows on the railing and stared at the two mountains. Ana stood behind him, contemplating the slope of his back and the curve of his buttocks. Tentatively, she put her hand on his back and slowly stroked the long muscles on either side of his spine. Here, at the dacha in which she'd grown up, he belonged to her now as her dolls had belonged to her when she was nine or ten.

She eased her hip against his, barely touching. The warmth of his body brought a heady recollection of the kiss they shared when they lay on the slope at Garni. It had been a long time since such electricity had raced down her sides into her loins. A long time since she'd felt a man inside her. Why not now? What would it be like with an American? There would be no complications if she were in control.

He turned to face her, a question in his eyes.

"Come," she said, taking his hand and leading him back into the dacha.

Chapter Twenty One

Lake Sevan

Tom was conscious of smooth, warm skin molded against the length of his body. Ana's back was to him and his face was buried in the earthy fragrance of her hair. His hand rested easily on the ridge of her hip. He stroked her inner thigh with his fingertips and slowly drew his hand up the silky softness of her belly. She stirred, moving her hips and pressing herself back against him.

She had dominated their first lovemaking, hungry and aggressive, mounting him and forcing the pace until she was spent. In their afterglow, she allowed him to caress her and explore her body, but when they were joined a second time, it was again like war, her fingernails raking his back, her teeth sinking into his shoulder. For Tom, the way she challenged him was more like enemies doing battle than lovers expressing their passion. He fell asleep from the physical exertion, but deep within his mind was an awareness that she had made love to him rather than the other way around.

With the pale light of dawn filtering through the window, they made love again in the warmth of awakening. She was still strong and demanding, but unlike the night before, she let him lead, wrapping her legs around him. Then they fell asleep once more.

****

He awoke a second time to brighter sunlight and water running in the bathroom. Without Ana beside him, he was chilled and was about to get up when the water stopped and she returned, wrapped in a silk emerald green robe. She lifted the covers and slipped in beside him.

"Shall we remain here and make love all day? We would have to eat olives and drink wine because there is nothing more." She paused, but gave him no time to reply. "Or shall we go on to Lake Sevan and enjoy the picnic I have prepared--caviar and ripe fruit and vodka and fresh bread?"

She was idly stroking his back as she spoke and her fingers found the depression of a smooth, round scar. Her fingertip fit it perfectly.

"What is this?" she asked.

"What's what?" he evaded.

"A scar, yes?"

"Yes."

"You were a soldier? Wounded in war?"

"No," he said.

Ana took his curt answers to mean he wasn't going to talk about it, so she put away her question and jumped out of bed, pulling most of the cover from him as she went.

"Please get up now," she said, standing in the center of the room, hands on hips, out of reach, commanding.

In that moment, he realized that their relationship had changed and not just because they had slept together. There was something about the way it had been done that both fascinated him and made him uneasy. Conventions had been tangled. She had been assigned to him. Technically, she worked for him. It was her country, but he was a guest, as entitled to certain courtesies as he was obliged to offer certain courtesies himself. Other than his kissing her at Garni, it was she who had taken the initiative, leading him to her bed. Surely this was not part of her brief with Manoukian. There was no need. In making love to him, she expressed a savage urgency, a drive that surpassed physical need. Was she proving something?

****

Ana left Tom at the hotel entrance and drove back to her apartment. When she returned to pick him up, she parked the Zhiguli between the new hotel and the old one, hidden from the street, and used the key she'd kept from her days with Intourist to enter a seldom-used door at the far end of the new hotel. She climbed the stairs at the end of the building, avoiding Sofia's station at the head of the corridor, and tapped softly at Tom's door. He let her in, dressed but still toweling his hair dry.

She slipped into the room, carrying a small bag which contained a change of lingerie and a fresh outfit, and closed the door behind her. Tom stood in the narrow vestibule of the room, not letting her pass. She leaned back against the door and he walked to her until he stood touching her, the towel around his shoulders, his hands against the door. He looked into her almond eyes, fixing her in his memory, every pore, every eyelash. Then he kissed her slowly.

She pushed him back and made him go downstairs to wait for her to shower and change. Afterward, she slipped out the way she had come, threw her bag in the trunk of the Zhiguli and drove to the front of the hotel. She picked him up there, thinking herself quite clever.

Again they drove up Abovyan Street onto Miasnikian as they had on their way to Garni, but when they reached the interchange, they veered left instead of right. "We will be on the main highway to Tblisi soon," Ana said. "Sevan is more distant from Yerevan than Garni."

"Tell me about Lake Sevan," he said.

"Lake Sevan is most beautiful lake in the world. It will be more beautiful soon. In summer, people come to take sun and swim. There are hotels and restaurants and boats to go for fishing. It is place for relaxing, for taking the sun and for being with good friends. Drinking and eating. A fish called ishkhan lives there--king trout, I think you say. It is a very delicious fish."

The day was sunny and clear, almost cloudless, and they drove through wide expanses of rolling, high country with distant snow-covered mountains in every direction, a perfect day for an outing, yet there were almost no vehicles on the highway in either direction.

"I don't want to bring up an awkward subject," Tom said. "But it seems like Armenia used to be a pretty pleasant place to live. I can see that Yerevan used to be very much alive. Now, it's dead. Yesterday, we saw dachas, today it'll be the resorts at Lake Sevan. The trouble is, there's nobody there. It makes me wonder if you weren't better off under the communists."

"Yes," she replied. "Life was better before. Always there

was heat in winter and electricity and hot water and work to do. We had our automobiles and gasoline. I do not even have a position now. We have suffered much since independence."

"Do you wish it hadn't happened?"

She thought for a few moments before she answered. "It is difficult to say. You see us freezing in our apartments and many people leaving the country. What are you to think? That it was always like this? It will not even be this way in two months. The wildflowers will bloom, we will repair the broken fountains and put in water, cherries will become ripe and sweet and we will go to cinema and drink tea at sidewalk cafes. But not all of us will go to our work each day as we once did. We will not take vacations at Black Sea beaches. We will not buy new boots because it pleases us, but because the ones we have cannot be repaired. We will wonder what happens to our children. Will they go to university? Will they give us grandchildren? Will they leave us and go to America or France? What will happen to our country?" She paused to catch her breath and collect her thoughts. "One day, perhaps, if all we do now is fruitful, it will be better than before."

He put his hand on the nape of her neck, caressing it. She took a hand from the steering wheel and rested it on his thigh. They drove that way, in silence, feeling more than thinking, content to be in each other's company.

Ana maintained good speed and soon, topping a rise in the road, Tom saw part of the Lake. She slowed as they passed several hotels and restaurants, all closed for the season. "Look," she said, pointing to a promontory off to the right. "That is where we go."

"Oh, yeah. I see. Are those churches?" he asked.

"Yes. The large one is Arakelots' Church. That means 'Holy Apostles' Church. The little one is St. Karapet's Church. At the top is another one, Astavatsatsin Church. Once the hill where they are was an island. But now, water is not so much and we climb up instead of going by boat."

"I guess it was a better spot for a monastery when it was an island, huh?"

"The monks must have liked it more than Geghard, don't you think? Here, they could always see the lake. But there are no monks here any more."

"You guys do have the most unusual architecture," Tom remarked, taking in the primitive, stubby spires, the stones themselves stained and worn. "I've never seen anything like it before." They turned off the main highway and drove along a tree-lined parkway until they came to a shuttered restaurant. There was only one other car in the parking area, so they would have the site to themselves again. A steep, winding path spiraled precariously up the promontory on which the monastery sat.

"I guess you're going to tell me we have to climb up there," Tom said, pointing to the path that he thought would have challenged a mountain goat.

"Of course," she said. "Will you take the basket? I will carry the blankets."

An irregular trail of ancient stone steps was notched into the cliff face. No railing guarded against a misstep and Tom tried to keep his eyes locked onto the next stone, placing each footstep deliberately. Yet every time the winding path pointed him out toward the lake, he struggled against vertigo. Ana skipped up the stone steps fearlessly and was waiting for him when he finally emerged onto the barren top of the promontory.

Gratefully, he sank onto a bench and looked out over the glorious expanse of Lake Sevan. The lake was calm as well as deserted and the surface was disturbed in only a few rippled patches where a vagrant breeze dipped down. The clouds drifted lazily across the sky and the breeze whispered softly in the leafless branches of the trees on the lower slopes.

"I guess it was worth the climb," he said.

"Come," she said.

He hoisted the basket and followed her up the hill, past the larger of the two churches. She turned off the path and walked down into a grove of trees on the slope facing the lake to a secluded glen, hidden from the path but open to the lake. Ana stopped and spread one of the blankets.

"No one will see us here."

"It's perfect," he said, setting the picnic basket down. While Tom gazed at the shimmering, sea green water of the lake, Ana took small glasses and a bottle of Stolichnaya from the basket. She poured two drinks and brought them to where he was standing.

"Welcome," she said, handing him one of the glasses.

They drank the vodka down. Her glass in one hand and the bottle of Stolichnaya in the other, Ana raised her arms and rested her forearms on his shoulders.

Tom pulled her to him and kissed her lightly.

She returned his kiss, but only for a moment, then she pulled away.

"You must eat," she said, leading him toward the blanket.

They stretched out and found that the dry, matted grass made a soft, thick padding. Ana brought the picnic basket into the center of the blanket and began to lay out their lunch.

She tore an end from a loaf of bread, split it into two pieces and smeared it with caviar. She handed Tom the bread and poured their glasses full of vodka. "This will give you strength," she said. The vodka had already sent his taste buds into salivary paroxysms and he could barely keep himself from wolfing down the caviar.

"Oh, good grief," he said. "That is incredibly delicious. This bread's still warm. How'd you do that?"

"We make bread every day. I bought it when I left you at the hotel this morning and wrapped it in heavy cloth. It is good, yes?"

"Absolutely."

Next she spread on a plate two sliced ripe tomatoes, cucumber spears and four boiled eggs and sprinkled salt over it all. They had more caviar, drank more vodka, devoured the eggs and the vegetables and finished with a sliced apple, cheese and Armenian brandy.

After they'd eaten, Tom lay on his back, looking up through the leafless boughs of a tree at puffy clouds drifting slowly through the blue sky. Ana put everything back in the picnic hamper except the brandy and the little glasses, then pulled the other blanket up over their legs because the air was cooling quickly as the sun passed mid-afternoon. Snuggled between the blankets, she lay on her side and propped her head on her hand. Tom turned toward her and put his arm around her, but she pulled away.

"Please," she said. "We are from very different places and I must know about you now. I do not make love with strangers. Last night--and this morning--was not as it should have been. Wonderful, but not . . . how do you say? Not good behavior?"

Tom sat up, crossing his legs Buddha fashion. "What do you want to know?"

"You have always done this kind of work? Economist?"

"No. I was a student. Then I worked with my father for awhile."

Ana waited for him to go on, but he didn't. Finally, she said, "What did you do with your father?"

"He took gemstones from one place to another. I helped him, but I didn't care for the work."

Was Ana a stranger on a plane, one he'd never see again and so could speak freely of things he wouldn't tell his best friend, or was she beginning to mean something much more? He'd been lonely without Seline, more than he could ever describe, and Ana was so exotic she would never remind him of her. Was he trying to close the door on Seline and his father and Andre and begin again? Confession, a purge of festering and painful things might help the healing.

"Gemstones?" Ana asked. "For jewelry? Why was this not interesting?"

"It was dangerous," Tom said. "The last time I worked for my father, the stones I was carrying were stolen and I was almost killed. Some strangers found me and got me to a hospital just in time. I have a scar on my back for a souvenir--the one you asked about--but that's not the only scar."

"What others?"

"My father, I guess. He hadn't been much of a father over the years. Always traveling, never home. He didn't even come to see me in the hospital. So when the hospital said I could go, I went back to school and that's where I met my wife."

"You are married? You did not tell me that."

"Used to be married. Not married now. She left me. A couple of years ago."

Ana smiled.

"Tell me about her."

"Blond hair, blue eyes, pretty face. Beautiful smile and a wonderful laugh. We lived in London when I was at the London

School of Economics. We had wonderful times together. And then I became like my father, I guess. Always traveling, never at home. It wasn't what she bargained for in a marriage, so she left. Now it's your turn. All I know is that you worked for Intourist and that you had two postings outside Armenia--St. Petersburg and Budapest. You always look a little dreamy when Budapest comes up, so why don't you tell me about that?"

"Very well. Budapest," she said, sitting up on her knees, her calves tucked under her, her back as straight as in posture class. She clasped her hands in front of her before she began. "I was sent there in summer of 1987. I loved it immediately. Yerevan is not like Budapest--as you know. I felt so elegant there. They have beautiful palaces and wonderful restaurants and the Hungarians sing and dance and play wild music. We Armenians, I think, are more--how do you say?--solemn. And the river. I love our mountains and I love our Lake Sevan, but Danube River is also lovely."

"And then you met this guy . . ."

"Yes," she said. "Yes, I met someone. His name was Peter. Hungarian. Handsome. Elegant like Budapest. We became very much in love."

"So what happened?"

"We wanted to marry. But his family did not approve," she said sadly and then added with spirit, "I am from good family and proud to be Armenian. I am also Persian and Greek, so I am a daughter of empires that ruled the world many years before Hungarians stopped sleeping with their horses. His family made me feel--I do not know how to say--like peasant from farm. Peter said he would defy them, but he wanted me to be Hungarian, too. I could not do that. I loved Budapest and I loved Peter, but I could not be Hungarian."

She paused, feeling relieved that she had spoken what was in her heart, what she had not said out loud before, even to her mother. "How did you know there was someone in Budapest?" she asked.

"Well, I didn't know," he said. "But Budapest is a romantic city, so there had to be a hundred Hungarian guys following you all over town. And you were of an age--twenty-four or twenty-five?--when you would've found at least one of them reasonably attractive."

"And now that I'm an old woman of thirty-four?"

"You're surely wiser today," he said, grinning,

"Wiser. Yes," she said.

"What's the Hungarian's status these days?" he asked.

"He has no status. I came back to Armenia in 1988. We wrote letters. He believed I would change. I am sure he has married some Hungarian princess by now."

"And what about the KGB major--Avakian, right? I'd like to know about him. Self-protection, if nothing else. You said he was dangerous. So far nothing." Tom propped himself up on an elbow and stared at her.

"Yes. I had forgotten about that," she said.

He waited for her to go on. When she didn't, he said, "Please. I've told you things about myself I haven't told anyone else." Still she didn't respond. "If you keep ducking this question, it'll only make me wonder." She sighed deeply and began. "I was very young when I met him--only twenty years. He was older and exciting. To be with him was to be a woman. We were together for many months--wonderful months, I will say truthfully. I was very happy. Then I discovered I was not his only woman. She is the one who keeps the bar at the hotel--Marina Vartanian. I saw them together in the bed . . . That hurt me very much. Then he was sent to the war in Afghanistan. He came here again after his first year in Afghanistan and we tried to . . . how do you say? . . . rejoin, reunite?"

"Get back together."

"Yes, get back together. But I could not forget what he had done. After he returned to Afghanistan, he was wounded and sent to hospital in Kazakhstan, just before I was assigned to Budapest. He spent a long time in hospital, to make his leg well. At first, I tried to write to him, to help him, but his letters were bitter. Not only his wounds. He had trouble with people in KGB, I think. I don't really know, but my feeling for him was gone. Then I met Peter and I knew there was no hope for Aleksandr and me."

"He seems to think he still has some kind of claim on you," Tom said, rolling over onto his stomach. "Like he might bust through your door there at any moment and . . . well, who knows what."

"He has no claim on me," she said. "But he does think he can take me back to him." She shook her head vigorously. "He cannot. He has thrown away all the things that made him a good person. He brings drugs from Turkey and sells them to Russians, maybe Armenians, too. And not drugs for healing people. Drugs for pleasure, drugs that destroy people. Once he believed in our republic and in Soviet ideals. Now he only thinks of himself."

"Afghanistan," Tom said. "It was to the Soviet Union what Vietnam was to us. A lot of people--soldiers--came home with ugly scars. Not just from wounds. Psychological scars."

"Yes, I am sure. But that is not all of Aleksandr. He betrayed me while I was risking my life to do his work--across the border, in Turkey and Syria. Dangerous work and hard. I do not like to remember I was big fool. Marina is still his woman and probably she still tells him what happens in the hotel. I feel pity for her. He uses her as a thing, not even as a person."

"You said you were doing his work? I thought you were Intourist, not KGB."

"I was Intourist," she said. "I was not KGB, but whatever KGB asked of Intourist, Intourist did. Before Afghanistan, Aleksandr helped Soviet agents come and go across Turkey and Syria. They were spies. I was not spy, if that is what you are thinking. I do not lie to you. With what I did, I saved two women's lives. I do not know if they were good women or bad women. That is not for me to say. And I only did this two times. Once I went with Aleksandr to help a woman who was forced and beaten--how do you say?--raped?--by Syrian border guards. She was hurt badly. Aleksandr would have killed her not to be troubled, but the woman of the safe house and I, we helped her to be strong enough to come home. Another time--the time I learned about him and Marina--I went alone to help a woman running from your CIA. She broke her ankle. A silly thing. She stepped from the curb in Damascus. Perhaps she could have managed if she spoke Arabic or even French, but she did not. She spoke only Russian and English. Without help, she would have been caught and killed. I helped her to come back and the night we returned, I found him with Marina. In the bed together. Naked and sweating and stinking. I was so tired and what I saw broke my heart. I still cannot believe it." She paused for a moment, collecting herself, then she said, "And now I want to forget this, please. It is a long time over and best to stay that way. Perhaps if he has not tried to hurt you by now, he will not try at all. And you will leave in only a few more days."

She turned away from him and stared out at the lake. "Now you have made me unhappy. To talk of Aleksandr and to think of your leaving. We should go back to the hotel now."

"Come here," Tom said and she relented. He spread his legs and she snuggled between them with her back to him. His arms went around her and he rested his chin on her shoulder. He spread his hands against her rib cage, where he could touch the first swelling of her breasts.

They sat that way for a long time, looking out at the lake, each thinking his own thoughts. Tom moved his hands under her arms and tickled her. She squealed and tried to get away, but he wrapped his legs around her and held her fast. "Oh, please," she gasped in spasms of breathless laughter. "Please, Tom. Stop." She turned in his grasp and lay in his arms facing him.

"We don't have to worry about the KGB today, do we?" he asked, unwinding his legs from her.

As soon as he relaxed his grip, she jumped up and danced away a few steps, laughing. "Can you catch me? I am fast runner," she called over her shoulder as she ran away down the hill. She was indeed a fast runner, but in the end, Tom's legs were longer and he caught her on the slope below the grove of trees.

"The picnic things," she remembered, gasping for breathe, her heart pounding. "We must go back."

Tom knew she was making an excuse. But with an effort, he stood up, holding out a hand to pull her up.

"You are a fast runner, too," she said, starting to climb back to where their blankets lay. "I will give you brandy for your prize."

"What if you had won?"

"I would give you loser's brandy," she said and they both laughed.

They had two brandies, gathered up the picnic basket, folded the blankets and returned to the path. As they started their descent, Tom said, "Hey, you didn't tell me anything about these old churches. What kind of tour guide are you?"

"I am best tour guide you will ever know," she replied proudly. "Was it not a fine day?"

"Absolutely," he said.

They touched but talked little as they returned through the

fading light of the afternoon. Purple dusk was settling over Yerevan when Ana parked the Zhiguli in front of the hotel and turned longingly to look at Tom.

"*Sirelis*, it has been a wonderful day," she said.

"It has indeed," he replied. "Will there be another one?"

She smiled. "Yes. Perhaps."

"I'll hold you to that," he said, gripping the door handle. "By the way, what did you just call me?"

"*Sirelis*," she said. "It means 'dear one, darling,' something like that."

CHAPTER TWENTY TWO

Sarkis and Razmik

Sarkis gave her his hat and coat when he arrived. She hung them on a peg by the door and led him into the parlor, where three women of approximately her age sat stiffly, their backs straight, hands folded tightly in their laps. They were well-groomed and although their plush figures would have appealed most to grandchildren waiting for a bedtime story, all three were still quite handsome. "These are my friends," their hostess said from the archway leading into the parlor. "They would prefer not to give their names. And it is enough for them that I vouch for you. What you see on the tables vouches for itself."

"Of course," Sarkis said. "Ladies," he nodded to each of them in turn and smiled. They smiled at him uncertainly.

"Now, as you see," their hostess said to Sarkis. "We are having tea. May I pour for you?"

"Yes, thank you," he said. "Cream, please."

"Sugar?"

"Please," he answered, distracted by the display of jewelry he could see laid out on the four tables.

"I imagine the light in the parlor is not strong enough to examine the stones, so I made a place for you in the bedroom. You can also speak privately there with my friends."

Three hours later, Sarkis left the flat without a single dollar in his satchel. Instead, there were eleven pieces of jewelry. He was in no position to know international values, but he knew he'd acquired pieces of rare beauty and fine workmanship. Several were quite old, Byzantine probably, and the gemstones in several of them were of extraordinary quality. Now he could send the fax to Razmik that the money had been invested, that Razmik should come immediately to take the jewelry out to the West.

****

When Sarkis' fax arrived with the message that 'friends were awaiting him in Yerevan,' Raz canceled his classes for three days and booked a flight to Yerevan via Athens, sending his arrival information to Sarkis at the Museum with an invitation to dinner for him and Karine. He checked into the Hotel Armenia in early afternoon and was sitting in the bar, nursing a cognac when he saw Tom come through the door of the hotel with a stunning, dark-haired woman. "Tom!" Raz called. "Tom Yeager!"

Tom heard his name but did not at first see who had called. Then he spotted Raz Melikian striding across the lobby. "Well, I'll be damned," Tom said, grinning broadly. "What brings you to Armenia?"

"Family business," Raz replied, giving Tom a vigorous handshake.

"Ana," Tom said, turning to her. "This is Razmik Melikian. He's an old friend from Jordan. Raz, this is Ana Stepanian."

Ana extended her hand demurely and said, "I am pleased to meet you."

"Come, have a drink with me," Raz said, his eyes laughing. "I want to hear all about what's been going on."

They sat at a table in the lobby bar and Marina Vartanian came to wait on them. Ana and Marina ignored each other.

"So," Raz began when Marina left. "How do you like Armenia?"

"It's a tough situation. We spent today at the Central Bank, reworking the proposal for institutional development. I never imagined the transition from a command economy to a market economy would be so difficult. But we're getting there," he said. "What brings you here? Do you make this trip often?"

"No," Raz replied. "Not at all. I came here for the first time only a few weeks ago to lecture at the university. I have a cousin who lives here."

"Who is your cousin?" Ana asked.

"Sarkis Melikian," Raz said, as Marina arrived with glasses for Tom and Ana. "He's senior curator of the History Museum, just across the street. I'm taking him and his wife to dinner tonight at Dzoragiugh. I want you to come, too. Both of you. Don't even think of saying 'no'."

Tom looked at Ana and she nodded. "Sure," Tom said. "That's great. What time?"

"My reservation is for eight-thirty. Some place in the old city. Dzoriguigh, it's called."

"Do you mean the Mafia?" she asked.

"The Mafia?" Raz asked, puzzled.

"Yes. Dzoragiugh is the name of a restaurant we call 'Mafia'. But Dzoragiugh also means 'village on the gorge.' It is old Yerevan and there are other restaurants there. I only wondered if you meant Dzoragiugh Restaurant or Dzoragiugh district."

"I don't really know. The lady at the reception suggested it to me. She said Dzoragiugh."

"I will ask," Ana said. She got up and went toward the registration desk, where Marta was on duty.

They watched Ana until she disappeared from view beyond the elevators. Then Tom turned to Raz. "So how're things in Jordan?"

"Not much different from when you left. I ran into two of your friends the other night."

"Oh? Who's that?"

"The AID Director, Ferrari, and Walter Webb."

"You mean Chico Webb?"

"I guess so. I know him as Walter. He's difficult to describe. He looks so nondescript--brown hair, brown eyes, not too tall, not too short."

"That's him. 'Chico' is the nickname he got infiltrating the Guatemalan guerrillas. He looked so much like one of them they took him in. He can pass for an Arab, too."

"I'm sure he can. He's CIA?"

"He's a good man to have on your side.

Ana returned and said, "Yes, it is 'Mafia'. I added two people to the reservation."

"Perfect," Raz replied. Thirty minutes is enough time then?"

"Oh, yes. Quite enough," Ana replied.

"I was planning to take my cousins in a taxi. Shall we all go together?"

"We can join you there," Ana said "It is difficult for five to ride in taxi."

"You know the restaurant, then?"

"Of course. An old stone house on the edge of the gorge."

"Why do they call it 'Mafia'?" Tom asked.

"It is easier to pronounce than Dzoragiugh," she answered. "They have their own electricity."

From the corner of her eye, Ana saw Marina talking on the telephone and a sixth sense told her that she was speaking to Aleksandr.

* * * * * * * * * * *

Karine was in a panic, tears welling up in her eyes, threatening to overflow at any moment. "Sarkis," she said. "I have nothing to wear to Dzoragiugh. Please go without me. I will only embarrass you."

"My dear," Sarkis said calmly. "You'll be wonderful. Your hair looks beautiful and I'm sure there's something suitable in your wardrobe." Karine had gone to the salon that afternoon to have her hair rinsed and set and its natural highlights sparkled like diamond dust.

"I have no shoes," she wailed. "Oh, why didn't I buy new ones today?"

"Now, now," he said. "Let me help." While Karine stood there in her slip, still shaking, Sarkis ignored the confusion of dresses she'd thrown onto the bed and went to their wardrobe. He pushed the hangers back and forth until he found what he was looking for.

"Here, my dear. Try this." He held out a plain black dress with an oval-cut neckline.

The sight of it brought back a flood of memories, fresh tears burst from her eyes and she covered her face with her hands. Sarkis dropped the dress on the bed and put his arms around her. "Karine? Are you all right?"

"Yes, yes," she sputtered through her tears. "Do you remember the last time I wore it?"

"Of course," he answered. "You were the most beautiful woman there." The occasion had been the annual reception and dinner given by the Committee of the Museum for the senior staff in November 1988, a month before the earthquake, before their lives turned into a waking nightmare. "Come," he coaxed. "Put it on. I'll get your pearls."

Sarkis was straightening his tie in front of the hall mirror when Mrs. Kebussyan knocked at the door. He had only to reach out his hand and turn the knob to let her in.

146

"Good evening, Mrs. Kebussyan."

"Good evening, Mr. Melikian," the stout, elderly woman said, undoing the knot that held a kerchief around her head.

"Let me take your coat," Sarkis said, holding out his arms, just as Karine came out of Setta's room, wearing the black sheath dress and the pearls. She'd worried about fitting into the dress, but it was actually a little loose. She'd rouged her lips lightly and touched her eyelids with eye shadow. Sarkis was speechless for a moment, dumbstruck by his wife's loveliness.

"Good evening, Mrs. Kebussyan," Karine said, completely composed.

"My, you look wonderful," Mrs. Kebussyan said. "Like the old days, yes?"

"Karine," Sarkis exclaimed. "You're so beautiful. I'd almost forgotten." It wasn't the most gallant thing he could have said, but she flushed with happiness.

"Thank you," she said to them both, then spoke to Mrs. Kebussyan. "Setta is sleeping. I don't think she will be a bother."

"Don't worry, my dear. You two enjoy yourselves. I know how seldom you go out."

Raz came moments later and after warm greetings, Raz said, "I hope you don't mind. I've invited two other people for dinner--Tom Yeager, an American economist and an old friend of mine who's helping the government, and his interpreter, Ana Stepanian."

"Wonderful," Sarkis said. "Karine will be glad to have her company." Sarkis picked up a candelabra from the foyer, took Raz by the elbow and whispered, "I want to show you the pieces."

Sarkis closed the bedroom door and the drapes and went to the wardrobe, towering against the outer wall. It was a massive piece of furniture, but he moved it with ease. "Rollers," he explained, pointing to the base of the wardrobe.

He next removed a floor-to-ceiling panel of papered wall-board, revealing the outer wall. A jagged crack zig-zagged up the seams of mortared basalt stones, rising from the baseboard and running all the way to the ceiling. "The earthquake caused this," he said, tracing the line of broken mortar with his finger. "One of the stones even fell from the wall." He stooped down and with his fingertips, wiggled a stone three feet above the baseboard and slipped it from its place. "I hollowed out behind it and on each side. It makes a good hiding place. I keep my coin collection there. And things I sometimes bring home from the Museum."

Raz watched Sarkis withdraw a cardboard box from the niche in the wall and lay out the jewelry piece by piece on the little table by the windows. Raz responded with one appreciative muttering after another. When the box was empty, Raz stood back to survey the collection. "Sarkis," he said. "They're magnificent. All this for ten thousand dollars? It's unbelievable. And you haven't exhausted the supply?"

"I don't think so. I've been introduced to several people who are willing to part with jewelry of this quality. There must be an end to it somewhere, but not right away."

"Excellent," Raz said. "If I can get them out of the country, Anastas will know how to market them."

"You said 'if' you can get them out of the country. Will there be a problem?"

"So much national treasure has already fled," Raz said. "I'm told the government is watching much more carefully. Anastas is a well-known dealer. He would never have been able to come. With me, perhaps they won't notice."

Raz seemed to pass over the problem too easily. Sarkis began to sweat. If Raz were caught and the jewelry confiscated . . . Sarkis took hold of himself and vowed not to worry.

"Leave these two," Sarkis said, pointing to a carnelian seal and a heavy, gold necklace with a loop-in-loop chain connecting three gold medallions. The center medallion featured a large onyx stone. The two side medallions displayed crudely-engraved eagles, one with a blood-red garnet eye, the other with a bright emerald. "They're not of great value without a provenance and I need more time to do the research."

"The carnelian is interesting. What do you think it is?"

"It's the seal of an official in charge of storehouses. The inscription says it belongs to Nimur, chief storekeeper of a district in Persia. But I haven't connected Nimur with a particular Sassanian ruler. I think the seal is fifth century. It would be a powerful cameo, don't you agree?"

"Absolutely. And the necklace?"

"The eagles symbolize Parthian royalty. I believe it's first century, but I don't know which royal family yet. Aside from there being so much gold, the emerald looks very good. The onyx is impressive, but neither it nor the garnet are great prizes. Provenance is everything with these two."

"Can you bring them with you then?" Raz asked. "I have to leave tomorrow and I'd like to buy the tickets for you and Karine and Setta while I'm here so you can come to us in Amman right away."

"No," Sarkis said, his eyes growing large behind his rimless glasses. "It isn't enough. Please give me money to buy more like this," he said, waving his hand across the array of jewelry spread on the table. "At least another ten thousand."

CHAPTER TWENTY THREE

Dinner at the Restoran Dzoragiugh

The large, rough-hewn basalt blocks of the walls of the Restoran Dzoragiugh, locally known as 'The Mafia', gave it the look of a fortification rather than the residence it once had been. Aleksandr scarcely noticed as he walked across the cobblestone courtyard and entered the restaurant's reception area. He arrived well in advance of Melikian's party because he wanted a word with the maitre 'd.

"Avram," Aleksandr said. "You have a reservation tonight for someone named Melikian?"

"Yes, Major. A private party of five. In the Red Room."

"I want to use your office tonight. Deshnikov is parking the car and will be here presently. Send him up when he comes in. And send the waiter you've assigned to the Red Room."

"Yes, Major."

Avram's office was a small, obscure perch in the rafters that offered a view of all arriving patrons and Aleksandr wanted to know who was in Melikian's party. He didn't care if Ana and the American were with him, but if Sarkis Melikian joined them, he would be concerned. He'd have to learn who this other Melikian was and what he had to do with Sarkis. Perhaps it was just a family thing, but perhaps not.

He saw Deshnikov enter the restaurant and heard him clumping up the narrow flight of stairs.

"What about a drink, Aleks?" Deshnikov asked from the doorway of the tiny office.

"Go ahead if you like."

Deshnikov was about to go back down the stairs when a pale, painfully thin young man in a starched waiter's jacket appeared in the door.

"Sir?" the waiter asked, his voice cracking. "I was told you wanted to speak to me."

"What is your name?"

"Hayk, sir."

"Hayk, I want to know what is said in the Red Room this evening. As soon as your guests are seated, return here and I will give you instructions."

"Yes, sir," the young waiter said.

"Bring us a bottle of Stolichnaya and a glass," Deshnikov told the waiter. To Aleksandr, he said, "Sure you don't want one Aleks?"

Distracted by more troubling thoughts, Aleksandr ignored him. Deshnikov held up his thumb and forefinger, Hayk nodded and raced down the stairs. 'Lord God,' he prayed as he crossed the reception area and entered the bar. 'Help me to do as the Major asks. And if not, have mercy on my soul.' Hayk took a full bottle of Stolichnaya from the bar, checked two glasses to make sure they were spotless, put it all on a tray with a bottle of mineral water and hurried back up the stairs.

Deshnikov took the tray from him at the door, poured two glasses to the rim and offered one to Aleksandr. "What are we doing here, Aleks?"

"It's not your concern, Ivan," Aleksandr muttered.

Deshnikov did what any good soldier knows how to do--he waited. Aleksandr waited, too, and said nothing as the minutes dragged by. Just before eight-thirty, three of Melikian's party arrived. "Look at that," Aleksandr said as Raz, Sarkis and Karine came through the door and were greeted by Avram. Deshnikov got up and looked over Aleksandr's shoulder.

"Handsome woman," Deshnikov observed.

"She's supposed to be at home, not dressing to meet the Prime Minister. Who's taking care of her cripple?"

Avram led Raz, Sarkis and Karine to the Red Room, one of several The Mafia held for private parties. When he reappeared in the reception area of the restaurant, he looked up at Aleksandr and nodded. Tom and Ana arrived a few minutes later.

From his vantage point, Aleksandr saw her as he imagined she would have looked arriving as his wife at a diplomatic reception in London, Paris or Rome. She was wearing a long-sleeved burgundy dress with a high collar. A wide chain-link gold necklace lay close to the base of her neck. She was still so beautiful and with all he had in Switzerland, he could dress her more elegantly than she could imagine. His reverie was broken when she turned her face to the American. She smiled. In a certain way. Unmistakable. In an instant, his wistful thoughts of a new life with her sank like a stone in the dark waters of rejection.

Avram took Tom and Ana to the Red Room and returned to the reception area. Again he looked up at Aleksandr and discreetly showed him four fingers and a thumb. Aleksandr knew that Ana and the American had joined the Melikians.

****

Hayk took a deep breath and went into the candlelit Red Room. "Good evening," he said. "Welcome to Mafia. What may I bring you?"

"First bring Armenian Cognac and Stolichnaya," Raz told him, establishing his role as host. "And a plate of olives, mixed pickles and whatever else you prepare for appetizers."

Hayk dutifully wrote down what Raz was telling him. "We have a few *ishkhan* tonight," Hayk said. "But they will soon be spoken for."

"*Ishkhan*? Really?" Ana interrupted. To Tom she said, "Do you remember? The wonderful fish of Lake Sevan."

"Oh, yeah. Why don't we try it, Raz?"

"Of course," Raz agreed and said to Hayk, "*Ishkhan* for all of us. How will you cook it?"

"It is seasoned with pepper and garlic, baked in olive oil and lemon juice and garnished with potatoes and tomato slices."

Raz went on through the menu, ordering yogurt and barley soup, nivik and yalanchi. Hayk kept writing, nodding to Raz that he understood and was getting the order down. "Very good, sir. Will there be anything else? We have kataifi for dessert tonight. It came from Athens on today's flight."

"Yes, of course," Raz replied.

"Thank you, sir," Hayk said and left.

"I haven't the vaguest notion what we're going to eat tonight, Raz," Tom said. "Will you tell me or is it a surprise?"

"Ana said you knew about the fish and she'll have to explain it to me because I've never had it before."

"Ishkhan is king trout, very large. One will serve us all, I think.

152

Very good tasting fish, pink like salmon." For Tom's benefit, she added, "Nivik is chick peas and spinach, but prepared in a special way. And yalanchi is rice wrapped in grape leaves with pine nuts and currants and we serve it with lemon and yogurt. It is delicious."

Realizing he'd need to make an effort to include Sarkis, Tom turned to him and said, "Raz tells me you're the senior curator at the History Museum." Ana was so accustomed to translating for Tom that she picked up the burden without thinking about it.

"Yes," Sarkis replied. "My special responsibility is numismatics. I am running an exhibit of Cilician coins now. Please come to see it."

"I'd love to," Tom said. "I'm not an expert, but collecting coins is a hobby of mine."

"Oh?" Sarkis said, taking a new interest in Tom. "What is the theme of your collection?"

Anticipating that this discussion might go on for some time, Raz interrupted. "Ana, let me translate for Tom. I need the practice and you can relax and talk with Karine."

"Thank you. We were at the Central Bank today and there was much conversation. Would bankers do more if they did not talk so much?"

Raz laughed. "I doubt it," Raz said and turned to Tom. "Go on, Tom. I'm not as good at this as Ana, but she shouldn't have to work all evening."

Hayk came in bringing Stolichnaya, the finest Akhtamar Cognac and the appetizers. He took his time serving their plates and pouring their drinks so he could listen to the conversation.

****

"Well?" Aleksandr demanded when Hayk stood in the door of the office. "What are they talking about?"

"Old coins and Armenian kings, sir. The one with the mustache is doing most of the talking and the other one is translating for the American. The two women are whispering."

"Get back in there," he commanded and Hayk hurried back down the stairs.

****

When Hayk left the room, Ana told Raz, "The waiter is listening to everything. Be careful what you say."

Raz's eyes widened and Sarkis paled. Ana leaned close to Tom and said to him in English, "The waiter is listening. Do not say anything--how should I say?--that might be interesting to someone else. Do you understand?"

"Of course," he said. "I'll be careful."

Hayk next came bearing an enormous fish mounted on an outsized platter, the juices still sizzling. Conversation ceased and everyone feasted their eyes on the fish. "So that's ishkhan," Raz exclaimed.

"Yes," Sarkis said. "And quite a grand one, too."

Hayk showed the head and tail and began to bone the fish to serve their plates. Two other waiters came in with the other dishes--nivik, yalanchi and fresh tomatoes. Hayk served each plate and departed. He hadn't heard what they were discussing when he brought in the fish and he could not think of a reason to stay. He sincerely hoped the Major would not be distressed that he had nothing new to report.

＊＊＊＊＊＊＊＊＊＊＊＊

By the time they finished the entree, Karine was becoming concerned about Setta. She mentioned this to Ana, who volunteered to take her home.

"Raz," Sarkis said. "Would you excuse Karine to go back to our apartment? Ana has offered to drive her and return for us."

"I understand," Raz replied. "But surely it's an imposition to have Ana return here for us. We can call a taxi."

"No," Ana said. "It is no trouble and you would not find a taxi now. Have your brandy and smoke your cigars. Karine and I will have our own little chat on the way."

Tom had not understood a word, so Ana bent to his ear and whispered in English. "I will take Karine and return for you. Enjoy your friends."

Everyone rose to send the women off and Raz escorted them

154

to Ana's car. Tom and Sarkis smiled at one another, unable to say anything until Raz returned. When Hayk came in, Sarkis explained the situation to him and by the time this had been straightened out, Raz had returned.

Raz took three cigars from the breast pocket of his coat, "We can have a glass of brandy and smoke a cigar while we're waiting for Ana to return." Hayk lit each man's cigar and listened attentively while he poured the brandy and warmed it. To his disappointment, the three puffed on their cigars, filling the room with aromatic smoke, offered silent toasts to each other, drank them and said almost nothing. It was awkward to stay, so Hayk left the room and stood against the door, straining to hear what they were saying.

Raz paid the check and the four of them went back through the reception area. Avram bid them good evening and they walked into the star-sprinkled blackness of the cold Armenian night.

✱✱✱✱✱✱✱✱✱✱✱

Aleksandr watched them go. Soon after, Hayk appeared in the doorway of the little office. He couldn't enter because the legs of a soundly sleeping Deshnikov stretched across the threshold.

"Well?" Aleksandr asked.

"They were not always speaking Armenian, sir, but I think the men talked about the family business in Jordan. I did not understand it all, but perhaps that's important to you?"

"Yes. Yes, it is," Aleksandr said thoughtfully. In the afternoon, without any great effort, he had learned that the family business was jewelry. Clearly, Sarkis was up to something. And the American. What did he have to do with any of this? Aleksandr's stomach boiled with acid as he thought about Ana with the American. That would not stand. He would not allow it.

He stood up, kicked Deshnikov's foot and woke him. As Deshnikov scrambled to a standing position, Aleksandr took a handful of drams from his pocket and stuffed them into Hayk's white tunic. When Hayk counted them later, they amounted to almost twenty thousand drams, about forty-five US dollars.

∗∗∗∗∗∗∗∗∗∗∗

Aleksandr was silent as Deshnikov drove through the deserted streets. When they arrived at Aleksandr's apartment, Deshnikov asked, "Do you want anything else tonight, Aleks?" Aleksandr made no move to get out of the car, nor did he answer Deshnikov for some time. He stared at the empty street in the stark illumination of the headlights.

"Aleks?" Deshnikov asked again. Aleksandr seemed to hear him for the first time.

"Bring her to me," he said.

"Who?" Deshnikov asked.

Aleksandr didn't answer. He opened the door and got out. Deshnikov reached across the front seat and closed the door. He watched Aleksandr walk slowly up the steps of his building and disappear into the black hole of the entrance. Then he put the car in gear and drove back toward the Hotel Armenia.

Aleksandr unlocked his apartment and switched on a light powered by a gasoline generator on the balcony. Leaving the door unlocked, he hung his overcoat on a peg and in one step moved to a small stool just inside the foyer. He sat down, slipped out of his shoes and stripped off his socks. Only then did he stand on the silky Persian runner that stretched down the hall. He walked into the living room, enjoying the feel of the expensive carpet on his bare feet. He switched on a table lamp and lifted a bottle of Stolichnaya from the bar, unscrewed the cap and threw it across the room. It tinkled as it bounced off the wall and fell to the floor. Then he put the bottle to his lips and turned it up, drinking the vodka as if it were cool water on a hot day. A river of the fiery liquid coursed down his throat until he choked. Slamming the bottle back onto the bar, he pulled off his jacket and tore away his shirt. Buttons flew in every direction, landing softly on the carpet and pinging against the hardwood floor. A low animal growl rose from deep within him and echoed around the silent room.

Half an hour later, Marina slipped through the door, removing her shoes and coat almost in one motion. She was tingling with excitement and anticipation. It had been weeks since Aleksandr had made love to her and she was hungry for him.

"Aleks?" she called. There was no answer. She saw his shoes and socks and started down the hall toward the bedroom. Then she saw him sitting cross-legged on the living room floor, his shirt hanging in a tatter around his shoulders. Something about his eyes, the vacant stare, sent a lightning bolt of fear through her, replacing the heat of passion with a chilling urge to flee.

"Aleks?" she said again, timidly this time. "Are you all right?"

Without speaking, he uncoiled and rose from the floor. He came toward her and she knew instinctively that he was going to hit her. She was too frozen with fear to move, even to flinch, and the blow from the back of his hand knocked her to the floor.

Still on her back, she tried to scuttle away from him, trembling and holding her jaw. It was numb, but her mouth was suffused with a warm, salty taste she knew to be her blood. She bumped against a wall and could move no further. He took three steps and towered over her.

"Aleks," she whimpered. "Why? I've done nothing."

"Who is he?"

"Who?" Marina asked, now trembling uncontrollably.

"The American."

"I told you," Marina wailed. "The Ministry of Finance. Ana is his interpreter."

Aleksandr reached down and pulled Marina up by her hair. Fear strangled her scream, which emerged as a low, anguished animal sound. He flung her away from him and she landed on the floor again. Adrenaline and blood were beginning to flow in her body and she was becoming aware of the pain in her jaw and her hip where she had hit the floor the first time. She wiped her mouth with her hand and found a smear of blood. She would have run, but Aleksandr stood between her and the door. He walked toward her. She crawled backward, trying to keep distance between them. He took a step and she crawled away. He took another step and she became aware that he was pressing her toward the bedroom. She knew he would take her there, but not with passion and love, certainly not with tenderness. Her mouth filled with fear and dread and she could only try to think of how to keep it from being worse, how to appease him.

"Aleks," she pleaded. "Please. Please, don't hurt me. I'll do whatever you want. Anything!"

"Whore," he spat out. Suddenly Marina understood that he wasn't cursing her. He was cursing Ana. Aleksandr hadn't hit her just now. He'd hit Ana. He hadn't yanked her by the hair. It was Ana's hair. And it wasn't her that Aleksandr was about to savage. It was Ana.

CHAPTER TWENTY FOUR

Mariah

The metallic squawk of the cabin speakers ignited a crackle of tension throughout the aircraft and woke Mariah from a deep sleep. She didn't understand the urgent words of the language being spoken, but from the aircraft's sudden angle of descent, Mariah knew they had a full-blown emergency. Suddenly alert, adrenaline pumping, she checked the cabin for smoke and found none. She looked out the window on her side of the aircraft and saw no fire. It was pitch black outside, so she had no clear idea of their altitude, but the plane was definitely going down. A stewardess was speaking hurriedly in a high-pitched voice and Mariah could feel the passengers around her becoming agitated and anxious.

She saw the Tupolev's landing lights come on, illuminating wisps of cloud flashing by the window. The aircraft seemed under control, making a straight-in approach--to somebody's runway, she hoped. Then she began to see scattered lights below and estimated that they still had several thousand feet of altitude. Identifying with the flight crew, she was glad they couldn't hear the rising crescendo of panic or smell the fear in the cabin. Once they were on the ground the stampede of passengers might be more dangerous than the actual landing, even if it were wheels up. Mariah marked an emergency exit two rows forward and breathed a sigh of relief when she felt the wheels go down and heard them lock. That meant the hydraulic system was still working so they had a chance of landing normally. She felt the plane decrease its angle of descent and slow under the increased drag of the landing gear. The flaps cranked down. Then she heard the explosion, followed by a bedlam of screams and wails from the passengers.

Looking aft through the window, she could see flames shooting from one of the engines. It had blown. Then there was the screech of tearing metal and a jolt. The aircraft lurched to starboard, dangerously dipping the wing.

It must have taken an enormous effort to right the plane and not a moment too soon. The pilot chopped the throttles and the Tupolev sank, hammering its landing gear onto the runway. The plane bounced and yawed and Mariah was afraid the pilot was going to lose it on the ground. But he steadied it, stood on the brakes and hit the reverse thrusters on the two engines he had left. He handled some further yawing as the thrusters bit unevenly, controlled again and finally let it roll toward the end of the runway. The fire equipment racing along beside them was catching up now and it looked like they were down safely.

Long before the plane finished its roll, the passengers were out of their seats, fighting for their carry-on baggage, hopelessly snarling any possibility of an orderly exit. Mariah extracted her brief case and laptop from beneath the seat in front of her and stood in the space vacated by her seat mate, who was struggling to join the mob in the center aisle of the aircraft. One by one, she kicked down the seats in the rows ahead of her until she reached the one with the emergency exit. She put her body between the exit and the aisle, seized the emergency handle, rotated it and popped the hatch. As soon as the other passengers felt the rush of cold air, they began to dive for Mariah's emergency exit, thrusting her forcibly through the hatch.

On the ground, a fireman's words were lost in the wail of sirens, but his beckoning arm was a clear signal to come. Mariah scooted down the cold, slick skin of the wing, dropped off the trailing edge into a rescue net and was led away toward a grassy area beside the runway where a bus was already waiting. When she looked back, she saw why the fire hadn't spread after the initial explosion. The whole engine had fallen away. She hoped it had come down on the approach, not on somebody's apartment complex. She boarded the bus, unable to understand a word being said to her by excited rescue workers. She kept repeating, "I'm OK. I'm OK," hoping they'd understand that she didn't need medical attention. Finally, it seemed to work and she sat on the bus, watching her fellow passengers pop out of the exits and straggle away from the crippled aircraft. 'What a mess!' she thought.

****

A sleepy Bob Lange groped for the phone beside his bed, knocked the alarm clock onto the floor and finally got a grip on the handset. "Who is this?" he mumbled.

"It's Sam Rhodes. Sorry to wake you up, but I'm at the airport waiting for Mariah Carroll and there's a problem."

Lange was slowly reaching consciousness, like a swimmer rising to the surface from a deep dive. "Gimme a minute," he said, throwing back the covers and bringing himself to a sitting position by putting his legs over the side of the bed. He looked at his watch--it was two in the morning. "Give it to me slow. What's the problem?"

"Her plane made an emergency landing in Tblisi. It lost an engine--literally. The thing exploded and fell off. Anyway, she's stuck up there and Armenian Airlines hasn't figured out how to get them down here. The latest rumor is they're going to send a bus."

"Shit," Lange said. "Tblisi's not that far. So she'll be here later today. Come on back, get some sleep and we'll see her when we see her."

"Well, the thing is that they don't think they'll be able to send a bus right away. The passes between here and Tblisi are iced over, so they're talking about waiting until they clear. That could be two or three days."

Fully awake now, Lange heaved an impatient sigh. "Why don't they send a plane, then?"

"Everything's flying right now. No spare aircraft."

"Why can't the Georgians fly them down?"

"Look, I'm just telling you what they're telling me."

Lange heard the edge in Rhodes' voice and realized it wasn't Rhodes' fault Armenian Airlines couldn't recover their stranded passengers. He made an effort to think it through and stop reacting. After a few moments, he said, "Do you know if she's OK? Have you talked to her or just the airline?"

"Just the airline. They say nobody's hurt. I can try to get through to her, but I ought to have something to tell her."

"Right. See if you can get Armenian Air to patch you through to her. I'm going to see about sending the Cheyenne to get her. She'll have to know to look for Jameson. Tell her not to try to make her own arrangements. We don't want her lost in Tblisi. Tell her what we're trying to do and to keep cool. Call me back in half an hour."

As they spilled from the busses and were herded into a transit lounge, the passengers became a frenetic, jabbering mob. Some of the women were wailing, others crying softly while the men put on fierce expressions. Mariah eased away from them and found a molded plastic chair beside a bank of windows, letting her briefcase fall to one side and her laptop to the other. Her traveling experience told her the thing to do was relax. Whatever the system was, you couldn't fight it and expect to win.

Presently, an airline official wearing a shirt with epaulets appeared and spoke to them. Mariah didn't understand a word he said, but the agitated body language and frantic verbal protests of her fellow passengers told her clearly that they weren't leaving anytime soon.

It was the early morning hours and with no scheduled flights coming in or going out, the shops and café were shuttered. She turned sideways in her chair to look out the window but the darkness of the night made the glass a mirror.

She put her chin in the palm of her hand and struck a thoughtful pose. The face that stared back at her in the glass could have graced the cover of a fashion magazine. Her eyes told her that. Her heart told her that behind the mask was an incomplete woman. I don't even know where I am, she thought. Somewhere behind enemy lines from the sound of it. Yet she was strangely at home, too. The people around her might have known where they were, but they were frightened and out of place.

She often heard her father's voice at times like these. That poor man who'd loved her dearly, but had been so far out to sea in knowing how to raise a girl by himself. What he would tell her now, she already knew by heart. It was Winston Welles, her old mentor from Vaquero Petroleum, who came to mind.

He'd made fun of her at first, a girl still wet-behind-the-ears flying a Beech Musketeer around Vaquero's drilling sites in the Venezuelan outback. She made him a believer the time she evacuated him in a hellish electrical storm from a site out in Boqueron. He told the story often after that, how he hadn't believed she could land and when she did anyway, how he was certain she couldn't take off. He was in agony trying to pass a kidney stone and he claimed at the time he preferred a quick death with Mariah at the controls to the damned kidney stone. He'd made her promise not to botch the job. She'd brought him safely into Caracas and after that, she was Winston's protégé. He wouldn't fly with anyone else.

It was some months after their stormy flight that they made a run down to Ciudad Bolivar. Her contract with Vaquero was coming up for renewal and she'd asked him if she had a future with them. He told her, "Honey, you've got a natural born talent for flying airplanes. No doubt about that. But you've got a higher calling than that. Don't you sign up again with Vaquero. You take a hard look at the people around you. Why are they poor? Well, lots of reasons, but the oil business is more part of the problem than it is part of the solution. You need to go back to school and learn something that'll help these poor folks down here."

She took his advice to heart and almost never looked back. That time with Cameron was the worst, she thought, when her compass went crazy and she thought life was passing her by. She still had her moments when she felt she'd do as much good hauling kids to soccer practice and going to PTA meetings as slogging around the backwaters of the world. Was anywhere a better place because of what she did? Had a net present value calculation ever filled a child's empty belly? Indonesia had scarred her, too. Too many poor people in Paradise. What the poorest of them did to survive . . . It trivialized her work, made her efforts futile and inconsequential.

What the hell was she doing here in some dead end corner of the old Soviet Union?

In some magical way, a reflection of Tom's face appeared in the window, looking over her shoulder. Suddenly she was like all the rest, lonely and afraid, lost at sea. She needed him to hold her again, to stroke her hair the way her father had, to whisper to her that everything was going to be all right. She choked back her panic and swallowed hard. Tom's appearance in the momentary void of her loneliness gave her something to hold on to and she determined to get it straight with him this time, no more holding back.

Ross Jameson wasn't hard to spot. Mariah had been told to look for a heavy-set man with a walrus mustache. It turned out that he was also wearing a leather flight jacket and cowboy boots. She got up and walked toward him.

"Are you Ross Jameson?" she asked.

"Hey, you betcha," he replied, grinning beneath the bushy mustache. "You Miz Carroll?"

"The very one," she said, holding out her hand. "You going to fly me down to Yerevan?"

"That's the plan," he said. "Where's your stuff?"

"All I've got now is my briefcase and my laptop. There's a carry-on bag in the cabin, a big bag and a computer in the belly of that plane out there. So far, there's no sign of any of that. I'd leave it, but the computer's special and I've got to have it to do the job out here."

"You just sit right down and I'll see what I can do," Jameson said and walked toward a door without a sign.

He returned half an hour later, bearing two glasses of tea and some hard-boiled eggs which revived Mariah's flagging spirits. "Talked to my buddies here. We'll have to be patient about your stuff a little longer. Called Yerevan and told them the story, so they'll be expectin' us later today." While they waited, Mariah established that she was also a pilot and asked Jameson how he wound up in the Caucasus, flying for AID.

"I used to fly for the oilies down in the Gulf," he told her. "But they're crazy and I wasn't gettin' any younger, so when this embassy type told me about the job up here, I signed on. Real stupid. I've got two more months on my contract. Then I'm outta here, even if I gotta walk."

"I flew for Vaquero a long time ago. I know what you mean about those guys. But what's the problem here?" she asked.

"It's not the people. It's the place. Tough flyin' and tough livin'," he said. "It's cold, I wanna tell ya. And the weather's freaky in these mountains. You don't wanna go to the toilet around here without a weather report. They had a Cessna Three-Ten when I came on board. Bitch of a plane. No good for this climate and she'd Dutch roll on you in a heartbeat. Ever fly one?"

"Once. No doubt about it. You have to muscle it around."

"That's the Three-Ten. We never cracked it up, but it woulda been real easy to do up here."

"What happened to it?" Mariah asked.

"We sold it to some Russian named Deshnikov. I see him once in a while down in Yerevan. Used to be Sov Air Force. Probably running dope out of Turkey. The AID weenies think they struck a blow for free enterprise in Armenia when he bought the plane. I don't know what the hell they think he does with it, but I ain't gonna tell 'em."

"How come you guys have a plane?" Mariah asked. "I've been around a lot and I can't remember another AID Mission with its own plane, much less a Piper Cheyenne."

"Well, you can go to Moscow from everywhere out here, but these days it's hard to go from one old republic to another. When you're covering three countries like this regional mission is, the AID boys have to have a way to get from one to another without going all the way to Moscow. That's why they got the plane."

At that moment, Mariah saw a shaggy baggage handler with sunken cheeks and a three-day beard pushing a flatbed dolly toward her with her carry-on, hardcase and the crate with her desktop computer.

"Hey, Jameson," she said, rising stiffly from the plastic chair she'd occupied for several hours. "Here's my stuff. Unbelievable."

"Are you sure it's all here?"

"Yeah, this is it."

"OK. Let's get this guy to haul it out to the Cheyenne and we'll boogie on down to Yerevan."

****

Tom, Ana and Bob Lange were sitting in the lobby bar of the Hotel Armenia when Mariah arrived a little after five in the afternoon. Tom had been fighting his concern all day, going on with his schedule of banking appointments. His anxiety fell away when he saw her walking upright with all her body parts in the appropriate places and no visible signs of breakage. Ross Jameson rolled through the door

165

after her and was steering her toward the reception desk. Tom cut them off, standing up and calling across the expanse of the lobby, waving both arms.

"Mariah! Hey!" When she saw him, he grinned and shrugged, his palms open to the sky. "Welcome to Armenia," he said.

She stood in the middle of the lobby and looked at him for a long minute. A smile started around the edges of her mouth. She shook her head slowly and started to walk in his direction, briefcase in one hand, laptop in the other. "You bastard," she said softly when she was close enough for the world not to hear. "You go to dangerous places."

He gathered her up in a bear hug. "It wasn't my idea, remember?"

She slumped against his shoulder, hands still at her sides holding her briefcase and laptop. "Yeah. Well, sorry about that."

He stopped squeezing her but held onto her shoulders. "Think you could stand a brandy?"

"I need about a quart--intravenously."

"I'll see what I can do. Come on, there're some people you need to meet."

With Jameson tagging along, Tom led Mariah to the table where Lange and Ana were standing. "Here's the wayward one," he said. "Mariah, this is Ana Stepanian and Bob Lange. Ana's my interpreter and Bob's the deputy Mission director."

Ana forced a smile, making a quick assessment of Mariah's good looks after allowing for travel fatigue and the stress of a plane crash. She hadn't been prepared for the stab of jealousy she felt seeing another woman fall so easily into Tom's arms. She was surprised that she resented the familiarity, the obvious history between them, but she felt it nevertheless. Mariah was pretty and American. She wore clothes in that casual Western way so envied by the rest of the world-- tight jeans molded to a flat belly and firm buns, rough hiking boots, an expensive leather jacket hanging loose over a cable knit sweater. Her amber hair was tousled and she looked more like a Hollywood starlet than a stodgy economist. Against her will, Ana felt threatened and confused.

Lange put out his hand to Mariah and smiled broadly. "We've

been a little worried about you," he said.

"So was I. Thanks for sending old Ross here," she said, wrapping an arm around his girth.

"Well, we're glad you're safe. Here," he added, pouring her a glass of Akhtamar Cognac. "This'll get you started."

Mariah took the first shot down and held out her glass for another. "One more," she said. "Then I'll tell you about the bouquet and the finish. Right now I'm firing for effect." Lange poured her another. She drained it and relaxed in her seat, looking at Tom. They began to laugh, slowly at first. A chuckle grew into a mouth-wide-open, full-fledged spasm. The rest of the table--except for Ana, who didn't understand--found it contagious and were soon roaring with them. When it subsided, so did the day's tension.

"Here's to happy landings!" Lange said, raising his glass.

"Amen to that, Brother," Mariah said and tossed her brandy down. When it hit bottom, she shook her head and remarked, "Whew. Three of those on an empty stomach. You may have to curl me up in the corner and throw a tarp over me. Man, a hot shower and I'll sleep until next Tuesday."

"Not yet, young lady," Bob Lange said. "I want to hear your story first. I've been worrying about you since about two o'clock this morning."

Mariah gave him a bleary smile and told them the short version--from the time she woke up with the plane going down until she spotted Ross Jameson ambling into the terminal, punctuating the story from time to time with shots of brandy. When she finished, she looked to Tom as if she were about wasted.

"Come on, people," he said. "I think our girl is about done in. I'm going to get her something to eat and see that she gets to bed. Ana, can we get something sent to her room?"

Ana nodded. "I will see to it. Meat and bread, I think. Yes? I will find out what room they have given her."

Ross Jameson shook hands all around and left. Bob Lange pushed his chair back and followed Ana to the bar. She used the phone to call in an order for ground lamb and levash and bottled water. Mariah's room was on the same floor as Tom's, but on the opposite side of the fourth floor lobby. Sofia's little desk would be between them.

"Can I give you a lift home?" Lange asked when she turned around to find him behind her.

Ana looked back at Tom and Mariah, still sitting at the table, heads together, laughing over some private joke, and felt excluded. After a moment's hesitation, she looked up at Lange and said, "Yes, thank you. It is not far."

* * * * * * * * * * *

In the elevator, Mariah leaned heavily against him. "Pardner," she mumbled. "One helluva long day. I'm about out of it."

"I'll bet," Tom said, shifting his grip on her briefcase and laptop in one hand to steady her with the other. "The good news is you've got time for a hot shower. That'll perk you up."

"Sounds wonderful. Little sleep first, though."

"Bit of a problem there," he said. "The hot water's only on from seven to nine in the evening and the morning." He looked at his watch. "It's eight-thirty. If you conk out now, you'll miss it."

Leaning against him, one hand splayed against his belly, she looked up. "What kind of a place is this?"

He grinned at her. "The Wild, Wild East, lady. You've heard the stories and they're true." The elevator stopped with a lurch and the doors opened slowly. Tom took her weight and walked her into the fourth floor lobby.

She was sagging, her eyes almost closed. Tom got the key from Sofia and followed her down the hall to Mariah's room. Smelling the aroma from the tray Sofia was bringing, he realized he hadn't eaten either and wondered if there was enough for them both.

Mariah went in first, bouncing off the walls in the narrow entryway and heading directly for the bed, somehow managing to miss stumbling over the wooden crate that contained a desktop computer and her large hardcase. Sofia followed and set the tray on the small table. In dismay, Tom watched Mariah keel over onto the bed, her head falling with a thump on the pillow, legs dangling over the side of the bed, still on the floor.

As Sofia closed the door, he called to Mariah, "Whoa, whoa, whoa. Not yet, babe. You've got to have something to eat." He took her by the shoulders and pulled her into a sitting position.

She opened her eyes halfway and gave him a smirk that passed for a smile.

"Are you up?" he asked, taking his hands away from her shoulders. "Can I let you go?"

She lifted her arms and put them around his neck, pulling him down to eye level. "I wish you wouldn't," she said, the smirky smile still in place.

"You need something to eat," he said. "You killed half that bottle of brandy by yourself. On an empty stomach."

She kissed him then, a soft, wet, fully articulated kiss.

For a moment, he kissed her back, a remembered passion flashing through his loins like heat lightning. Then he pulled away.

She frowned. "That's what I need," she said, pouting. "I thought I'd bought the farm, Tom. Not getting killed always makes me horny. I need you. Really."

He shook his head. "You're a tempting morsel, kiddo, but you're sloshed. Between the brandy and the adrenaline, you don't know what you're doing. Take another shot at me when you're sober. Now come on. You've got to eat." He put his hands under her arms and stood her up. "Two steps and you're at the table. Come on."

She didn't protest and once she began, she devoured the meal and drank the entire bottle of water. She crossed the silverware, pushed the plate away and turned to him. "Look, daddy. I ate all my peas and carrots. What're you going to give me?"

"A pat on the head and a goodnight kiss," he told her, getting up to go.

"Not good enough," she said, pushing the chair back. She tried to stand, but lost her balance and fell into his arms. "Oh, shit," she said. "You're right. I'm sloshed."

Tom helped her make the two steps to the bed and held her up with one hand while he pulled back the covers with the other. "Can you get yourself undressed?" he asked.

"Uh, uh," she said in a sleepy voice. "You do it. I want to be tucked in."

"That's not on the agenda," he said.

"Neither was the damned plane crashing in Tblisi," she said, eyes closed, her head on his shoulder.

He sighed and slipped her leather jacket off. When her arms slipped out, he lost his grip and she toppled onto the pillow like a fallen tree. She was like a Raggedy-Ann doll, loose at every joint, floppy in the middle. He couldn't just leave her like that. First the hiking boots. That was the easy part. He made quick work of the laces and slipped them off along with her heavy socks.

He was at a loss about what to do next. He opened the double-glassed window a crack to let some fresh air into the room, then considered how heavy the blankets were. Should he get her sweater off? Maybe so.

He pulled the cableknit sweater up toward her head, bringing her arms with it, and looked down at her, trying to ignore the abbreviated, white lace brassiere that seemed more decorative than functional. How the hell was he going to get her jeans off? No need to take off her jeans, just loosen them. He popped the top button and unzipped the fly.

He pulled back the blankets and taking both legs in one arm, slipped them under the blankets. That would have to do. Anything more would be . . . well, it wouldn't be right.

CHAPTER TWENTY FIVE

Hotel Armenia

Mariah walked straight to Tom's table, past the burly maitre d' who would have stopped any man--or homely woman--who ignored him so cavalierly. Mariah, of course, was neither. She was wearing a camel colored sweater with a matching knee-length pleated wool skirt that hugged her hips and swung gracefully with every step. The maitre d'--and everybody else in the room--watched with growing fascination as she crossed the large room.

Conversations stopped and the sudden silence caused Tom to look up from the magazine he'd bought in Amsterdam, now two weeks old. He checked his watch. Thirty minutes almost to the second since he'd tapped at Mariah's door, heard the shower running and left a note to tell her where to find breakfast.

"Right on time," he said. "And nobody would guess that your airplane had crashed or that you'd guzzled half a quart of brandy in the last twenty-four hours."

"Did I do all that? I can't remember a thing. How did I get to bed last night anyway? I woke up half naked." She didn't wait for his answer. "How's the coffee?" she asked.

"I don't recommend it," Tom said, relieved that she was ignoring the business of getting her undressed last night. "The tea won't give you a jolt but you can swallow it without gagging."

The maitre d' came to their table, a waiter at his elbow, and aimed a question at Mariah. "In hotel?" he asked.

"Yes," Tom answered for her, nodding. To Mariah, he said. "Show him your key. He needs to get your name and room number."

Mariah turned the base of the wooden key fob toward him and said, "Carroll. Mariah Carroll." The maitre d' repeated a heavily accented version of her name and checked it against the morning's list. "Thank you," he said, giving Mariah a never-before-seen smile that featured two gleaming gold teeth. He departed, leaving the waiter standing silently but attentively beside her, pad and pencil poised to take her order.

"Coffee, please," she said to the waiter and to Tom, "What else can I have?"

"The buffet is behind you, by the windows. Goat cheese, apricot juice, cold cuts of mystery meat, bread, stuff like that. I have ordered fried eggs and crisp bacon with toast, but what I got was scorched eggs, limp bacon and cold toast. The buffet is the safe bet. This morning, I'm having blinis, which they do quite well."

Mariah turned back to the waiter, pointed at items on the menu that were in English and made good use of sign language. "Two fried eggs, crisp bacon and toast. OK?"

The waiter nodded solemnly and went away.

"Didn't you hear what I said?"

"I'm a risk-taker."

To Tom's astonishment, Mariah's eggs were perfect, her bacon crackled and her toast was golden brown. The waiter even brought sugar for her coffee, which he never--ever--did.

"I thought you said they burned the eggs," Mariah said, mopping up the last of the yolk with a piece of toast. "Bacon was great, too."

"Bacon causes cancer," Tom snarled.

"I'll remember that. What's on the schedule for today?"

"You ready to work?"

"No heavy lifting, please. I may be out of it by noon, but we can get started and hope for the best."

"OK. You and I need to go over the Statement of Strategy and the projects that're in the loan request," Tom went on to brief her on the Committee turf war and what he wanted to do to make peace.

"I don't know, Tom," Mariah said when he'd finished. "What's running an optimal solution going to accomplish? It looks sexy, but they're not going to understand it, are they?"

"Look, everybody wants their stuff to go first, but if we dazzle them with a few reams of computer printout and a bunch of charts and graphs, we can find a way for these guys to save face and get behind a good program. Any minister who comes in second has to argue with your solution, not the minister who's his rival. We'll depersonalize it. And if the Committee agrees on the implementation sequence, the rest of it is a piece of cake."

"Boy is that a long shot," Mariah said.

"Not here it isn't. These people are smart and they're rational. They're just caught in a shit storm without a rudder. They don't have market instincts and they don't know the World Bank liturgy, so when they get stressed, they fall back on old Soviet bureaucratic methods. We've gotta help them over that hurdle. I figure you and all your numbers will make them feel like they're getting the word straight from Central Planning."

"OK. I'm here and my hotel room is paid until next Friday, so let's get on with it. You want to walk me through the strategy thing?"

Ana appeared at the door of the dining room, saw Tom and Mariah and came to their table.

"Good morning," Tom said. "I'm just starting to brief Mariah. Want some coffee or tea?"

"*Chai*," Ana said to the waiter, who rushed to their table when she arrived.

"Have you found an interpreter for Mariah?" Tom asked.

"Yes," Ana replied. "But perhaps it would be proper for Miss Carroll to say her requirements." Ana gave Mariah a cold stare and waited.

Mariah felt the chill and read the message--she didn't think they were going to be friends. "Please," Mariah said to Ana, eager to put her at ease and avoid conflict. "Call me Mariah. May I call you Ana?"

"If you like."

"Well, Ana," Mariah said. "I'm going to be doing a lot of quantitative work--mathematics, you know--so I need an interpreter who's familiar with mathematical terms."

"Katya Ivanova helps scientists who visit here--physics and mathematics, sometimes chemistry. She is Russian, not Armenian, but her English is satisfactory. She is waiting outside."

Tom and Mariah exchanged a look of surprise.

"She's here now?" Tom asked. "Are we not hurrying?"

"Let's go get her, then," Mariah said.

Katya and Mariah made an unlikely pair. Mariah was petite and small boned, with delicate angles in the lines of her face. Katya had a face as cheery and round as a ripe apple and a frame worthy of a tractor pull. She adopted Mariah on the spot and they launched a dialogue on mathematics, interspersed with real words, that left Tom and Ana mystified and excluded.

****

The morning passed quickly. Tom finished briefing Mariah on the strategy and suggested a set of initial values for the objective function she'd be trying to optimize. Mariah met Levon Abovyan at lunch and they fell together on either side of Katya like old friends. Late that afternoon, Ana and Katya went downstairs to pick up after-hours building passes, leaving Tom and Mariah alone in the office. Mariah sank into one of the large chairs and heaved a deep sigh. "Pardner, the needle on my tank just bounced off 'empty'. I'm gonna have to call it a day."

"You've done great," he said. "How soon can you start crunching numbers?"

"We leave next Friday night? It'll have to be right away. That's eight days going flat out. Not even eight if we have to do exit briefings with the Ministry and AID on Friday. Everything's got to go click, click, click."

"Levon's been pulling stuff together for a week so I trust you're not going to run into too many data problems. But we do have to get the Committee's blessing. So you need preliminary results by close of business Tuesday--five days from now. We can put it to Manoukian Wednesday morning and take it to the Committee Wednesday afternoon." Tom paused for a minute. "It's gonna be tight."

"And what are you going to be doing all this time?"

"I'm beefing up the institutional development program. The financial sector types here are definitely not ready for prime time. And we have a report to do, right? So while you're doing your dance, I'll write, Ana'll translate it, we'll drop your stuff in at the end and be outta here Friday night, just like the pros from Dover."

Mariah wanted to ask if there was something going on between him and Ana. She didn't really think Ana was Tom's type, but there was no denying she was beautiful. And exotic. Those eyes were something to behold. And the way she looked at him . . .

174

Her recollection of Tom's putting her to bed was hazy, but she was pretty sure she'd offered and he hadn't stayed. Was it Ana? Or was he really that much of a gentleman?

CHAPTER TWENTY SIX

Geghard Monastery

On Monday afternoon Sarkis left his office early and drove his old Zhiguli to Geghard Monastery. He parked beside the ancient wall, turned off the Zhiguli's rattling engine and opened the door to a frigid blast of air pouring down the narrow gash of the valley.

The entrance to Geghard Monastery, so often cluttered with a gauntlet of old men selling religious medals and hand-carved wooden crosses, was deserted. Sarkis pulled his black wool overcoat a little tighter and let the wind propel him up the cobblestone ramp beside the wall toward the main entrance. The leather soles of his shoes slipped on the stones as he hurried through the gate into the shelter of the courtyard.

Brother Arteshesh was waiting just inside the sanctuary. His coal-black eyes peered out of a heavy jet black beard that rose up his cheeks almost to his eye sockets. "I had expected Director Hajinyan," he said. The beard so obscured his face that Sarkis couldn't see his lips move and, echoing off the stone walls, the monk's voice seemed disembodied.

"The director sends his apologies," Sarkis said. "He asked me to make a preliminary assessment of what you've found."

"I see," Arteshesh mumbled, making little effort to conceal his disappointment that the director had sent an underling. "I believe we have uncovered a previously unknown library or at the least a copying room. I made them stop work immediately when I saw the fragments. I know the measures taken to preserve the Dead Sea Scrolls and I'm convinced we may have something equally important here."

He took Sarkis by the elbow and steered him back through the portal into the courtyard. "We must go to the Chapel of the Upper Tier, where the lance was kept when Geghard was its repository."

"Yes, I remember."

They rounded the outside wall of the Main Room of the Church and began climbing, first a series of steps, then a path up the face of the cliff into which many of Geghard's caves and cells had been carved.

"We were repairing a wall and part of it gave way," Brother Arteshesh explained as he guided Sarkis past a barrier that closed the Chapel of the Upper Tier to the public. On the floor inside the entry, he found a pressure lantern, pumped it a few times and lit it. The room took form in the eerie chartreuse glow and a narrow opening became visible in one of the walls.

"This is what we found," Brother Arteshesh said, coming to a halt in front of the opening. "A small passageway was carved through the stone and then sealed again, so cleverly that it went unnoticed all these years. Hundreds of years, in fact."

"Where does it lead?" Sarkis asked.

"I will show you."

The chartreuse light of the hissing lantern and the dank smell of the cave enveloped Sarkis and he felt a twinge of anxiety as he ducked his head, pulled in his shoulders and squeezed through the narrow tunnel behind Brother Arteshesh. After a few steps, they entered a small room where it was possible to stand upright. The light from the lantern cast an unearthly glow over the ancient walls.

"The stone bench suggests it was a copying room," Brother Arteshesh said, pointing toward a ledge of stone jutting from one of the walls. "There was a skylight and an air shaft when it was in use, but, like the entrance, they were sealed as tight as a tomb. Here, against this wall, we found fragments. I can see no writing on them, but they are so darkened with age . . . and the light is inadequate to make out the markings. Still, no one has touched anything. As soon as I saw the fragments . . . "

"Yes, quite right, Brother Arteshesh," Sarkis said, kneeling down to inspect one of the rusty brown chips of parchment. He shook his head. "I'll have to take them back to the museum to see if there is anything we can do. I'll call someone from Matenadaran Library to help. Are these all?"

"All we have been able to see, but please look above the bench," Arteshesh said, maneuvering the lantern to direct the light onto a niche carved into the wall above the stone bench. There sat a rectangular box made of the same stone as the walls. "We have not opened it for fear the air would damage the manuscripts. I thought it would be useful for you to see it in situ, as the archaeologists say."

The box was perhaps twelve inches long, six inches deep and six inches wide--and heavy.

"How do you know there are manuscripts in there?" Sarkis asked.

"Surely the evidence suggests . . ."

"Yes, I see," Sarkis agreed. "And better safe than sorry. I can open it at the museum where I have a clean room with humidity control. It's the best we can do. I'll take the box as it is. I'll collect the fragments on the floor, too, and hope they can be restored. Could you shine the light down here?"

Sarkis removed a packet of small plastic envelopes and a pair of tweezers from his coat pocket. While Arteshesh held the lantern, he lifted one fragment after another, put them in plastic sleeves and returned them to his coat pocket. Some were no larger than his thumbnail, but a few were several inches long and might yield some idea of the material.

"So what do you think?" Arteshesh asked, resting the lantern on the table and rubbing his hands together anxiously.

"Finding this room is very interesting," Sarkis said. "And the fragments, too, of course. But I have no idea what they mean at this point."

"You know the Church is electing a new Supreme Catholicos. The Assembly begins in only a few more days. It would be wonderful to present our discovery at the time of the celebrations. It would make the occasion so much more . . . Well, I'm sure you understand."

"I understand, Brother Arteshesh," Sarkis replied. "But I can't rush the science." He gestured with one hand and added, "This room has kept its secrets for many years--hundreds, you think? And you have no notion of why it was sealed, do you? That alone is a fascinating mystery. Perhaps in a few days, we'll have some idea of what the answers to those questions might be."

Arteshesh didn't reply for a few moments and Sarkis had the feeling he regretted having sent the note to the museum. "The box is heavy," he said at last. "If you are going to take it now, I'll light the way."

Sarkis followed him through the narrow passageway, struggling with the heavy stone box. At the entrance to the Chapel, Brother Arteshesh extinguished the lantern and went out into the gray light of early evening. At the foot of the stairs in the courtyard, he placed a heavy hand on Sarkis' shoulder. "I'll be involved with the National Assembly next week," he said. "Perhaps I could stop by the Museum on Friday or Saturday? Before the National Assembly convenes?"

"Come on Saturday," Sarkis said, anxious to leave.

"Then go with God, my son," the monk intoned, his dark eyes again seizing Sarkis.

Sarkis hurried away toward the gate. He descended the slippery cobblestone ramp toward his Zhiguli awkwardly, fearing he might slip, drop the heavy box and spill its contents. He could imagine an ancient scroll tumbling out into the darkness, its brittle parchment shattering as it rolled down the ramp, the swirling winds carrying the fragments out into the valley. The vision of disaster haunted every step of the way down the uneven surface. Finally, he reached the car, placed the box on the floor of the front passenger seat, walked around the car and slid behind the steering wheel. He released a great sigh and, to his surprise, found himself perspiring in spite of the cold.

****

Karine was waiting when he came through the door of the flat, concerned about where he'd taken the car and his late arrival home. But the scolding words froze in her throat when she saw him bringing an encrusted block of stone through their front door.

"Sarkis," she said. "What on earth?"

"I'll explain later," he said, panting from the exertion.

She wasn't satisfied, but she held back. "Your dinner is cold. What should I do with it?"

"I'll come right away," he said, pulling off his coat and hanging it on a peg by the door. "I'm just going to put this out of the way."

Karine stared resentfully at the stone box sitting on the carpet of the foyer, looking quite out of place. She stooped down and brushed away the flakes of clay it shed on the carpet and returned to the kitchen.

Sarkis picked up the box and turned toward the bedroom. Suddenly, a corner of the box crumbled in his hand and he lost his grip. The stone box crashed onto the parquet and turned on its side. The lid fell away. Sarkis held his breath. Nothing had broken. Nothing had spilled from the hollow of the box.

Karine came running at the sound of the heavy box striking the floor and found Sarkis standing over it, transfixed.

"Are you all right?" she said, one hand clasping his shoulder.

"The box . . ." he said, scarcely breathing. He went to his hands and knees, sat the box upright with trembling hands and cautiously peered into its cavity, half expecting a genii to appear.

What he saw caused him to gasp. Seven gold coins lay embedded in a lining of dark wood, casting a dull glow in the half light.

Without shifting his gaze, he said to Karine, "Bring the candelabra. Hurry."

When Karine returned, Sarkis pointed to the small table by the window and told her to clear it and put the candelabra there. He rose unsteadily then and took a pair of cotton gloves and a soft cloth from their bedside table. He spread the cloth over the tabletop and positioned the candelabra so that its light spilled directly into the cavity of the box. The coins fit snugly into their carved recesses of the dark wood lining, too snugly for him to lift them out with his fingertips, so he devised a lever from a strip of heavy paper to prize up the edges of the coins. Then he pulled on the cotton gloves to prevent any of his body oils from touching the coins.

He inserted the paper lever into the recess that held the largest coin. It tipped up readily and the fingertips of his left hand found the heavy coin's rim. Slowly, he removed it and placed it gently on the soft cloth. He judged the coin to be about 2.5 centimeters in diameter. In the candlelight, its surface was a golden mirror. Even the patina of centuries of storage under less than ideal conditions had scarcely dulled the polished finish. It was unquestionably a proof, a *fleur* de coin. He'd never seen such a beautiful one.

Karine, who had been watching in silent awe, caught her breath. "Oh, my," she said. "Sarkis, what is it?"

Reverently, he turned the coin over. He saw a most unusual three-quarter profile of a man, then the Roman 'Chi-Rho' in the lower right hand quadrant. Sarkis turned the coin again to examine the side of the coin he'd seen first. His magnifying glass revealed an intricate engraving of Christ on the cross, head slumped forward. The figure below was a Roman soldier, piercing Christ's side with a lance. Sarkis' skin tingled and his throat went dry--the engraving was so fine, so exquisite. How could the eyes of any ancient be so sharp or his hand so steady and gifted to create the image he saw in his glass?

He held his breath as he turned the coin again. The three-quarter portrait must be Christ Himself. Sarkis peered through the magnifying glass and the face emerged in fine, lifelike detail. It was also unusual that the 'Chi-Rho'--a Roman coinage tradition using the Greek letters

'Chi' and 'Rho' to represent the first three letters of CHRist--appeared in the lower right hand quadrant. He could not think of a single Roman coin that featured the 'Chi-Rho' on the reverse in combination with a portrait. Sarkis knew he was looking at a rare example of coinage, a path-breaking design, flawless in its execution. He sat at the little table for some time before he could pull himself together enough to think of the other coins, the ones still resting in the recesses of the polished wood lining of the stone box.

He inserted the paper lever into the second recess and brought up the next coin in his gloved fingertips. The obverse depicted two men--not soldiers--holding a lance between them. On the reverse, a man standing, holding a lance, and another man prone. At the top of the coin, in Armenian letters, was the name 'Abgar' and at the bottom of the coin, the name 'Thaddeus'. The coin showed Thaddeus healing King Abgar V of Edessa! The images flew back and forth in Sarkis' mind before comprehension came to him. The coins were telling a story.

Sarkis placed the second coin beside the first and reached into the stone box for the third coin. It was smaller than the second and weighed perhaps ten grams. The obverse portrayed an intricate landscape--a church, a lake, and a man holding a lance. The portrait on the reverse was labeled 'Thaddeus' in Armenian. Sarkis found the scene obscure until he remembered that Jude Thaddeus established two of the earliest churches in Christendom, one at Artaz and the other at Sewniq, near Lake Sevan. The third coin had to represent the church at Lake Sevan.

The obverse of the fourth coin held a profile labeled 'Tridat III'. The reverse depicted two women, one holding a cross, the other wearing a tiara. They had to be Rhipsime, the beautiful Christian girl, and Princess Khosrov.

The fifth coin showed a man wearing a crown being ministered to by another man in a long robe--Grigor healing King Tridat III. The reverse showed Mt. Ararat, symbol of the Armenian nation, flanked by the King and Grigor--the conversion of Armenia to Christianity.

The Armenian alphabet covered the reverse of the 6th coin. Three men, two standing and one seated at a desk were on the obverse. One of the men was a Supreme Catholicos because he wore a triangular cowl--a veghar. The other standing figure wore a crown and had to be a king. The seated figure was at first a mystery. Sarkis turned the coin both ways several times before he understood. The seated figure was Mesrop-Mashtotz, creator of the Armenian alphabet, which probably made the two standing figures Sahak Partev, the Supreme Catholicos who encouraged Mesrop, and King Vram Shapur, who sponsored him.

Vram Shapur might have commissioned these coins. If so, they would be almost 1,600 years old. The importance of their age, however, was insignificant beside the fact that they might be the only coins minted--and until now completely unknown--during the 400-year reign of the Arascid dynasty.

There was one small coin left in the stone box. Sarkis removed it and brought it under his magnifying glass in the light shed by the candelabra. On its obverse men and women, encircled by the Armenian alphabet, were holding hands. The reverse displayed Mt. Ararat topped by a cross. Could its message signify 'Armenians united in Christ and culture'?

Sarkis stared into space, absorbing the enormity of this discovery. He had become part of an epic event. It had always been a mystery that no Armenian coins had been minted in any metal during the long reign of the Arascid dynasty, from Tridat I in AD 52 to Artaxias IV in 428--arguably the time when the most brilliant pages of Armenian history were written. Sarkis was holding in his hands the golden coins--the only coins--from that golden era. Their existence did not solve the mystery, it deepened it. Why had they never been minted?

He looked up at Karine, her eyes shining in the candlelight. "These are the most marvelous coins I have ever seen in my life."

He began the process of authenticating the coins immediately, writing down the circumstances of their discovery, describing each coin in detail. The candles guttered and died before he fell into bed, exhausted.

✳✳✳✳✳✳✳✳✳✳✳✳

He came awake with a start. The coins! He threw off the comforter and bolted out of bed. To his great relief, they were still there on the table, gleaming softly in the sunlight streaming through the window.

In the bathroom, he splashed cold water on his face, brushed his teeth and combed his hair. He was stiff and sore from the hours of intense concentration last night. The mirror told him he needed a shave and that his eyes were limned with dark circles. He stripped off his shirt and washed his chest and armpits with cold water, walked back to the bedroom, put on a fresh undershirt and joined Karine in the kitchen.

"The coins," she said, without turning from the stove where she was scrambling eggs for their breakfast. "What is it all about?"

"I scarcely know myself," he said, pouring a glass of tea and sitting down at their breakfast table. "But whatever I tell you, you must give me your solemn promise not to say a word of it to anyone."

Karine looked up and stared at him with bright eyes. "Oh?"

"You must promise, Karine," Sarkis told her sternly.

"Very well, then. I promise."

"They were just discovered at Geghard. No one knows about them. No one. Brother Arteshesh thinks the box contains manuscripts. And the workmen who discovered the room where they were hidden do not know even that. They could be of unbelievable importance, but I have to study them carefully and authenticate them before the discovery is announced."

"I understand," she said, giving him the smile he'd hoped for. "Of course I'll keep the secret." She scooped eggs onto a plate and brought it to him with bread and cheese. "Here, I'll fix more if you're still hungry. You didn't eat a thing last night."

"I'm going to stay home today," Sarkis said as he began to eat. "Would you call the Museum and tell them I'm ill?"

"The Museum doesn't know?"

"As I said, I am the only one--and now you--who knows of their existence."

✱✱✱✱✱✱✱✱✱✱✱

In the sunlight, Sarkis had a better view of the coins. He'd been impressed with the quality of the workmanship last night. Now he saw they were masterpieces. But were they real or an elaborate hoax? These coins were so nearly perfect that Sarkis immediately ruled out the possibility that they were cast forgeries--the crudest form of counterfeiting. Besides, these coins were unknown. They had never been circulated.

Sarkis began his authentication with the idea that the coins were special proofs, fleur de coin of the finest quality, which meant they had been struck from dies and polished with great skill and care. But even proof coins of the highest quality would show evidence of the strike in tiny stress marks radiating away from the raised images on the coin. These coins showed no stress marks. He used his loupe to examine the coins and in the sunlight, he began to consider the possibility that he wasn't looking at proofs, but patterns--the original designs themselves, the direct product of the engraver's art, the example shown to the sovereign for his approval.

'Patterns,' Sarkis thought. 'If these are the patterns for coins that were never minted, they're unique, priceless.' He paced the bedroom,

183

trying to contain his excitement so that he could move on to the basic elements of the task of authenticating them.

Dating ancient coinage, which typically didn't display a mint date, was always a challenge and he considered the information he had. The inscriptions were in Armenian so he knew the coins were struck--or the patterns engraved--after the invention of the Armenian alphabet in 404 AD. And no coin depicted the translation of the Bible into Armenian, which had occurred in 433 AD. Given the coins' religious theme, one of the coins would almost certainly have depicted that event. So the evidence suggested a dating between 404 AD and 433 AD. The earliest known numismatic portrait of Christ was on the gold solidus of Justinian II, who reigned from 685 to 695 AD. If the Armenian coins were earlier, their portrait of Christ would predate Justinian's solidus by 250 years.

If this were so, Sarkis realized, the coins shimmering on his makeshift worktable were of global historical significance, not simply priceless Armenian artifacts. He stretched and took deep breaths, walked around the room and tried to relax. At last, he forced himself to focus on the box, which he had neglected until now.

He hadn't questioned its size or shape. It was relatively flat, but still quite thick to be a container for only seven coins, laid horizontally in recesses. He picked up the box and took it to the window to let the sunlight shine into its cavity. He saw the seven empty recesses in the dark wood--Persian walnut, the most desirable for storing coins. A Carbon-14 dating of the wood liner would help him date the coins. It wouldn't be conclusive, but if Carbon-14 tests indicated that the tree had been cut in, say, 400 AD plus or minus a few years, he'd have another piece of evidence for his provisional dating. He looked at the liner and wondered how he could take a sample of the wood without doing grave damage to it. He couldn't just carve out a piece of it. The box itself would be an important historical artifact if the coins were genuine. He turned it over to look at its underside.

The liner that had seemed so firmly implanted fell out onto the floor. With it came fourteen heavy bronze dies, clattering and clanking together as they crashed against the floor.

****

Taking a deep breath, Sarkis set the stone box aside and carefully retrieved the Persian walnut liner. He placed it on the seat of his straight chair and remained calm enough to remember to put on his cotton gloves before he picked up the dies. They were heavy bronze, annealed and ready, once they'd been mounted, to receive a planchet-- the blank of metal that would become a coin when hammered between the two dies. He put each die under his loupe and examined them carefully one by one. They were pristine.

He picked up the stone box and looked into its cavity again. Neat rows of recesses lay exposed on another plate of Persian walnut into which the dies had been fitted. Their presence explained why the box had been so heavy, why the thickness and width of the shell had so greatly exceeded what would have been required to harbor a single set of gold coins.

He wondered if there might be another layer. He slipped the blade of a knife from the kitchen between the wall of the stone shell and the edge of the walnut base in the bottom of the box. He drew the blade of the knife all the way around the edge of the walnut before he attempted to wedge it away from the stone. It didn't come easily, and when it did come free, it flipped into the air--bringing with it a cascade of gold coins.

Sparkling in the sunlight, the tumble of coins flashed in front of his face and fluttered down. Most of them landed softly on the carpet, but one rolled away, singing across the parquet floor. It struck the baseboard beside the door with a solid 'thunk' and fell exhausted on its side. Sarkis moved slowly and deliberately, scarcely breathing. He picked up the coins and placed them in a row on the cloth cover of the table beneath those he'd extracted from the recesses of the wooden liner. Then he got up to recover the coin that had rolled across the floor. He placed it with its mates on the cloth-covered table, careful to array the second set of coins below the first and to check obverse and reverse of the second set against the first. The designs of the two sets matched exactly. When he re-examined the second set of coins under the magnifying glass, he detected the tiny stress marks of the strike. The implications were clear. He had the patterns, the dies and the first--probably the only--set of proof coins struck from those dies.

One more layer of walnut lined the bottom of the box and again using Karine's kitchen knife, he eased it from the stone shell.

Finally, there was only stone beneath the wood. The box had surrendered all its secrets at last. For Armenia and the world of numismatics, the discovery was monumental. Sarkis' knees buckled and he sat down heavily.

It was more than he'd ever dreamed about--his golden chance to become an icon in numismatics. If the coins were genuine--and in his heart he knew they were--his name would be known around the world. As suddenly as that thought swept over him, the chill realization that what he had done with Aleksandr, for Setta, put all that at risk. For a moment, panic gripped him and he didn't know if the coins were blessing or curse. He shook it off. He had no choice but to go on with the authentication.

The coins themselves were only faint testimony. Carbon-14 dating of the walnut liner wasn't conclusive. Tests could show it to be 1,600 years old, but the wood could have come from somewhere else entirely to support the hoax. The tiny room at Geghard and the manner of its discovery lent credence, but didn't constitute conclusive proof. Sarkis needed a more complete 'story.'

If the coins were fifth century, they belonged to the same era as the carnelian seal and the Parthian necklace. In his search for their provenance, he'd spent many hours at the Matenadaran Library, digging through the collection of fifth century manuscripts which included those from King Vram Shapur's reign. If Vram Shapur had commissioned the coins, there might be a record.

He could do nothing more until he could return to Matenadaran Library and he was suddenly very tired. He wanted to sleep, but he didn't dare leave the coins out as he had the night before. The safest place in the apartment was the niche behind the wardrobe and he set about making room for the stone box there. He removed his coin collection and Karine's jewel case and tried the space. The stone box fit perfectly. He turned back to his work table where the coins, the dies and the Persian walnut plates were laid out and stared down at them. He slipped on his cotton gloves and took the largest of the coins between his thumb and forefinger to examine it just once more. Turning it slowly this way and that, it caught a ray of light from the window and a halo formed around the head of Christ. It was a magical moment. He wasn't sure how long he stood there, holding the heavy coin, but the light was almost gone when he came to his senses again. Gently, reverently, he placed it back on the table and set to work.

The bronze dies were set back in place and the top plate fitted over them. He replaced the lid of the stone box and set it inside the niche, resealed it with the basalt brick and rolled the wardrobe back against the wall.

He put Karine's jewelry case in the lower drawer of their bedside table and carefully laid the coins of his collection, sealed in their plastic cases, in the olive wood box that held the chess men he'd bought at the vernesazsh. He looked down on the rubles and staters and dirhams, the dinarii and tetradrachmas of his collection and felt a small satisfaction that he still counted them his treasures, that he hadn't been entirely carried away by the seven gold coins that remained on the work table--the patterns. The precious, priceless patterns. For the time being, he would give them a special place of repose.

CHAPTER TWENTY SEVEN

Hotel Armenia

On Saturday morning, just after seven o'clock, Tom heard a tap on his door and found Mariah there, looking tired and pale, as though she hadn't slept.

He swung the door wide and stepped back to allow her to come in. "You look like you could use a cup of black coffee," he told her.

"I told the lady in the hall to bring two cups. The café is jammed. Who are all these people in black? They're all over the place."

"They're electing a new pope. They're the delegates, from all over the world. I knew they were coming before we left, but not exactly when."

Mariah looked around Tom's room, identical to her own, and felt a twinge of relief that Tom was sleeping alone. One of the twin beds was littered with file folders and books. The upholstered armchair was loaded with dirty clothes. Patches of yellow Post-Its covered one wall.

"What a mess," she said.

Tom's laptop sat on the tiny desk he'd made into a workspace, its screen filled with text. She bent over the table to see what he was writing. "Any of this printed out?"

He took a stack of pages from the right hand corner of the desk and handed them to her.

She took them, dumped his dirty clothes on the floor and sat down.

There was another tap on the door and Tom went to answer it. Sofia was there with coffee and a plate of muffins. He welcomed her with a grin and made space on the bedside table for the tray.

When Sofia had gone, he poured coffee for them both and handed one to Mariah, slouched in the chair, paging through what he'd written. Tom left his coffee on the bedside table and bent to touch his toes, swung his arms from side to side, pulled one elbow behind his head, then the next, trying to relax the muscles in his back and neck.

Mariah cocked her eyes up at him and gave him an amused expression. "You should make funny faces to go with those contortions."

"I've been up since four," he said. "I'm as stiff as a three-day-old pretzel."

"Come here," she said, putting the report aside. "Sit down in front of me. I'll put my magic fingers to work."

"I won't turn that down," he replied and sat on the floor between her legs. She came to the edge of the chair, dug her fingers into his tense neck muscles and began to knead them. "Mmmmmm," Tom groaned. "That's wonderful."

"It's looking good," she said.

"What is?" he asked, eyes closed, relishing the strength of her fingers massaging his neck and shoulders.

"The game plan. You're taking this seriously, aren't you?"

Tom didn't answer for a few moments. His report was almost finished and, whether the Committee signed off on the implementation schedule or not, the end of his mission in Armenia was in sight. "I busted my buns on the financial sector. They didn't have a clue what to do with it. Sorry I haven't been around to give you a hand with your stuff. That'll be the pièce de la résistance. How's it coming?"

She reached around him and unfastened the top buttons of his shirt, pulled it away from his shoulders and began to massage his chest, caressing more than kneading, drawing his head back between her thighs. "We got lucky with the first set of weights for the objective function," she said. "The first few passes were ragged, but it solved. I should finish tweaking it in a couple of days. I'm pretty sure it'll make sense. It might even be compelling."

"Good show," he said, eyes closed. "You getting along OK with Levon and Katya?"

"They're aces. Real workaholics. And they walk me back to the hotel every night. They both have families, but they're right there with me all the time. I couldn't ask for better. How's Miz Ana holding up?"

"We're pretty much through with the Central Bank now, so I gave her some time off. I told her to come by this morning and pick up what I have so she can start translating. All this has to go into Armenian, you know."

"Mmmm hmmm," Mariah muttered absently. "I think I'm going to sack out over there for awhile," she said in a sleepy voice. "You don't mind, do you?"

"In my bed?" he asked, straightening up and turning around.

"Why not? Miz Ana would understand would she?"

"Why shouldn't she?" Tom replied. "Go ahead. But wouldn't you be more comfortable in your own room?"

"I like the way your stuff smells. Aroma therapy." With Tom still sitting on the floor watching in bewilderment, she got up and took the two steps to the side of his bed. With her back turned to him, she undressed, letting her clothes fall in a heap at her feet. She gave him a fleeting glimpse of one breast before she slipped beneath his sheets and pulled them up to her chin.

"You're a rascal, Mariah Carroll."

"Wake me up in an hour," she said, giving him a wink and a sultry smile before she closed her eyes.

From the sound of her breathing, he thought she must have fallen asleep immediately. Maybe she really was too tired to make it back to her room. He doubted it. She was making a statement for Ana. And what a statement, he thought. But he wasn't going to play her game. He'd head Ana off before she got to the room.

He buttoned his shirt and pulled a sweater over it. Then his eye caught the case which held the Rolex. Impulsively, he opened it, slipped on the watch and fastened the catch. It fit perfectly, as if his wrist and Gunter's were the exact same size.

"What's that?" Mariah asked, eyes half shut, but watching him.

"Something from my father."

"Let me see." He sat beside her on the bed and held out his wrist.

"Good gravy," she said. "Is this a real Rolex?"

"I guess so. Handsome without being pretentious, don't you think?"

"Not something you want to leave lying around."

"No, I suppose not. Go to sleep now."

He printed what was on his screen, gathered up the loose pages of the report and closed the door softly. At Sofia's table, he went through an amusing, but articulate charade to explain to her that Mariah was asleep in his room and, pointing to the Rolex, that she should knock on his door in an hour to wake her.

Sofia cackled, flashed her gap-toothed grin and nodded that she understood.

Tom took the stairs to the lobby and sat down at a table in the lobby bar where he could watch for Ana. Marina brought him coffee and, for the first time in days, he thought about the incident in the Business Center.

Ana had warned him that Avakian was dangerous, but he hadn't felt a single vibe, not a whisper. Maybe Avakian realized he was out of line and was lying low. It was true that Tom hadn't given him much opportunity for payback. His days were taken up in meetings at Government House or in nearby buildings and the nights were spent in his room, pulling together his notes from the day's meetings. It wasn't as if he were prowling the streets after dark, laying himself open to attack. Still, he thought discretion demanded that he see what Ana had to say about it.

He saw her through the windows, coming down the sidewalk, her dark hair bobbing as she walked. He laid some drams on the table for Marina and met Ana on the steps outside.

The sun had come up strong, eager for spring, and it was a glorious day. "Let's stay outside a while," he said. "I've been cooped up too long." He took her hand and led her to Anniversary Park. Beside the cascade of fountains, two women sat on a bench talking, flanked by prams with babies snuggled in their blankets. Further along, the same gaggle of old men he'd seen before huddled around a chess match. No one paid any attention to Tom and Ana and midway down the promenade, he chose a vacant bench drenched in sunshine.

"Let's sit here," he said. "If we get cold, we can walk some more." He handed her the dozen pages and said, "Here's what I've got so far. Do you want to translate it today or wait until I'm finished?"

"May I read it now?" she asked

"Of course. I want you to," he replied, leaning back on the bench to let the sunlight strike his face. Eyes closed, he concentrated on the rustle of the dead leaves of the sycamore trees and listened for the pages turning. When he judged she was almost to end, he opened his eyes and looked at her.

She was on the last page and when she finished it she looked at him with her glossy almond eyes. "It is very good." She sat forward on the bench and turned to him. "And exciting. It gives me hope. If the World Bank gives us money . . . our people can . . . how do you say? . . . prosper? We can be proud nation again."

He smiled at her enthusiasm. "Prosper would be just dandy. It's a long way between here and there, though."

"I know, but I want to begin now. I want to see how it will be in Armenian. Should we go to the hotel?"

"I'm feeling a little cooped up there. It's Saturday. Can we get into Government House today? You could translate there, couldn't you?"

"Yes. Government House. But better that I go alone to concentrate. I will find you in hotel when I am finished. Not long."

****

In search of breakfast, Tom found the second floor restaurant packed, a complete contrast to all the previous days. He went downstairs to the café. He got the last table on the balcony, one near where he and Ana had had brandy several days ago. He ordered blinis and coffee and settled in for a long wait, wishing he had brought something to read.

He'd folded his hands on the table top and was staring at them when he felt the presence of someone beside him. He looked up into the face of a man in a black suit with a straight, high collar and a tab of white at the throat. Not the waiter.

The man spoke to him in a language Tom didn't understand, but gestured toward the empty chair and Tom understood that he wanted to sit down or take the chair to another table.

Tom nodded. "Of course," he said, spreading a hand toward the chair. The man pulled back the chair and sat down, smiling mostly with his eyes since the heavy beard obscured his mouth.

"Thank you," he said in a heavy, Slavic accent that might have been Russian.

Tom caught the waiter's eye and waved at him, pointing to the new arrival. The harried waiter stopped at the little table on his way back toward the kitchen and the two conversed rapidly in Russian.

Tom saw the new arrival's eyes fix on the Rolex.

"My name is Pavel. Do you prefer English?" he added in that heavy accent.

Every muscle now taut, Tom replied. "Yes, I do."

"Is beautiful watch," Pavel said.

"It was my father's."

"What is your father's name?"

"Gunter," Tom replied.

Pavel's hand slipped beneath the napkin, balled it up and passed it across the table to Tom. "Come to Room 512. *Dasvidanya*," Pavel said, pushed back his chair and left.

****

Mariah had gone by the time he returned to his room. Holding the red and white checkered napkin in his hand, he stared out through the double windows at the far ridge, the one with the huge statues. *"Why did I respond? I could have played dumb and been out of it. Just couldn't say 'no.' He didn't owe Andre and he didn't owe his father. Whatever was in this napkin was his if he could hold on to it. Was that why he put on the watch? Was that why he took the napkin? Was it just rank avarice?"*

He spread the napkin on the bedside table and opened it. A single diamond. What else had he expected? It would have been nice to have a diamond light, but that was only for the sake of curiousity. Like smoking or making love, what he knew about diamonds had never been erased This one looked like D-flawless, probably about a carat. He'd never seen the blood diamonds coming out of the savage war in West Africa but he wouldn't have wanted to touch them if they had, regardless of value. This one was not West African, though. It had been delivered by someone who spoke Russian, who was making the drop in a former republic of the Soviet Union, so the stones were probably stolen from the Aikhal mines in Siberia. This sample was good quality, cut and polished, not diamond rough. Gunter had told him it would be a brush pass, though, and it wasn't. Was he walking into a trap? Well, no guts, no glory.

He used the stairs to climb to the next floor and found room 512 quickly. The floor attendant wasn't at her little desk. He tapped twice at the door. Pavel opened it immediately, as if he had been waiting with his hand on the knob.

Tom moved swiftly into the room and Pavel closed the door behind him.

"Show me the rest," Tom said.

Pavel unfastened his belt and let his trousers slip down a few inches, taking a suede leather pouch from a pocket in his crotch. He handed the pouch to Tom with one hand and gave him a loupe with the other.

Tom moved to the window and cleared away the bedside table. The light from the window was nothing like a diamond light, but it would probably suffice.

One at a time, Tom removed the stones from the pouch and examined them with the loupe. There were twenty-five diamonds, half round-cut and the rest marquise-cut, the two most valuable. Most would grade D-Flawless around one carat, but there were two that Tom judged might cut to more than two carats. All diamonds have some inclusions, but there were no large ones Tom could detect with the loupe in the available light. The goods were as advertised, even better. He didn't know what Andre had paid for them, but he guessed the value to be around ten thousand dollars a carat for the D-Flawless, one-carat stones, so almost a quarter of a million, not counting the two-carat stones. They would go for proportionately more because of their size.

Tom looked up from the table and nodded at Pavel. "Payment has been made, yes?"

"Yes," Pavel answered. "But you must telephone and say that you have received the stones."

"We just have to get a line. Who am I to call?"

Pavel handed him a card with a name and telephone number in Zurich.

Tom nodded and said, "May I take the stones now?"

Pavel nodded and Tom tucked the suede bag into his trousers pocket.

"Follow me," Tom said and led Pavel into the hallway. The floor lobby was still vacant, but they took the stairs to the mezzanine rather than the elevator. Tom opened the stairway door to the mezzanine slowly. The main lobby below was crowded with delegates milling about, talking and smoking. The old Intourist offices were dark; the gift shop was doing a brisk business and no one appeared to notice when Tom and Pavel crossed the mezzanine, passed through the double doors and entered the lobby that connected the old hotel and the new one. Ghostly silent now, the area was dimly lit in sepia tones. Tom imagined that in happier times, it had been filled with theater-goers and conferees and the sound of lively conversations.

There was a line of delegates waiting for the international cubicles that had been installed in an old suite, as dimly lit as the silent lobby. Tom was grateful for that because it reduced the possibility that he would be seen with Pavel. Once he was connected to Bruner's Bank, he spoke to Klaus Bruner and confirmed receipt of the diamonds. His business with Pavel was then complete. They did not shake hands and as they walked back to the main hotel, they did not walk together. Tom did not expect to see Pavel again, ever.

CHAPTER TWENTY EIGHT

Government House

Tom returned to his room and was relieved to find Mariah gone. The maid had even been in to make the bed and plump the pillows. Now he had to figure out what he was going to do with the diamonds. He couldn't very well carry them around in his pocket for a week. He hadn't brought anything with him that would conceal the diamonds passing through customs--hollow-heeled shoes, a false-bottomed briefcase, a coat with a hollow seam. He'd have to use his money belt, leaving the ankle wallet to hold the thick stack of dollars he still had. He locked the door, ripped off his belt, removed the bills it held and began threading the diamonds, one by one, around the inner lining of the belt. They would be immediately apparent if he had to take off the belt and lay it out on a customs officer's table, but otherwise probably not.

He had just finished with the diamonds when there was a knock at the door. The folded hundred-dollar bills still lay in an untidy pile on his bedside table. He quickly threaded his belt back through its loops and slammed a book down on the pile of hundred-dollar bills.

"Just a minute," he said.

It was Ana.

He swung the door open and she came in.

"I have finished the translation. The report is now ready for the minister."

"That's great," Tom said, shifting his weight from one foot to the next to seat the diamond-laden belt more comfortably.

****

The team worked through the weekend and it was all business between Tom and Ana as they joined forces with Mariah, Levon and Katya.

On Monday morning, they appeared in Manoukian's office.

Manoukian himself came to usher them in and while they settled around the conference table, Manoukian told his assistant to bring tea and nervously lit a cigarette.

"The Minister welcomes you all," Ana translated. "He is eager to hear what you have to report."

"Minister Manoukian," Tom said. "I'd like you to meet Mariah Carroll, who joined our team last week. As I mentioned to you before, she's a world class mathematical programmer and she's already close to solving the dilemma we have with the Committee."

Manoukian appraised Mariah. Through Ana he said, "Welcome to Armenia. I am sorry that your arrival was not more, ah, orderly. I understand you made an unscheduled stop in Tblisi?"

"Thank you, Mister Minister. Yes, we had a little excitement there. I trust leaving Armenia will be much less eventful."

"We'll give you a progress report in a minute," Tom said to end the small talk. "But I'd also like you to review this proposal for financial sector development. I want to replace the one in the current loan request with this. We'd like to know your suggestions as soon as possible." Tom slid the twenty pages of Armenian text across the table to Manoukian.

"Excellent," he said through Ana. "I was told you were talking with people in our financial sector. I am pleased to have your recommendations. I will give it careful attention. Now, you're scheduled to leave at the end of this week, so I'm anxious to know what progress you've made."

Tom brought Manoukian up to date and described their plan of work for the final few days of the mission. "By late Tuesday, we expect to complete a draft of a working document based on Mariah's analysis. We want to review it with you Wednesday morning if you can make time. If you approve, we can put it to the Committee that afternoon. Mariah will show them an implementation schedule we think they can agree on and one the World Bank will probably accept and be impressed with. I can't guarantee the Bank will grant the loan, but if they like the Statement of Strategy and the Implementation Schedule, I feel pretty sure they'll give you an approval in principle, subject to the feasibility studies."

"Excellent," Manoukian exclaimed. "I will call a meeting of

the Committee for Wednesday afternoon.”

CHAPTER TWENTY NINE

Government House

Ana came to breakfast looking fresh and rested. How, Tom could not imagine, since the night before she'd translated and typed his Committee presentation and all the revisions to the loan request he'd made in the last two days. He watched her walk from the door to his table by the window, her stride sure and strong, her straight, gray wool skirt loose enough for comfort, but tight enough to reveal the lines of her thighs and hips as she walked. Watching her come toward him, he sensed that the tension of the last few days had dissipated.

He stood up as she neared the table. "You have no right to look so beautiful," he ventured, thinking an extravagant compliment couldn't hurt.

She surprised him with a smile. "You are kind," she said, sitting down and smoothing the starched white tablecloth with her hands. "I feel exhausted."

Sam Rhodes appeared as they returned from the buffet.

"Good morning," Rhodes said, including Ana in his greeting. "I figured I'd better check up on you to see if you were going to pull this thing off. Mr. Lange asked me about you yesterday and I had to admit I hadn't seen you in a while. I've been up in Spitak with the UN housing guys."

"As of this dawn's early light, I think we're going to make it," Tom told him. "Mariah and Levon got an optimal solution last night. It makes economic sense and I think it'll make political sense to the heavyweights on the Committee. The draft's written and translated, so it shouldn't take long to plug in whatever changes they want. Incidentally, we also have a new section on financial sector development that we've already run by Manoukian. It includes mortgage origination units in the banks and a secondary mortgage market for the housing sector. That's the good news. The bad news, Sam, is that there's no funding for housing development."

"You're actually recommending institutions for the mortgage market?" Sam asked.

"Uh huh," Tom said.

"That's fantastic," Rhodes said, suddenly excited. "Does that mean you actually heard some of that stuff I told you a couple of weeks ago?"

"I guess so," Tom grinned.

Rhodes shook his head slowly from side to side. "This is great. It's hard to believe. A total turnaround for the program out here. You're a bloody miracle-worker."

"Well, don't hang that tag on me. The real miracle-worker's coming through the door right now."

Mariah's tousled, honey-colored hair came straight from the shower and gave her a relaxed look in spite of the fatigue she felt in every bone.

"I was just telling Sam that you had an optimal solution," Tom said as she sat down.

"Yeah. The numbers crunched up just fine last night. But you're the one who set the parameters. You and Levon."

"Success has many fathers," Tom intoned. "But failure is an orphan."

"Success has mothers, too," Mariah added. "I don't mind taking a little of the credit."

Tom turned to Rhodes. "Come what may, we're going to need an appointment with Lange or Marcos on Friday to do an exit briefing. We're outta here Friday night."

"I'll set that up," Rhodes said, bringing himself back to the liaison business. "Ten o'clock?"

"Sounds fine. Will you send the Jeep to pick us up?"

****

The buzz of conversation in the conference room ceased when the team walked in. The Committee members knew of Mariah's arrival, but they were meeting her for the first time. The highlights in her amber hair sparkled in the sunlight and she'd dressed for effect in a tailored business suit with a double-breasted coat over a white silk blouse that buttoned to the neck. Her above-the-knee skirt and high heel shoes were designed to showcase her sleek figure. She pretended not to notice the effect she was having on the Committee and demurely allowed Tom to introduce her to Minister Zadigian. Zadigian seized the moment and introduced her to each of the Committee members individually.

Manoukian bustled into the room, a sheaf of papers in one hand, a lighted Marlboro in the other. "Good morning, gentlemen," he said, the hush upon the room making it unnecessary for him to raise his voice. Almost to himself, he added with a little smile, "I see you've met Miss Carroll."

The members read through the two-page summary of the implementation schedule dictated by Mariah's analysis and when Tom asked her to explain mathematical programming to them, every man's attention was riveted on her. Ana handled the translation and it was almost as if Mariah were speaking to them in Armenian. The Committee was completely captivated.

After Mariah finished, Tom walked them through the logic. The schedule was crafted to mollify the Minister of Transportation, the Minister of Communications and the Minister of Energy by including key elements of their favorite projects in the first tranche. The Minister of Industry, who expected nothing, was enthralled by the program for promoting Armenian products abroad and developing market analyses. At a minimum, he'd get an all-expense-paid tour of the major capitals of the Western world. The Minister of Construction was disappointed that no funds were recommended for housing, but was placated by Manoukian's enthusiastic endorsement of the financial development proposals. The Ministers of Health, Education, and Tourism were also left out, but Manoukian thought they'd thrown enough bones to the big dogs to keep these minor ministries at bay.

When Tom finished, Manoukian rose. "As you know, the President is in Paris, negotiating assistance with the French government. Otherwise, he would be here with us today, in this room. I spoke with him last night about the Committee's progress. From the stormy cabinet meetings we've had over the last few months, I am sure you know the importance he attaches to this loan."

Manoukian chuckled softly and was joined by several others who'd been burned by the President's anger when the original loan request had been rejected. "I told him I thought we had the formula for success in hand and he assured me that he would be pleased if we did, in fact, reach agreement on the implementation schedule." Manoukian sat down and a silence that almost crackled fell upon the room.

After Manoukian invoked the specter of the President's iron fist, he stared out the window, his eyes refusing to meet those of anyone around the table. Other eyes were shifting, anxious to see who would break the silence. Finally, the Transportation Minister, who had started the stormy controversy over the implementation schedule, cleared his throat to speak, fixing his cold gaze on Tom.

Ana moved close to Tom, her lips at his ear, waiting to translate what the Transportation Minister was about to say.

"I remain convinced that all my transportation projects are vital to our economy and its recovery," the Minister began, holding Tom's summary up in the air over his head. "But I also see the wisdom in the balanced approach set out in this plan," he added gruffly, slamming the papers onto the conference table. "So . . . on behalf of my ministry, I approve this implementation schedule and urge my colleagues to approve it also."

Ana's translation quickened at the end of the Minister's remarks and the tension went out of her.

Manoukian's head snapped around, his dark, sunken eyes boring into the Transportation Minister's as a smile crept over his face, softening his features. After that moment of unspoken thanks, his eyes darted from one minister to another, pressing them to concur, to seal the agreement.

The Minister of Communications and the Minister of Energy felt compelled to give speeches before they signed on, but by noon, the deal had been done. Zadigian took the formal vote to adopt the implementation schedule and the entire group adjourned to the President's spacious anteroom for a buffet lunch.

Manoukian had the obligation and the honor of making the first toast. He raised the small glass of vodka he was holding in his hand and shouted, "Comrades! You have done well! With a little capital from the West, our national resolve will write a new chapter in our long and glorious history." He paused for only a moment and then shouted,

"Armenia!" The room roared back, "Armenia!"

The windows rattled and the bottoms of vodka glasses were turned to the ceiling. White-jacketed waiters rushed through the group, refilling them. Manoukian had not yet yielded the floor. "For my own part as well as the President's, I want to thank Dr. Thomas Yeager and Miss Mariah Carroll for their assistance in helping us formulate this new program." Manoukian smiled at Tom and Mariah, lifted the glass above his head and shouted, "America!" The room echoed the toast "America!" at a decibel level only a fraction less than the cheer for Armenia.

Again the waiters scurried about, refilling glasses. Manoukian was now looking expectantly at Tom.

Taking the cue, Tom responded. "Gentlemen," he said with Ana translating. "Your struggle is a difficult one and we welcome the opportunity to help you realize your dreams of a prosperous independence. We couldn't have come this far without some talented colleagues. Levon Abovyan."

Tom turned to Levon and saluted him with his glass but did not drink. The room roared back, "Levon!" Tom turned to Ana and saluted her, catching her unawares. "And Ana Stepanian." The Committee laughed at her embarrassment and pounded the tables mightily, showing their affection for her. "And Katya Ivanova." Again the Committee pounded the tables. "Finally, I want to recognize Minister Manoukian for his help and support. We wouldn't have finished our work so quickly--perhaps not at all--if he hadn't been willing to make the time whenever we needed to see him, to correct our mistakes and show us the best way to help Armenia. So I now give you . . . Krikor Manoukian!" Happily, the room roared its response--"Krikor! . . . Manoukian!" Finally, Tom raised his glass and drank.

Manoukian put an end to the toasting by saying, "Thank you, Dr. Yeager. Now let us enjoy the food prepared for this fine occasion." As the Committee began to serve their plates, Manoukian put his arms around Tom and Mariah. "I want to thank you personally," he said in English. "We are deeply grateful for all you have done."

"Thank you, Mister Minister," Tom replied, groping for the appropriate words. "I'm happy to have had your confidence and support. You have a long way to go to make the money move. There are all those feasibility studies and negotiations to get through. Still, I'll bet you're going to make it."

Manoukian grasped Tom's shoulder affectionately and turned to Mariah. "And now Miss Carroll, let me thank you, too. Dr. Yeager told me you were the best in the world at this mathematical thing," Manoukian said, a mischievous grin on his face. "You made the Committee's decision come easily." Manoukian paused only a moment before he added, "They were bewitched from the moment you walked into the room."

Mariah blushed, and said, "Whatever it takes, Mr. Minister. Whatever it takes."

****

The luncheon didn't break up until three in the afternoon and Tom was reeling with end-of-mission fatigue by the time he and Ana and Mariah emerged into the brisk air of Republic Square.

"I'm ready to sleep until take off time," Mariah said. "Really. Is there anything you need from me now?"

"I can't think of a thing," Tom said. "Go ahead and crash."

"Try a different term. I've already crashed once this trip."

"Sorry," Tom said. "Shall we all get together in Maran tonight? Eat some chicken? Listen to some good music?"

"Sure. Eight o'clock?"

Tom looked at Ana. She nodded.

"See you there."

When Mariah moved away toward the elevators, Ana said, "I want to show you something. Will the revisions take very long?"

"No," he answered. "I'm so blitzed from that long, liquid lunch I'm not sure I could concentrate on writing anyway. What do you want to show me?"

"One of our monuments."

"Is it far?"

"No, not far. Just across the river."

CHAPTER THIRTY

Swallow's Fortress Park and
the Genocide Memorial

They walked to Ana's apartment, picked up the Zhiguli and drove across the Razdan River to Swallow's Fortress Park. Ana drove into a parking area at the base of a hill and they got out.

"We will walk from here," she announced and Tom followed her into a wide walkway paved with smooth black stones that led up the hill. "This is the Avenue of Mourning. It leads to our Memorial to Victims of the Genocide, one and half million Armenians slaughtered by the Turks."

"When did this happen?" he asked.

"Most in 1915, but it began before and continued after, really until 1922."

"Genocide. You mean they tried to kill you all?"

"Yes," she replied. "They killed us because we were Armenians, like Hitler killed Jews. That is genocide, yes?"

"Yeah, I think so."

"It began with the last Sultan of the Ottoman Empire, Abdul Hamid, but the militaires--Enver and Talat--the Young Turks who deposed the Sultan--were worse. We supported them at first because they made us believe they would save us from the Sultan. But they betrayed us. It was their idea to kill us all from the beginning."

"But why?" he asked. "There must have been something--like Hitler blaming the Jews for Germany's problems."

"To say 'why' is difficult. Some say because we wished to remain Christians and keep our language. Perhaps we died for that. They said we were disloyal, but I think it was our land they wanted. Hitler wrote about Aryans being the Master Race. Enver and Talat thought something like that about ancient Turks and Mongols--Attila, Genghis Khan, Timur, those old barbarians. They wanted to put Turkey and Central Asia together, but Armenians lived in between, in the Caucasus and Eastern Turkey. And we were different. Not Turk, not Muslim. Whatever excuses they made, they meant to kill us and take our land. When war came to Europe--you call it the First World War--Europeans, even Russians, were too busy killing each other to care about Turks killing Armenians.”

As they approached the top of the hill, the monument itself came into view, first a needle-shaped stone obelisk and then a gigantic circle of stone steles leaning inward to guard an eternal flame. It was set in a massive plaza of paved stone, bereft of any other adornment.

“This is awesome,” he said as they walked into the huge plaza and felt the full impact of the hilltop site and its commanding view of Yerevan.

“The stones are said to bow in grief and to protect the fire that burns there to help us remember those who died. And there,” she said, pointing to the obelisk. “The needle is to make us think of our future and our hope, how we must rise up--tall and strong and sharp. It says we must stand against the storm and not be beaten down like grain.”

“The design’s magnificent,” Tom said. They were alone on the great plaza under an overcast sky, a chill wind swirling around them. “And this is very important to you, isn’t it?”

Her eyes fixed on his. “I will always be Armenian because to be anything else would dishonor those we remember here. I want you to see this because perhaps it has something to do with how I am.”

“I want to know more about it then,” Tom said. “But it’s cold out here. Why don’t we check out the eternal flame?” They crossed the expanse of the square, entered the circle of giant stones and sheltered against the wind. “Go on. I’m still with you.”

“To hate is not good,” she said. “So I do not hate Turks. What happened was many years ago and there were many good Turks who helped our people even then. But it is difficult to understand the awful things soldiers did when they took us from our villages.” She paused and Tom saw her faraway gaze, as if she were trying to go back in time to share the pain and the terror.

“Sometimes soldiers locked us in our churches and set them on fire. At Trabzon, they burned the churches but they also drove us into the harbor to drown us and shot us if we tried to swim to the land. In this way and in other ways, soldiers of the Sultan killed two hundred and fifty thousand of us. But the Young Turks who came after him killed even more. Do you want me to go on? It is written here--in

English and other languages. Perhaps it is better for you to read it."

"No," he said. "Go on."

Ana stared into the flame. Finally, she spoke again. "Many Armenians were good soldiers in Ottoman army. Good fighters. Brave fighters. But the Young Turks took away the guns from Armenian soldiers and put these good fighters into work battalions. They made them carry supplies and ammunition like animals and dig in the earth for--how do you say?--trenches. They did not feed them properly and made them sleep outside in cold and rain. If one became ill, Turkish soldiers shot him. The Turks could not kill fast enough this way so later, they marched our young men to a place where people would not see and told them to dig graves. Then they shoot them."

Ana paused and sighed deeply. "It was not enough to kill Armenians who could be fighters. Older men, ones left in the cities and villages, were put in prisons. These men were taken out at night and shot or hanged or beaten to death. In Ankara, to hide the dead bodies, they cut them--butchered, yes?--and threw the pieces into a river. A road went beside that river and they could not let people pass along it in daytime because no one could stand the sight or the smell. Even at night, when travelers could not see below, the smell was horrible."

Tom swallowed hard, fighting the nausea rising in his throat. "That's as bad as anything I know about Hitler's Holocaust," he said.

"These things were not all they did to us. They took our houses and our possessions, like Hitler took from Jews. And when there was no place for women and children and old men to sleep, they were sent away. 'Deported' I think you say. They were made to leave everything they could not carry and walk to Syria with little food or water or medicine. Summer for that year--1915--was very hot and many people died of hunger and thirst and sickness. The Turks did not give us medicine or try to make us well. Some arrived at Ras al'Ain, a Syrian town where Turks made a camp, but our people were so weak, many more died with fevers. Ones who lived were sent on--still walking--to another camp in the desert at Dier az-Zor, in Syria. Not many lived at Dier az-Zor." Ana stopped and didn't go on for several moments.

"There is more to tell," she said. "But it is enough for you to know that horrible things were done to us. Perhaps Americans and Europeans did not know what Hitler was doing to Jews, but I do not think so. Americans and Europeans did know what happened to Armenians. And if they remembered what happened to us, why did they not do more to help Jews? So many Armenians should not have died for nothing. Perhaps you will explain this to me some time."

CHAPTER THIRTY ONE

Hotel Armenia

Nikolai Danilov arrived from St. Petersburg on Friday morning, weary from the long flight. In the first light of day, he went into Republic Square for fresh air. Returning from his walk, he reached the sidewalk in front of the hotel and froze, unable to believe his eyes. The face he saw through the hotel doorway was older, but there was no question in his mind. He'd followed the man for weeks and he remembered that final night clearly. The man's raincoat where it landed when his shot threw him forward onto his face. Rolling him over, cutting the handcuff chain and taking the briefcase. Stunned brown eyes looking up at him, blood spreading a dark pool over the stones. Then the eyes glazed and their lids closed. No one in sight up or down the narrow cobbled street. No lights coming on suddenly in the apartments above. The taxi with its doors open, engine idling softly. Yes, he remembered it all quite well, even the heat of the silenced 9mm against his side and the weight of the briefcase as he walked away, his assignment complete, the last link in the chain broken.

His eyes now put a lie to that.

The Russian stepped off the sidewalk, finding partial concealment by the fender of the white, UNHCR Jeep. He took a cigarette from the case in the skirt of his suit coat and was surprised when he flicked his gold lighter and found his hand trembling. That diamond courier in Yerevan! A ghost from the past come to haunt him.

As he smoked nervously, confusion gave way to calculation. Had the game mutated and gone on? He'd been reassigned after Vienna, but he saw Glazunov from time to time for years after and Glazunov had never intimated that . . . But then Glazunov was retired and what was left of the old Soviet Union's treasures was being pillaged by anyone in a position to do so. The Siberian diamond mines might be leaking stones again. But why pass them through Armenia? Surely there were easier routes to the West these days. Unless . . . unless Avakian were part of the chain. Was he swapping Turkish drugs for Siberian diamonds and stealing Armenian antiquities on the side? Avakian--the idealist, the true believer--was ravaging the Soviet carcass like all the other jackals. And using an American courier for the diamonds. It was outrageous, hilarious, ingenious.

Danilov watched the American disappear behind the elevator doors and hurried up the stairs to wait for Avakian.

****

The Russian led Aleksandr into the sitting room of the corner suite and offered him tea. "Shall we?" Danilov said, indicating the balcony overlooking Republic Square. "Spring has almost come here. It will be at least two more months in St. Petersburg."

Aleksandr followed the Russian onto the balcony without commenting. But it was true. Warmed by the morning sun, the air had the moist promise of a maiden's kiss.

Danilov stared across the empty square at the History Museum where the Scout was parked in front of the massive fountain, still barren and dry. "So you have a private tunnel that leads to the vaults, eh?"

Aleksandr sighed. "Have you come to do business, Russian, or pry into my affairs?"

Danilov turned to face him, the sun winking off one of the lenses of his rimless glasses. He smiled and said, "Now, Sasha, don't be impatient. Of course I've come for business. I'm anxious to see what you have."

Aleksandr set his tea glass on the stone railing of the balcony and slipped one hand into the side pocket of his suit coat. He withdrew the brooch, still nestled in the square of black velvet, and settled it in the palm of his hand. He peeled away one corner of the cloth and then another until the little brooch lay exposed to the morning light.

The Russian took it and held it to his eye. "Magnificent," he said. "It's a good example of royal jewelry, Celtic design. The stones are small, though." He took a jeweler's loupe from his pocket and fitted it to his eye, examining the piece more closely. At last, he removed the loupe from his eye and returned it to his pocket. "Is there a provenance?"

Aleksandr handed the folded sheet of paper Sarkis had drawn up to the Russian.

Danilov scanned it quickly. "Excellent," he said. "With this, it should bring seventy-five thousand US, possibly a hundred with the right buyer. I'll give you ninety because I want to talk to you about something else."

The Russian was offering more for the brooch than Aleksandr had expected. And it was his opening offer. How high was he prepared to go? He decided to let the bargaining wait and see what else Danilov had on his mind.

"I'll consider it," Aleksandr said. "What's the other matter?"

"Consider it?" the Russian said, frowning. "My offer is more than generous. Give me 'yes' or 'no' before we move on. I'm not in the mood to haggle. Do you think your Frenchmen would give you so much?"

"They have not had the opportunity. Who knows? They might jump at the chance. I have a relationship with them."

The Russian smiled knowingly in a way that made Aleksandr uncomfortable. "I know more about your affairs than you imagine, Sasha," Danilov said.

"You're trying my patience, Russian. Come to the point."

"Very well. You're trading drugs for diamonds. Diamonds that are being stolen from our Siberian mines. I don't know if you're trading them on to your Frenchmen, but this morning I learned that you've recruited an American as your courier. Wonderfully devious. I compliment you, Sasha, and I apologize. I underestimated you."

Aleksandr laughed out loud.

"Where did you get such an idea? I have nothing to do with diamonds, not even in antiquities like that one," he said, pointing to the brooch that Danilov still held in his hand. "And American couriers? What makes you think that?"

The Russian kept his eyes fixed on Aleksandr, but he blinked them rapidly several times, the only indication that he was no longer sure of his footing.

"I saw him," he said, at last. "Here. This morning. I thought I killed him twenty years ago, but I saw him in this hotel an hour ago. Who else but you would bring a diamond courier to this God-forsaken rock pile of a country?"

"Look, Russian," Aleksandr said. "I know nothing about an

American diamond merchant. There are only two Americans in this city and they're economists, not diamond couriers. You've just seen someone who looks like one of your ghosts, that's all."

The Russian shook his head stubbornly. "There's no mistake. My last assignment in Glazunov's division. I followed him for weeks. I would know him anywhere."

"Twenty years ago," Aleksandr scoffed. "People change."

"Not this one. Yes, he's older, but he is the same one."

Aleksandr stared at the Russian, evaluating the information, turning it over in his mind. Images from the Mafia Restaurant flooded his mind--the Jordanian, Sarkis, his handsome wife, Ana, the American. Ana and the American. Sarkis and the American. Ana betraying him with the American. Was Sarkis now betraying him with the American? And that Jordanian toad--who was he? Marina had said he and Sarkis had the same last name.

"Tell me what you know about this American," Aleksandr demanded, his expression hard, his body tense.

The Russian shrugged. "Why not?" he asked of no one. "I'm sure you know that the world's diamond supply is controlled by the De Beers cartel in London. It's always been a leaky sieve and after we began production in Siberia in the nineteen-sixties, these Englishmen became concerned that we would break their control of the market. But the cartel had an appeal to our way of doing things, so we allowed them to market our diamonds along with the rest. Of course, they watched us like hungry hawks to see that we didn't cheat. That was how we discovered the diversions from our mines in the Yakut region, particularly Aikhal."

The Russian snapped open his gold cigarette case and held it out to Aleksandr. Aleksandr shook his head and the Russian took one for himself, lit it with a small gold lighter and watched the smoke drift out into Republic Square before he went on.

"The cartel's own security people pinpointed several outlets in Western Europe where diamonds were reaching the market outside its channels. Most were African stones, from the great mines in South Africa and Botswana and Namibia, what they called 'illegal' diamonds--that is, stolen from their mines. When small amounts of our production began to show up passing through these sources, they accused us of cheating on the agreement."

Danilov shrugged and put on a sly smile. "It turned out that there was great thievery going on, but the stones weren't passing through any of the sources the cartel had marked. But that's another story. After the screaming was done, we cooperated with them and I was given one of the sources to watch, to backtrack the chain. It was an Armenian, now that I think about it. His name was Petrossian. I sat on him for four months before anything promising appeared. Then one day, I saw two men at Petrossian's who didn't seem to be like his usual clients. I began following them. They turned out to be Americans posing as German. The older one was very good, very hard to follow. I tracked him around Europe for weeks. But the younger one was good, also."

Aleksandr sighed impatiently. "Get on with it, Russian. I don't care how clever you were."

"Eventually, the younger one showed up in Vienna. He met a Czech airline stewardess at Demel's. They didn't even sit down, much less sit together. It was almost a brush pass and I'd never have seen it if I hadn't been looking for it. Then we followed the Czech and she led us to a clerk at Almazjuvelexport in Moscow, you know, the trading company. Almazjuvelexport received diamonds from Aikhal and made up the shipments to De Beers in London. From time to time, we learned, there was a package of diamonds over and above the documented shipment--'cream' that had been skimmed at the Aikhal mines."

"Damn it, Russian," Aleksandr growled. "What about the American?"

"I'm coming to that," Danilov said, taking a drag from his cigarette. "Once we had identified the chain, I worked my way back down it, cutting the links. When the next shipment of diamonds arrived from Aikhal, I waited for the Almazjuvelexport clerk to pass it to the stewardess, then I 'cancelled' him. I flew with the stewardess to Vienna, followed her to a hotel and garroted her, leaving her and the package for the American. I think he panicked when he saw her dead. He took the package, though. I followed him out, put him down and took back the diamonds."

"If you 'put him down,' how is it that he is here?"

"Obviously because he didn't die after all. He was pouring blood. I saw his eyes glaze. There was no one in sight. He should have died. But he didn't. He's here. In this hotel."

Aleksandr was silent, staring intently at the Russian. "There are no diamonds here," he said. "I would know. Something else perhaps."

Danilov turned his back to the balcony rail and leaned against it, watching Aleksandr process the information.

"Perhaps what you say is true," Aleksandr said. "I suspected this American before you arrived. But I've had him watched day and night and nothing he's done indicates he's anything but what he claims to be--an economist working for the Ministry of Finance. Perhaps you taught him a lesson, Russian. Perhaps he's no longer active."

"You say you would know if there were diamonds here," the Russian said. "But what if the first shipment hasn't arrived yet? I've seen to Petrossian and the other American who worked with him for many years. The American who's here now is his son. They are like lizards who lose their tails but grow another. Where will these diamonds go? Not back to Petrossian. Perhaps on to Israel. Their diamond industry has become quite important."

"Or to Jordan and then to Israel. The Melikian who is here now--Sarkis' cousin--is part of a family that deals in gemstones. I saw them all together," Aleksandr said. "In the meantime, I'll show you my appreciation for the information by giving you the brooch at the price you offered. Ninety thousand. Send the wire. Dollars. When Zurich tells me it has the money, you'll have the brooch. I'll see you here as soon as I've heard from Zurich. Perhaps I'll have something more by then. Are you prepared to deal?"

"It will have to be immediately. I was able to get a room here only for tonight. There is an international meeting in Yerevan-- something about the Armenian Church. They're even putting people out of their rooms to accommodate the delegates."

Aleksandr was puzzled at first, then he remembered.

"The National Ecclesiastical Assembly." He paused to think a moment. "Everyone not with the Assembly is being put out of the hotel?" "That is what they told me," the Russian replied.

"That means the American will have to leave, too." Aleksandr held out his hand to take back the brooch. "There's no more time to waste."

CHAPTER THIRTY TWO

Sarkis' House

Karine's puzzlement turned to terror when Aleksandr and Deshnikov threw her back into the room and slammed the door.

"Where is he?" Aleksandr asked in a soft, sinister voice.

"Who are you?" Karine began. "You have no right . . ."

Aleksandr slapped her hard with the open palm of his hand, knocking her to the floor. Karine put a hand to her stinging face and shook her head to clear it.

"I have every right," he said, standing over her. "I'm the one who supplies your sister with narcotics. And your husband is betraying me. I'm going to show you how much that pains me while we wait for him to return."

"I don't know what you are talking . . ." Karine tried to protest, but Aleksandr raised his hand to strike her again and she stopped in mid-sentence.

"Tie her hands," Aleksandr said to Deshnikov. "And tape her mouth shut. Now, where is the little cripple?" he mused, looking first into Sarkis' and Karine's bedroom. He continued down the hall until he came to Setta's bedroom.

A tremor ran through Setta's body when Aleksandr appeared in her doorway. She stared at him with frightened, bulging eyes. Who was he? A new doctor? She didn't like him.

Aleksandr smiled when he saw the fear and confusion in her eyes. A droplet quivered from one of her nostrils and her face glistened with sweat.

"Here she is," he said. "Needing it badly, too, aren't we? We can go to work right away." He opened his briefcase and removed a vial and a hypodermic needle. "This is going to make you very wide awake and aware of absolutely everything. You'll feel things you haven't felt in years, doped up on morphine." Setta's lips curled into a snarl and she struck at him feebly.

"Get away," she said, her voice an angry, animal growl, her

wasted arms flailing. Aleksandr easily subdued her, seized her wrists and taped them together.

"Karine!" Setta screamed just before Aleksandr sealed her mouth with a strip of tape. He threw off the blanket and the sheet covering Setta, revealing her useless legs. With the hypodermic in one hand, he spread the toes of one of her feet with the other and injected the contents of the syringe. "Now we'll see how you feel in a few minutes. We'll bring your sister in to watch." Aleksandr called back to Deshnikov. "Ivan, bring the other one."

Setta began to fidget even before Deshnikov entered the room pushing Karine ahead of him. Karine's hands were tied behind her and her mouth sealed with a slab of tape.

Aleksandr grinned, "It's working already. This will be interesting."

"What's going on?" Deshnikov asked.

"An interrogation technique we used in Afghanistan--a 'cocktail' that amplifies the agonies of denial and withdrawal. She's been on heroin so long she's ripe for it. In half an hour, she'll be in agony. Her sister won't want to watch that. We'll find out what we want to know soon enough."

Setta's eyes began to roll wildly, pleading with Karine.

"Now, Karine," Aleksandr said a few minutes later. "I want to know what Sarkis is doing with this American I saw you with at Mafia. You understand what I'm going do to your little sister if you don't tell me? I'm going to take her right into the furnace of Hell and let the flames strip the flesh from her body. Can you imagine that, Karine? You can tell me what I want to know right now and Setta can go back to dreaming. Do you understand?"

Karine nodded and Aleksandr viciously ripped the tape from her mouth. Even Deshnikov winced. Karine's mouth stung from the force of the tape being torn from her skin and tears came to her eyes.

"We know nothing about the American," she whimpered. "Our cousin, Razmik Melikian, invited him. My husband has nothing to do with him," she gasped desperately.

"Karine, you will tell me eventually," Aleksandr said, shaking his head. "You're just prolonging Setta's agony." To Deshnikov, he added, "Tape her up again. This little one has not yet suffered enough."

"I'm telling the truth!" Karine screamed.

"Shut her up," Aleksandr said. Deshnikov pressed another piece of tape over Karine's mouth, but he looked at Aleksandr with revulsion.

Setta began to keen and moan through the tape over her mouth. Her eyes flicked frantically from side to side and seemed about to explode from their sockets. A seizure wracked her body and brought her rigid in the bed. Tears streamed from her eyes and an agonized moan escaped from beneath the tape across her mouth.

"Yes," Aleksandr said, watching. "She's feeling it now. Every blood vessel in her body is twisted in knots. I've seen blood pressure go almost off the meter. That's happening to her now. The whine in her head must sound like a jet engine."

With one eye on Setta's torment, Aleksandr filled a hypodermic needle from the vial containing the powerful stimulant, shook it vigorously and set it to one side. Then he took a bag of heroin from his briefcase. He melted the white powder in a spoon and filled a syringe with it. He smiled at the craving in Setta's eyes as she watched him prepare it.

"Now, Karine, look at your little sister's eyes. Look through those windows into her tormented soul. She's at the gates of Hell. She can feel the heat. See her sweat? The flames are licking her skin, Karine. Soon she'll think it's melting off her body. You can make it stop." He held up the syringe with the heroin. "This needle, Karine, has what Setta needs to stop her pain. It will put out the fire. But this other needle has my little 'cocktail' in it. I've already given her one and you see what it does to her. If I give her another, her pain will become much more intense, but she won't pass out, Karine, she'll go further into the fire. I'll keep her there until you tell me what I want to know. You will tell me, Karine. You know that don't you? Nothing Sarkis has is worth letting your sister suffer this way."

Karine's eyes were almost as wild as Setta's. She knew nothing of any arrangement between Sarkis and the American. But she knew about the coins. Karine tried to speak through the heavy tape and although she could not make her words understood, Aleksandr saw she was trying to tell him something. Again, he ripped the tape from her mouth.

"Yes?" he sneered.

"Coins," Karine gasped. "Gold coins. From Geghard."

"Where are they?" Aleksandr demanded.

"I don't know," Karine wailed. "Please stop torturing Setta!"

"Tell me everything you know. Now!" Aleksandr hissed.

"He brought them home. In a stone box. From a secret room in Geghard Monastery. Very old. Very beautiful. No one has ever seen them before. They aren't here. He must have taken them to the museum."

Aleksandr turned to Deshnikov. "Call the Museum and ask to speak to him. Tell him to bring the coins, that I'm here with his wife. He'll know what I mean."

Deshnikov shrugged and went to the telephone. When he got through to the museum, he was told that Mr. Melikian was ill.

"He's not there. They said he's sick."

Aleksandr glared at Karine.

"You're lying to me Karine. Where is he? Where are the coins?"

The tears streamed down Karine's face and her expression revealed her terror and anguish.

"Speak, bitch!"

"I cannot tell you what I do not know," Karine pleaded.

"Has the American come to take these coins out? To sell them? What about the cousin? Is he after diamonds?"

"We don't know anything about the American."

Aleksandr snorted. "Tape her up again. She's not telling me everything yet. She knows what Sarkis and the American are doing. We'll take her sister a little higher and see if that improves her memory." Aleksandr jabbed the needle into Setta's shoulder and emptied it.

"No! Please!" Karine screamed. Straining frantically against Deshnikov's efforts to tape her mouth closed, she felt her bonds loosen. Deshnikov was holding her shoulders back against the chair, but from the side of her eye she saw where her knitting needles lay on the table beside Setta's bed.

Another seizure struck Setta like a hammer. She quivered and shook and then became rigid in the bed, emitting a shriek through clenched teeth that they heard even through the tape over her mouth. Aleksandr stared at her as the violent seizure intensified. Suddenly, a stream of blood spurted from her nose and her head fell to one side on the pillow. With a desperate burst of strength, Karine broke free of the cords that tied her hands to the chair, seized one of the knitting needles and lunged at Aleksandr. He caught the movement from the corner of his eye and threw up his arm an instant before the long needle pierced his heart. Karine struck with such force that it passed all the way through the flesh of his arm. The hypodermic fell from his hand, the needle point striking the floor and breaking.

Deshnikov caught Karine by the hair and pulled her away from Aleksandr.

"Bitch!" Aleksandr spat at Karine. Grimacing with pain, he withdrew the bloody knitting needle from his arm and struck Karine with the fist of his other hand. With Deshnikov holding her head by the hair, the blow twisted her neck and severed her spinal cord in the region of the cervical vertebrae. Her body crumpled and she died instantly. Deshnikov felt her dead weight and recoiled, releasing her to fall to the carpet.

The only sound in the room for a long moment was the drip of blood on the parquet floor from Aleksandr's wounded arm. Deshnikov knew Karine was dead. He looked at Setta. A trickle of blood oozed from her nostrils and she was completely still. They were both dead.

"We're leaving. Come on," Deshnikov said, taking the stunned Aleksandr by his uninjured arm and dragging him into the kitchen, out through the back door and into the parking area behind the building.

CHAPTER THIRTY THREE

The USAID Mission; Government House;
Hotel Armenia; Republic Square

"We're grateful for the fine job you've done here, Dr. Yeager," George Marcos said, standing in the doorway of his office. "You, too, Miss Carroll. I imagine the Armenians are pleased."

"We're glad it worked out," Mariah said.

"We'll get you two out here again soon, I'm sure. This is going to be a big program. The contracting people will sort all that out," Marcos said, looking at his watch and stepping back into his office. "I'm off to Baku for a few days. It's exciting juggling three countries with different problems, two of which are at war with each other. Sometimes I can't remember which is which." He thought that was funny and laughed.

"Good luck with the juggling act," Tom said to Marcos and steered Mariah toward the stairs.

Bob Lange followed them down and stood with them in the courtyard of the Mission. "I hope to see you two down the road," he said, holding out a hand to Mariah, then to Tom. "Sorry the whole thing got off to such a rough start. Oh, I forgot to tell you. It's a good idea to get to the airport early. It's a free-style operation. You never know the drill until you get there. It's whatever they feel like that day."

"Thanks for the heads up."

"Got a ride to the airport?" Lange asked.

"Yeah. We're going to take our stuff over to Ana Stepanian's, have dinner there and then she's going to take us."

"I forgot to ask," Lange said. "Did you exit with the Minister of Finance?"

"Didn't really need to," Tom said. "Ana's over there now, just to make sure. We'll go over if there's anything else he wants to talk about. I doubt it, though. He worked very closely with us on this one and he was headed out to his dacha for the weekend. What do they do out there anyway? It's too early for gardening."

"Decompress," Lange said. "I'm going to do a little of that myself this weekend--eat some shashlik, drink a little vodka, tell a few lies, play some cards." Lange looked through the small courtyard, past the steel gate. "I see Sam's waiting for you in the Cherokee. Have a good flight."

****

Manoukian smoked steadily as he chatted with Ana. "Your work was superb," he said. "The stakes were very high."

"Thank you, Mr. Minister," she replied. "It was an exciting challenge and I was proud to help my country."

"You realize I will continue to need your help with these World Bank people and their feasibility studies. I've decided that you should join my personal staff."

Ana smiled broadly. "I'm very flattered, Mr. Minister. When?"

"Immediately. This afternoon if you like."

"That's so . . . so thrilling," Ana exclaimed. "But please, Mr. Minister, to begin so soon . . . As you know, we worked many hours these last few days and I am quite tired. And Mother is in St. Petersburg with my aunt. I have planned to spend two weeks with them there."

"Well, I'm disappointed," Manoukian said and went silent for a few moments. "You're right, of course. You should take some rest. But your country needs you, young lady. Don't forget that," he said, smiling and wagging his finger at her.

"Thank you, Mr. Minister. I'm honored that you would say these things to me. And I appreciate your understanding. I promise to call when I return. I do not think the World Bank can reply sooner than that."

Ana breezed out of the Minister's office and floated down the corridor on a cloud of exhilaration, forgetting her fatigue. 'How incredible,' she thought. 'A job, a permanent job, on the personal staff of the Minister of Finance, who could be the next President of Armenia.'

****

Mariah had released her room to accommodate the next wave of incoming delegates and brought her bags to Tom's room just after two o'clock that afternoon. She was dressed for travel--jeans, jogging shoes and a sloppy sweater. Tom, too, had packed his ties, his blue blazer and

221

gray slacks and was wearing comfortable clothes--khakis, desert boots, and an Oxford-cloth shirt with a button-down collar.

"Want some air?" he asked when she'd settled her gear at the foot of one of the beds.

Fatigue rimming her eyes, Mariah replied wearily, "Yeah, that might be just the thing."

Outside they inhaled the cold mountain air and, out of habit, Tom steered them toward Government House. As they passed behind Lenin's empty pedestal, Mariah slipped her hand into his and stared down the cascade of fountains. "It could be a pretty place, couldn't it?" she said.

"This time tomorrow, we'll be in Amsterdam," he said. "The tulips should still be in bloom. Some of them at least."

"Is that what you've got in mind for Amsterdam?" Mariah asked. "Tour the tulips?"

"Not necessarily," he said. "We can prowl the canals, drink beer, do the Rijksmuseum. Vermeers and Rembrandts and Steens. They've got a ton of Indonesian restaurants. I never seem to get past satay. You could show me how to order."

"Forget that. I don't care if I ever taste peanut sauce again."

"Hey, it's a good time of year to be in Amsterdam. I'm wide open to suggestions."

"We could do a lot of things in Amsterdam, but there's one thing I definitely want to do."

"What's that?"

"We said no holds barred, didn't we?"

Tom nodded, the intensity that had overcome her fatigue bringing half a smile to his face.

"I want a no-holds-barred conversation with you," she said. "There are some things I need to tell you and some things I want you to tell me."

"For instance?"

"I used to think that all that mattered was what two people were when they were together, but seeing you at the lake changed my mind about that. I didn't know you had a place at the lake. I didn't know you rode horses. I didn't know you played golf or cooked lamb with Montrachet cheese or a million other things. I've been thinking since then that it's why our relationship is so damned shallow. I don't want it to be. I want to know if you're an ex-con, if the kids threw rocks at you when you were in school, I want to know if you can drive a stick shift." She stopped and caught her breath. "And I want you to know why I got engaged to Cameron. And why I broke it off."

"And that's all?" he asked, choking back a laugh, hating himself for it. She was intently serious.

She caught a little of his mood, relaxed and said, "No. I want to find out all these things in a great big bed in a great big room with a great big bathtub. A Jacuzzi. And room service. Maybe you could get them to send in tulips and a picture postcard of the windmills. Most particularly, I want a bottle of pisco añejo. Among this inexhaustible supply of things I want to know about you is where things stand with Ana."

Tom led her onto the sidewalk in front of the arch where Mt. Ararat occasionally appeared. There were fewer people milling around the phones than there would have been at mid-morning, but two foreigners still drew attention.

"Tommy," Mariah said, pulling him to a stop. "I'd be dead stupid if I didn't know there might be some connection between you and Ana. That said, I'm not going to let this slide. For the record, you need to know that I really care about you. Maybe it's not ever going to work out for us, but that doesn't mean I don't love you." There. She'd said it. Now she looked up at him, her eyes shining, waiting for him to . . . do something.

"Why did you get engaged to Cameron What's-his-name?"

That wasn't what she wanted to hear. Fatigue swept over her again, as if she'd only had that little bit of reserve to fling down a gauntlet. "I'm not ready for this. I just wanted to set an agenda."

"Oh, no you don't," he said. "You're not going to leave me hanging like that now. I've wondered about it for a long time."

"Why'd you wonder?" she parried.

"Don't answer a question with a question. You said you wanted to tell me why you got engaged to Cameron."

She let go of his hand, folded her arms and fixed her eyes on his. "I got engaged to Cameron because I could never catch up with you. Don't you realize that after Peru, we went for a whole year--fourteen months, actually--without seeing each other? I called that damned answering machine of yours a hundred times."

"And I called yours--from all over the frigging world," he shot back, stung and suddenly a little angry. It wasn't his fault.

She ignored his defense and shook her head. "I started to feel like we'd had a one-week stand, just something that happened because Seline walked out on you, and we weren't ever going to have anything more. Maybe it wasn't anybody's fault . . . yours or mine. But it hurt. And I heard my clock ticking. It was stupid of me, but I went to a class reunion and there were girls I went to college with, ones who batted their eyes and spread their legs for the football team instead of grinding out A's. They were living in nice houses in nice suburbs, getting ready to watch their kids graduate from high school. I felt left behind, like I was missing something."

She sighed. "I know, I know. They haven't done half the things I've done. I've been around the world a dozen times, met interesting people and some downright bizarre ones. I've eaten stuff that would turn most stomachs--you know. Once in awhile I actually feel like I did some good. But at that moment, I felt like I was a dandelion gone to fluff and the wind was blowing."

They stepped off the sidewalk to avoid the crowd in front of the Post Office and walked a little ways into the square.

"Cameron What's-his-name showed up about that time, right?"

"He did. Every girl's dream husband. After all those years. Would you believe that my first date ever was for the senior prom. And I had to ask the guy. He didn't even go to my school."

"Unbelievable," he said. "I would have guessed you'd have been in somebody's back seat every night."

"A lot you know," she said. "And I don't appreciate your disrespectful opinion of my virtue. I was the last person on earth to be a slut."

"I was thinking about talent, not virtue," he said.

"Look, buster, I didn't lose my virginity until I was a sophomore in college. I was a scrawny kid. I wore glasses and braces and the full complement of my body parts didn't arrive until I was almost eighteen."

He chuckled. "I really don't believe that."

She shrugged. "After those two dates in Washington, you can't imagine what Peru meant to me. I was a complete sexual novice. Surely you noticed. I was no match for you at all."

"If that's true, you are truly gifted. You deserved a master's degree in the subject when I left for La Paz."

"I've always been a quick study. But after that incredible week there was nothing. No contact. We couldn't even make the phones work."

"Maybe that explains why you got engaged, but why'd you break it off?" he asked.

"Tunisia," she said, suddenly discovering that the crowd of people on the sidewalk had drifted into a loose semi-circle around them.

"Oh, my God," Mariah said. "We have an audience. Half of bloody Yerevan is watching us."

Tom laughed. "They don't know what we're saying."

"You're not sure about that," she said. "Let's get out of here."

Tom waved to the grinning crowd, threw his arm around her shoulder and walked her away from their curious eyes. Her arm went around his waist and they fell into step. They cut the corner at Tigran Metz, ducked into the arcade of Government House and walked in the shadows, finally reaching a quiet corner.

"You were saying you dumped Cameron because of Tunisia," he prompted.

"OK. I've come this far. I might as well finish it." She took a deep breath and let it go. "I took that gig to prove to myself that I was over you, that I was ready to have a normal life with Cameron. He wanted me to be a stay-at-home mom. Pick him up at the train station. Play bridge with the neighbors. I could see that I was going to be bored out of my skull in no time."

She shook her head. "It's important for me to try to do something worthwhile. And it's important for me to be who I've become. I don't want to haul all my baggage around with me. I'm not making sense, am I?"

"It'll work out," he said. "Just keep talking."

"I took the job flying for Vaquero because I couldn't stand the idea of living where I grew up. People you know as a kid always remember you as a kid. Out here, people see you for what you are, not what you were when you wore braces and didn't have tits."

He smiled. "What else?"

"You were what else. I fell in love with you all over again in Tunisia. Or maybe I'd never stopped. Anyway, I wasn't over you. By the time I got that stuff sorted out--how I wanted to live and who I loved--you were gone again. Chile, I think it was."

"You never told me any of this," he said.

"I know. That was my fault. But that's why I'm telling you now. I don't want to make the same mistake twice." She searched his eyes for some clue to what he was thinking. She desperately wanted him to say something loving, but he just smiled at her. There was love in his eyes, wasn't there? What the hell was he thinking?

She swallowed and played her last card. "Tommy, I'm going to go to dinner at Ana's house tonight and I suppose I'll have to endure watching the two of you saying some kind of gushy goodbye. I won't like that, but I want you to know that whatever happens, I'll be there for you if . . . well, no ifs. I'll be there for you, no matter what."

He put his arms around her, drew her to him and whispered into her hair. "You make me feel very cariñoso. Remember your Spanish?"

She drew back from his embrace. "Cariñoso. Affectionate, loving?"

"That's it. But for me, there's a little more. It's also feeling warm when the air is cold and the storm is blowing all around you. When I was little, I used to go out on the porch when a blue norther came through. The temp would drop thirty degrees in ten minutes. The thunder would roar like some great awesome beast on the prowl and the lightning would explode around you, singe your hair and light up that ugly, dark sky. You'd be right there on the edge of chaos, watching the universe at war. One day I was out there in a norther and my grandmother brought out an old sheepskin coat and wrapped me up in it. Then she put her arms around me and stood there with me. I could smell the storm raging all around but I was warm and safe in that coat and she was there with me. I still have it. It was my grandfather's."

"You wore it at the lake," she said and smiled at him in wonder, her anger gone. "Tommy, my dear heart, I've never heard you talk like that. It's practically poetic."

He looked into her eyes for a long time, as if he were trying to see into her deepest, darkest places. "Think I should kiss you now?"

Her eyes misted. "Damned well better," she said, standing on tiptoes to lift her mouth to his, kissing him fully, wanting to make sure he'd never forget it.

CHAPTER THIRTY FOUR

Aleksandr Avakian's House

Aleksandr's arm began to throb before he and Deshnikov reached his apartment. He'd said nothing during their flight from Sarkis' flat, though it had taken only a few minutes for him to recover from the shock of seeing both women die so suddenly. He went straight to the kitchen and put water on to heat. Deshnikov followed in a trance, still stunned by what they'd done. Aleksandr found the vodka, took a long drink from the bottle and passed it to Deshnikov. Deshnikov upended it and drank until he choked. Coughing and sputtering, he took the bottle from his mouth and fell into a chair.

Aleksandr peeled away the blood-soaked shirt sleeve from his punctured arm. The knitting needle hadn't struck an artery, but there was a knot of swelling and blood was still seeping from it. He inspected the wound and went into the bathroom. He found peroxide, gauze, tape and a bottle of pain pills in the medicine cabinet. He swallowed two pain pills, took a towel from the rack and went back into the kitchen, where the water had begun to steam. He dipped the towel in the water and sponged the wound clean, bathed it in peroxide and tried to rally Deshnikov. "Ivan, come on. Help me," he said. When Deshnikov stared stupidly at Aleksandr's arm, Aleksandr screamed at him. "Do it, man! What's the matter with you? You've seen blood before."

Deshnikov shook it off and said dully, "Don't worry. I'll fix it." He fumbled through the task of making a bandage to cover the puncture, then examined the wound closely before he taped the bandage on. "You need a doctor for this," he said. "That's a hole in your arm, not a scratch. If it gets infected, you could lose it."

"Later," Aleksandr said. "Right now, we have to find out where that sonofabitch is keeping those coins. We should have searched the apartment. He wouldn't have taken them to the museum. They're still in that damned apartment."

"Go back if you want to," Deshnikov said. "But I'm not going with you."

"We don't have to go back. He'll come home eventually. We'll follow him from there."

"And then what?"

"I don't know," Aleksandr conceded. "Go to the hotel and bring Danilov here. I want to talk to him."

****

"That's what she said. That they were very old, came from a secret room and that no one had ever seen them before," Aleksandr said.

"She said gold? And very beautiful?" Danilov asked.

Aleksandr nodded. "Can you guess what they are?"

"I don't deal in coins," the Russian said. "But I know a little. When I was here before, I saw an exhibit at your museum--Coins of the Kings, I think it was called. There were three gold coins in it, two tahekans and a half tahekan. I think the plaque said they were the first gold coins minted in Armenia. By King Levon I, around twelve hundred AD. But they're crude affairs. Not in the Greek style, but the Roman. No one would think to describe them as beautiful."

"So what do you make of it?"

The Russian lit a cigarette and paced across Aleksandr's carpet, seeming to give more attention to it than to the question.

After some moments, he stopped pacing and fixed Aleksandr with his dark eyes. "Never seen before?" he asked.

"That is what she said."

"If that is what your man told her, they could predate the gold coins of King Levon. If they are truly unknown--never circulated--and I assume your man would know--they could be patterns. Incredibly valuable."

"What do you mean by patterns?"

"The model for a coin that is presented to the monarch for approval before the coin is issued. The patterns typically go into the royal treasury and are kept as the personal property of the king--the crown jewels of coinage," the Russian said. "If they were never issued, collectors would be wild for them. Particularly if there were a story to go with them. The 'secret room' conjures up a fabulous vision. Are you sure she didn't say anything more?"

"That was all."

"Pity you killed her."

"It was an accident," Aleksandr protested. "The bitch tried to kill me."

The Russian nodded. "I've told you as much as I can then. What will you do now?"

"The coins explain why your American is here. Sarkis is making a deal to send the coins out of the country. I feel it in my bones. They were talking about coins at the Mafia that night. Yes. That's it. So Sarkis will come home this evening from wherever he has been. He won't know anything has happened. We could take him then or wait until he tries to leave. I'll make him tell me where the coins are." He looked at the Russian. "Are you prepared to deal for them?"

Danilov shrugged. "I have to see them first, but they're interesting, of course."

Aleksandr looked out the window and made his decision coldly. It was time to leave. His Swiss account held more than fifty million dollars and he liked the Armenian winters less and less. Back to Mexico. A place on the beach, in the sun. Pacific breezes. But he was going to punish Sarkis for his betrayal. The Russian could have the coins. Let Sarkis try to explain what happened to them. The American was different. He'd see him on his knees, puking and begging for his life before that was done.

He picked up the phone and dialed a number. "This is Avakian," he said when a voice answered. "I want to speak to Zarkarian. Right away."

There was a long pause. Finally, the voice came back on the line. "If you are Avakian, you will remember what years you were in Afghanistan."

"Idiot! Of course I remember. Eighty-five to eighty-seven. Tell that fat-assed sonofabitch to pick up the phone and talk to me," Aleksandr sputtered, exasperated. Before the telephone talker could cover the mouthpiece, Aleksandr heard the roar of laughter he remembered from long ago and knew that the head of the Armenian Mafia himself posed the identification question.

"Aleks," Zarkarian said into the mouthpiece. "It's been a long time."

"I don't have time to play your games," Aleksandr said. "I've decided to retire. If you want my Turkish network, it will have to be today. What's your answer?"

"Of course I want it, Aleks," Zarkarian said. "How much?"

"The money's secondary. Right now I need manpower--about twenty of your best to help me clear up some last minute details."

"For how long?"

"If your people are any good, they should be through tonight."

"This is interesting, Aleks. What's it about?"

"You don't need to know. Your men won't get hurt unless they shoot each other. Do we have a deal?"

"I'd like to know about the money, Aleks. You can have the men, but I won't pay an outrageous price for your Turkish operations. They're not worth much without you."

Aleksandr paused for a moment. The price was for honor. He didn't need the money. "A million US, payable to my account in Zurich. I'll give you the number and trust you to send the money. When the money's deposited, I'll give you a list of my agents and their commissions and inform them of the change of control before I leave."

"Throw in the airplane," Zarkarian said.

"You can have the plane for what I paid--seventy five thousand US--but the pilot goes with it and he's in for five per cent of the Turkish operations. I'll expect you to honor that."

"Agreed. When and where do you want the troops?"

Aleksandr rattled off his account number and explained to Zarkarian how to deploy the men. "I want two of them to watch an apartment building, pick up a man and bring him to me. There's another man in the Hotel Armenia--an American. Six men for that. And four men to block the American Embassy. I don't want him running into that rabbit hole if we can't take him in the hotel. The others will go to Zvartnots Airport, to passport control and the ticket counters. I want it done quietly, Zarkarian. I don't want the riot police called out. Have your detail leaders report to me here in the hotel, room five-twenty-five, and I'll tell them who they're looking for. We need communications equipment, too."

"Ah, Aleks, always thinking of everything. Four details, right? And radios. Yes, Aleks, we have enough for that."

CHAPTER THIRTY FIVE

Matenaderan Library

Sarkis felt a tingle as he rolled the microfilm through the fragments of the diary of Petros, a monk of Geghard Monastery who made his last entry in 422 AD. Sarkis had reached the entry for June 11, 410. Fr. Petros was recounting the progress of construction of a special workroom in the Chapel of the Upper Tier. The day before Sarkis had discovered a Treasury order dated April 15 transferring 30 Roman ounces of fine gold to the custody of the Abbot of Geghard Monastery. It was plausible that this was the gold that had been used for the coins.

Piecing together Fr. Petros' account of who was to occupy the workroom and for what purpose took Sarkis another hour paging through the journal. He learned that the new occupant of the workroom was a Sicilian dwarf named Palitus, who had come to Geghard under the special protection of Vram Shapur, King of Armenia. Who Palitus was and what he was doing in his special workroom, however, was a mystery to the brotherhood at Geghard until the summer of 413 when a wandering penitent recognized the dwarf and revealed his identity and the story that went with it.

Palitus had been a master engraver at the Royal Mint in Syracuse. He had offended the Roman Emperor, Honorius, by making Honorius' nose too large on a new issue of coinage. In a fit of pique, Honorius stripped Palitus of his position at the mint and banished him from the territories of the Empire.

The penitent knew nothing of how Palitus had found his way into the court of the King of Armenia, but he gained favor with Vram Shapur, who made a place for him at Geghard. The penitent's story created a stir among the brotherhood, but Fr. Petros' references to Palitus disappeared for several years.

Sarkis strained his eyes through page after page of Fr. Petros' cramped handwriting in frustration before he found an account of Palitus' sudden disappearance and the sealing of the workroom in 416 on the order of the Abbot. No other monk was ever permitted to enter the workroom and the Abbot was the last to leave it. Fr. Petros made no mention of what Palitus had done there.

If Palitus had been the engraver of the gold coins discovered at Geghard--and it seemed obvious that he was--he was an extremely talented one. The artistic style of the coins was certainly in the classical Greek tradition, but they were pathbreaking in many respects, too.

He wrote down the references for the journal, copied the text from the relevant dates onto a pad of paper and went on without finding another reference to Palitus.

Then Sarkis went back to the source material on Vram Shapur's reign, looking for an explanation for why the coins had never been issued. After an hour, he found a listing of messages for the year 416 passing between the court of King Vram Shapur and the Roman Emperor in the East, Theodosius II, whose uncle, Honorius, reigned in the West. What piqued his interest were two messages from Honorius, who would not ordinarily have been communicating with the Armenian king. Armenia was in the sphere of the Eastern Empire.

It took another hour's searching, but it was worth the effort. Honorius had learned of Palitus' presence in the Armenian court, probably through the reports of the penitent who had recognized Palitus. Although the records were incomplete and Sarkis' command of Latin was limited, he was able to deduce that Honorius had issued a general prohibition over the issuance of any coins designed by Palitus. Vram Shapur had protested the Roman emperor's meddling in the affairs of the Armenian state, but Theodosius II had weighed in on Honorius' behalf and, in effect, denied Vram Shapur permission to issue coinage. There was no mention of specific coins, much less the gold coins Sarkis now had in his possession, but Palitus disappeared and the workroom at Geghard was sealed that same year. Both the king and the Abbot of Geghard died the following year, taking the secret of the coins and of Vram Shapur's humiliation by Honorius and Theodosius II to their graves.

If his interpretation was correct, it illustrated how Armenia's independence was restricted by the Romans. How Vram Shapur must have chafed to have been threatened by the Roman Emperor. Just as Tigranes had been humbled after his defeat by Lucullus at Tigranocerta and forced to kneel to Rome, Vram Shapur's Armenia had still been subject to Roman whim.

More than any tangible object Sarkis could imagine, Palitus' gold coins symbolized Armenia's repressed independence--by Roman, Persians, Turks and Russians.

He sat back, his head throbbing from squinting into the harsh light of the microfilm reader. His neck and back were cramping as well, but it was a small price to pay for being able to prove that the coins were not only genuine, but venerable symbols of the essence of Armenian independence.

The prize he'd always dreamed of was there before him. Armenia was once again independent, but beset on all sides. What these coins would say to the world and to the Armenian people was that their freedom was only delayed, not denied. Perhaps the new government would want to use Palitus' patterns for a new issue of coinage, one that would validate the nation's new freedom. And he, Sarkis Melikian, had become their deliverer. He would achieve the pinnacle of his career, become a hero to his nation.

His elation lasted only a moment. He knew the victory would be denied him. Nothing could heal the breach of trust he'd committed to feed Setta's addiction. Fame did not await him, only duty. He had to complete his authentication and deliver the coins to the government. Then he and Karine and Setta would quietly leave Armenia and disappear into some far away corner of the world.

****

"Karine," he called as he came through the front door of the flat. "I'm home." There was no answer and the apartment was dark and cold. "Karine?" he called again, an anxious feeling seizing him. He hurried through the rooms--their bedroom, the kitchen, finally Setta's room. His heart stopped.

Setta lay rigid in the bed, her arms stretched out in front of her, wrists taped together, a trail of blood from her nostrils caked on the pillow. Karine's body was a twisted rag doll crumpled on the floor, her head at an unnatural angle, a chair turned on its side nearby. He went to his knees beside Karine and touched her cheek.

"Karine?" he said softly, as if to wake her. "Karine?" He straightened her head and carefully lifted her onto his lap. Her body resisted. The apartment was cold and rigor mortis had begun to mold her as she had fallen. "Karine," he whispered, rocking her slowly back and forth. "Oh, Karine. Karine. Oh, God, why? Why you, my darling?" he asked, tears streaming down his face.

After a time, his weeping subsided, but he continued to hold her in his arms. He sat there, rocking her gently, until the room grew dark and he realized that the dream was over. No little girl of their own with Karine's eyes, no warm skin beneath the cover on cold nights, no more laughter, no one to share . . . everything.

"Karine," he sobbed. "I miss you so much."

He knew there was no one but Aleksandr who could have done this. In an agony that went beyond what he could endure, he also knew that Karine had told him about the coins. Aleksandr would come for them. If he lost these precious coins to Aleksandr, they would disappear into the vaults of some greedy collector, never to be seen again. Armenia's loss was too great to imagine.

Sarkis lifted Karine in his arms and stood stiffly. He hadn't realized how little she weighed. He put her body next to Setta's and covered it with the blanket from the foot of the bed. He knelt down beside the bed and said a last goodbye to her. "My love, my dearest heart, I cannot stay to honor you. But I know you understand. I will always love you. And I will avenge you. I will come down on Aleksandr with all the wrath of an angel of God."

He rose, stumbled into the bathroom and threw cold water on his face. There were things he had to do.

He lit the candles in the candelabra on the table in his and Karine's bedroom, rolled the wardrobe away from the wall and removed his coin collection, the dies and the gold coins of Geghard. Then he sat down in the straight chair at the little table and began to write.

Outside, one of Zarkarian's troops clicked the 'send' button on his radio and reported that a light had gone on in the apartment.

CHAPTER THIRTY SIX

Ana's House

Ana had just put on her leather coat, picked up her shoulder bag and was preparing to leave for the hotel to pick up Tom and Mariah when she heard a knock at her door. She found Sarkis, his battered satchel in one hand, a slender olive-wood box in the other.

"Barev, Sarkis," she greeted him, swinging the door open to allow him to enter. "Come in. I was wondering when you would come. I called the museum today, but they said . . . " Her last words trailed off. Sarkis seemed haggard and dazed.

"Sarkis? What is it? What's wrong?" she asked, taking his arm and pulling him into the foyer, closing the door behind him.

"This must go with the American," Sarkis said, holding out the olive wood box. "Can you take it? My coins. For Razmik. He must protect them until I come. It is so important."

"Of course," Ana said, taking the box from him. "Come. Sit down, Sarkis. You don't look well."

He stumbled into the living room and Ana helped him into a chair. When she had him seated, she relit one of the candles she'd just extinguished and the room came back to life.

Sarkis blinked against the light and looked around, trying to orient himself. He looked at the satchel in his lap and seemed to focus. He unfastened its straps, pulled back the flap and reached inside, withdrew two cloth-wrapped packages and held them out to Ana. One contained the Parthian necklace. The other, smaller package, held the carnelian seal. "I bought these for Razmik," he said. "The American promised to take them to him. These must go, too." He handed her two envelopes, sealed with red wax.

Ana took them absently and tucked them away in her leather shoulder bag. "Would you like some cognac? You look awful."

"Yes, please," Sarkis said. Ana rushed to a cupboard, brought out a bottle of cognac and, with trembling hands, filled a glass for him. He swallowed the amber liquid, but scarcely showed more signs of life than when he'd stood in the door.

"Karine is dead. Setta, too," he blurted, his voice cracking. "Aleksandr killed them."

Ana was stunned. "I don't understand," she said. "Dead? How?"

Ana knelt down beside his chair again and took his hand. "Sarkis, tell me what happened."

In a confused, disjointed way, Sarkis mumbled the story of how he'd been led to Aleksandr in search of drugs to relieve Setta's pain and how he'd been stealing artifacts from the museum to pay for them. Finally, he told her in sketchy terms about his enterprise with Raz to escape from Aleksandr and Armenia. His mind seemed to clear a little as he talked.

"Why didn't Setta go to the hospital?" Ana asked. "My mother is a doctor. We have wonderful facilities."

Sarkis shook his head slowly. "They gave her morphine for too long. When they could do nothing more for her, they sent her to a place for addicts. But the blockade . . . they had no drugs for them. It was horrible--a cage for lunatics. Karine couldn't leave her there."

"But stealing from the museum . . ."

"I had no other way," Sarkis said, hanging his head. "And Aleksandr had no pity on us. He only wanted more and grander things from me."

"Why do you think he killed Karine?" she asked, not wanting to believe Aleksandr was responsible.

"It could have been no one else. And he must know what I have now. Karine was tied to a chair. They tortured her." He broke down for a moment, sobbing, choking. When he recovered himself, there was cold fury in his voice. "This thing must be done first. Then I will find him and kill him--with my bare hands. I want to squeeze the eyes from his head."

Suddenly, the glass in Sarkis' hand exploded. Ana, still kneeling beside him, tried to jump back and lost her balance, ending up sprawled on the floor.

Sarkis was shaken from his savage fury. "I am so sorry," he said, reaching out to help her up with a hand dripping blood. A shard of glass was still imbedded in its heel.

Ana pulled away and rose on her own. "Sit there. Stay there," she commanded. "I'll get a bandage."

She ran to the bathroom, returning with a damp cloth, iodine, gauze and adhesive tape. She plucked the glass shards from his hand and cleaned the wound as best she could, then bandaged it. As she finished, she asked, "Have you called the police?"

Sarkis looked at her with frightened eyes.

"No. They would put me in prison. Don't you understand? I have taken things from the museum. I am a thief."

"But what about Karine?" Ana said, horrified that her dead body was lying in a cold, dark apartment.

"I can't go back now. I left money for Mrs. Kebussyan. Our neighbor. She will take care of Karine and Setta."

"Where will you go?"

"To the mountains. Beyond Garni."

"Did you see anyone on your way here?" Ana asked, suddenly alert. Without waiting for him to respond, she went to the bedroom window that faced onto the street and stood to one side of the curtain. Drawing it back enough to peer out, she saw Sarkis' Zhiguli at the curb. Across the street the glow of a cigarette made an orange dot in the black night. Someone was watching. Her heart began to pound as she slowly let the curtain fall into place.

"We must leave," she whispered to Sarkis. "Quickly." She took his arm and tried to pull him from the chair. Slowly, he rose and stood beside her as she dragged him toward the back door.

"Wait," he said. "This must go, too. Give it to Razmik." He pressed a third envelope into her hand.

She plunged it into her shoulder bag. "We have to leave now."

"The coins," Sarkis said. He picked up the olive wood box and handed it to Ana again.

She took it and yanked his sleeve hard. "Move!" she hissed.

A shoe scraped on the stairs leading into her building. Even Sarkis noticed and began to move at last. Ana saw the handle of her front door turn and was thankful it locked automatically. She led him through the back door of the apartment onto the balcony and into the night. Still holding his sleeve, she took one slow, careful step after another until the railing of the balcony came into her outstretched hand. Two more paces put her on the top step of the stairs. Sarkis shuffled along behind her. She heard the door of her apartment crash open and knew the lock had been forced. Her heart pounding, adrenaline rushing into her veins, she managed the six steps down to the courtyard and broke Sarkis' fall when he stumbled on the last one. They struggled up quickly. Ana's Zhiguli was only a few meters away.

"Get in, Sarkis," she whispered to him urgently, opening the driver's door and sliding in. She fumbled in her shoulder bag for the keys. 'Where are they?' she screamed silently, willing them into her hand. At last, she felt a sharp, serrated edge, gripped it firmly and yanked out the key ring. She found the ignition key and inserted it. The engine roared into life with the first explosion of spark and gasoline.

'How I love you, little Zhiguli,' she muttered to herself and put the car in reverse. Behind her, she heard a noise and a clatter, then a shout of pain. Someone had fallen down the stairs. She backed the car out of its space, pulled the gear lever into low, glimpsing a man's angry face in her side window as she accelerated out of the parking area. She waited until she turned the first corner before she switched on the headlights. She had no idea where to go, but she had the accelerator down and was thankful there was no traffic to impede their flight along Sarian Street.

Soon she saw the headlights of a car in her mirror, rapidly closing the gap between them. She pressed her foot to the floor and the Zhiguli leaped forward like a racehorse given its head.

"Sarkis," she said. "There's a car coming very fast behind us. I think it's the people who broke into my apartment. I'm going to try to lose them but I can't take you to Garni. That road has no turnings past the dachas and they would know where we were going. I can race them out Miasnikian and lose them in the apartments near the zoo. They won't know if we've turned back for the city or gone on to Garni or Abovyan. You'll have to jump out and get to Garni on your own. Can you do that?"

"Yes. I can do that."

Sarkis was unable to hold himself straight in the seat and was being thrown about as Ana swerved to avoid holes in the road. By the time she passed the zoo, she'd widened the gap between the two cars. She downshifted, cut her lights and made a skidding turn into the apartment complex by the zoo. She turned again and reached across Sarkis to open his door.

"Jump," she yelled at him.

He rolled out of the car onto the sidewalk, falling heavily on his satchel. The fall knocked the wind out of him and he lay gasping as Ana sped away, closing the passenger side door with the thrust of the car's acceleration. With an effort, Sarkis pulled himself up and watched her turn around in the narrow street and drive back the way she'd come. He thought he saw her hand wave to him as she passed. Then the Zhiguli swung into Miasnikian Avenue.

She drove as quickly as she dared without lights to the cloverleaf, turned toward Garni, then back toward the city on Safarian Street. There she turned on her lights again and sped into the neighborhood of Nor Marash. The pursuit was nowhere in sight. She breathed deeply and began to work her way toward the hotel.

CHAPTER THIRTY SEVEN

Hotel Armenia

"Got away?" Aleksandr screamed into the radio. "You idiots." In disgust, he let the hand holding the radio fall to his side and hang there.

He had appropriated the Russian's hotel room for his command post and now paced aimlessly around it. Gritting his teeth, he raised the radio to his mouth and clicked the send button. "Where did you lose them?"

"In the apartments near the zoo," came the metallic, disembodied reply.

"The zoo," he said. "Was that the way she was going when you caught up with her?"

"Yes, out Miasnikian."

"Then she was headed toward her dacha, on the road to Garni. There is only one way in and out. Go there and block the entrance. If she tries to leave, stop her and bring her here."

Deshnikov was outside, leaning on the balcony railing, smoking. Danilov lounged on the sofa, silently enjoying Aleksandr's agitation.

"Why is Ana involved in this?" he sputtered. "Zarkarian's men said Sarkis had a satchel and a box. Do you think she's the cutout between Sarkis and the American?"

"That's how it looks, comrade," Danilov said.

"But why the dacha?"

"Think, Aleks. Zarkarian's people interrupted the exchange. They should have just watched and waited instead of breaking down the door. Didn't they say dinner was prepared? The plan was probably to have Sarkis meet the American at the woman's flat and pass the goods there. Then the woman--Ana?--would drive the American and the goods to the airport. What I don't understand is why this Sarkis fellow went ahead after you killed his wife. Now they're improvising and there's no way to guess what they might do." Danilov shook his head in dismay. "All you had to do was wait for them to leave for the airport. You could have taken them on the road, in the dark. Do you think they've alerted the American?"

"I don't think they had time. He's still in his room with the other one. It doesn't matter whether he knows or not, Sarkis still has the coins."

"Might Sarkis abort the exchange?"

"I don't know," Aleksandr muttered. "But I don't like it that Ana's involved. She's clever. Maybe she only wanted us to think she went to the dacha." Aleksandr brought the radio to his mouth again.

"Hotel detail," he barked.

"Hotel detail," was the response from the street below.

"Anything to report?"

"Nothing."

"Call me immediately if you see a white Zhiguli anywhere in the area."

"Half the Zhigulis in Yerevan are white."

"Just do it," Aleksandr screamed and closed the circuit.

They didn't know that Ana's white Zhiguli was already parked behind the hotel or that at that moment she was climbing the abandoned back stairs to the fourth floor.

＊＊＊＊＊＊＊＊＊＊＊

Mariah was dozing on one of the twin beds and Tom was slouched in a chair, staring vacantly at CNN world news when Ana knocked on the door. Mariah awoke and Tom got up.

"Hi," he said to Ana, opening the door. "I was beginning to wonder . . ." He stopped in mid-sentence when he saw she was flushed and out of breath. "What's the matter?" he asked, pulling her into the room and closing the door.

"It is so awful," she said, still trying to catch her breath. "Sarkis. Karine."

"Whoa, whoa," he said. "Calm down. Let me get you a drink."

"Vodka," she said. "Big one."

"I haven't got any. There's some brandy left."

"Yes. Anything." Tom poured a tea glass full from what was left in his bottle and handed it to her. She drained half of it in one long swallow.

"What's up?" Mariah asked, sitting on the side of the bed, suddenly

243

alert.

Tom, kneeling beside Ana's chair, waved her to be quiet and waited for the color to return to Ana's face. "Better?" he asked. She nodded. "What happened? What's this about Sarkis and Karine?"

"Karine is dead. Her sister, too. Sarkis believes Aleksandr killed them. Because of something between Sarkis and Raz. And now you, I think."

"What?" Mariah exclaimed.

"Wait a minute. Wait a minute," Tom said. "I don't understand. Take it from the beginning."

Ana tipped up the glass and drank the rest of the brandy.

"Yes. Yes," she said. "I will try." She took a deep breath and said, "I was on my way here. But Sarkis came. He brought things for you to take to Amsterdam. For Raz. Yes?"

Tom nodded and Ana rummaged about in her shoulder bag, drawing out the cloth-wrapped packages that contained the Parthian necklace and the carnelian seal. She held them out to him and he took them absently. "Where's Sarkis?" he asked.

"Gone to the mountains."

Mariah was wide awake now, taking in Ana's every word. Over the next few minutes, Tom coaxed the story from her of men breaking into her apartment, the car chase and her escape through Nor Marash.

Back in control of herself, she looked at Tom and said, "Could Aleksandr connect you and Sarkis? Could he know you would be taking these things?"

"I can't imagine how. I only met Sarkis once, that night at dinner. And there are only two little pieces. It's not enough to get excited about unless one of them's the Hope Diamond."

"But why would Aleksandr kill Karine and Setta if not for something very valuable?" She thought further. "These are jewels, are they not? Sarkis said that Aleksandr made him steal a brooch--an old and valuable one--to give to a Russian."

Tom's eyes widened. "Are you saying this stuff was stolen from the Museum? I never agreed to carry stolen goods."

"No. Sarkis said he bought them with Raz's money. But Aleksandr might not know that." Ana's expression suddenly changed. "The restaurant. Mafia. The waiter. Do you remember? I told you he was listening to what you said. Now I am sure Aleksandr knows about you and Sarkis. And Raz, too. And there is the time in the Business Center when you humiliated him. That will make him more determined."

"Let's see what we've got here," Tom said, picking up the smaller of the two parcels and unwinding the cloth wrapping. The carnelian seal glowed dully in the light. "Well, there goes the Hope Diamond theory. It might be historically valuable, but it's just red chalcedony. Carnelian I guess. It's carved, but there's nothing inherently valuable about carnelian." He wrapped it up again. "Let's see the other one." He spread the Parthian necklace on the bed and stood back from it. "There's a fair amount of gold," he said. "Old, but no major stones."

Mariah had come to stand by Tom, looking over his shoulder at the large Parthian necklace. "That looks like half the Comstock Lode," she said. "Let me hold it. Must weight a ton."

Tom passed it to her and she weighed it in both hands. "Not as much as it looks."

"There are papers," Ana remembered. "Perhaps they will say." She dug the two envelopes from her shoulder bag. They were sealed with red wax and stamped. She started to rip one open but Tom stopped her.

"Wait," he said. "Don't break the seals. Let's take it on faith that they're worth a lot to somebody and go from there. I don't want to screw up the documentation of their provenance if that's what's in those envelopes."

A look came over Ana and she went to the window.

"Put out the light, please," she said and Tom flipped the switch for the overhead light. Ana turned off the bedside lamp and opened both sets of windows. Cold air flooded into the room.

"Hey, be careful," he said, rushing to take hold of her as she crawled over the wide window ledge to look below.

"I cannot see the front entrance from here." She shinnied back into the room and closed the windows. "Aleksandr may be watching the hotel."

"Did you see anyone when you came in?"

"I did not come through the front entrance. I came my secret way. Tom," she said. "I am so sorry. I do not know what I have done. They followed Sarkis to my apartment. And they know I will come here, to you. I have put you in terrible danger."

"You haven't put me in danger."

"Hey, wait a minute everybody," Mariah said. "This is getting a little over the top for me. What's going on, Tom? Dead people? Somebody watching our hotel? The Mafia?"

"It's not that complicated, Mariah, and I really don't think we're in any danger. Raz is a friend of mine from Jordan. Sarkis is Raz's cousin. He's the senior curator of the History Museum. Antique jewelry and coins. We all had dinner together the night before you arrived--at the Mafia, which is just a restaurant--and Raz asked me to take a couple of things to Amsterdam for him. No big deal. But now Ana's telling me that Sarkis also had something going with this KGB Major . . ."

"KGB?" Mariah exclaimed, jumping off the bed. "What's the KGB got to do with this? And who says you're not in danger if those guys are interested in you?"

"He's ex-KGB," Tom told her patiently. "There's no KGB in Armenia any more. Anyway, Sarkis came home and found his wife and his sister-in-law dead. He thinks the KGB guy did it . . ."

"He probably did," Mariah said excitedly, finding nowhere to pace in the small room. "And I'm sure as hell sorry he knows your name. 'Cause if he knows your name, he probably knows my name and I didn't even get to go to dinner."

"Tom," Ana said. "You must leave. Now."

"She's right," Mariah said. "We need to fly far, far away. As fast as we can."

"Hold on, people. No need to panic. Let's get the hard facts on the table," he said, turning to Ana. "Is there any doubt in your mind that a car followed you?"

"I cannot be positive about the car, but I know people broke my door. And if you had seen Sarkis, you would know something terrible happened to him. He said he found his wife and her sister murdered. I believe him. I do not know if Aleksandr killed them. But I believe he could do it. If he wants what Sarkis was bringing to you, he will come to this room and take it if you stay here. If you do not give it to him . . ."

"You're saying if. We don't know that Aleksandr's after this stuff. Or that the people who broke into your apartment are his people or, whoever they are, that they're anywhere near this hotel." The jewelry was one thing. Tom was thinking that the diamonds might be the hotter item and that they were the larger prize.

"Well, I for one am not eager to stay around to find out," Mariah said. "He could be coming through that door in the next two seconds. Let's get out of here."

"Mariah is right," Ana said to Tom. "But, Mariah, I agree with Tom, too. Let me take you to Sofia's room while I find out about Aleksandr. He will not think to look for you there. Bring only what you must carry if we have to run."

"That makes sense," Tom said. "Let's do it."

He tucked Sarkis' jewelry and the sealed envelopes into his briefcase and hitched up his rollaway, leaving the big hardcase, his laptop and printer on the luggage rack. Mariah left her hardcase and laptop, but brought her briefcase and duffel.

Sofia's door was ajar and a Russian program was blaring from the television.

"Sofia?" Ana called. Sofia came into view around the corner. "*Barev, Sofia.* I need your help."

"*Barev tzez*, Miss Stepanian," Sofia replied.

"I want you to let Dr. Yeager and Miss Carroll use your room for a few minutes. You must tell no one--absolutely no one. Do you understand? Sit at your desk outside and let no one into your room. Men may come looking and I don't want them to be found."

"I understand."

Ana motioned to Tom and Mariah to come in and Sofia welcomed them with a toothy smile.

"Thanks, Sofia," Tom said. "Sorry for the inconvenience."

"I will see if unusual things are happening in the hotel. Wait here," Ana told Tom and Mariah.

****

With the beam of her flashlight dancing ahead, Ana flew down the service stairs to the mezzanine, opened the stair well door a crack and slipped out. She moved quietly past the dark space once occupied by Intourist to the shelter of one of the large marble columns. From there, she could look down on the main lobby. It was teeming with black-cassocked priests and lay members of the Assembly dressed in coat and tie forming into groups to go to dinner. There was so much activity in the hotel it was difficult to pick out the people who might be there for other reasons, but she spotted three men in leather jackets who seemed to be watching the central staircase, the elevators, the corridor leading from the cafe and the front entrance. One of them had something in his hand that looked like a small radio. As if he felt someone's eyes on him, he looked up toward the mezzanine. Ana quickly ducked behind the column, her heart pounding. When her courage returned, she peered around the column again. The man showed no sign of having seen her.

Vahram had been waiting on two priests and a man in street clothes. As they left his shop, talking and laughing, Ana squeezed against the column and they passed down to the lobby without noticing her. She dared not cross the central staircase to Vahram's shop because it would expose her to the lobby below and to the porter who sat at the top of the stairs beside the door to the old hotel. Usually, one could count on his being asleep in his chair, but probably not tonight. Vahram took out a cigarette and was about to return to his customary posture, leaning on the glass counter top. Hidden from the lobby by the big marble column, but visible to Vahram if he chose to look up, Ana waved frantically and hissed at him.

The match flared, he squinted through the curl of acrid smoke and threw his head back to take a deep drag. As he exhaled, he caught sight of her. She beckoned him to come to her. Looking to his right and his left, Vahram came around the counter and crossed the short distance to the column where Ana was hiding. As he neared, she put a finger to her lips for him to be silent.

"What is it, Ana? What's wrong?" he asked.

"Come where we can talk," she whispered and led him back to the service stair landing.

"I can't leave my shop. I have customers for the first time in weeks."

"Only for a minute. Please. Vahram, have you noticed anything different in the hotel tonight?"

"Of course," he snapped. "There are people here for a change."

"I mean . . . Have you seen any of Aleksandr's men?"

Vahram didn't answer immediately. He stared at her face, unfamiliar in the shadows cast by the deflected beam of the flashlight. "Aleksandr doesn't have any men. Only his pilot. Maybe another one. Zarkarian's the only one who has men. You know that."

"Then have you seen Zarkarian's men here tonight?"

"There are always a few, coming and going," he said. "I haven't noticed tonight."

"There are three men in leather coats in the lobby, watching the stairs and the entrances. They don't do that usually, do they?"

"Why would they?"

"Please look outside for me, Vahram. I have to know if the hotel is being watched."

"What's this about, Ana? I don't want any trouble with Zarkarian or Avakian."

"You will not make trouble for yourself, Vahram. Please. Just go outside the hotel and look."

"For our friendship, Ana, but . . ." She knew this was his limit.

"Thank you, Vahram. Hurry. I'll wait here. Knock on the door when you come back."

She waited an eternity in the dead air of the dark, musty space and when Vahram's tap on the steel door came, it sounded like cannon fire. She jumped, her nerves sparking. When she opened the door, Vahram slipped into the stair well.

"You may be right," he said. "There are more of Zarkarian's boys than usual. I saw four standing outside the hotel, but not together, talking, the way they usually do. One down by the cafe entrance, one at the end of the block, by Anniversary Park, and two inside, by the entrance."

Her heart sank. "Thank you, Vahram. I'll never forget you for this." She rose on her toes and kissed his stubbled cheek.

"Whatever you are doing, Ana, be careful," he said.

****

She rushed back up the service stairs and found Sofia sitting tensely behind her table. "Has anyone come looking?"

"No, Miss Stepanian," Sofia said. "People are going down. No one is coming up, but Marta called to ask if the American was still in his room."

"Did she say why?"

"He is due to leave the hotel tonight. I think she wants his room for one of the delegates."

Ana went past the little desk into Sofia's room. Tom and Mariah had been talking but they stopped and looked at Ana when she came in.

"What's the story?" Tom asked, a line of tension around his mouth.

"There are men in the lobby and men watching the hotel. We must leave now. Marta has called to see if you are in your room. Aleksandr surely knows where you are."

"You know," he said. "This is getting 'way out of our league. Why don't we just call the cops and let them handle it?"

"No!" Ana said.

"Why not?"

"Leave the country tonight, as you plan. It is safer to answer police questions from a distance. You could be suspected in Karine's killing. You might be put in prison."

"That's crazy. I didn't have anything to do with it."

"Our police do not know that. And they would not permit you to leave Armenia until they were sure."

Tom had no reason to mistrust the Armenian police, but on general principles, he knew her advice was sound. Justice might be blind, but it could also be capricious. "Then let's call Manoukian and have him vouch for us," Tom said. "Wouldn't that work?"

"Yes, it might." She rummaged in her shoulder bag until she found a small notebook. "I have the telephone number at his home." She dialed the number and listened to Manoukian's telephone ring. And ring. And ring. She looked at Tom and Mariah and shook her head. "He is not answering. He is already at his dacha and there is no telephone there."

"What about that guy who's chairman of the committee?" Mariah suggested. "Zadigian?"

"Zadigian would not help. He would not take responsibility for helping you in a matter with the police."

"OK, then," Mariah said. "Call the bloody American ambassador,

Tom. Tell him we need the Marines."

"Why not? They won't send the Marines, but they might have a suggestion. Ana, can you get the phone number?"

****

Aleksandr was growing impatient. The detail leaders were reporting no contacts. Five white Zhigulis had come to the hotel, all of them picking up delegates, none of them with a dark-haired woman.

They had run out of vodka and Aleksandr called Marina to bring another bottle.

Marina felt the tension as soon as she entered the room. "Aleksandr, what is it?" she asked. "What's wrong?"

"Nothing to concern you," he growled. "Ana's showing us how stupid Zarkarian's men really are." To himself, he muttered, "She won't feel like playing games when I'm finished with her. And that American . . . I'm going to enjoy taking care of him. I'll even let her watch."

Marina heard what he said and understood what it meant. She still bore the bruises from his beating and brutalizing her only a few nights ago.

As if he read her thoughts, he turned his cold eyes on her. "Have you seen the American tonight?"

"He left with the American woman this afternoon, but they came back about four o'clock. I have not seen them since," Marina said, feeling a cold shiver run down her spine. "They are leaving tonight, though. Everyone not with the National Assembly is being put out."

"I know that," Aleksandr snapped impatiently. "I want to know if he is leaving the country tonight. Find out."

"I'll ask," she said, leaving the room quickly, knowing exactly what she was going to do.

Danilov poured a drink from the fresh bottle of Stolichnaya and amused himself by watching Aleksandr pace back and forth.

Suddenly, Aleksandr stopped his pacing and said to no one, "She's not at the dacha."

"How do you know that?" Danilov asked.

"I know her," he replied. "She'll double back. I don't know where she is, but she's not hiding in that dacha." Aleksandr shouted at

Deshnikov, who had remained on the balcony, moodily drinking vodka and smoking, trying to salve his conscience for what had happened that afternoon.

"Go to the airport, Ivan," Aleksandr commanded. "Pay the pilot of the Amsterdam flight to leave early--an hour early at least. If Ana connects with the American and they reach the airport, they'll find the flight already gone. Then we will have run them into a rabbit hole."

"How much will you pay?" Deshnikov asked.

"Five thousand US should be enough, don't you think?"

"Perhaps," Deshnikov replied. "But if I were the pilot, I'd want to see the money."

"All right," Aleksandr growled. "We'll go to my apartment. I have it there. But only five thousand. If he wants more, he'll have to wait." Aleksandr turned to Danilov. "The people we're using are incompetent and they don't know what the American looks like. Go downstairs and make sure he doesn't leave the hotel. The others should be able to keep Ana from entering if she gets past the roadblock at the dachas, assuming I'm wrong and she is there."

As the three men hurried down the hall, Aleksandr asked the Russian, "Do you think the American is armed?"

"Possibly. It's difficult to travel with weapons these days. So much security. But a resourceful man can manage."

"Do you have a weapon?" Aleksandr asked Danilov.

"Of course. I'm a professional."

****

Tom hung up the phone and looked at Mariah and Ana. "The Duty Officer said they'd be delighted to protect us just as soon as we're inside the gates of the Embassy. But he has only two Marines on duty tonight and there's no way he can authorize a rescue sortie to put us on the airplane. His suggestion was to get on the plane and leave tonight."

"If the Embassy can't help us," Mariah said. "The AID Mission sure can't. Marcos is out of town anyway."

"Yeah," Tom replied. "And Lange's out drinking with a bunch of his buddies. There'll be a duty officer but . . ."

"We must not wait," Ana said. "I do not think they know I

have come to hotel. Probably they are still looking for me in the city. If I could get you to the airport, I could take you through the VIP Lounge to the airplane. You would not pass through customs inspection or sit in waiting areas where they would look for you."

"Are you sure?" Tom asked.

"Of course," she said. "At Intourist, I escorted high ranking visitors through the VIP Lounge many times. Recently I took a French delegation that way. Perhaps other VIPs are leaving tonight, but I think it is little risk. VIPs are coming in for National Assembly, not going out. Wait. I know what to do." She leaped up and left the room, conferred with Sofia for a moment and came back smiling.

"What's the deal?" Tom asked.

"You will see soon enough," she said, smiling. She went out of the room and spoke to Sofia.

When she returned, Tom said, "Let's not get ahead of ourselves here. We have the offer of protection from the Embassy. If you could get us to the airport, you could get us to the Embassy, too, right? All we're worrying about right now is getting past the heavies who've got the hotel staked out."

"How long do you think it'd be before we got out of there?" Mariah asked. "Didn't we have a Catholic cardinal in our embassy in Poland for forty years or something?"

"It wouldn't be forty years, Mariah. A few days, maybe."

"But if the police wanted to question you, it might be longer," Ana said. "You would have to tell the police why you were in danger. Because you were taking valuable Armenian artifacts from our country, yes?"

"She's right," Mariah said. "Let's go for the flight."

Tom turned to Ana. "You're in danger here, too, aren't you?"

Ana shook her head vigorously. "Aleksandr only wants the jewelry. If you take it away, he has no reason to hurt me."

At that moment, Sofia came into the room carrying a bundle of black garments.

"What's this?" Tom asked.

"Here," Ana said to him, smiling. "Try this." She held up the largest priest's black cassock. "And you, Mariah," she added, holding out another, smaller cassock.

Tom slipped off his leather jacket and held the cassock up at arm's length. "Where did these come from?"

"Sofia has the keys to all the rooms on this floor. Do you not remember? I hate to take them, but it is for good reason. I will return them before I leave for St. Petersburg."

The black cassock fit Tom perfectly. It even covered the tops of his tan desert boots. The cassocks Sofia had taken for Mariah and Ana, however, were too snug around the breasts. They would need cloaks.

There was another problem. Mariah's hair was blond and short, but not cut like a man's. That was a larger problem for Ana, whose hair fell to her shoulders. And none of them had the heavy black beards worn by Armenian priests.

"Should we take their veghars, too?" Ana wondered aloud. "Yes, why not? It will hide the hair."

"What's a veghar?" Tom asked.

"The hat, the pointed hat," Ana replied, meaning the cowl that celibate Armenian priests wear when formally dressed. She held up her hands to make a triangle over her head, dashed into the hall and almost collided with Marina Vartanian.

"I'm so glad to find you," Marina said, gasping for breath. "You must get away. Aleks is going to hurt you." Having blurted her warning, Marina suddenly fell silent, staring at the black cassock.

"Why are you telling me this?" Ana shot back.

"Ana," she said, eyes pleading. "I'm sorry for all the bad feelings that have been between us. I know Aleks never loved me, only you. And now he has changed so much. So I must warn you. He will not let anyone else have you. Please believe me, Ana. He has men looking for you. Go with the Americans tonight."

Tom heard the commotion outside and went to the door. He found Ana and Marina Vartanian face to face. "Ana?" he asked, his eyes fixed suspiciously on Marina.

"It is nothing, Tom," Ana said.

"This is Aleksandr's girlfriend. What's she doing here?"

Marina noticed that Tom was also wearing a cassock, but she pressed past Ana and took him by the arm. "Please. Take Ana. Aleksandr hurts her. Hurt you, too." Marina's bar English lacked fluency, but it carried the message.

Tom stared at Ana, believing it now and feeling stupid and selfish that he hadn't seen the danger. "Why should she lie, Ana?"

"I don't know," Ana conceded.

"You're not forgetting the people who broke down your door, are you? They weren't selling cookies, were they?"

"They wanted Sarkis, not me," she said.

"Tom," Mariah said, squeezing his arm. "Let's not take that chance. Ana comes with us."

"It is not possible. I have no ticket. No visa."

"If you can get us on the airplane," Tom said. "I'll make sure it takes off with all of us on board. And I'll get you into Holland somehow. But you're coming. End of discussion."

It didn't matter that she made no reply because Tom wasn't waiting for one. He had spoken. Until now, she'd seen him only as logical, reasonable, accommodating. Never this way. Certain and commanding. She liked it. And Mariah. Now her friend?

To Marina, Tom added, "I'm sorry, but you're going to have to stay here for a while. I'm really grateful that you came to warn us, but you know what we're doing and I can't take the chance you'll tell Aleksandr. It's for your protection, too."

****

Sarkis left the road and moved cross-country over the hills toward Garni. He stumbled often. The bandage covering the hand he'd cut was soaked with blood and his knees were scraped and bleeding. After climbing for almost an hour, his legs turned to rubber and his breath came in ragged gasps that burned his lungs. Finally, he reached a flat area cluttered with stones dislodged by the earthquake and his way became easier. He closed his eyes and thanked God for that but in the darkness, his mind was numb to the danger of the black ribbon that ran across the disturbed field of stone. He stepped into it and fell headlong into the crevasse. He did not even have breath to scream as his body struck first one side of the the narrowing gash in the mountain and then the other. When he could at last fall no further, the satchel that contained the dies and the patterns lodged against his chest and collapsed his lungs. In the inky blackness of the crevasse, he saw a bright path of light--and

Karine, his lovely Karine, waiting for him.

CHAPTER THIRTY EIGHT

Zvartnots International Airport

No one saw the three priests emerge from the darkness of the doorway at the north wing of the Hotel Armenia. The moon had not yet risen, but even if some small light had shown in their direction, their beardless faces would have been hidden by the brooding cowls. Ana doused the Zhiguli's dome light and Tom loaded his rollaway and Mariah's duffel bag into the back seat. Mariah put their briefcases and Ana's shoulder bag on the floor and slipped into the back seat herself. Tom tried to get into the passenger seat but knocked his veghar askew and nearly lost it.

"What the hell do I do with this thing?" he muttered.

"Take it off," Ana hissed at him. "You do not need it here. But at airport, yes."

Tom removed the helmet that gave the triangular shape to the silk fabric of the cowl and tried again to get into the passenger seat. His head went in, but his feet became tangled in the olive wood box.

"What's this?" he whispered, as Ana took her place behind the wheel.

"Oh, I forgot. Sarkis' coin collection. You must take it to Raz."

"No way. We're traveling light. Sarkis is out of luck on this thing."

"I will take it then. I only have my shoulder bag to carry and Sarkis has lost so much already."

"The thing weighs a ton," Tom exclaimed, lifting the box onto his lap.

Ana started the Zhiguli, wincing at the sound of the exhaust echoing between the two buildings. She flicked on the parking lights and backed slowly into the open space between the new hotel and the old. With the engine revving slowly, she put the car in gear and resisted the urge to accelerate. She let the idling engine carry the car slowly to Zakian Street. There she turned left, drove past Taterakan Park and across Victory Bridge. When she turned onto the road that would take them to Zvartnots International Airport, she finally accelerated through the gears and released a whoop of exhilaration.

"Does that mean we're in the clear?" Mariah asked.

"I think so," Ana answered, smiling widely. "But we should not go into the airport immediately. There is an apricot orchard near the terminal. We can hide there until it is time for boarding."

Tom looked at his watch. "It's eleven o'clock. The flight's at oh-two-hundred? How long to the airport?

"A few minutes only."

"And we go in about one o'clock?"

"Half past one o'clock, I think," Ana said. "We should not be long in the VIP Lounge. Armenian priests have beards, did you know? If someone looked at us, they would know we are not priests."

"Will Marina be all right, do you think?" Mariah asked, leaning forward between the front seats.

"We've given her some cover," Tom said. "If she sticks to her story about coming to my room to see if I was leaving Armenia, our tying her up ought to be a pretty good out for her. If Aleksandr breaks the door down and finds her that way, she looks like a brave soldier. If he doesn't, Sofia can pretend to find her and cut her loose in the morning. It seems cruel after what she did for us, but letting her go was too much of a risk."

✳✳✳✳✳✳✳✳✳✳✳

The leafless apricot trees were trimmed low to the ground, but they offered little concealment. The white Zhiguli would have been seen by anyone looking directly at them. And the sky was growing lighter by the minute as the full moon rose. They soon ran out of conversation and drowsed, thankful that their body heat warmed the air inside the car. Shortly after midnight, they heard the approach of the flight from Paris and got out to watch it land. This was the aircraft they'd be taking to Amsterdam once it had been serviced. From the edge of the orchard, they saw the Tupolev's landing lights blaze as it turned onto final approach. Then the runway lights came on and the outline of the terminal became sharper with illumination as the ground crews prepared to receive the flight.

The headlights of a few cars could be seen approaching the airport. Ivan Deshnikov was behind the wheel of one of them. In his coat pocket

258

was $5,000 from the safe in Aleksandr's apartment.

****

"Tom," Ana said softly. "It is time to go."

Tom awoke alert. "Let's do it, then. The sooner we're airborne, the better."

They eased out of the apricot orchard, bouncing over the uneven ground, until they reached the main road leading to the airport. As Ana switched on the headlights, they saw a Tupolev taxi onto the active runway, its landing lights piercing the night. The plane sat at the threshold a few moments while the engines ran up to full power. Tom watched through the side window of the Zhiguli as the pilot released the brakes and began his takeoff roll, the lighted squares of cabin windows winking a mute goodbye.

"I wonder where that one's headed," he asked idly.

"I do not know," Ana said slowly, looking at her watch again, an empty feeling starting to grow in her stomach. "There is no flight between the Paris arrival and the Amsterdam departure."

Tom looked at her, hearing the disquiet in her voice.

"What're you saying?" he asked.

"Nothing," she replied.

A few cars were still waiting for passengers from the Paris flight to clear customs when Ana drove into the parking area. She removed her veghar and Tom and Mariah ducked their heads to avoid being seen through the car windows. Ana stopped in the darkest part of the parking area she could find and turned off the engine.

"Come," she said softly. "There is a door. Inside are stairs to the VIP Lounge."

Their *veghars* back atop their heads and their cloaks billowing, the 'priests' glided through the moonlight like three black triangles. They encountered no one, but heard baggage handlers moving luggage and air freight nearby. Ana gripped the door handle and turned. To her great relief, it was unlocked and swung open with a shriek of rusty hinges. They slipped through the door and Tom eased it shut. Ana found the flashlight in her shoulder bag and flicked it on. Iron stair railings stood only a few feet away. Following her light, they climbed a long way, one short flight of metal stairs ending in a landing to be followed by yet another flight of stairs. At last, Ana stopped in front of another steel door, took the handle and turned off the flashlight.

"Wait," she said. The door opened with the whoosh of a vacuum being broken. No flood of light came into the stairwell from the corridor. She looked in both directions, opened the door and went through it. Mariah came next and Tom followed. The only light reaching the second level was reflected from below.

"This way," Ana said. They followed her along a curving catwalk past an enclosed area housing vacant terminal offices and finally reached a set of double doors padded in leather. "Wait here," she said, marching up to the doors and opening them boldly, as if she owned the room. Moonlight filtered through an expanse of slanting skylights and the lounge was deserted. "Quickly," she whispered, beckoning them into the room. Safely inside the lounge, Tom checked the Rolex. "Thirty minutes to take-off," he said. "What's our next move?"

"Those doors lead to jet bridges," Ana said, throwing the beam of her flashlight on another set of double doors. "When there are VIP passengers, an attendant takes their documents to passport control and returns them here. Then they walk directly onto the aircraft."

"What about all this?" Tom asked, holding out a corner of his cloak. "Shouldn't we get out of these now?"

"Yes," Ana said. "I will see which is the gate for the Amsterdam flight."

While Mariah and Tom stripped off their cassocks and rolled them and the veghars up in the cloaks, they could hear Ana talking on a phone nearby. They didn't understand what she was saying, but her tone began to alarm them both. They were watching her anxiously when she hung up the phone.

"The plane is gone," she said.

Tom and Mariah were too stunned to comprehend.

"What do you mean, gone?" Tom asked at last.

"The plane we saw take off was the flight to Amsterdam."

"That's not possible," Tom said. "I've never heard of a flight leaving an hour early."

"Our pilots decide when to fly," Ana said with a shrug. "Perhaps a weather report told of storms or he is meeting someone in Amsterdam. It does not matter now. The next flight is to Athens at six o'clock."

"How the hell did they have time to refuel it? We only saw it land an hour ago," Tom said.

"We have no fuel here. The gasoline they take at Paris or

Amsterdam brings them here and back to Bucharest. They take fuel at Bucharest to fly to Amsterdam," Ana explained.

"What about all the passengers who got left behind?" Mariah said. Ana shrugged. "Only two airlines fly here--Armenian and Aeroflot. It does not matter to them."

"Well, we've got to check out the Athens flight," Tom said. "I don't suppose we dare try to change these tickets? Too much risk of being spotted. We'll just have to buy our way on board. Count your money, Mariah, and I'll count mine. Got any dollars, Ana?"

"I have German marks. I bought them yesterday for my trip to St. Petersburg."

"Marks will do fine."

"Twenty-two hundred and change," Mariah said.

"I've got sixteen hundred," Tom added.

"Four-thousand-two-hundred marks," Ana said.

"The mark's about one and a half to the dollar, right?" Tom said. "That means you've got twenty-eight hundred dollars. Together we've got sixty-six hundred. That's got to be enough to get three of us to Athens."

"Yes," Ana said. "Even too much."

"Then we're funded," Tom said. "So we sit tight here, slip onto the jet bridge, bull our way onto the flight and show 'em the money. What do you think?" he asked.

"What about visas?" Mariah said. "The last I heard, Greece still requires a visa."

"First things first, huh? Let's get in the air and get out of here. We'll worry about the paperwork later. But while we're on the subject-- Ana, you wouldn't happen to be carrying your passport would you?"

"Of course," she replied. "We carry our passports always. For identification."

Tom turned to Mariah and gave her a smile. "See? All we need is some bureaucrat's OK at the other end. If Ana hadn't had her passport . . ."

"It's not going to be a walk in the park," Mariah said. "But I'm a hundred percent with you on getting out of Armenia."

"We cannot stay here in the VIP Lounge so long," Ana said. "Aleksandr's men will search here before the morning. Perhaps we should go back to the orchard."

"You've got a point. It's not good to be sitting still, whether it's here or in the orchard," Tom said. "And we're going to lose the night in a few hours. Is there another road out of the airport? Could we drive to Lake Sevan? Tblisi? We're cornered here."

"There is no other road. If Aleksandr is watching the airport, he would also block the road." Ana said.

"Any other ideas about hiding inside the airport?"

"No," she replied, eyes wide and anxious.

"Let's have a look outside," Tom said, heading for the double doors. They emerged onto the catwalk and looked down on the terminal floor just as Aleksandr, Nikolai Danilov and a squad of Zarkarian's men came through the main entrance.

"Oh, shit," Tom said. "That's him, isn't it?"

"Yes," Ana replied, looking down at the men spreading out in the terminal.

Tom stared at Aleksandr in quiet contemplation, studying the man, watching him pointing like a general disposing his troops on the battlefield. The man standing next to him looked up and a chill ran through Tom. The rimless glasses, the nose, those eyes. He would never forget those eyes. God! How could it be? Was he hallucinating?

He grunted, the breath going out of him, the memory filling his brain. The cobblestones smashing against his cheek. Wet. Something, a foot, turning him onto his back. He saw the face. Handsome in a cruel way. Rimless glasses. Eyes back in their sockets. Aristocratic nose. The briefcase with the diamonds in one hand and a long-barreled pistol in the other. And there he is.

From a great distance he heard Ana speaking to him.

"The tall man he's talking to now is Ivan Deshnikov, his pilot. The others are Mafia." She stopped. "That one . . ." she added, looking at Danilov. "I saw him in the hotel. He is not Mafia."

"No," Tom said slowly. "He isn't. He's after diamonds." He stared down at the scene below for a long moment, then forced himself to focus. "How long before they make it up here?"

"They will search below first."

"Wait a minute," Mariah said.

"You said Deshnikov, didn't you?" she asked Ana. Ana nodded. "That's it," Mariah said. "Deshnikov. He's the one with the Cessna. Jameson--the AID pilot who picked me up in Tblisi--said they used to have a Cessna 310 but they sold it to a local drug smuggler named Deshnikov."

"So what?" Tom asked.

"Tommy," Mariah said, her eyes bright and alive. "I can fly us out of here if you can steal that airplane."

CHAPTER THIRTY NINE

The Tarmac, Zvartnots International Airport

Tom, Mariah and Ana left the cassocks and veghars in the VIP Lounge, but put the black cloaks back on over their leather jackets. They moved through the interior doors of the VIP Lounge, walked along the carpeted corridor to the now-deserted jet bridge and used its exterior stairs to descend to the tarmac.

"OK, Mariah," Tom said in a low voice. "I'm ready to steal the plane. But where the hell is it?"

"They keep little planes away from big planes. We have to go around the terminal until we find where it's parked."

They moved into the shadows of the inactive area of the building, their way lighted only by the rising full moon. The runway lights had been doused as soon as the Amsterdam flight retracted its landing gear. Even the control tower was dark. They walked for some distance before Mariah stopped stock still and held out her arm to bring Tom and Ana to a halt. She pointed to the outline of a small, twin-engine aircraft sitting on tricycle landing gear. Mariah nodded her head vigorously and Tom got the message that this was the Cessna 310 they were looking for.

There was one small problem. A sentry paced slowly around the aircraft, an AK-47 rifle slung over his shoulder.

They retraced their steps and crouched beside the terminal building. "We're going to have to take him out," Tom whispered. "I need a piece of pipe or something. Did either of you see anything like that?"

Both Mariah and Ana shook their heads. The ramp was clean along the way they'd come. Tom looked at the olive wood box under Ana's arm. "Let me see that." Ana handed it to him. The edges of the box were sharp. "It's heavy enough. If I can get close without him seeing me, I think this ought to do the trick. But we're going to need a diversion."

They looked at each other for several moments. Finally, Ana

whispered, "I saw this in a film. If I pretend to hurt my ankle and fall down, I can ask him for help. When he comes to me, I will keep him distracted. Can you hit him then?"

Tom shrugged. "I can't think of anything better. Mariah, pitch in if I miss. Ana, I'll follow you as close as I can, right up against the building. With any luck, he won't see me until the last minute." Tom stashed his rollaway bag against the wall of the terminal and gave Ana the nod to go ahead.

"What happens if you miss?" Mariah asked.

"There are three of us, Mariah. And he's not that big."

Ana removed her cloak, put it over her arm and stepped into the bright moonlight. With a normal stride, she launched off in the direction of the Cessna. Tom crouched in the shadow of the terminal wall and scurried along behind her, keeping pace. The sentry came into view, standing near the wingtip of the Cessna. He saw Ana immediately. She called out a greeting to him in Russian and waved. Coming toward him, she fell.

"Oh! Oh!" she cried out. The sentry trotted toward her, unslung the AK-47 and bent down to look at her leg. With the sentry's attention distracted by the act Ana was putting on, Tom circled to a point where the sentry's back was to his approach and sprang forward. He covered the twenty paces between the wall and the spot where Ana lay and swung the olive-wood box at the sentry's head.

The sentry heard a swoosh of fabric or the scrape of a shoe as Tom closed on him because his head came around just as Tom swung the box. The blow caught him square on the bridge of his nose and he fell back with a groan, stunned but not unconscious.

"Shit," Tom muttered.

Mariah and Ana pounced on the hapless sentry, ignoring the blood spurting from his broken nose.

"Get his arms," Tom said, pulling a handkerchief from his pocket and stuffing it in the sentry's mouth. The handkerchief would stifle his calls for help, but he was recovering from the blow and struggling to get free of Ana and Mariah.

"Sorry, pal," Tom said. "I'm gonna have to hit you again." He struck the base of the sentry's neck and felt the box crack. This time the sentry went limp, out cold. Mariah and Ana felt him relax and released their grip.

"I hope you didn't kill him," Mariah said.

Tom laid two fingers on the pulse in the sentry's neck. It was there, beating strongly. "No, but he's going to have one hell of a headache tomorrow."

"What are we going to do with him now?" Mariah asked.

"You check out the plane. Let Ana and me worry about this guy."

"Right," Mariah said, sprinting toward the Cessna.

Tom looked at Ana. "We've got to tie him up. Get my bag. There's a spare belt and some ties."

Ana ran back to get it while Tom kept watch over the sentry, ready to hit him again if he started to come around.

Mariah scrambled out of the airplane and trotted back to where Tom and Ana were ransacking Tom's rollaway bag. "Ana," she said breathlessly. "I need your flashlight."

Ana plunged a hand into her shoulder bag and found the flashlight. Mariah grabbed it and ran back to the plane.

Tom came up with a belt and two ties. "These ought to do the trick. Here," he said to Ana, handing her the belt. "Tie his ankles. I'll take care of his hands."

As they finished with the sentry, Mariah put her head out the cabin door of the Cessna and called to them. "Come on. Let's get outta here. Bring my briefcase and duffel. They're by the wall."

Ana scrambled up the wing, crawled through the cabin door and slipped into the rear of the passenger compartment behind the two front seats. Tom came quickly behind her, pushed his rollaway, the two briefcases and Mariah's duffel into the seat beside Ana. He was about to get in when Mariah turned to him.

"Pull the chocks. Check for tie downs."

"Tom," Ana said. "Sarkis' coins. They are by the sentry."

"OK. OK," he said and scrambled back down to the tarmac. He pulled the chocks, but saw no tie downs. The sentry was beginning to come around and Tom grabbed the olive-wood box from the ramp near where he lay. The force of the second blow had cracked it at the hinge and Tom had to use both hands to hold it together. Climbing back up the wing, he sat down next to Mariah and pulled the cabin door shut.

"Clear?" Mariah asked without looking at him.

"Clear," he said, out of breath. He passed the box back to Ana. "Here," he said. "Be careful. I fractured it. Next time I see Sarkis, I'll tell him his coin collection is a knockout."

Mariah was still running the flashlight over the instrument panel, locating gauges and switches. "Tom, find us some charts while I figure out this panel." He felt under the seat, in the side pocket of the cabin door and in the shelf under the instrument panel before he found what felt like a folded chart.

"Shine the light here for a second," he said.

Mariah turned the flashlight on him, saw instantly that they had a chart and went back to the panel. "OK. Let's give it a shot," she said and prepared to start the engines.

"Battery on, generators off," she said aloud to herself as she went through a make-shift pre-flight check list from memory. "Ignition on. Prime port engine. Now, start for Momma," she said, pressing the port engine starter button. The starter whirred for a moment before the engine caught, coughed and settled into a reassuring growl. With the port engine firing strongly, Mariah primed the starboard engine, cranked it up, smoothed it out, turned on the generators and brought up the panel lights.

"That's more like it," she said, still talking to herself over the rumble of the engines. She located the 'six-pack'--three instruments for each engine that registered oil pressure, cylinder temperature and oil temperature. The needles on all the gauges had to come into acceptable ranges in 30 to 60 seconds. Mariah allowed them a little extra time because of the cold, then muttered, "Six-pack's in the green."

From Tom's side of the cockpit, he could see the sentry struggling with his bonds.

"Better move it," he told Mariah. "Our boy's gonna be loose pretty soon and I left the damned AK-47."

"Roger, dodger. We're rolling," she replied, releasing the brakes. "Wish I could check the tabs on those fuel tanks." She ran up the starboard engine, held the brake on the port wheel and let the plane turn smartly about. She released the brake, equalized the throttles and began to taxi away from the terminal.

"Thank God for this moon. A radio check and a weather report would be nice, though," she mumbled. She taxied onto the runway, the full moon illuminating the stretch of concrete almost as clearly as runway lights.

Tom wondered what the boys in the control tower were thinking now and looked back. The tower, rising from the center of the terminal, was dark.

Mariah lined up at the threshold, set the brakes and ran up the engines. They made an ear-splitting, teeth-jarring racket, but so far from the terminal, no one seemed to notice. She checked the gauges for manifold pressure, RPM and fuel flow. "Power normal," she told herself. "Here we go." She released the brakes, rammed the throttles forward and the Cessna gathered speed quickly. In seconds, they were airborne.

"Oh, man," Tom said, exhaling a breath he thought he'd been holding for half an hour.

Mariah retracted the landing gear, saying to herself, "Gear up." She trimmed the aircraft's control surfaces and finally turned to Tom with a grin a mile wide. "Yeeeee-hah, pardner," she said.

Ana was laughing. "It is like a carnival ride," she said. "How wonderful."

They took a few moments to relish their escape. Then Tom turned to Mariah and said, "Now that I've stolen the airplane--as promised--and you're flying it--as promised--could I ask if you've given any thought to where we're going?"

"It won't be all that far because the fuel gauges say the main tanks are empty and the auxiliaries are less than half full. Rough cut, I guess about fifty gallons. Tblisi's our best shot. Got any friends up there?"

"Never been there," Tom replied. "You have, though."

"Don't remind me," she said. "Wasn't Marcos going to Tblisi this weekend?"

"He said Baku." Tom turned in his seat and shouted to Ana over the roar and vibration of the engines.

"Got any connections in Tblisi? That's our best choice."

"No," she said, shaking her head. "I am sorry."

"Then we'll just have to throw ourselves on the mercy of the

American ambassador in Tblisi."

Mariah set a northerly course and began climbing, but almost immediately, she encountered towering, dark clouds, obscuring the moon. "Now I really wish I had a weather report," she said. "That looks ugly."

Ana leaned forward between the front seats and said, "Caucasian storms are common in this season. Tblisi could have snow even if Yerevan does not." As she spoke the words, heavy snowflakes began splatting against the Cessna's windscreen.

"Oh, shit," Mariah said. "We're gonna have to get out of this stuff. I don't think I can climb over it and I sure can't fly through it. We'd bore a hole in some mountain in no time. I'm wide open to suggestions, folks."

"How far will fifty gallons take us?" Tom asked.

"I'm guessing she'll burn about thirty gallons an hour at a ground speed of one-seventy-five. Two hours with sixty gallons gets us three-hundred and fifty miles. Tblisi can't be much more than a hundred. It's a chip shot as far as the gas is concerned, but that storm says we're gonna have to find someplace else. I don't think we can count on sixty gallons so get out that chart and tell me what's inside three-hundred miles."

Tom began unfolding the chart. "Hold the flashlight, Ana. Keep it on the map." To Mariah, he said, "All these markings look Greek to me."

"It's an aeronautical chart," Mariah said. "Ignore the funny markings. There's a regular map underneath and a mileage scale. We've got to get a course charted. What about Baku?"

"Armenia is at war with Azerbaijan," Ana reminded them.

"Just be quiet a minute," Tom said. "Ana, give me that box. I need to figure some distances, here." Tom smoothed the chart over Sarkis' box, putting Yerevan in the center, and located the scale. He used the ruler in his pocket notebook and laid out straight line distances to all the major cities he could find on the map before he spoke.

"Tabriz isn't much farther than Tblisi, but I'm not keen on dealing with the Iranians, are you?" Tom asked Mariah.

"Not if there's an alternative."

"In Turkey, we can make Erzurum, Trabzon and Van for sure.

Diyarbakir is a stretch."

"Turkey would not be friendly," Ana said. "The Turkish border is closed to Armenia. If we land there, we will have trouble."

"If you can squeeze three-hundred miles out of this thing, we could make Qameshli, in Syria," Tom said. "There's a fair chance we could buy our way out of official objections to our unconventional arrival and the state of our papers. Why don't you turn this baby around and fly a heading due southwest to a town in Turkey called Agri, take it south-southwest across Lake Van and find a nice soft sand dune in the northeast corner of Syria? Make sure it's Syria, not Iraq. We don't want to blunder into a 'no-fly' zone left over from the Gulf War."

"Tom," Ana chimed in again. "Turks and Kurds are fighting at Van. We must go more west." Ana's forefinger traced a line from Agri to Mus. "At Mus, Mariah can fly south to Qameshli. And I am sure it will be as you say. We can pay."

"That might be more than three-hundred miles," Tom said. "Mariah, what do you think?"

"Gas gauges are notoriously unreliable. We might have seventy-five gallons and we might not even have fifty. But I hear what Ana's saying. I just left one war zone. I don't want to come down in the middle of another one. And I sure as hell don't want to try to explain things to an F-14 Tomcat in a 'no-fly' zone. Let's give it a shot Ana's way." Mariah turned the plane on its wing and flew west toward Turkey. Ice had already built up on the Cessna's windshield and wings and the aircraft wasn't responding well to the controls.

"What about Turkish radar?" Mariah asked once they were straight and level again. "I forgot about that."

"What about it?" Tom asked.

"This used to be the Cold War front lines, in case you don't remember. We probably have so much radar in Turkey looking in on the Soviet Union that we know when Khruschev changes his shorts."

"Khruschev is dead," Tom said.

"So are we if they think we're Soviet terrorists and send up a pair of fast-movers itching for target practice."

"Ana," Tom said, turning back to her. "Didn't you say that Aleksandr uses this plane to smuggle drugs?"

"That is what people believe. The plane flies to Turkey and

returns to Yerevan."

"What do dope smugglers do about radar?" he asked Mariah.

"Fly under it. Radar doesn't go right down to ground level. Drug runners coming out of Columbia fly about 100 feet off the water and the radar never sees them. Here, I guess they hug the valleys--'map-of-the-earth' flying. But you really have to know what you're doing. My daddy taught me that little bit of wisdom. If there's a lot of drug traffic through here, maybe they won't scramble fighters to check out one little plane," she said. "Let's scoot under the radar as we cross the border, then take back some altitude and hope they don't bother us."

"You're the boss," Tom said at last.

"Give me a heading for Agri," she said.

****

Ten minutes after Mariah put the wheels up on the Cessna 310, the sentry loosened the necktie that bound his hands and struggled free of the belt around his ankles. In great pain, but no longer bleeding, he staggered into the terminal. A search team came across him in one of the loading bays and when he explained through a blood-caked mouth and broken teeth that three people attacked him and stole the airplane he was guarding, they sent word to Aleksandr.

"I cannot believe this," Aleksandr muttered angrily. "Where did they find a pilot?" He turned to Danilov. "Does the American fly?"

The Russian shrugged. "It's possible."

"The guard said three people. Sarkis, do you suppose? Bring him to me," he commanded one of Zarkarian's minions standing near by.

A nurse had been found to set the sentry's broken nose and clean the cuts on his lips and mouth. He had a huge knot on the back of his head from Tom's second blow. Both his eyes were swollen and beginning to blacken from his first encounter with the olive-wood box. The nurse had given him a sedative and he was groggy by the time he was brought to Aleksandr. Containing his fury, Aleksandr found a comfortable chair for the wounded sentry and called for tea.

"It's too bad this happened to you. Arkady is your name?" The sentry nodded. "Three people?" Arkady nodded again. "A man, a woman and what? Another man?" Arkady tried to speak, but found moving his lips or indeed any part of his face painful, so he made the shape of a woman with his hands.

"One man and two women?"
Arkady nodded. "The other American," Aleksandr said. "Of course. The one who came a week ago. Where would they go?" he asked, turning to Deshnikov.

"Not far," the pilot answered. "The main tanks were dry and there were only two hundred liters in the auxiliaries, probably less. It only takes one hundred and fifty liters to fly to Patnos and return. I was going to fill the tanks there on my next trip."

"All right, but where would they go?"

Deshnikov thought for a moment. "Tblisi is the nearest with a major airport, but they're closed. Snow. The pilot will run into that soon. They won't reach Tblisi."

"Where else?" Aleksandr snapped impatiently.

"Turkey or Iran. Let's see." Deshnikov took Aleksandr back to the Flight Operations Office, where he spread a chart on a table against the wall.

Deshnikov stared at the chart for several minutes. "Their maximum range is about four hundred and twenty kilometers," he said. Then he set a pair of calipers against the chart's scale to mark off the distance, put one leg of the calipers on Yerevan and made a circle. "Baku is beyond their range and there are better alternatives--Tabriz and four cities in Turkey--Trabzon, Erzurum, Van and maybe Diyarbakir. It's dangerous to fly into Van these days, but they might not know that. I don't think they'd try for Tabriz, either."

"Why not?"

"They are Americans, yes? Since the Ayatollah, Iranians and Americans do not like each other. But Americans and Turks are allies in NATO. The Americans would think they would be more friendly than the Iranians. Still, the Turks might give them some trouble about their papers if they land at a commercial airport. The Syrians would be more understanding about such things," Deshnikov added, rubbing his thumb and forefinger together.

"Could they make Syria?" Aleksandr asked through clenched teeth.

"If there's more gas in the tanks than I thought or if they have strong tail winds from this storm coming down from Georgia."

"Damn it, yes or no?" Aleksandr snapped.

"Yes," Deshnikov snapped back. Looking again at the chart, he added, "There's an airfield at Qameshli, just inside the Syrian border. Nothing else."

Aleksandr looked at Danilov, who had followed them into the Flight Operations Office. "You've hunted this man before, Russian. What's your opinion?"

"Turkey, I think. After that, I have no idea. From there they could fly anywhere. Even take a ship. Who knows? Forget these people, Sasha. You've lost them."

Aleksandr stared coldly at Danilov's smug smile, thinking how he'd like to rip out his larynx. That would stop him smirking. "No. The game's not over. Look, Russian, I want that American and what he's carrying. Help me and I'll make you a present of the brooch. You said it might be worth a hundred thousand US? When did you ever get paid that much for a few days work? And I'll even let you kill the American when I'm through with him. I should think you'd welcome a second chance to finish the job."

Danilov drew on his cigarette and appraised Aleksandr for a long moment. He thought about the possibility that the American was moving diamonds, part of a new network. He'd need to to something about that. "Do you have a plan?"

"We'll book seats on the Athens flight now. I'll tell you what I think on the way to the hotel to pick up your baggage. If you don't like what I propose, go back to St. Petersburg."

"What about the brooch?"

"If you return to St. Petersburg, nothing is changed. When I hear from Zurich that the money's been credited, I'll have Deshnikov bring it to you. On a silk pillow."

CHAPTER FORTY

Under the Radar in Turkey

They crossed into Turkey without incident. The moonlight helped Mariah skim the treetops over the border and there was no sign they were detected by Turkish radar. Headset clamped over her honey blond hair, Mariah was locked onto the Van radio beacon, the engines were growling sweetly and they were settled into the flight. A moonlit Mt. Ararat loomed majestically on their left. Mariah was giving the smaller peaks along their route a wide berth and Tom and Ana were sitting quietly, allowing the drone of the engines to unwind the nervous tension of the past few hours.

In the glow of the instrument panel, Tom's thoughts turned back to the man he'd seen in the airport, the one who'd shot him in Vienna and taken the diamonds. He hadn't thought about it in a long time, not until Ana had asked about the scar on his back when they were at the dacha. And now. Was the sonofabitch still looking for him or was it some grisly coincidence? He'd sworn to himself if he ever saw him again . . . and here he'd had the opportunity and no way to seize it. He had to get Mariah and Ana out of there. The odds weren't in his favor, either. For the moment, it didn't matter. They'd escaped. But was he going to be looking over his shoulder now, everywhere he went?

Ana leaned forward and spoke in his ear over the roar of the engines. "I have checked behind to see if there are narcotics on the plane. I do not see any."

"Good girl," he said. "It's one thing to buy a visa and another to deal with a drug smuggling charge. Did you see any tape to hold this blasted box together?"

"Yes," she said. "There is tape."

Tom handed her the olive-wood box and she began to wrap it securely. "Look, Tom," she said. "The box has blood on it."

"Tape over it," he said.

"Your hands," Mariah said, turning toward him. "You've got blood all over them."

"The damned sentry. His nose was a gusher." Tom took the flashlight from Ana and ran it over her clothes. "A few spots," he said. "But they're small. I don't think they'll be noticed." He inspected his own sweater and khakis. "Can't see anything on my sweater, but I've got some on my pants. Shit. We don't want to walk into Syria looking like we just came out of an abattoir."

"Maybe it'll flake off when it dries," Mariah said. "Keep rubbing your hands together and if you still look like Jack the Ripper when we land, keep them in your pockets."

"What about my pants?" Tom said.

"Maybe we can squirt a little engine oil on you before we pass through customs."

"Great idea," he snarled.

Mariah picked up Mus and adjusted course to line up with Qameshli. "We've been out for an hour and I'm doing one-seventy-five miles over the ground, so we must have covered about that many miles. I'm guessing we're down to twenty gallons of gas, which means we run out at about two hundred and ninety miles. Where's that gonna put us?" she asked Tom.

He took the olive-wood box from Ana and spread out the chart. He laid his makeshift ruler on it and made his calculations. "It looks like a hundred and eighty kilometers from Mus to Qameshli. What's the conversion factor? Point six-two? That's a hundred and ten miles, so at a hundred and seventy-five at your current rate of fuel consumption, that's fumes at Qameshli. We need nineteen gallons and you're not sure we have as much as twenty. That's cutting it close."

"I've got the mix as lean as I dare and I think I'm close to optimal altitude for this bird. We may not have any choice but to put down in Turkey. What's that other place, Diyar-something-or-other?"

Tom laid his ruler on the chart again. "Diyarbakir is a hundred and fifty kilometers from Mus. That's a little over ninety miles--fifteen gallons. Not much better than Qameshli."

"Anything in between?"

"Nothing. We're in the Turkish boondocks."

"I know a man in Diyarbakir who would help us," Ana said.

"What about going back to Mus?" Mariah asked.

"I know no one in Mus," Ana replied.

"What's the terrain look like between Mus and Diyarbakir and between Mus and Qameshli, just in case we can't make either one?"

Tom inspected the chart and exhaled his concern. "Flying a straight line between Mus and Diyarbakir, you've got mountains. If you try for Qameshli, it looks flatter and flatter as you go south."

No one said anything for a while and the engines droned on as if they could run forever. Finally, Tom said, "These aren't lovable choices, but we can't take all day to decide. The Syrian border in that corner is wild and woolly and Qameshli's the most civilized place to cross. The others, including Ras al'Ain, aren't much more than flyspecks. To get to Diyarbakir, we'd have to fly west, then go back east to get to Mardin and Ras al'Ain. Jump in here anywhere, Ana, if I'm getting this wrong."

"No, Tom," she said. "You are right."

"You're saying head for Qameshli and hope for the best?" Mariah asked.

"If we come up short, the terrain looks more accommodating and Mardin is closer. So's the Syrian border. I hate betting the farm on a couple of gallons of gas, but that's how it looks."

Tension hung heavy in the cabin until Mariah said, "OK. Qameshli here we come." Now wide awake, Ana leaned forward between the front seats and squeezed Tom's arm.

****

"Tommy," Mariah said. "This gas gauge may be goofy, but the needles have been on their pegs for awhile. My gut tells me we're real close to empty. We need to be thinking about a place to put her down. This Cessna isn't a brick, but it's not noted for long-distance gliding."

"We just went through all this twenty minutes ago," Tom protested.

"Don't know what to tell you," she said. "Check the gauges yourself if you want to."

"Well, hell. Gimme the box, Ana."

Mariah was looking at the landscape below, its contours vague, but visible in the moonlight. "It doesn't look promising down there. I don't see any lights or roads. If I could land on a road, even a two-lane, we might find some gas and take off again."

"All I see on the map are mountains and some big lakes. The roads are winding, too. They definitely do not look like runways. There's a circle around Diyarbakir. What's that mean?"

"That means an airfield. What we need is a circle somewhere around here."

"There's a little circle at Mus and one at a place called Batman, if you can believe there's a place called Batman, but it's almost as far as Diyarbakir. That's it, babe. Want to go back to Mus?"

The port engine coughed. "Does that tell you anything?"

"We're on fumes," he answered.

"Should I 'May-Day' us? Nobody knows we're here. If I send a 'May Day,' they'll pick us up. Or find what's left and notify our next of kin."

"If you do and they pick us up, they'll put us in jail. If you don't--and if you can get us on the ground in one piece--we can still make Syria."

"Yeah, if. Easy for you to say."

"I'll take a chance on you," Tom said. "I don't fancy spending any time in a Turkish jail."

"OK. No 'May Day.' But I've got to go down for a look," Mariah said, her voice icy with tension. "Snug up your harness." She turned her head to call into the back seat. "Ana, tighten your seat belt as tight as it'll go."

"I will," Ana answered from the rear seat.

Tom was poring over the chart. "I can't see anything that looks like level ground, but there are these big lakes. What about putting it in the water?"

"You see any pontoons on this plane?" Mariah shot back.

"No. But I don't see any level ground around here, either. What's wrong with putting it in the water? It's not like it's our airplane. You'd be striking a blow for a drug-free Armenia."

"These things sink, you know. We only have one door and it's somewhat small in case you haven't noticed. Even if I don't kill us in the crash, we could drown before we got out."

"I thought these things would float."

"Sometimes," Mariah conceded. "Actually, there are a few

cases where the damned things would've become hazards to navigation if somebody hadn't gone out and sunk 'em. It could go either way, I guess. We could go down in two minutes or two hours or two days."

"Do you really mean two minutes?"

"Yeah."

"Two minutes is a long time."

"Not if one of us breaks a leg or gets knocked unconscious in the crash. We'd never get that one out of the harness and through that itty-bitty door in two minutes."

"OK," Tom replied. "But how much can go wrong if you land in the dark on some mountainside? This thing isn't boulder-proof, either. And it won't win any battles with a tree. What then?"

"You've got a point, but at least we wouldn't drown. Hey, I see the lake." Mariah pointed to her left as they crossed a long mountain ridge. "Big sucker, isn't it?" In the vee of two mountains, a large, long body of water shimmered in the waning moonlight.

"Does it have a name?" Mariah asked.

"As near as I can tell, it's the Batman Baraji. What's a baraji, Ana?"

"It means something to hold back water."

"Ah, a dam. These big lakes are reservoirs."

The starboard engine coughed.

"Oh, shit," Mariah said, her voice trembling. "I've never done this before."

"Don't worry, babe," Tom told her. "You can do it. I know you can."

"Thanks for the vote of confidence, but I can't tell what the ground looks like on the side of this mountain. The moon's too far down. Maybe you're right. Maybe I can put her in the water close to shore. At least I can take a long flat run at it, can't I?" Mariah was talking to herself now. "OK, guys. Hold tight. I'm gonna put it in the lake. I'll ease down and try to stall it in. Please, God, keep Your hand on my shoulder." For an instant, she also saw her father's leathery face and felt him with her in the cockpit. How she wished he was actually beside her. A lot was riding on what he'd taught her. She wondered if it would be enough.

She put the Cessna into a shallow dive toward the water below, leveled off at 300 feet and began easing the plane down. She hit the switch for the landing lights, illuminating the water. It looked smooth and calm. Both engines were coughing now, threatening to die at any moment. Tom folded the chart and handed it back to Ana. "Stick this in a briefcase," he told her.

"OK. OK," Mariah muttered to herself, both hands gripping the yoke. "Kill the power. Feather the props. Turn the blades so they won't dig in when we hit. Tom, hit the starter button on the starboard engine until the prop's level. I've got the port. Atta boy. Full flaps now. Easy. Easy now. Nose up. Nose up. Easy. Easy. Nose up. Nose up, girl."

Without the roar of the engines, the only sound was Mariah's nervous coaching and the wind whistling across the plane's surfaces. When the Cessna hit the water, the shock and the sound of the impact ran through them like a freight train. The plane bounced off the hard surface of the lake and Mariah struggled to hold it level as it lost airspeed and wallowed. All they'd need was for a wingtip to dig in and cartwheel them. Mariah managed to hold it level and the Cessna struck the water flat the second time, but with less force, and bounced again. When she got it onto the water again, she held it there, skidding along on its belly, the nose and wingtip tanks throwing up a great spray before the plane came to a sudden halt and began to settle. In the silence, the Cessna rocked back and forth as it floated. All three of its passengers were stunned by the force of the landing. Mariah came to her senses first and began yelling at the others.

"Out! Out! Get out of here! Tom, get the door open. You OK, Ana?"

Tom popped the quick release for his seat belt and shoulder harness, pushed the door open and looked out. Water was sloshing across the wing. He put one leg out to test it. The wing dipped in the water when it took his weight, but it held, the empty wing tanks giving it buoyancy. Through the darkness, he could make out the shore line twenty yards away.

Squatting on the wing, steam from the dead engines rose around him, the landing lights shed an eerie glow beneath the water. Tom fumbled for his wallet and stripped off the ankle wallet that held his remaining fifties and hundreds. He handed them to Mariah and said, "Get your passports and money into a briefcase. One way or another we're gonna get wet. I'm going to see how deep the water is," he said.

“Wait a minute before you come out.”

The water was icy cold and he gasped as he slipped off the trailing edge of the wing. He found rocky footing when the water was around his chest. He was freezing and spewing water that sloshed into his mouth. “Cold! Damned cold!” he gasped. “Y’all are going to have to swim. Too deep for you. Gimme the briefcases. I’ll try to walk ‘em in.” Ana handed them to Mariah and Mariah slid down the wing to give them to Tom. He held them over his head and began wading for shore, praying he wouldn’t step in a deep hole and go down.

“Come on, Ana,” Mariah said. “The plane’s floating now, but I want you in the door in case she starts to go down.”

“We should take the cloaks,” Ana said, handing them out to Mariah. “It is very cold and we will be wet.”

“Right,” Mariah agreed. “Maybe we can get a fire going and dry out. Might as well try to get Tom’s bag and mine out, too. For dry clothes. Let’s put ‘em on the wing for now.”

The Cessna continued to float, but the fuselage was belching great bubbles as water displaced the air in its cavities. They couldn’t see Tom on the shore, but they heard him coming back. “My God, it’s cold,” he sputtered. “Can you swim?”

Mariah and Ana returned a chorus of “Yes.”

“OK. Give me some stuff. I can make one more trip before I hit hypothermia.”

“Can you take the two bags and the cloaks?” Mariah asked. “We’re gonna need it all.”

“And my shoulder bag?” Ana added.

“Give ‘em to me. Come on. I’m freezing my ass off out here.”

Tom began wading back to the shore balancing the awkward pile atop his head. Mariah went over the wing as soon as he was clear and yelped when she hit the frigid water.

“Oh, my God,” she gasped, feeling her heart seize with the shock. She began to stroke for the shore with all her might.

Ana let her swim clear of the plane and went into the water. The weight of the olive-wood box took her to the bottom and she had to spring off the rocks to reach the surface. With a great effort, she side-stroked, sank, bounced to the surface again and eventually reached the shallows. On the shore, she fell to her hands and knees, choking and sputtering.

Tom helped her up. He couldn't stop his teeth from chattering. The night air was still, but all three of them were shaking badly from their icy soaking.

"We've got . . . to make . . . a fire," he managed to say in chattering spurts. "Any matches?"

"In my briefcase, maybe," Mariah said.

"Still got your flashlight?" he asked Ana.

She rummaged in her shoulder bag, found it and handed it to him. He flicked its beam back and forth across the shore, looking for anything that would burn. The moon was setting and the flashlight proved to be a Godsend. He laid it on the ground and used both hands to gather twigs and bits of brush.

Closer to the shoreline, Ana and Mariah found a relatively clear place on the shore and Tom unloaded his collection of firewood and kindling.

"I found the matches," Mariah cried.

"G-g-g-great," Tom said through chattering teeth. "P-p-put some rocks in a circle for a fire pit and get some paper handy. I'm going for more wood."

With freezing fingers, he built a pyramid of twigs over several wrinkled sheets of paper, struck the first match and cupped it in his shaking hands to shelter it from the wind. The paper flared, the twigs sparked and caught fire. Quickly, he added larger bits of wood until they had a roaring blaze.

"The cloaks are pretty dry. Let's get out of this wet stuff and wrap up in them," Mariah said. "We'll get warm faster. I'm freezing."

"Right," he said. "But get dry clothes out of your bag and change under the cloak. You don't want your skin exposed to this air. Get your boots up against the fire, too. Maybe they'll dry by morning. We'll build up the fire and lie down together."

"Mariah," Ana said. "Please, may I have some of your clothes? I have nothing."

"You bet," Mariah said, pulling the zippers on her duffel.

Out in the lake, they heard the Cessna release its last pocket of air and slip to the bottom. The plane rested in less than six feet of water, its tail sticking up at an angle above the surface. It would be completely visible from the air, but days, even weeks, might pass before the wreck was discovered.

They dug away the rocks around the fire and burrowed into the sand next to each other, drawing the cloaks over them to hold their body heat.

"Mariah," Tom said when they'd done their best to find comfortable niches. "I gotta tell you that was one hell of a job of flying back there. To say I knew you could do it in no way diminishes it. Now, if we just had a big juicy steak and a bottle of Armenian brandy . . ."

"Oh, shut up and go to sleep," Mariah said. "My stomach's as empty as that Cessna's gas tanks."

"I keep thinking about the dinner I made," Ana added mournfully.

Tom looked at the Rolex and was happy it was a 'Submariner,' able to withstand immersion in the cold waters of the baraji. The luminescent hands said the time was two-thirty-five.

****

Aleksandr slammed the phone onto its cradle. "Damned Syrians. I'll have to call Vasily in Damascus. He should know how to handle them."

Aleksandr and the Russian were waiting in the first class lounge of the Athens international airport. They'd slept little on the flight from Yerevan and both were irritable. Aleksandr's arm was throbbing and he'd taken half a dozen pain pills to keep going. Arriving shortly after nine that morning, they discovered there was no flight to Damascus until early evening--a Cyprus Air flight that connected through Lanarca with a two hour delay. They'd reach Damascus about midnight, Saturday.

Aleksandr dialed the numbers of the Russian embassy in Damascus from an entry in his address book. He verbally brutalized the receptionist who answered the phone and was soon connected with his old comrade in arms, Vasily Lipetsky.

"Vasily? Vasily, it's Aleksandr Avakian. . . . Yes, Vasily, a long time. . . . I'm in Athens, but I'm coming to Damascus. I need your help. My airplane was stolen and I'm chasing the thieves. I think they've flown to Syria, but the Syrian police are no help. Obviously, I don't know who to talk to. . . . Captain Achmed al Hussein. . . . Yes, Vasily. I know how difficult it must be these days, even in the embassy. Perhaps I can help. . . . Of course, Vasily. Dollars, not rubles. . . .The plane did not have much fuel, so if they are coming to Syria, it would have to be Qameshli or the northern region in general. They flew from Yerevan. . . . No, Vasily. I am not certain they are coming to Syria but I want you to call Qameshli airfield and ask if a small, two-engine plane landed there today with three people--an American man and two women, one American and the other Armenian. I want to trace them. I think they will try to come to Damascus, to catch an international flight. They will have to fill out forms to enter. Find out what they say. Can you do that? . . . Excellent. . . . The Armenian woman is Ana Stepanian. Thirty years old. Dark hair and eyes. Very pretty. I do not know the American woman's name, but she has blond hair and blue eyes. About the same age. Also attractive. The American man is older. Tall. Thin. His family name is Yeager. I do not know the given name. . . . I understand, but what I have just told you should be enough. . . . Of course. The Mukhabarat. Better than the police. They will understand what I need. . . . Vasily, I arrive in Damascus at midnight tonight and we should talk then. Would you book two rooms for me at the Semiramis Hotel? . . . Yes. An associate is traveling with me. Give me the telephone number in your apartment. . . . It will be good to see you, too." Aleksandr hung up the phone and looked at the Russian, who'd heard Aleksandr's side of the conversation.

"Old friend?" the Russian inquired.

"He served under my command in Afghanistan. He would help me because I ask, but I do not have to test his loyalty. He needs the extra money to keep his wife happy in Damascus."

"What if they don't go to Syria?" Danilov asked. "I think they'll go through Turkey. So much easier to be lost in the crowd than in that God-forsaken wilderness on the Syrian border. You think Qameshli only because Deshnikov said they might have enough gas to get there. I'd give them more credit than that."

Aleksandr stared at the Russian, not wanting to concede the point. "They might go to Diyarbakir," Aleksandr said grudgingly. "But Eastern Turkey is crawling with militia fighting the Kurds. They'd be picked up at the first checkpoint. Ana will know that." He fell silent for a few moments, thinking. Suddenly his expression changed. "Selim. Why didn't I think of that? She would try to use him if she went through Diyarbakir."

Aleksandr flipped through his notebook until he found a number, snatched the phone from its cradle and began punching the keys. He listened for a few moments, then slammed down the phone.

"What's the trouble?" the Russian asked

"There are no lines to Diyarbakir."

CHAPTER FORTY ONE

Turkey, Beside Batman Baraji

Tom woke with a start, adrenaline pumping. A man was standing a few feet away, staring at him with brilliant blue eyes. A dirty turban crowned a weathered face with a large nose and a full, scruffy beard shot through with gray. He wore baggy trousers and a misshapen suit coat over two layers of wool sweaters. He was carrying a British Enfield rifle of World War II vintage.

"Good morning," Tom said, coming to a sitting position and disturbing the cloaks that covered the women. His movement and the sound of his voice woke them. They blinked at the bearded man standing in the bright sunlight of early morning.

"Who's he?" Mariah asked sleepily.

Before Tom could answer, Ana unleashed a stream of Turkish and the man replied. He and Ana exchanged a few more short bursts of language before Ana explained. "This man is a shepherd. His oba--his tent--is nearby. He has invited us to eat with him and we should go. He is a Kurd, but not a guerrilla, I think."

Tom watched him as he spoke with Ana. "Then let's get all this stuff together. Ask him how far."

"He says not far."

"Tell him to give us a few minutes to get ready."

Ana and Mariah walked out of sight of the men and while they were gone, the Kurd tried to talk to Tom with words and gestures. Tom couldn't understand any of it and he thought it interesting that the Kurd didn't make signs or sounds like the airplane he might easily have seen sitting twenty yards out in the reservoir. Since they'd come in dead stick, without power, it was just possible the Kurd had no idea how they'd washed up on this particular shore.

Mariah and Ana returned wrapped in their black woolen cloaks. Tom had put on another pair of Levis with a fresh shirt and a dry sweater. His leather jacket was still damp, but he wore it anyway and slung the heavy cloak over his shoulder. With his desert boots and khakis, he might pass for a trekker if he could dump the briefcase and the rollaway.

"He hasn't noticed the plane," Tom said to Ana. "I'd like to leave it that way, but I don't think we can. We need a story, but what the hell is it?"

"Why not tell him the truth?" Mariah said. "Bad guys were chasing us, we ran out of gas and fell in the lake. Now we need a ride to civilization. Something like that."

Ana agreed. "But we should not tell him more than he needs to know. Even if he has not seen the airplane, he must believe we did not walk here. Look at us. Why not show him the plane and tell him we were flying, but not where we came from. We can tell him we want to go to Diyarbakir, where we have friends. He does not need to know about bad men. It will only raise the price of his help."

"That works for me," Tom said and, assuming that Kurdish society was male dominated, took the initiative. The Kurd had his back to the water, but Tom pointed out into the reservoir where the tail section of the Cessna was standing tall. When the Kurd turned around, Tom gave his best sign-language impression of an airplane, arms outstretched, accompanied by engine imitations he hadn't made since he was a boy. The Kurd pointed at Tom, Tom nodded and the Kurd grunted, as unimpressed as if small airplanes came down in the baraji every day. Tom shrugged and turned to Ana.

"Tell him we're ready and let him know whenever you think it's appropriate that we'd like his help getting to Diyarbakir."

Ana nodded and spoke a few words to the Kurd, who struck off up the slope.

They soon saw a wisp of smoke from a cooking fire. In the Kurd's camp two women and four children were working around a black wool tent, a billowy, irregularly shaped affair with protruding poles. The women glared at them with tight-lipped suspicion. The Kurd issued half a dozen gruff commands and the women and children went scurrying off in different directions. But around a corner of the oba, Tom noticed two small boys peeking at them with unconcealed curiosity.

****

The Kurd invited Tom to sit by the fire on a spread of colorful carpets at the entrance to the oba. When Ana and Mariah remained standing at a distance, he waved them over to the fire and gestured for them to sit down also. One of the Kurdish women brought a tray of hot milk, tea, flat bread and a weeping ball of white cheese. The woman, clad in a bright-colored dress, her hair covered by a kerchief, quickly retreated, scarcely acknowledging the foreigners in their camp. The Kurd, sitting cross-legged with the Enfield on his lap, motioned for Tom to take tea and eat.

The tea was arguably the best he had ever tasted. He knew it had something to do with the fact that he'd eaten nothing in almost twenty-four hours, but he relished it anyway. He scooped a gob of cheese onto the flat bread and poured fat-rich hot milk into his tea glass. Ana and Mariah had to be as famished as he, but here the men ate first, so the sooner he finished, the sooner Ana and Mariah would be allowed to eat.

After smelling the food and being obliged to watch Tom wolfing his portion, they could scarcely maintain their dignity when the tray was passed to them. The Kurdish women sat apart from the visitors and went about their work, taking no part in what was transpiring around the fire, but they furtively cut their eyes to watch the two strange women in their camp. When Ana and Mariah finished eating and more tea had been poured, Tom thought it might be socially acceptable to get down to business.

"Would you thank him for his hospitality and let me know if you think it would be OK to ask him to help us get to Diyarbakir?" Tom asked Ana.

She spoke for some time and Tom watched the Kurd nodding. She must have been pretty persuasive because the Kurd was almost smiling. He gestured toward Tom several times during the conversation and finally fell silent. Ana turned to Tom. "Thanks have been given and received. He is inviting us to stay the night. Put one of your hands over your heart to show you are grateful. Point to your watch and I will tell him we would like to stay but our friends in Diyarbakir will worry if we do not arrive. I will also ask if he would show to us where is the nearest road."

"Should we offer him money?"

"Yes, but wait. Let me see how he answers."

Tom spoke the words of regret, holding one hand over his heart and pointing to his watch, and stated their need to be in Diyarbakir.

After a long conversation with the Kurd, Ana turned to Tom and said, "His son will guide us to the highway. It is not far. He also says his son is bright boy and he will go away to school soon. I am sure he would accept something for this boy's education."

"Great. One other thing," Tom said. "We need a big sack. Our luggage is hugely out of place here, particularly the briefcases and my rollaway. We must look like aliens from outer space to these people. We might as well fly a flag that says 'We don't belong here.' If we can trade him my rollaway for a strong bag of some kind, I can stuff the briefcases in it and consolidate my clothes and Mariah's in her duffel, which isn't so conspicuous."

"I will see." Ana said.

They talked for a few moments and finally Ana looked at Tom. "He believes you worry about bandits and I think he understands. He is good man. He will take your rollaway bag, but he also wants your briefcase. For his son to take to school, I think."

"Let's see what he's got first," Tom said.

The Kurd went into his oba, returning with something that looked very much to Tom like a pair of saddlebags. They were worn and discolored, but they looked large enough to handle everything his briefcase contained and probably his clothes and Mariah's briefcase as well.

"Damn," Tom muttered. "That briefcase has been with me a long time. I got it in Argentina. I hate to let it go." To Ana, he said, "How long do we have to bargain over this?"

"He will be disappointed if it is done quickly, but I can explain again why we are hurrying."

"Make the deal then."

Thirty minutes later, the Kurd handed over the saddlebags and Tom went about repacking. When he finished, he turned to Ana. "Ask him when his son will be ready to take us down the hill."

The Kurd's shout brought a young man quickly to his side. The boy's name was Jamal, a blue-eyed copy of his father.

"Does this mean we can leave?" Tom said out of the corner of his mouth to Ana.

"Yes," she replied. "I think so."

Tom and the Kurd shook hands in front of the oba while Jamal gathered up Mariah's duffel and, in his eagerness, was about to take everything, but Tom slung the saddlebags over his shoulder and Ana held tight to her big purse and clutched the broken olive-wood box to her breast. Jamal understood and waited to lead them to the highway. In the commotion over the bags, Tom was able to find his hoard of fifty-dollar bills and whispered to Ana, "What should I give him? Fifty? A hundred?"

"One hundred will be generous," she whispered back.

Tom managed to put two fifty dollar bills in his hand as if they were the only ones he owned and handed them to the Kurd, whose eyes widened as he took them in his gnarled hands. He bowed his head and repeated a word--sepas--several times. Tom assumed that meant 'thank you'. Then the Kurd rattled off a long command to one of the women.

"He is happy with the money and with his trade for your luggage," Ana said. "He is telling his woman to bring food for our journey. You should accept it."

"He won't have to offer twice."

The trek to the highway was no more than five kilometers, but it took them almost two hours along a narrow, winding goat trail. About eleven o'clock they cleared the top of a ridge and saw below them the twisting two-lane ribbon of asphalt that Jamal said would take them to Diyarbakir. He pointed to several trucks parked beside a teahouse and told Ana he would get them a ride in one of them.

They stopped to catch their breath and rest before taking on the steep descent. Tom knelt at the edge of the ridge, studying the peaceful scene below. Ana squatted beside him while Mariah stretched out on her back, her arms shielding her eyes from the sun.

"If my friend in Diyarbakir can fix our papers to show entry into Turkey, we could fly from Diyarbakir to Ankara or Istanbul," Ana said. "From there we could go to many places, I think."

"Would your Armenian passport be a problem? The blockade and all, you know."

"Perhaps. But Selim is good with such problems. I am more worried about the Turkish army and the Kurds."

"There's nothing we can do about that until we connect with

your friend. The Kurdish business brings up another point," Tom said, pointing to the road below and the trucks parked at the teahouse. "What do you think the odds are those trucks are going to hit checkpoints or roadblocks between here and Diyarbakir?"

Mariah had been listening to their conversation and sat up quickly. "Checkpoints? What next?"

"I have been thinking about that, too. We should try to make Jamal understand our problem."

CHAPTER FORTY TWO

Diyarbakir, Turkey

Fifty dollars and a few supportive words about the Kurdish cause earned them a three-hour ride concealed in the aromatic splendor of a load of Turkish tobacco from Bitlis. They hit only one checkpoint between Silvan and Diyarbakir and since the driver was a regular on the route, the soldiers waved him through. When the truck pulled onto the side of the road and came to a halt inside the Mountain Gate of the ancient city of Diyarbakir, Tom crawled through the rows of strung tobacco that filled all but the small space against the cab where they'd hidden. He opened the tarp an inch to see if a squad of soldiers was waiting to welcome them. It was clear, so he vaulted over the tailgate and dropped to the ground. Ana and Mariah handed him the saddlebags, Mariah's duffel and Sarkis' olive wood box and Tom helped them climb out. He told the driver they were clear by pounding the side of the truck and they joined the people moving along the roadside. The driver revved the engine and roared into the city in a cloud of black smoke.

Mariah, blinking in the afternoon sunlight, exclaimed, "Am I glad to be out of that tobacco barn. I don't think I'll ever get the smell off me. Where to now?"

"To the house of a man I know," Ana said. "I will ask for his help. If we are not welcome, I do not know."

"Where's your friend's house?" Tom asked.

"Across the city, near the Mardin Gate."

"Then let's get moving before we attract attention," Tom said, waving down a dust-covered Mercedes taxi.

As the cab pulled to the side of the road and stopped for them, Ana told Tom and Mariah, "Say nothing in the taxi. I will speak for us." Ana and Mariah piled into the back seat with the bags and Tom sat up front. The driver ground the gears and worked his way back into the stream of traffic heading into the center of the city while Ana gave him directions in Turkish.

The slanting rays of the afternoon sun caught the columns of dust brought up by the wind from the lonely plain of the Tigris River and sprinkled its golden motes over the mix of costumes and conveyances of the ancient crossroads city. The cacophony of car horns beat a dissonant rhythm for the lazy shuffle of Kurdish men in baggy trousers and their women in colorful traditional dress. White and checkered kaffiyeh head scarves and long jellabah robes of Arabs up from Syria and Iraq bobbed along in the pedestrian flow. Modern Turkish men on motorcycles whizzed past veiled women covered in black chador.

The taxi worked its way through the traffic into the center of the city, crossed the main intersection and continued south toward the Mardin Gate, affording a slow, rolling tour of downtown Diyarbakir. The tawdry chaos of signs along their route, the narrow alleys, the black and white bands of the stones of the mosques accentuated Diyarbakir's foreign, frontier feeling.

Within sight of the Mardin Gate, Ana tapped the driver on the shoulder and told him, "Burada, burada." The driver pulled over to the side of the street and Ana gave him a ten-mark bill from her hoard of crisp Deutche marks. She got a fistful of soiled Turkish lira in change. They got out of the taxi and tried to blend into the milling stream of pedestrians passing the shops along the street.

"What was the silent treatment for?" Mariah asked, finally feeling free to speak.

"I did not want the driver to remember two English and a woman who spoke poor Turkish. He might report us to the police. Or tell the army. Do you see so many soldiers? Too much Kurdish business. We turn here."

As they followed her down a narrow side street, retail shops gave way to apartments and private houses. She stopped before the gate of one of these and pulled a cord that rang a bell on the other side of the wall. After the second ring, a peephole in the gate opened and part of a face became visible. "Evet?" the face asked.

Ana replied in Turkish. The peephole closed and the gate opened for them to pass into a quiet courtyard. A large, round man draped in an ivory-colored jellabah scowled at the three dusty, highly aromatic travelers who had interrupted the serenity of his afternoon.

Then a smile of recognition spread across his face and he and Ana spoke for several minutes.

"Selim is my friend from a time past. I have asked him about our papers and he says it is not possible. If not for the guerrillas, perhaps he could help, but the Turkish Army is in charge here and they cannot be bought so easily. We will not have papers, but he says he will help us reach Mardin and cross the border. His expenses will be two thousand dollars."

"That's a major chunk of our bank roll," Tom said.

"We cannot bargain. He is the only one I know," Ana said.

"Then we don't have a choice," Tom said. "We wouldn't last thirty minutes on the street. There is one thing, though," Tom said, scanning Ana's and Mariah's anxious faces. "Does the deal include a bath and something to eat, possibly a bed with clean sheets? We smell like a cigar factory."

Ana smiled at him, tension easing, and answered, "Yes. But we should not stay here long. Selim said nothing about being contacted and we should leave before anyone calls. Do you understand?"

"You think he's still out there?" Tom asked. "We made it. We escaped. I don't see how he thinks he can still find us."

"You do not understand him as I do. He has many contacts in Turkey, even in Persia and Syria. And we are not so difficult to see, yes? Selim will help us to change our clothes, too, but that will not be enough to stop him from looking for us."

A frown wrinkled Tom's forehead as he tried to assess the situation.

"Tom," she said. "We have no choice."

"Yeah. I guess so. Do we pay him now?" he asked.

"Let me give him my German marks. To make it seem I am escorting you." Ana went into her shoulder bag and removed a leather wallet. She counted out three thousand marks and handed them to Selim, who took them without expression, not even a smile of thanks.

"Does he speak English?" Mariah asked.

"Yes, some English," Ana replied. "I will not introduce you. He does not need to know who you are. It is safer that way."

"If this deal is done, could we take delivery of the bath?" Mariah asked. Fatigue had overcome her and she was almost out on her feet, swaying silently in the afternoon shade.

"There is one room with bath. We must use it in turn," Ana told her. "Please hurry."

Ana put her hand on Mariah's shoulder to indicate to Selim that Mariah would go first. Selim motioned to Mariah to follow him, leaving Tom and Ana standing alone in the walled garden.

Selim sent a servant to them with tea and hot towels. The servant led them to a bench near the house and they sat down beneath the shade of tall, leafy trees. The murmur of a fountain gurgling quietly in a small pool surrounded by plantings soothed their weary spirits. But they took only a little time to relax.

"Let's get back to Aleksandr," Tom said when it seemed they were alone. "If the damned plane hadn't conked out on us, we'd be flying out of Damascus right about now. Instead, we're on the ground in bloody Turkey and we've already lost--what?--twelve hours or more. And you're worried that he'll call here and this fellow, Selim, will blow our cover."

"Aleksandr might think I would bring you here."

"Then he could be ahead of us, waiting." And the Russian might be with him, he thought.

"Yes. It is true. So we must behave as if he knows what we are doing."

Tom nodded. "OK. We'll use every trick we can think of, but I need a shower and something to eat."

They fell silent, allowing their minds and their bodies to respond to the garden's serenity.

"You've been here before?" Tom asked at last.

"Two times," she said.

"With Aleksandr?"

"Yes, when we went to Ras al'Ain. Another time I came alone and with the woman who broke her ankle in Damascus. It is now a long time ago. Selim is older and more fat."

Tom nodded, letting the tension go out of his body, accepting the numbness of fatigue.

Selim returned and took Ana upstairs. Lulled by the gentle gurgle of the fountain, Tom was soon dozing. When Selim touched his shoulder, it seemed he'd only closed his eyes for a minute. Selim led him into the house, up a narrow staircase and along a cool hallway to a room at the rear. When he opened the door, the delicious fragrance of humidity and soap greeted him. This was the room with the bath and the women had just departed. He fervently hoped there was still hot water.

****

They rallied for dinner downstairs and ate like starving animals, scarcely speaking. As they finished, Selim loomed in the doorway.

Ana greeted him in Turkish and they spoke for a few moments. Then she turned to Tom and Mariah. "He has arranged for transportation to Mardin in the early morning. It will be uncomfortable, but Mardin is only one hundred kilometers so only one hour or two. He asks what clothes we want. He will try to bring them."

"We're going to have to overnight here?" Tom asked. "I thought you were worried about you-know-who calling."

"Yes, I am worried," Ana said. "But Selim says there has been much activity by Kurds. Last night, they attacked a police post and made an explosion in the telephone building. Now it is not possible for calls to come to him. Perhaps for several days. It is bad luck that we cannot go on right away, but I think we are safe here now."

"Wait a minute," Mariah said, her voice edged with anxiety. "I thought we were going to get a plane out of here to Istanbul."

"Without a stamp in our passport that says we entered Turkey properly and with no Turkish visa, we'd be dead ducks at the ticket counter," Tom explained. "Want to check out a Turkish jail?"

"No, thanks. I saw that movie, *Midnight Express*. That's close enough for me. But what're we going to do?"

"Selim's going to smuggle us across the border into Syria. We'll buy visas on our way in."

"Why can't we do that here?" she asked, frowning.

"Because we're in the middle of a civil war and the Turkish Army looks askance at foreigners showing up unannounced. Considering that you're two out of two in crash landings, I wouldn't think you'd be so eager to get on another airplane."

"I'd chance it. More and more, this place feels like we went the wrong way in a time tunnel."

294

"Tom," Ana interrupted. "Selim asks again what clothes to bring for us."

"We don't want to stand out, but we're not gonna pass for Turks or Kurds," he said. "Suppose we go for the Euro-trash look, seedy, traveling light? I saw some types like that yesterday as we were driving through the city. My khakis and your jeans ought to pass muster. Let's have jackets from the local market, too. We can stow our leather ones. You need different shoes, too, Ana. Something sturdy. Your boots are way too elegant for this. And backpacks. I want to get rid of these saddlebags and Mariah's duffel won't make the long haul. Can he do that for us?"

Ana launched a long explanation. Selim replied and Ana looked at Tom and Mariah. "He can do it," she said. "And he has agreed to return the priests' cloaks."

"For two thousand bucks, it's a bargain," Tom grumbled.

****

Ana suggested they take their coffee to the roof where they could see the city and have a breath of air before they went to sleep. Mariah begged off, pleading exhaustion, so Tom and Ana went up alone.

Leaning against the parapet, they gazed out across the ancient city walls at an evening star glittering in a pale purple sky. Below, smoke from the cooking fires made smudges against the sky and the lights of the city slowly winked on and multiplied, casting a yellow glow over the city. To their left, the sounds of traffic on one of the main commercial streets was muted and the garish neon could be ignored by turning away from it. It was cooler than they had expected and Tom put his arms around her. Ana leaned back against him, encircled in his embrace.

He inhaled the fragrance of her hair, still scented by curing tobacco. "You're awfully quiet," he said to her at last.

"I was thinking about ghosts," she replied softly.

"Ghosts?"

"Yes. Ghosts of Armenians who lived here long ago. Once many lived here. Now very few."

"The genocide?"

295

"Yes," she said, looking over her shoulder at him. "Do you remember what I told you at our memorial?"

"Most of it," he said. "Pretty grisly stuff."

"Yes, that is true. Our people were sent walking in 'convoys' away from their homes in Cilicia. They came through this place. Diyarbakir. I see them falling and dying by the road--long lines stretching to Syria, the way we go tomorrow. To Ras al'Ain. It was refugee camp for people who survived the long march in 1915. A small place. I have another contact there who will help us cross into Syria."

"How is it that you have a contact in Ras al'Ain? With that kind of a history, I'd think that'd be the last place for an Armenian."

"I did not choose it," she said, coming out of Tom's arms and resting her forearms on the parapet. "It was for spies. I was told that a British spy--Kim Philby--used it as a secret way to come to Soviet Union. It is called the Philby Gate. Others followed."

In the silence, Tom was both amused and disoriented. He was standing on a rooftop at dusk, gazing out over an ancient, walled city in central Turkey with a woman who'd helped people spy on the United States, traveling a route pioneered by a British traitor and paved in blood by Armenians on their way to die in the Syrian desert. It was true. They had come the wrong way through a time tunnel.

In Yerevan, facing the prospect of never seeing Ana again, he'd felt the pain of her being pulled away from him by a relentless tide of events. Here, standing beside her, so aware of her scent and the warmth of her body, he felt instead a vast distance, one he couldn't at the moment imagine bridging. Perhaps he could see in his mind the long lines of refugees all those years ago, but he could never feel their pain and sorrow as she did.

With the sounds of the city muted in the distance, he let the cool breeze whisper in his ear and soothed his eyes by tracing the lines and features of her face. He took her in his arms again and she came eagerly, as though he were her last, best refuge. Silently they watched the night fall on Diyarbakir.

CHAPTER FORTY THREE

Damascus, Syria

Weary from the long journey and the lack of sleep, Aleksandr and the Russian presented their passports to the night clerk at the Hotel Semiramis in Damascus and asked that they be returned as soon as possible. A fifty dollar bill peeked from the pages of Aleksandr's passport to ensure the clerk's cooperation. Upstairs, Aleksandr went immediately to the telephone, tossing his briefcase onto the bed.

"Vasily will be here shortly," Aleksandr muttered, replacing the instrument as Danilov came in. "They didn't pass through Qameshli, at least not yet."

"They've outsmarted you again, Sasha," Danilov said, smirking.

"It's not over," Aleksandr snarled through clenched teeth. "It's not over."

The Russian shrugged and went back to his room. Aleksandr took two more pain pills, slipped off his shoes and fell back on the bed. The adrenaline that had been keeping him going gave way to the pain pills, his anger turned to ashes and a wave of melancholy enveloped him.

He reached out for memories of the Mexican beaches and deep blue waters of the Pacific, but they failed to banish his growing sense of loss. A vision of Ana descending a wide staircase in a long velvet gown came into focus. A room full of people, diplomats of a hundred nations, glittering crystal chandeliers. Conversation stops. Every head turns. Every eye on her, his Ana.

A groan escaped from the well of his being. He'd seen the haunting vision many times before. In Afghanistan when the misery was too great and the opium pipe came easily to hand, he would dream of how it would be when he took the post in Europe he'd been promised.

The vision swam away. He tried to hold it, but the American forced his way in. Ana was looking at him. Her eyes, so luminous, lusting for the American. He saw her naked for a moment and then the American put out his hand and took her away. The screen on his eyelids darkened and oozed blood red.

Vasily tapped at the door and Aleksandr forced himself back to consciousness. Vasily knocked again, louder this time. Aleksandr rose from the bed to let him in. "Major Avakian. How good to see you again," Vasily said.

"Come in, Vasily," Aleksandr mumbled, still groggy.

"Your arm, Major," Vasily said. "You've been hurt?"

"Only a scratch. Now," Aleksandr said. "You're sure they didn't land at Qameshli?"

"I called the airfield myself. Nothing unusual. I've asked the Mukhabarat to help and my contact there will be more cooperative than Captain Hussein. There is the expense, however. He also wanted descriptions. I could only tell him what you told me. He would have preferred to have more, even pictures. The Detain for Questioning list cannot be distributed for some hours, but I have been assured that they will pass the order by telephone to the posts on the Turkish border."

"Do you have confidence in these people?" Vasily shrugged.

"They are the best on offer."

"Very well. Can you get me a car?"

"Of course. What kind?"

"Most of the services here are Mercedes, so something like that. And strong field glasses. How much will it cost, Vasily?"

"I ask nothing for myself, Major, but I have already promised my contact at the Mukhabarat a thousand dollars just to issue the Detain for Questioning order, so perhaps you could advance funds to me for that and these other expenses. The car, for example."

Aleksandr snapped the locks on his briefcase and handed Vasily two banded bundles of fifty dollar bills that amounted to ten thousand US. "I'm not rich, Vasily, but I want these people."

Vasily took the money and looked closely at Aleksandr. "A personal thing, Major?"

"Yes. Personal."

The hotel operator rang at mid-morning with a line to Diyarbakir. Half an hour later, Selim came on the line.

"Selim, it's Aleksandr Avakian here . . . Yes, I hoped so. I'm trying to get in touch with her. . . . Early this morning? To Mardin? Not to Istanbul, then? . . . Yes, I understand how difficult it is with papers now. The Kurds and all. Where will she cross, Selim, Ras al'Ain or Qameshli? . . . No, no, Selim. I left it to her to decide. It's just that there's been a change of plans. If I knew where she would cross, I could meet her . . . . I understand the difficulty, Selim, but it's urgent. Call me here in Damascus if you learn her route or hear from her."

Aleksandr was elated when he hung up. "You see, Russian? I know this woman. They're coming to Syria. And then Jordan. Probably their plan all along was to take the morning flight to Athens and then Amman. We flushed them early, that's all. And now they're on the ground, running. We need only spring the trap." As Aleksandr took three quick strides to the window and looked out, another thought struck him. "I wonder what they did with the plane."

The Russian shook his head. "You are very lucky. Finding a needle in a haystack."

"No, Russian. I know this woman. I taught her all she knows. And I can guess where she will go next. She'll cross at Ras al'Ain. Where the hell is Vasily with the car?" he shouted, pacing the room.

When Vasily failed to appear by eleven o'clock, Aleksandr stormed downstairs and inquired about the driving time to Ras al'Ain. He was assured that it could not be done in less than seven hours. He bought a road map of Syria, returned to his room and called Vasily's apartment. Vasily's wife told him that Vasily was 'out' and she didn't know when to expect him. He got the same answer from the Russian Embassy. Seething, but subdued, he went to the Russian's room.

"Vasily's still not here with the car and I can't reach him," he muttered.

"So what?" the Russian grumbled, groggy from sleep and in ill temper from being awakened. "Let the Mukhabarat pick them up at the border."

"Yes, yes," Aleksandr replied. "I want the Mukhabarat to track them, but the Mukhabarat is very good at making things disappear-- people, money, rare artifacts . . . We might never see the coins if we aren't there when they run Ana and the American to ground."

****

Tom wasn't sure he'd ever walk again. The road was rough between Diyarbakir and Mardin and they'd been sealed in coffin-like crates, surrounded by empty vegetable cartons and covered with fodder. They could breathe and even if the air reeked of decay, they weren't cold. The backpack that now carried his few remaining clothes and the contents of his briefcase had been jammed into the crate at his feet. They'd been stopped three times at roadblocks and been passed through each time without a search. Perhaps money had changed hands between the driver and the sentries. But the delays made their confinement last almost three hours, not two. The ordeal ended in a damp, dark warehouse in the main market of Mardin where four men dug them out of the fodder and set their crates on the floor. The truck drove away and the rolldown door of the warehouse rumbled down and clanged shut. Tom heard Arabic being spoken.

"Leave the crates here," one man said. "Osman will see to them."

"Who are they?"

"Don't ask."

The crate's cover had been tacked closed and Tom easily pushed it away, the nails shrieking as they left their sockets. He sat up, looking to the two startled Arabs every bit like a corpse returned to life in its coffin. Wide-eyed, they left quickly by a side door.

"Ana? Mariah? Are you OK?" he asked.

"Yes, but please help me," Ana replied.

"Me, too" Mariah called.

"Just push the lids off," Tom said. "They're barely tacked."

The other two crates popped open immediately, the lids clattering onto the concrete floor. Ana and Mariah sat up and looked about the surrounding gloom. Dim light filtered in from the larger warehouse beyond.

"I don't care if this does look like Dracula's cave, I am so glad to be off that truck," Mariah said, rolling over the side of her crate onto all fours. Ana was able to stand. She went directly to Tom.

"Are you all right?" she asked, kneeling beside him.

"I think so, but give me a hand getting out of here, will you? I've got back cramps something fierce." Ana gripped his wrist and pulled. With her taking some of the strain, he got his feet under him, but the muscle spasms in his back kept him from straightening up.

They hadn't fully regained their mobility when the side door opened and a large, weathered man wearing a kaffiyeh came into the room. Three days' of dark stubble covered his face and his eyes had a cruel slant that bothered Tom.

"Good morning," the man said in accented English. "I am Osman Kayir. I will take you where you can change your clothes and have something to eat. We can talk on the way."

A dented Ford Fairlane sedan sat idling outside the warehouse and Tom's ear told him that the Ford's battered body housed a well-tuned, powerful engine. Mariah recognized its sweet sound, too, and raised her eyebrows to Tom as they piled into the car. Osman took the front seat beside the driver and they snaked slowly through the trucks and wagons crowding the market.

Osman leaned over the back of the seat and spoke to Tom, ignoring the two women. "You wish to cross secretly into Syria?" he said.

"We cannot cross from Turkey in the usual way because we have no Turkish entry visas," Tom replied. "We also have no visas for Syria. But I understand they can be obtained at the border."

"How did you come into Turkey?"

Tom shrugged and said, "Does it matter?"

"You are in Turkey illegally?"

"We're just passing through," Tom replied.

"Illegal entry is a serious offense. Perhaps you are not welcome in Turkey. Perhaps you are wanted by the police."

"No. Not in Turkey or anywhere else." Tom hoped it was true that Aleksandr hadn't reported his airplane stolen in Armenia.

"Crossing the border is difficult these days," Osman said at last. "When do you wish to go?"

"As soon as possible," Ana interjected.

Osman looked at her for the first time. In his family, women did not become involved in men's affairs. He ignored her and turned back to Tom. They appraised each other as the Ford crept through narrow defiles between pale limestone buildings. Osman wanted to know the story-- why they were in Turkey, how they came to know Selim in Diyarbakir, why they wanted to go to Syria. But in the end, he made his decision on the American's hard eyes.

"American, yes?" Tom nodded.

"I don't understand about the women," Osman said.

"They're with me," Tom replied, trying to close the subject. "Can you help us? Yes or no."

"How do you expect to get visas? Do you think you can walk into any border post and they will do as you ask?"

"It used to be just about that easy," Tom said. "Pay a little baksheesh and trouble has a way of disappearing."

"But you must know who to pay," Osman said. "This is what I can do. Give me your passports. I will see to the visas in Senyurt. I have a friend there. In your case--your papers not in order--perhaps he will only charge one hundred US for each."

"So you'll take us across the border for three hundred dollars?"

Osman smiled. "No, my friend. It is three hundred dollars for the visas and one thousand five hundred for the transportation."

"Fifteen hundred to cross?" Tom protested. "It's only a few miles."

"Listen, my friend. You are crossing a frontier illegally. Three of you. If not for Selim, I would not even speak to you."

Tom felt a trickle of sweat run down his rib cage. Fifteen hundred was another big chunk of their remaining bankroll. Plus three hundred for the visas. Six thousand had seemed like so much when they started.

"Give us a minute," Tom said and whispered to Ana, "What about your friends in Ras al'Ain? I thought you were going to have them get our visas."

"Yes," she whispered back. "But perhaps this is better plan. It is more business for him."

"And you think a bigger payday might help him play straight?"

"He has offered to get the visas. I am afraid now to tell him no."

"I see your point." He turned back to Osman and said, "OK. You've got a deal."

"You are a wise man. Now we go where you will be safe for a few hours. If it is quiet at Senyurt, perhaps we will cross tonight. Do not leave the house where I take you. And be ready to leave at any time this evening after the sun sets. Do you understand? You pay now."

"Three-hundred now for the visas," Tom said. "I'll pay the fifteen hundred when we're safely across the border in Syria.

"Half now, the rest in Syria," Osman countered. "I will return your passports when you cross the border."

"Five hundred now. The rest later. My final offer. There are other ways to get into Syria." Tom wondered if Osman would bail out on them for five hundred bucks and a pair of US passports, which were as good as gold on the black market. He decided he had to take the chance.

Osman gave Tom a shrug and the slightest sideways nod of agreement as the Ford pulled into an alley so narrow that none of the car doors would open. The driver stopped the car and Osman stared at Tom while the Ford idled softly.

Tom pulled up the leg of his pants, undid the Velcro of the ankle wallet and withdrew all the bills he could touch. He counted out three hundreds and four fifties and handed them to Osman. He still held two fifties in his hand.

Osman took the money and nodded, but he also looked at the two fifties, wondering where Tom kept the remaining thirteen hundred dollars he'd been promised. "I must have your passports."

"Tom . . ." Mariah said. "Are you sure we ought to be doing this? If this guy bails out on us, we're up Shit Creek without a passport. You know what kind of trouble that puts us in."

"No guts, no glory, Mariah. Hand it over."

Osman gathered the passports, taking a little extra time to inspect Ana's. "Armenian. This one will be more difficult. I thought you were all US. I should have charged you more. But I have given my word. It will be as we agreed." Then he muttered something to the driver and the Ford moved slowly down the narrow alley into the courtyard of an ancient apartment building. A dozen ragged boys, none older than seven or eight years, were playing soccer on the hard-packed earth of the courtyard. They stopped their game and ran away when the car appeared.

"Wait here. A woman will show you," Osman said, opening the back door. "Do you speak Turkish or Arabic?"

"Yes," Ana said. Osman scowled at her again. There was malice in his gaze and she wished she'd left it to Tom to answer for her.

They got out of the car and retrieved their backpacks. The Ford turned around slowly and eased back down the alleyway to the street, leaving Tom, Ana and Mariah standing alone in the middle of the courtyard. Tom let go a deep breath and turned to Ana. "I thought you said you had friends in Mardin."

"This Osman is not my friend. But Selim told me he did not think my people were active now. If Osman had been difficult, I would have tried to find my old friends."

"You think he was being easy back there? What would he have had to do to be 'difficult?'"

"There is much he might have done. When the car stopped between the buildings, we could not have opened the doors to leave. He could have cut our throats and taken our money. Who would complain?" she said.

"So now you trust him because he didn't cut our throats?" Mariah asked.

"I do not trust him," Ana said. "We could have tried to find my friends here in Mardin. But it is a risk to go searching. Like Diyarbakir. If the police or the army stopped us on the street, before we reached Selim's house, we would be in jail. Here it would be worse. They would think we were here to help Kurds."

"And the Sheik of Araby has our passports," Mariah said, shooting Tom an accusing look.

A woman called down from a balcony and they turned to look up at her. Ana answered and the two women spoke briefly in Turkish. "We are to go up," Ana said and they straggled toward the stone staircase leading to the second floor.

The woman gave them flat bread and cold rice with a few chunks of mutton laced with congealed grease. The tea revived them, but there was no bath worthy of the name, only a room with a concrete floor and a drain where they took turns douching in cold water from a single tap and dabbing at themselves with threadbare towels. Their sleeping room was furnished with pallets teeming with tiny insects eager to hitch a ride. To avoid the pallets, they spent the afternoon leaning on the railing of the second story balcony discussing their plans. The children returned and resumed their boisterous play in the courtyard below.

Mariah had contained herself through the negotiations with Selim and Osman. Now she spoke.

"Tom," she said, an edge in her voice. "We're so far out on a limb . . . Have you given any thought to what we do if that guy, Osman, doesn't come back?"

"That's gonna have to be a little sketchy for now," he said. "Let's skip to the part when we cross into Syria."

"I'm glad you said when, not if," Mariah said.

"Syrian visas are the first priority," Tom said. "If Osman comes through, we've taken a major step forward. Then we need transport to Damascus." He paused for a moment, watching dust swirl as two of the boys below wrestled their way through an argument, then went on. "Once we get to Damascus, we're not home free, but if our papers are in order, we can get off this underground railroad, check into a hotel, get some money. Take a bath. What do you think about transport to Damascus, Ana?"

"We should hire a service. It would not attract attention. We could go to Aleppo, then south to Damascus. But perhaps we should leave from Aleppo," she said. "Please remember that Aleksandr does not know you only have two small pieces. He would not have killed Karine for so little. We also made fool of him because we escaped from Yerevan." Ana paused and looked at Tom. "And he is angry that I am with you. Marina said he will kill you. He may still know people in Syria who would help him find us."

Without lifting his elbows from the railing, Tom turned his head to her and asked, "Like who?"

"*Mukhabarat*--it is like KGB. They will understand each other."

"So we need to be on the lookout for the secret police," Mariah said. "Do they wear blue blazers and name-tags or what?"

✱✱✱✱✱✱✱✱✱✱✱

Vasily appeared at the Semiramis with a dusty Mercedes sedan at two that afternoon. He parked it in front of the hotel and went straight to Aleksandr's room.

"I'm sorry for the delay, Major. There was some difficulty with the car. It couldn't be helped. But the Detain for Questioning Order has been issued to all Mukhabarat posts, police stations and border crossings. It will take some time to distribute the descriptions to airport security, train stationmasters and bus depots, but the process is underway."

"Never mind. I know where they will try to cross."

"Really?" Vasily asked.

"They will come to Ras al'Ain in the next twelve hours, I am sure," Aleksandr said confidently. "All you have to do is send a few

Mukhabarat to the house of Ali Hashemi. That's where she'll go for help." Aleksandr pounded his fist into his palm and grinned. "Tell the Mukhabarat to hold them and treat them--and their goods--with the utmost respect. We'll drive to Ras al'Ain as soon as they're in custody." He turned to the Russian and exclaimed, "We've got them, Russian."

Vasily smiled and reached for the telephone. Aleksandr watched with growing impatience as Vasily's exasperation mounted. After an hour, he put down the telephone.

"They have no one available to send. The closest offices are in Aleppo and Dier az-Zor. They have alerted the border guards and there is a resident operative at Ras al'Ain. They will be taken into custody when they try to cross."

"Do they think they're going to walk up to the frontier? They won't cross in the normal way. Idiots! We should have driven there ourselves."

The Russian stubbed out his cigarette and arose from the chair where, with detached amusement, he'd been watching Vasily's futile efforts to move the Syrian Secret Police. "It's four o'clock now. You wouldn't reach there until eleven at night. There's nothing you can do but wait and see what the Mukhabarat turns up. They still have to run the gauntlet of the Detain for Questioning order."

CHAPTER FORTY FOUR

Ras al'Ain, Turkey

Osman appeared as the moon was rising, bringing bad news.

"It was not possible to get your visas," he told Tom.

"Why not?"

"The PKK raid on Diyarbakir has made everyone nervous. My friend said he could do no business for me. Most of the Turk forces are east of where we will cross. I can put you into Syria tonight, but I cannot help you with papers."

Tom gave Ana a questioning look.

She shook her head and said, "We have another way. It will be all right."

Osman shrugged and returned their passports.

"What about the three hundred dollars I gave you for the visas?" Tom asked.

"There is more risk crossing now. I will not make you pay for what I did not give you, but I will keep the money until we are at the border. Don't worry, American. I am an honorable man. I am not yet sure if you are."

Tom had no choice, so they loaded the backpacks into the trunk of the Ford and rode as before--Tom, Ana and Mariah in the back seat, Osman and the nameless driver in the front. The Ford moved slowly through the town, but once they cleared the outskirts, they flew toward Kiziltepe at 80 miles an hour, the engine humming effortlessly. The driver slowed passing through Kiziltepe, crossed the Urfa highway, then turned onto an unpaved road outside Senyurt, the last Turkish town before the Syrian border. They bounced along a track littered with rocks washed up from recent rains, headlights off, the driver steering by the moon. Scrub lined both sides of the track. They'd have no warning of a Turkish border patrol until they were face to face. After half an hour of this punishing passage, Tom asked Osman, "How much more of this?"

"It is fifty kilometers from Senyurt to where you will cross. Another hour."

It proved to be a little less. A man dressed as an Arab stood in the center of the track and the Ford stopped. He came to the passenger-side window and greeted Osman in Arabic.

"*Salaam aleekum, Osman.*"

"*Wa aleekum al-salaam, Hamid,*" Osman replied. "Is it safe to cross?"

"We must hurry. Syrian patrols are everywhere, looking for the PKK who attacked Diyarbakir. They don't want them crossing."

"It was clear coming from Senyurt," Osman said. "The Turks are concentrating elsewhere. Let me finish the business, Hamid, and I will give them to you."

"Who are they, Osman?"

"Two Americans and an Armenian woman. The man seems capable, Hamid. Do I make myself clear?"

"Yes, Osman. I understand."

Osman turned back to Tom and said in English, "This man will guide you across. Now it is time to pay."

"I said I'd pay the balance once we were across the border, in Syria, not in Turkey. Come with us and you can collect on the other side or the guide can bring you the money."

"You are a difficult man, my friend," Osman said. "We will do it as you say, but I must see the money." He touched a forefinger to his lower eyelid to emphasize the point.

"All right," Tom replied, removing his ankle wallet. Osman held a small penlight while Tom opened the wallet and took five hundreds from it. He made a fan of them while Osman used his forefinger to check the money.

"Now, are you coming with us or do I give the money to the guide?" Tom asked.

"I will come with you," Osman said.

So far Tom had heard nothing sinister in anything Osman had said in English or in Arabic. In fact, his warning to the guide, Hamid, had been reassuring. In silence, they stumbled after Hamid for half an hour before the scrub cleared and they halted at the edge of a field of wheat stubble. "Welcome to Syria," Hamid said, his smile visible in the moonlight. "I will go to the road to wait. When the truck arrives, I will signal you to come."

Tom reached into his pocket and retrieved the ten hundred dollar bills. He handed them to Osman and whispered to him in Arabic, "*Shukran jazilan, Osman.* You were true to your word." If Osman were surprised to hear Tom's well-accented Arabic, he gave no outward sign of it. He replied in Arabic, as if he'd known all along.

"Maa salama, Ameriki. Allah maak."

A Toyota pickup truck was stopped on the road, thirty yards away, engine idling. Hamid spoke to the driver, turned and waved them forward. They crunched through the field toward the road. Hamid lowered the tailgate and motioned them into the back of the pickup. Tom scrambled in and offered his hand to Ana and Mariah.

"Where do you wish to go?" Hamid asked Tom. Ana replied in Arabic, giving him the name of a restaurant near the main market. Hamid nodded and got into the front seat. Tom looked back over the way they'd come, but Osman was gone. "Where are we going?" Tom asked Ana as the truck, running without lights, rumbled down the road while the cold desert air lashed at them and brought tears to their eyes.

"Why do you ask?" she said, an edge to her voice. "You speak Arabic. Why did you not tell me?"

"What comes after the main market?" Tom asked, smiling.

"The house of Ali Hashemi."

The Toyota passed through the empty streets of the bedraggled border town of Ras al'Ain and stopped beside the main entrance of a dark and deserted market. Tom bounced out of the truck, unhooked the tailgate and helped Ana and Mariah down. He rehitched the tailgate, patted the fender and the Toyota pulled away, leaving them standing alone in the street.

"I hope I remember the way," Ana said when the truck was out of sight.

"So do I," Tom said, shifting the backpack to a more comfortable position.

****

They made their way through dark streets, rousing dogs as they passed. A few blocks from the main market, Ana stopped in front of a small house set right on the sidewalk. She used her flashlight to read the name on the brass plate by the door. "This is the house,'" she announced softly. She knocked on the door, short, sharp raps, then waited. She tried again. At last, a light came on and muffled sounds could be heard. Someone was awake and stirring. The door opened a crack and a sleepy-eyed young man snarled at her. "What do you want?"

"I am sorry to disturb the house at such a late hour, but I must see Ali Hashemi," Ana whispered.

"He is with Allah. Three years past. Go away."

"And Leila Hashemi?" Ana asked, her heart sinking and a rivulet of sweat beginning to run down her spine.

"She's asleep. What do you want?" the man asked, annoyance growing in his voice.

"Please," Ana begged. "Please tell her Ana is here."

"Wait here," the man growled and closed the door.

Ana turned to Tom and Mariah and shrugged.

"What if she doesn't remember you?" Tom asked.

"I do not know," Ana replied.

The door was flung open and a woman of fifty years appeared, wrapped in a heavy robe.

"Ana?" the woman said. "Is it really you?"

"Yes, Leila. It is me," Ana said and the two women fell into each others arms.

"Come in. Quickly," Leila Hashemi said and was surprised when Tom and Mariah materialized and slipped through the door behind Ana.

"These are my friends," Ana explained, seeing Leila's surprise. "We need your help."

"Who are you?" the young man who'd answered the door demanded, wrapping himself in as much dignity as his sleeping clothes would allow.

"Achmed," Leila said to him. "This woman is more than a sister to me and one of your father's friends from long ago. Do you not remember? We must help them if we can."

Ana smiled, finding a lost memory of the young boy who'd shown her around Ras al'Ain the last time she was here.

"You," he said, the recollection softening his features and bringing a reluctant smile to his lips. "We went to the springs one day. You read poetry to me."

"That was a fine day," Ana said. They stood looking at each other for a time, Ana willing him with all her strength to remember her fondly enough to help them.

To Ana, Leila said, "Achmed was only nine years old when you came here. Now he is grown and an officer of Mukhabarat."

Tom sucked in his breath and tried to hold it, appraising Achmed. He was scarcely more than a boy. If he was in the Mukhabarat, he had to be pretty junior and so far, he seemed friendly enough, remembering Ana, but . . .

Mariah didn't know what was being said, but she felt Tom tense. She had to struggle to contain the rush of fear that turned her knees to jelly and caught her breath.

"Achmed takes care of me now that Ali is gone," Leila continued. "There is no more of your work for us to do. At least not until tonight. What do you need?"

Ana's throat was suddenly dry, but she swallowed, looked directly at Achmed and forced herself to say, "Visas for Syria and someone you trust to drive us to Dier az-Zor."

Tom cut his eyes at Ana when she mentioned Dier az-Zor. They'd agreed to go through Aleppo.

"Achmed?" Leila turned to her son.

Achmed's friendly expression suddenly changed, his eyes widened and he backed away. "No! Now I know who you are. A bulletin has been issued to detain you. It came yesterday. Two Americans and an Armenian woman. A man named Yeager and an Armenian woman named Ana Stepanian. That is who you are."

Tom coiled the muscles in his legs and the small of his back while he measured the distance between himself and Achmed. The options ran quickly through his mind. A hard right to the jaw, a lunge and strangle hold or a vicious kick to the crotch. Or wait a minute more to see how it played.

"The bulletin said our names?" Ana asked, horrified.

"Yeager and Stepanian, but it said there was another American, a woman," Achmed said, glaring at Mariah.

Tom came onto the balls of his feet but held himself in check. If Achmed made a move toward the door, he'd have to take him.

"And what does the bulletin say we did?" Ana asked, her heart pounding.

"It does not have to say. 'Detain for questioning' is the order." Achmed growled. As the thought of how the apprehension of three wanted foreigners would look on his record flashed through his mind, he felt Tom's eyes on him. The American was coiled like a snake and his eyes were just as cold. To capture them, Achmed would have to fight him.

"Achmed," Leila hissed. "What are you saying? Ana is our friend. She is asking your help."

"Be quiet, woman," he told his mother. *This is a Mukhabarat affair.*"

"No," Leila insisted, pulling the sleeve of his night shirt. "It is an affair of your family's honor."

Achmed stared down at her coldly, frowning.

"Your father is in Paradise with Allah because this woman saved him from mortal sin," Leila scolded, pointing at Ana. "But for her, they would have murdered the woman those border guards treated so badly and your father would now be burning in Hell. And you . . . do you not know that the sins of the fathers are visited upon the sons?"

The long silence that followed was broken only by the audible breathing of the five people crowded into the small room.

"All right," Achmed said at last. "I will get the visas."

"Thank you," Ana said, holding his eyes with hers. What she saw in his expression was only half reassuring and she was glad she'd lied to him about Dier az-Zor.

As Achmed turned to leave the room to dress, Tom moved, too. Achmed looked at him, questioning. "I am going to dress," he said.

"I'll come with you," Tom said in Arabic. "You might need help."

****

The dogs in the neighborhood spread a dissonant chorus as soon as Tom and Achmed left the house. Though the streets were dark, Tom felt naked and exposed by the barking sentries tracking their passage toward the border.

Achmed stopped when they reached the main street and

pointed to his right. "The border is there," he told Tom. "Give me the passports and the money and wait here. You will have to trust me to do as I promised."

Tom looked in the direction Achmed pointed and saw the red and white striped poles stretched across the two-lane blacktop road. A low-wattage bulb glowed in the mud brick building that housed the border guards and customs inspectors. He saw no one in the sentry box and he had a clear view of the counter through the windows of the customs office. There was no one visible there either. He shrugged.

"Go ahead," he told Achmed and watched him cross the empty street and enter the office.

At its most active, the border crossing at Ras al'Ain was never busy and it was now after midnight.

Achmed looked through the glass and saw no one. He opened the door carefully and stepped into the room. On the other side of the counter, he saw the young border guard on duty sound asleep, his head down on one of the desks. A regiment of Kurdish guerrillas could have marched past without waking him. Achmed slipped behind the high counter that contained the stamps and forms he needed to place temporary visas in the passports. Before his appointment to the Mukhabarat, he had worked as a customs officer and knew the procedure for granting an entry visa--six blue stamps and two brown ones, canceled with a blizzard of ink blots. Achmed went about the work quietly, facing the windows to allow Tom to see him. He opened the ledger and, looking back and forth between its pages and first one passport and then another, he wrote in large Arabic script:

Two US, one Armenian. On Detain List. Armed. Traveling to Dier az-Zor. Alert Mukhabarat.

He signed his name beneath the entry, left the ledger open on the counter and slipped out the door, leaving the border guard sleeping soundly as before.

Achmed rejoined Tom in the darkness beyond the customs house and handed over the passports without a word.

"What about transportation?" Tom asked.

"My uncle owns a service. He will take you to Dier az-Zor."

CHAPTER FORTY FIVE

Aleppo, Syria

"We've changed our plans, Uncle," Tom told Mahmoud when they were several blocks from Leila Hashemi's house. "We're going to Aleppo, not Dier az-Zor."

"As you like," Mahmoud replied and made a series of turns to take them away from the desert road to the one that ran beside the frontier.

"What the hell is going on, you guys?" Mariah hissed from the back seat.

"Junior back there was Syrian KGB," Tom told her. "They've got us on a 'detain for questioning' list. Your name's not on it at the moment, but now that he's seen your passport, it will be as soon as he gets to a phone. I doubt his mother can keep him in line. What do you think, Ana? And incidentally, that was a stroke of genius to tell him Dier az-Zor. Do you suppose he bought it?"

"Yes, I think so. But he will call Mukhabarat, too. Leila will not be able to stop him unless he truly believes he will dishonor his father. Women do not matter much here."

"Yeah," he said. "It's kind of a foot race now, huh? You guys get some sleep. I'll keep an eye on our boy behind the wheel and see if I can come up with a Plan B. That Detain for Questioning order just cancelled Plan A."

****

They covered ninety kilometers before the sun rose behind them. Tom, riding in front with the driver, had dozed off and awoke with a start when the car turned off the main highway. Mahmoud grinned at him through stained teeth and wished him a good morning.

"*Sabah al-khayr.*"

"*Sabah an-nur,*" Tom replied. "Where are we?"

"I am turning to pass through Suluk. It is a small town, not so many eyes as in Tell Abyad and we will save a few kilometers."

Tom looked at his watch. It was a few minutes before seven. "How much farther to Aleppo?"

"About two hundred kilometers. Two hours, Insh' Allah. The road is better after Suluk."

"We need some food. Can we stop for breakfast?"

"There is a place off the road. We can make tea. I have bread and cheese."

On the other side of Suluk, Mahmoud pulled into a wadi and drove down it some distance before stopping, out of sight of the highway. He took a Coleman stove from the trunk, fired it up and poured water into a medium-sized metal pot with the long, curved spout characteristic of Arab coffee pots. The women went one way down the wadi to answer the call of nature. Tom and Mahmoud relieved themselves a few steps away from the car.

The tea was brewed by the time the women returned. Mahmoud ignored them, leaving them to help themselves, but he ladled two spoons of sugar into a small glass and poured the steaming brew for Tom.

While Mahmoud put away the stove and the tea glasses and prepared to leave, Tom took Mariah aside and said, "We need to talk. We have to believe the Mukhabarat is on our trail by now and we've got to do some maneuvering. Achmed saw your passport, so we have to assume your name will be on that detention order by the end of the day. With luck, they're looking for us on the road to Dier az-Zor, not Aleppo. And it takes awhile to print and distribute those lists. Anyway, I want to get you on a plane before that happens."

"No, Tommy," she said, protesting. "I'm not going to bail out on you. Get us to Aleppo and we'll steal another plane. They never lock them. We can all be in Jordan in no time. We just have to make sure we steal a plane with gas in it."

Tom shook his head. "Hear me out. This is Plan B. Before your name shows up on that list, we can get you on a plane to Cairo direct from Aleppo. Once you're outside Syria, I want you to make two phone calls. The first and most important one is to a guy named Walter Webb at the US embassy in Amman. People who know him call him Chico and you might need to use that name to get through. Tell Chico I'm in Syria and I need help getting across the border into Jordan. Tell him everything about the situation he wants to know and ask him--please--to meet me at the café in Dara'a where the bus stops. Then call your partner, Karekin. I don't know what he can do, but I want him to help every way he can. He's supposed to have a lot of influence."

"Why don't you call them yourself from Aleppo? You know better than I do what you need."

"First of all, you have to show your passport, which I'm not real anxious to do right now. And for all I know, the Mukhabarat may monitor international calls. It'll be safer all the way around to have you make the calls once you're out of Syria."

Mariah frowned at him.

"Ana and I will go on the way we planned. We'll have a different profile. We won't be a man and two women, just one man and one woman. Aleppo's big enough to give us some cover, too." He gripped her shoulders with both hands and added, "And I want you out of the crossfire."

"What crossfire?" Mariah asked. "Why don't you just give the guy this stuff and be done with it? You don't owe the Melikians this kind of loyalty."

"There's a little more to it than that. I had a run-in with Avakian in Yerevan early on, before you got there. He and Ana were lovers once. I didn't know that at the time, but he was about to hit her and I stopped him. Somewhat forcefully. That's probably why he wants to kill me. The jewelry is secondary."

"Wants to kill you?" Mariah said. "You're kidding, right?"

"There's a bit more. One of the guys I saw with him at the airport in Yerevan almost killed me once. Either Avakian has brought him in on this or he's been tracking me for one hell of a long time. There's also the outside chance that it's a very wild coincidence."

"Holy shit, Tom. You're really scaring me," Mariah said, her blue eyes wide, fixed on him. "Tommy, please. Don't be coy with me about this," she said. "I want to know about this. I really need to know."

Tom looked over his shoulder and saw Ana watching them. He took Mariah by the elbow and led her a little way down the wadi, found a boulder resting against the bank and sat her down on it.

"I used to smuggle diamonds. It was my father's trade and

he wanted to teach me the business. The guy who's with Avakian is a Russian enforcer. His job used to be--and may still be--tracking down and eliminating leaks in the system. There's a chance he pulled a hit and run on my father in London. In any event, my father is dead now. You remember that I needed a couple of days at the beginning of this job to see him in the hospital. He was partners with a guy in Amsterdam--an Armenian it turns out--and my dad told me he had something for me. It turned out to be the Rolex." Tom held up his wrist to show her.

"To make a long story short, I picked up a package of Russian diamonds in Yerevan. I've been out of the game for a long time, but I'm guessing that they're worth about a quarter of a million dollars. The Russian may know I've made the pickup. He may want the diamonds back and he may want my head to go with them."

"I knew I needed to know more about you, but I never imagined . . ."

"It was a long time ago and I haven't done anything like this for roughly twenty years. But when I was working, it was mostly in Europe and the Middle East. Jordan mainly. That's where I met Raz Melikian and his brother Anastas. And Chico Webb. He was back for another tour when I worked there last year, so I hope he's still in country. If not . . . getting across the border into Jordan is going to be a lot harder."

He paced back and forth in the sand of the wadi while Mariah watched him like a tennis match in slow motion. "What's the rest of the story, Tom?"

"OK," he said. "I'll try to fill in some spaces. The Melikians are jewelers, but Raz's father was also an intelligence source for Chico. Anyway, Chico asked me to do a favor for the old man--move a briefcase full of gemstones out of Jordan up to Amsterdam. Raz's father thought another Israeli war was coming and he wanted to get his goods out of country without paying a Jordanian export tax. Turned out to be the Yom Kippur War, 1973. The stuff was consigned to another Armenian named Petrossian in Amsterdam and Melikian paid me thirty thousand US for the favor. That was a lot of money in 1972."

"And that was it?" Mariah asked.

Tom shook his head. "It was the end of it with Melikian. But Petrossian wanted me to move goods for him. Russian diamonds. I didn't know they were Russian diamonds at the time and I didn't ask too many questions. I was trying to build a relationship with my father, who was doing this kind of stuff and, besides, I was getting a princely sum for every delivery and I didn't give a damn if they were being stolen from the Russians. They weren't our buddies in those days, if you'll remember." Tom put his hand on his forehead. "This isn't easy to tell quickly."

"I'm following you," Mariah said. "Go on."

"The Russians must have gotten on to the business. Anyway, I was making a pickup in Vienna, from a Czech stewardess for Aeroflot. I'd picked up from her before, always a different place--Demel's coffee house, the Judenplatz, the damned Spanish Riding School once. This time it was a hotel room at the Palais Schwarzenberg. When I got there, the door was part way open. I went in and found her dead, but the diamonds were right there beside her, so I shoved them in my briefcase and ran. I must have panicked and made it easy for him. I grabbed the first taxi in the line outside the hotel and told him to go to the airport. A little way from the hotel, the cabbie turned into an alley and stopped. He jumped out and ran. I knew I was in big trouble then so I jumped out and ran, too."

"But somebody shot you," she said.

He nodded. "Something that felt like a truck hit me in the back and sent me sprawling. Knocked the wind out of me. It didn't hurt at first. Shock, I guess. But the next thing I knew, somebody was twisting my arm up and cutting the chain on my briefcase. Then the guy I saw at the airport in Yerevan the night we skeedaddled rolled me over. We stared at each other for what seemed like a long time. Me trying to get air, him looking at me like I was something he'd scraped off his shoe. I could see him holding my briefcase in one hand and a long-barreled pistol in the other. Then I blacked out."

"What happened then?"

"A young couple out walking found me and called an ambulance. If they hadn't, I'd have bled to death. The sonofabitch who shot me and took my diamonds left me there to die. Anyway, it was a clean wound and I recovered pretty quickly. Petrossian was understanding about the loss but I'd had enough and got out of the business. I left money with him, though and he kept reinvesting it for several years after that then I cashed out and did my own investing. It's how I paid for the lake house. Anyway, that's the story. For some reason, they didn't come after him until just a few weeks ago--in fact I found him dead in Amsterdam on my way out here."

"But here you are helping Melikian again and if this guy is still on your tail, the story's not over," she said. "How did you get yourself into this?"

"Hell's bells, lady, you're the one who talked me into taking this job."

Ana appeared and stopped some distance away, frowning at them. "Tom, we must go. We are here too long."

"Right," he said, looking back at her. Then to Mariah, he said, "I need you to make those phone calls. I need you out of here to change our profile. And I want you out of harm's way."

"I guess this means Amsterdam's off, huh?" she said, her voice quavering.

****

Nikolai Danilov ate a leisurely breakfast alone, grateful for the privacy after enduring Aleksandr's constant agitation. Afterward, he walked outside the hotel to take some fresh air and to smoke. He returned to the hotel just before ten and rapped on Aleksandr's door.

"Why didn't you wake me up? It's almost ten o'clock. Damned pain pills," Aleksandr muttered, dragging himself toward the bathroom. "Call the desk and see if there are messages for me," he called over his shoulder. "We should have heard from Vasily by now."

Aleksandr went into the shower and Danilov was about to pick up the phone when it rang. He answered it.

"Yes. . . . He's in the shower. Is this Vasily? . . . I see. I'll tell him. Where can you be reached? . . . Yes. I've got it."

Danilov put his head into the bathroom and shouted, "Vasily just called. Your birds flew over the border last night and the Mukhabarat missed them."

Aleksandr shut off the shower. His good arm emerged from behind the curtain, groping for the towel rack. The Russian took one from a stack and slapped it into his hand.

"Damn, damn, damn," Avakian cursed and climbed out of the shower. Still dripping, he threw on the hotel robe and said, "Order some breakfast, Russian, while I get dressed."

"I'm not your valet," Danilov shot back.

Aleksandr's angry eyes fixed on him. "Why do I put up with your surly arrogance?" he muttered.

Aleksandr went to the phone beside the bed and reached Vasily at the embassy. "Tied up the Mukhabarat resident? I can't believe it. . . . So are they blocking the roads to Dier az-Zor? . . . No flights, eh? . . . Only charters. Well, that's their first mistake. . . . Still, Dier az-Zor. Are you sure? That's not the shortest way to Damascus. . . . Yes, they might think they could fly directly into Jordan, but it could also be a false scent. Tell them to watch the other roads, too. . . . Yes, yes, Vasily. I'll wait here." He slammed the phone back onto the cradle.

Danilov sat by the window, blowing acrid smoke from his cigarette into the room. Aleksandr scowled at him, took two more pain pills and called room service.

****

On the eastern outskirts of Aleppo the Mercedes joined the flood of traffic around the airport. If there were Mukhabarat watchers at the airport, they would be looking for two women and a man together, not separately, so as they reached the terminal, Tom told Ana to duck down in the seat and sent Mariah into the terminal alone. He told Mahmoud to move off as if they were leaving the airport, then bring the Mercedes around again. Tom got out on the next pass and Ana continued with the driver to a nearby parking area. Inside the terminal, Tom waited for Mariah among a group of bleary-eyed young Germans sprawled across a waiting area. His three-day beard and wrinkled clothes fit with their scruffy appearance. Half an hour later, he saw Mariah turn away from the Egypt Air counter with tickets in hand. He caught her eye and they made a rendezvous among the Germans.

"I'm booked on Egypt Air to Cairo at noon," she said. "I get there at one-forty. Air France goes to Paris at six this evening."

Tom looked at his watch. "It's almost ten now. I'm glad you don't have long to wait. Clear passport control and customs right now and board the plane as soon as you can. It may not help much--your name's on the passenger manifest now, but with any luck, it hasn't made the Detention List at Passport Control. If you get past them, you'll be OK."

"Don't fret about me, Tom. You're the one I'm worried about."

"Yeah. Well, so far, so good. I think we've got them off balance and I'm going to throw Mahmoud a curve, make him think we're going to Latakia, then hole up and get some rest," he said. "Remember to tell Chico that I'll wait for him tomorrow at the café in Dara'a where the bus stops. He'll know the one."

"Bus Stop Café in Dara'a. I got it."

"We better split now," Tom said, looking into her eyes. "You're the best, babe." He pulled her into his arms and gave her a fierce hug.

"It'll make a hell of a story when we get home," she whispered, not trusting her voice. She hung onto him for a long moment, pushing out of her mind the rasping crackle of the public address announcements and the crowd milling around them. Then she leaned back in his arms and looked up at him. "Tommy, I'll be in Agadir at the Tikida Beach Hotel," she said. "Remember that, won't you?"

"I'll remember," he said and let her go. He gave her the jauntiest, most confident smile he could muster and slipped through the glass doors into the midday sun. The Mercedes appeared almost immediately, Ana's anxious face peering over the seat. Tom jumped in beside her and Mahmoud sped away.

＊＊＊＊＊＊＊＊＊＊＊

"Tom, look," Ana said, pointing excitedly as they entered Aleppo, an ancient city of cream-colored stone buildings. "Those signs are in Armenian." She stared in wonderment as they passed one shop sign after another lettered in the distinctive script. "I was told that many Armenians still lived here. It must be true."

"But you don't know anyone here?"

"No one."

"Then we need to do some research," Tom said, peering at the shops along their narrow route into the old city. "Mahmoud," he said. "If you see a bookstore, stop."

"As you wish," Mahmoud replied.

Sidewalk vendors' merchandise spilled into the street along their route and Ana spotted several tables piled high with books. "There," she called out in Arabic. Mahmoud eased to the side of the street and stopped.

"I see it," Tom said. "Give me some of your Deutche marks. If this guy remembers me, he's going to remember me as a German, not an American." He got out of the car and walked back to where a jumble of books, new and used, were stacked in the shade of a striped awning. Behind the sidewalk bazaar, a more conventional shop occupied the ground floor of a French Mandate-era building. Tom squeezed between the tables and entered the shop. He went to the clerk and asked in German, "*Sprechen Sie Deutche?*"

"*Ja, mein Herr,*" the clerk replied.

Tom continued in German. "I want a guidebook for Syria, in German."

"We have Baedeker's," the clerk replied and came around the old-fashioned high wood counter to find the book. Tom took it immediately.

"This will do," he said. "Will you take Deutche marks?"

"I cannot give you the difference in marks."

"Syrian pounds will do," Tom said. He offered a 100DM bill and waited for the clerk to make several computations on his hand-held calculator. The clerk spoke softly to him so as not to be overheard. "The book is four-hundred pounds and I can give you ten pounds for each Deutche mark. You have given me one-hundred marks which is a thousand pounds. The difference is six-hundred pounds. Ja?"

"*Ja, danke,*" Tom said, scooping up the Syrian pounds in one hand and taking the guide book in the other. He disappeared through the door so quickly that the clerk's "Danke, mein Herr" was spoken to the back of his head.

"What book did you buy?" Ana asked as Mahmoud slipped the dusty black Mercedes back into the slow-moving stream of traffic and pulled away.

"A guide book. I want to see what it says about Latakia and the best way to get there," he replied in Arabic to make sure Mahmoud heard.

"Latakia?" Ana asked.

"Mahmoud," Tom said. "Take us to the train station, please. You can leave us there and return to Ras al'Ain. Thanks for everything."

"As you like," Mahmoud replied.

****

Tom and Ana moved quickly through the doors of the train station and stood in the shadows watching Mahmoud's Mercedes move away into the traffic.

"Tom," Ana said. "I don't understand. We are going to Latakia?"

"No, but I want Mahmoud to think so."

"Oh, I see," she said. "Of course."

"We have to believe that Leila's son has the hounds after us by now. When they don't find us on the Dier az-Zor road, they'll figure Aleppo. I just need to buy us a little time. I'm so tired I can't think straight. I'm going to make a stupid mistake if we don't get some rest. Let's find a place to sit down and check the hotels. But not here. I don't want to hang around the train station. They might be watching it."

"But won't the hotels have our names? We will have to show our passports."

"I'm looking for a cheap one, one that might have hourly rates, if you know what I mean."

"No. What is that?"

"Never mind. Just trust me on this. We only need to stay long enough to get a shower and a couple of hours sleep. I know it's a risk, but so's everything else." He quickly read the two pages on hotels, skipping those where Americans might be expected to stay. "This one looks like our speed. The Hotel Yarmouk. It's cheap, renovated and has hot showers. What do you think?"

"Say the part about the hot showers again."

He grinned at her. "My thought exactly. Let's get a taxi."

****

The clerk at the desk of the Hotel Yarmouk looked at them in stony silence when they entered the small lobby, which was clean and freshly painted. Tom was disappointed--it was altogether too reputable for a hideaway. "Good day," Tom said to the clerk in Arabic. "Do you have a room for the afternoon for two people?"

"The rate is the same if you stay a short time or all night," the clerk replied.

"All right," Tom answered. "How much is it?"

"Three hundred pounds," the clerk replied, still inspecting them. "Fill this out," he said, giving Tom a registration card to complete. "And I must see your passports."

Tom scrawled an illegible signature across the registration card and laid a fifty dollar bill on top of it before he pushed it across the desk to the clerk. The clerk looked down at the bill, then at Tom. Their eyes locked as the clerk tried to decide who they were.

Ana laid her blue Armenian passport on the desk, open to the pages that were covered with Syrian entry visa stamps and kept her hand on it, hoping to satisfy him with the valid visa and keep him from looking at her name. But the clerk snatched it from her and flipped it closed to examine the cover. He looked up and smiled at her. "*Barev, hayrenakits,*" he said in Armenian.

"*Barev,*" Ana exclaimed. "How wonderful to meet a compatriot."

"You're from Yerevan?" he asked in Armenian, the tension falling away. "How is it there now? We've heard life is very difficult."

"It is still difficult, but better than before.

The clerk turned to Tom and spoke to him in Armenian, the hint of a friendly smile playing around the corners of his mouth. "And do you have work in Yerevan? We've heard that most men are unemployed."

Ana hurried to explain that Tom wasn't Armenian. "Please," she said, her eyes begging the clerk's compassion. "We can pay, but no one should know we were here. Do you understand? My father . . ."

The clerk looked at Tom again, the smile gone. He cocked his head in disbelief but he took the fifty and tore up the registration card. He laid a room key on the counter and turned away. They hurried to the small elevator and breathed a sigh of relief when the doors closed and the elevator started up.

"What did you say to him?" Tom asked.

"I tried to make him think we were running from my father. Anyone would understand that a father would not want his daughter to run away with an American," she said with a straight face.

"Thanks a lot," he said. "I don't want to let our guard down, though. Let's get a shower and some rest. I'm starving, but food's going to have to wait."

****

Mahmoud drove a few blocks from the train station and stopped near a collection of small shops. He double-parked, left the engine running and went inside to ask directions to the Post Office. From there he called Achmed in Ras al'Ain.

"Achmed, they made me take them to Aleppo."

"Not Dier az-Zor?"

"No. I'm in Aleppo at the Post Office. They are going to Latakia by train. What shall I do?"

"Go to the Mukhabarat office in Aleppo. It's near the police station in the Jdeide Quarter--the Christian section. Ask to see the Lieutenant on duty and tell him what you've told me. I'll call him and explain that you're coming."

Mahmoud found the Mukhabarat headquarters, but far from being accorded the respect due a patriot of the Syrian Arab Republic, he was placed under suspicion and rudely locked in a cell while they sent a beggar boy to fetch the Lieutenant. The Lieutenant arrived at his post shortly after three o'clock that afternoon, just as Mariah was asking the receptionist at the desk of the Air France first class lounge in Cairo for a telephone. The Lieutenant questioned Mahmoud and called Damascus for instructions. An hour later, Damascus told him to dispatch men to the airport and the train station and to alert the Latakia police.

Chapter Forty Six

Damascus

Tom and Ana showered and lay down damp and naked between cool, clean sheets. Tom threw an arm around her shoulders and drew her to him, her skin quickly warm where he touched her.

She pressed her body against his along its length and put her hand to the back of his neck, drawing his head to hers. "My sirelis," she said and kissed him, her lips swelling for a moment as if passion were going to overtake her. Then, exhausted, their legs entwined, they fell fast asleep.

Tom awoke with a start two hours later. Feeling him stir, Ana came awake, too.

"Time to go," Tom said, his heart suddenly pounding. "Hurry," he added. "I've got a bad feeling."

They dressed and slipped through the door, the pungent smell of fear following them into the empty corridor. Tom pointed to the stairs and Ana nodded. The clerk who'd received them was still on duty when they slipped through the lobby and he let them go without comment.

The late afternoon sunlight fell softly on Al Maari Street and the air was pleasant. Tom turned to his right and walked toward another major cross street, which he thought was Baron, aiming for the park he could see across the intersection. When they were seated on a bench, he looked at Ana and, shaking his head, said, "I don't know what got into me. I just felt we were in danger."

"I felt it, too," she said, sitting sideways to face him and holding his hand.

"We need to keep moving," Tom said. "We can hire another service or catch a bus. Let's see what the guidebook says." He took the Baedeker's from his backpack and turned to the section on Aleppo. "The bus station is just over there." He pointed across Al Maari Street, then went on with his reading. "It says five hours to Damascus. It's three o'clock now. If there's a bus anytime before early evening, we can get to Damascus in time to find a place to hide out tonight and make the dash to Dara'a in the morning. If Mariah gets in touch with Chico from Cairo and if he's waiting for us in Dara'a, we'll be OK. Dara'a is about the same distance from Damascus as it is from Amman, so if we leave Damascus the same time Chico leaves Amman, we ought to connect and not have to risk being spotted in that little town."

"What if this man Chico does not come?"

"I've got a couple of ideas, but I'd rather not have to try them," he said.

"Mahmoud will tell the Mukhabarat that we are here. We should find another service, Tom. They must be watching bus stations by now."

"Maybe, but wait here while I check it out. If it looks clear, the bus will save us some money and we won't fall into a pattern that might give them an edge."

Tom returned from the bus station with two skewers of kebab and a large bottle of a local soft drink. "Oh, food," Ana exclaimed. "I had almost forgotten how hungry I am." They wolfed the kebabs and drank the soda greedily.

"Can we go by bus?" Ana asked when the edge of her hunger and thirst was dulled.

"I didn't see anybody who looked like police, so I bought tickets on the next one--leaving at five o'clock. Just in case, I'm going to speak German from now on and as little of that as possible. You don't need to answer. Just nod once in a while. Don't speak to me in English, whatever you do. Make it Arabic if you have to say anything. I think we'll be OK here in the park unless the Mukhabarat is hunting us on the street. With any luck, they think we've gone to Latakia."

Thirty minutes after the five o'clock bus left the station, a black official car began making the rounds of the downtown Aleppo hotels. The night clerk at the Hotel Yarmouk had come on duty by the time the Mukhabarat arrived and had seen no guests like the ones they described. After grilling half a dozen desk clerks in the area, the car drove slowly around the park where Tom and Ana had waited and stopped at the bus station. Two burly men piled out and went in to question the ticket agents.

****

At eight o'clock that evening, Vasily called Aleksandr at the Hotel Semiramis in Damascus. "Aleppo, huh? . . . Only one man and one woman now? . . . What about the second woman? . . . To Cairo, eh? And the other two went to Latakia? . . . But they didn't turn up there? What about the hotels in Aleppo? . . . And nothing at the airport or the train stations or the bus stations? . . . That's the only thing? Someone who might have looked like them at a bus station? Might have. . . . But speaking German? Well, that doesn't sound promising."

"Who was speaking German?" Danilov asked. He'd been listening to Aleksandr's side of the conversation.

"Who was speaking German, Vasily? . . ." Aleksandr looked at Danilov and raised his eyebrows. "The man. So what? There are Germans all over the Middle East."

"The American speaks beautiful German. If these two look like the ones we want, it could have been him."

"What did they look like, Vasily? . . . Dressed as the driver said? . . . Then it's them. It's got to be. Where did they go, Vasily? . . . Five o'clock bus for Damascus? . . . How long does it take? . . . Five hours?" Aleksandr looked at his watch. "Is there only one station or several? . . . Then we've got them. Bring a detachment of police and meet us there."

As they hurried through the door, Aleksandr said, "It's only the American and Ana. Vasily said the woman was dark. The other woman was blond-haired. We have them now, Russian."

****

Tom and Ana slept most of the way to Damascus, waking only when the bus made its regular stops in the historic cities of Hama and Homs. The bus was only half full and the passengers were tired and kept to themselves. During his waking moments, Tom had been thinking hard about what to do once the bus reached Damascus. He had to assume Mahmoud would put the Mukhabarat on their trail. The Latakia ruse probably delayed them and he might have gotten away with the German disguise at the bus station, but he had to assume it didn't take five hours to make a phone call from Aleppo to Damascus.

****

Ana tensed as they entered the outskirts of the city. Tom took her head in both his hands and whispered in her ear. "We're going to get off this bus before it gets to the station. Follow me as soon as I make the move." Ana nodded.

When apartment blocks began to give way to shops and office buildings, Tom knew they were nearing the central city. He got out of his seat, took their backpacks from the overhead rack and began to make his way up the swaying aisle. Ana followed closely behind. He reached the driver's shoulder as the bus stopped for a traffic light. Tom put a 100-pound note in front of the driver's face and spoke softly to him in Arabic.

"We will get out here."

The driver tried to look up at Tom, but couldn't twist his neck around far enough. He sensed menace in Tom's voice and decided against reciting the law about letting passengers out between stations. Taking the hundred Syrian pounds, he pushed open the door.

"Be quick about it," he hissed at Tom, who needed no encouragement. In an instant, they were in the street, hurrying away.

"Walk back the way we came," Tom said to Ana. She followed, half trotting to keep up with his long strides. He found what he was looking for midway down the block--a darkened arcade housing a collection of small shops. He pulled Ana off the sidewalk into the arcade entrance.

"Let's see if we can figure out where we are," he said. "Still got your flashlight?"

Ana stirred the contents of her shoulder bag until she found it, vowing to carry a flashlight for the rest of her life, no matter what.

"Can you make out that street name?"

"Al-Thawra Street."

"OK," he said, focusing the beam of the flashlight on the map of Damascus in the guidebook. "I see that. It runs beside the Old City and the souk, provided we turn the right way."

"Where will we go?"

"Well, no more hotels and I don't see any parks where we could bed down for the night. This is a big city. We could walk ourselves numb trying to find one. Why don't we head into the souk and find a dark corner where we can lay up and wait for morning? The Christian Quarter is probably the quietest part of the Old City. Let's try it."

Tom flicked off the flashlight and they emerged from the darkness of the arcade onto the sidewalk. The traffic had thinned considerably because of the hour, but they saw a cruising taxi, flagged it down and asked the driver to take them to the Bab Touma, the Thomas Gate of the Old City.

The driver sped down the main avenue running along the Barada River to the *Bab Touma*. Tom paid him and watched the cab drive away. He and Ana walked into the Christian Quarter, feeling as if they were making a journey into time. Every shop was shuttered. Every restaurant, every café closed for the day.

"We're out of luck as far as food goes," he said. "There's not going to be anything open this late. What a dumb idea I had to come here."

"A hotel would not be safe. Where else should we go?"

"I don't know," he said, despair and fatigue falling heavily on him. They went deeper into the Quarter until they found a narrow side street. "Let's try this. I doubt it's on the police patrol route."

He soon found what he was looking for--an inset doorway, unusual in the Old City where most shop doors were flush with the walls of the buildings. "Here," he said. "We'll be out of sight and no one will stumble over us in the dark."

"As long as I am with you, it does not matter," she said, exhausted in spite of sleeping on the bus.

He put an arm around her shoulders and squeezed her as they sat down in the entry, propping their backpacks against the wall and leaning against them. "I wish we still had the cloaks. It'll be cold before morning," he said, pulling her to him to shelter her.

"It will be all right," she said, pressing her face into his chest, breathing his warmth.

They didn't see the old man smoking quietly on a tiny balcony opposite the doorway in which they were bedding down, but with eyes adjusted to the darkness, he had watched them come along the narrow street and wondered who they might be. When he saw them settle in the doorway, he knew they were homeless for the night. He smoked on, pondering what to do. His house was empty since his wife died. His children, grown with children of their own, came to visit often. Then the house came to life with laughter and happy chatter. But most of the time, he lived alone with his memories. Often they were too vivid to allow him to sleep. So he sat on the balcony outside the bedroom where he and his wife had made their life together for almost fifty years. In remembering his days with her, she returned and sat with him there. It helped to pass the time while he waited to join her.

What would she have thought of the two people down below, huddled in a doorway? She would have known they were hungry and would have taken them food. And they obviously needed shelter because the air was cold tonight. He was already feeling it in his bones, in spite of his heavy, wool sweater. Yes, she would offer the hospitality of their house and he almost felt her urging him to get up.

Tom came awake when he heard the door open across the narrow street. He saw the man coming toward them in silhouette. An old man, Tom thought, from the way he shuffled and from the stoop of his shoulders. Tom's heart was pounding, but he was not afraid.

"*Salaam aleekum,*" came the old man's voice, deep and sweet.

"*Wa aleekum al-salaam,*" Tom replied.

Ana woke with a start, hearing the exchange of greetings.

"Are you hungry?" the old man asked in Arabic.

"*Aiwa, shukran,*" Tom answered and continued in Arabic. "We arrived too late. All the restaurants were closed."

"And you have no place to sleep?"

"We are going on in the morning. Only a few more hours."

"Have you traveled far today?" the old man asked.

"Yes," Tom said, trying to think how far they had come. This was Sunday night and they'd left Yerevan Friday night. "We have been traveling several days."

"Please," the old man said. "There is room in my house, just there. You are most welcome."

Tom wasn't certain about the etiquette of the situation, but he knew that you were less likely to give offense if you accepted Arab hospitality than if you didn't. "Shukran," Tom said. "You are very kind." He and Ana struggled to their feet, shouldered their backpacks and followed the old man across the street and through the gate that opened on his small courtyard.

Exhausted, they dropped their backpacks by the door and followed their host into the kitchen. There they collapsed into chairs around the dining table while the old man puttered about the kitchen. Finally, he set a bowl of tabouleh sprinkled with chunks of lamb in front of them.

"I am Aram Toranian," he said.

Ana looked up at him in surprise. "Toranian?" she asked. "Armenian?"

"Yes," the old man said, looking at Ana with renewed interest.

"Barev, hayrenakits," she said. "I am Ana Stepanian." The old man's wrinkled face broke into a broad smile and he shook his head slowly in wonderment.

"Oh, no. I don't believe this," Tom said, offering his hand. "Mr. Toranian, I'm Tom Yeager. American, not Armenian."

"American? You speak Arabic well," he said and turned back to Ana.

"And where do you come from? Now and before," the old man asked in Armenian.

"Yerevan, now," Ana replied. "Many years ago, my family came from Van. You are so kind to offer us your hospitality, even without knowing we were countrymen."

"I am a Christian first, even before I am an Armenian," Aram said, beaming at Ana.

Tom finished his tabouleh while Aram and Ana chatted away in Armenian. Since he could understand nothing of what they were saying, he excused himself and went into an adjoining room furnished with chairs and low tables and, most importantly, a divan. He stretched out on it and fell asleep instantly.

＊＊＊＊＊＊＊＊＊＊＊

The Mukhabarat surrounded the bus as soon as it arrived from Aleppo and cleared the few, frightened passengers through into the terminal. The bus driver was shaking and ashen when they dragged him into the station master's office to question him. He readily admitted letting two passengers off on Al-Thawra Street, but he claimed the man held a knife to his throat and that he really had no choice in the matter.

Aleksandr turned to the Russian and shook his head. "This American is either very lucky or very good. Perhaps he is both." To Vasily, he said, "Tell them to double the watch on the airport and every bus and train going south to Amman. We're going to Dara'a. Make sure they check everyone crossing the border there. I'll call you from Dara'a."

CHAPTER FORTY SEVEN

Dara'a, Syria

"Tom, Tom," Ana said softly, shaking his shoulder. "It is morning. Wake up."

He smelled strong coffee brewing and fought through his sleep-fogged brain to rouse himself. In the distance, he heard the muezzin calling the faithful to prayer:

"*Allah Akbar. Ashad an la ilaha illa-Llah. Ashad Ana Muhammadan rasulu-Lalu. Hayya ala-salah. Hayya ala-l-falah. Allah Akbar. La ilaha illa-Llah.*"

Slowly he came to understand where he was. Damascus, the Old City, the Christian Quarter, but within earshot of the Muslim call to prayer. Fifty miles from sanctuary over the Jordanian border and another fifty from Amman. As he thought about how close they were to safety, he gathered himself for the run down the Damascus road. He threw back the cover that someone had thrown over him, rolled off the divan, set his feet on the Oriental carpet and went in search of the toilet.

Once relieved and refreshed, he joined them in the kitchen. "*Sabah al-khayr,*" he said to Aram.

"*Sabah an-nur,*" Aram replied. "I apologize for allowing you to sleep on the divan, but I thought it best not to wake you."

"It was grand," Tom replied in Arabic. "You are most gracious."

"The pleasure is mine. I learned much last night about our homeland. I have never been there, but like our faith and our language, it is a beacon for all us Armenians. Our homeland. Very precious."

"Yes," Tom said. "I'm coming to realize that."

Aram gave them coffee and cheese and flat bread for breakfast and they ate greedily. When they finished, Tom and the old man talked while Ana prepared to leave. "What did she tell you about us?" Tom asked.

"She told me you were in danger from an Armenian man who once was in the Soviet KGB. She said the Mukhabarat were helping him but that it had nothing to do with politics and you thought you would be safe if you could reach Jordan."

"She is also in danger from this man," Tom said.

"Will you permit me to help you?" Aram asked.

"Your hospitality has been more than generous."

"I have a friend who owns a service. He can be trusted to drive you to the border."

Tom thought only for a moment before answering. Aram Toranian had the solution to their transportation problem, perhaps the only solution. "I accept," Tom said. "But how can I possibly repay you?"

"As I have said, it is not necessary," Toranian said, patting Tom on the shoulder, his eyes smiling. "I have been blessed in great abundance throughout my life, but it is good to be remembered, so when you tell your children about your adventures, perhaps you will tell them about me--an old Armenian whose path you crossed one night in Damascus."

"I'll do that," Tom said, smiling. "Of course I'll do that."

Ana emerged from the bathroom looking refreshed and they strapped up their backpacks while Aram telephoned his friend, Krikor Garbedian. They chatted for another half an hour and when it was time, Aram walked with them to the Bab Touma where Krikor waited in a Volvo service. Aram introduced them and explained that Krikor could not take them to Amman. "He can take you across the border, but only to Ramtha. There you must take a Jordanian service to Amman."

"I hope it won't be necessary for him to take us beyond Dara'a," Tom replied and turned to Krikor. "Do you know the café south of town, where the bus stops?"

"Of course," Krikor said.

Aram smiled and turned to Tom and Ana.

"*Maa salama*," Aram said.

"*Shukran jazilan*, Aram. *Maa salama*," Tom told him.

Ana took the old man's hand in both of hers, kissed it and spoke her thanks and her farewell to him in Armenian. There were tears in Aram's eyes as he waved them away into the morning traffic.

****

Aleksandr cursed Karine for the throbbing pain in his arm and struggled to rise from his bed in the Al-Ahram Hotel in Dara'a, where he'd slept in his clothes, awaiting a phone call from the Mukhabarat roadblock at the frontier. The room he shared with Danilov was scarcely larger than a closet, but it was the only one available by the time they returned from making sure the roadblock was in place. Every decent room had been taken by a French tour group destined for Bosra the next morning. Aleksandr turned on the only tap at the basin in the room, took two pain pills and splashed cold water on his face. Then he went down the hall to the toilet.

Danilov was still sleeping when he returned. With his good arm, Aleksandr lifted the foot of the Russian's bed six inches off the floor and dropped it. Who gave a damn if it woke up a Frenchman in the room below? Jolted from his slumber, the Russian grumbled, half-rising from the bed when it hit the floor. "What the hell?"

"Get up, Russian," Aleksandr growled. "We have work to do. I'm going downstairs to call Vasily. Be ready in ten minutes."

Aleksandr and Vasily were speaking Russian, but that cast only the thinnest veneer of privacy over their conversation on the public phone in the lobby of the Al-Ahram Hotel. "I know Damascus is a large city. . . . Nothing at the airport or the bus station? . . . And no sign they've come through to Dara'a? They must have a service . . . Another ten thousand? Very well, Vasily. When I return to Damascus. . . ." Aleksandr paused and said in a voice dripping with menace, "Vasily, I'm in Dara'a to stop them, but if I do not, I expect your people to keep them from crossing into Jordan. . . . Don't fail me, Vasily." He slammed the phone onto its cradle as Danilov came down the stairs.

"What news from the worthy Vasily?" he asked.

"No sign of them. They didn't show up on a hotel register last night, either in Damascus or here in Dara'a. And there's been no sign of them at the airport or the bus and train stations this morning. Of course, there might be a safe house in Damascus. You know how it's done. And it's always possible to bribe a hotel clerk."

"And if they have a private car?"

"That's why we're in Dara'a. We're going to take them before they reach the border."

"Why? You saw yourself that the roadblock was in place. Let the Mukhabarat take them when they try to enter Jordan. Why must we intercept them first?"

"You trust the *Mukhabarat?* The *Mukhabarat* had many hours of advance warning, but Ana and the Americans still got into Syria, then they slipped through their fingers in Aleppo and disappeared in Damascus. Why do you think the idiot Syrians can stop them at the Jordanian border?"

"All true enough. But how do you expect to see them as they come down the road? Even last night there was heavy traffic."

"We'll find a place south of here, so the only traffic we see will be what's going to Jordan. I have binoculars and I'll look at every car and truck that comes from Damascus. When we see them, we'll run them down and take the coins. The roadblock is the last resort--in case we fail."

Danilov shook his head. "I never did understand you damned stubborn Armenians. What makes you think you have any chance at all of spotting them? What if they're hiding in the trunk or somewhere you can't see them? They could be inside a shipping container on the back of a truck. Do you think the Mukhabarat is going to search the cargo of every truck crossing the border?"

"What I know," Aleksandr replied, his voice rising. "Is that we will not catch them if we sit here on our asses in Dara'a."

****

Krikor's Volvo hummed along the north-south highway, past the first green fringe of wheat sprouting in the fields. Tom and Ana drowsed in the back seat and soon found themselves in Dara'a. South of the town, Krikor drove into the parking area beside a sprawling roadside establishment--café, gasoline pumps and garage facilities. The parking area held three aging Mercedes, four Volvo sedans, a mud-splattered tour bus, several long-distance trucks and one dusty, sand-painted Land Rover with a heavy A-frame brush bar wrapped around the grill and a spare tire on the roof.

"Wait here, Krikor," Tom said to him and to Ana, "Stay in the car."

Chico Webb looked like any other Arab, dressed in baggy trousers and a locally-made woolen coat. He wore a red and white checked kaffiyeh like most of the men in the restaurant and the two days of stubble on his cheeks fit the Arab excuse for not shaving--'Allah likes a little beard.' As soon as he spotted Tom getting out of Krikor's Volvo, he rose and began moving toward the door. They met just outside.

"Allah be praised," Tom said to Webb softly in Arabic and to himself, "Thank God. She made it."

"The Rover," Webb said.

Tom climbed into the passenger seat. Webb got behind the wheel.

"Now, you crazy bastard," he said when both doors had slammed shut. "What's this all about?"

"First, I'm assuming you wouldn't be here if you hadn't talked to Mariah Carroll. Is she OK?"

"Sounded good to me. She was in Cairo, on her way to Paris and a connector to Casablanca. She told me to tell you to be careful, that she was charging a lot of new clothes to your Armenian connection-- whatever that is--and she wanted you to be around to pay the bill. Now how about putting me in the picture?"

Tom heaved a sigh and began. "The Mukhabarat has me on a Detain for Questioning list. They're helping an ex-KGB Major who wants to catch up with me because . . . This is a long story, Chico. Couldn't we just move it and let me fill you in later?"

"Give me the short version of the long story," Webb said, almost growling.

"I really haven't done anything to him except steal his airplane," Tom said. "But he's killed two people because he thinks I've got something he wants."

"Just an airplane, huh? KGB, huh? Only two bodies? Pretty touchy fellow, getting pissed over your stealing his airplane."

"I told you it was a long story. Honestly, I'd a lot rather tell you in Amman than in a parking lot in Dara'a. I just need to find a back door into Jordan. I'll fill you in and sort out the paperwork later."

"I thought I saw a little something extra at the border this morning. You're going to have to do better than that, sport. Your gal Mariah filled me in a little, but not enough. You're lucky I was in town and that she knew to call me Chico. I wouldn't have believed the story otherwise.

Tom drew a breath and went on. "There's another thing. I've got an

Armenian lady with me and she goes wherever I go. Will you help us get across?"

"I need to know a couple more things. Is any of this political--even remotely?"

"Not a bit of it. It's commercial, but not where I'm concerned. I'm an innocent, unpaid--dumb-assed--courier. A friend of mine asked me to take a couple of pieces of jewelry to Amsterdam--I was going to lay over there on my way back after this job in Armenia--and I guess the KGB guy thought there was a double-cross going on. My friend and the KGB Major were doing business with the same guy and the Major must think he has a monopoly on the trade. I don't know."

"Is the stuff stolen?"

"I've been assured that it isn't. It doesn't even look particularly valuable to me. For sure it's not enough to kill for." Tom avoided mentioning the diamonds. They were almost certainly stolen and might, in some circuitous way, be political. Chico might not care that they were stolen from the Russians, but he didn't want to take the chance. He needed Chico's help in the most critical way.

"Who're you carrying for?"

"The son of our old friend, Andranik Melikian. I guess you know that business back then almost got me killed." Tom almost told him about the Russian he'd seen with Avakian at the airport, but thought better of it. The situation was complicated enough. "I never did find out what Andranik did for you," he added to try to put the ball in Chico's court.

"You're not going to, either. Did you know the old shop's still there, downtown by the gold souk? His son, Anastas, runs the place. I tried to bring him on board when I got back out here, but he didn't inherit his father's love of adventure. I'm surprised he's involved in something like this."

"It's not Anastas. The deal's with Razmik. The younger son," Tom said. "I thought you'd met him. It doesn't matter. He didn't steal the stuff."

Chico stared at Tom for a long moment. "OK. So it isn't stolen, but is it legal?"

"If you mean are they antiquities, the answer is almost surely 'yes.' I can't figure out any other reason for the fuss. I don't have documentary permission to take them out of Armenia, but they're not exactly Armenian anyway. One's Persian and the other's Parthian. Old, but not like they just came out of an archaeological dig. Soviet law doesn't apply there any more and Armenia's got plenty of problems to deal with before they write new laws on antiquities. The stuff may not have export licenses and be wrapped with all the other legal ribbons, but it's not illegal either."

"How about you? Are you legal? Like, are you wanted by the Armenian cops?"

"I could be. I did steal the guy's airplane, but he's supposed to be a big time drug dealer and with a couple of dead bodies to his credit, I don't think he's gonna be in a hurry to file charges. He's got the pull in Syria to get me picked up by the Mukhabarat--that's the 'detain for questioning' thing--but the plane wasn't stolen in Syria and it didn't come down in Syria, so I don't see how the Syrians have any kind of legal jurisdiction. The Mukhabarat's got the muscle and what they're doing is probably a professional courtesy thing or something for old times' sake. I don't see how it could be official. They still might make us disappear just to stay in practice."

"Where is the plane, incidentally?"

"In five feet of icy water in the Batman baraji. In eastern Turkey, two or three hours from Diyarbakir. I told you this was a long story."

"No shit," Chico said, laughing softly. "Two dead bodies, a stolen airplane, an ex-KGB Major who's a drug dealer, the Mukhabarat chasing you. Did I leave anything out? I guess I'll have to help you to lay claim to the story. OK. There's a wadi around the bend we can follow and I know a place to cross."

"Great. Then can we light the burners on this thing and go get my lady? She's over in that old Volvo."

CHAPTER FORTY EIGHT

Dara'a and the Jordanian Border

Aleksandr had been perched on a knoll south of the restaurant since dawn, watching every car and truck driving south toward Jordan or parking at the restaurant. His binoculars picked up Tom as soon as he got out of the Volvo. From that point on, Aleksandr watched Tom's every move. He saw him meet an Arab outside the restaurant and get into the Land Rover that had come in from Jordan half an hour before.

"He's here, Russian," Aleksandr called down, keeping the binoculars in place against his eyes.

He watched the Land Rover move out of its parking space and drive up to the Volvo the American had come in. His pulse began to race when he saw Ana get out. The American took two backpacks from the trunk and stowed them in the Rover, then went back to the Volvo and spoke a few words to the driver. "They're in the Land Rover, Russian. We've got them."

Danilov was leaning against the fender of the Mercedes, smoking. He looked up at Aleksandr with studied indifference, then calmly removed his glasses and polished them with his handkerchief. He stubbed out his cigarette and drew the Glock 9mm from his shoulder holster, chambered a round and clicked off the safety. He opened the passenger door and got in as Aleksandr came scrambling down the knoll, creating a cascade of small stones and sand.

"I'll try to drive them off the road, Russian. If I cannot, shoot their tires," Aleksandr said, starting the car and throwing it into gear. Driving with his good arm, he eased the Mercedes onto the shoulder, watching the rear-view mirror for the Rover.

Chico held to the outside lane, going through the five gears methodically, running up to optimal revs before shifting and looking for the place he wanted to leave the road and head into the wadi. He passed the Mercedes as it sat on the shoulder, saw it accelerate onto the highway and move to the inside lane to come alongside him.

"We've got company," Chico said just before the Mercedes

drove into his lane and smashed against the front fender, driving him onto the shoulder. He wrenched the wheel back, crashing the Rover into the side of the Mercedes. Then he saw the ugly black snout of the 9mm pointing at him from the open passenger window. He yanked the Rover onto the shoulder just as a 9mm slug tore through the driver's side window and shattered the windshield into a thousand spidery prisms.

Ana screamed.

"Tom, kick it out. Kick out the windshield," Chico yelled as the Rover jolted over the shoulder onto rock-strewn scrabble. "I can't see."

Tom leaned back in his seat and aimed a kick at the fractured windshield. It popped out of its mounting and slithered off the hood. A rush of cold air filled the passenger compartment.

As Chico swung hard to the right, the Mercedes skidded sideways in the road, followed them onto the scrabble beyond the shoulder and took up a blocking position in front of them.

That was when Tom saw the man behind the barrel of the Glock. The Russian had come with Avakian. That's good, Tom thought. This time they'd be face to face, mano a mano.

Chico was turning back toward the highway, cutting behind the Mercedes when the muzzle of the Glock flashed again. He grunted as the heavy slug smacked into his right shoulder and drove him back in the seat. Ana screamed again and the engine died as Chico lost control. Two more shots tore through the cab of the Rover. Chico grabbed the door handle, opened the driver's door and rolled out onto the rocky scrabble. His left hand groped awkwardly for the weapon in the shoulder holster under his left armpit. "Tom," he yelled. "Drive on. I'll cover you. Go!"

Tom vaulted over the high console into the driver's seat and brought the Rover's engine back to life while Chico unleashed a barrage of covering fire. Vibration rushed through the pedals and Tom reshuffled the transmission into low gear, stomped on the accelerator and popped the clutch. But he didn't turn toward the highway--he drove straight at the Mercedes, accelerating, bouncing over the rough terrain, watching the Glock shift its aim from Chico, sprawled on the ground, still firing, to the Rover.

The Mercedes' wheels spun in the gravel as it tried to maneuver away from the Rover's collision course. Tom felt the whiz of a bullet as it passed beside his head and heard Ana's sharp cry behind him. He continued accelerating, tracking the Mercedes. He had the angle and the crash was inevitable.

The Rover struck the Mercedes square at the passenger door, throwing the Russian back into the driver, tangling the two men. Arms flailing, the driver tried to disengage from his passenger, but Tom kept the accelerator down, the Rover's four-wheel drive digging in, pushing the Mercedes to the edge of the deep gash of the wadi. It teetered briefly on the edge before tumbling down the embankment in a cascade of rocks and soil and Tom hit the Rover's brakes with both feet, throwing up a shower of gravel and stopping just before the front wheels went over the rim of the wadi.

He jammed the gearbox into reverse and backed away to solid ground. Teeth clenched, he turned to look for Ana. She lay slumped across the beige leather of the back seat, a rivulet of blood tracing a thin red line down her cheek.

"Ana," he shouted, throwing open the rear door, reaching in to her, lifting her into his arms. Her eyelids fluttered and focused on him.

"Tom? *Inchpes es kez zgum?*" she asked in Armenian, too addled to know what language she was speaking.

"Thank God," he muttered, pulling back the hair from the side of her head to find the source of the blood.

"*Lav em. Chem vnasvel,*" she said.

"It's just a crease, baby. You're going to be OK. Stay down and sit tight. I've got to see about Chico."

Thirty yards back, Chico Webb sat on the gravel beside the shoulder with his legs straight out, the .357 Magnum resting in his lap. One end of his red and white checked kaffiyeh was clenched between his teeth and he was trying to bind it around his right shoulder for a tourniquet.

"Good move, my man," he said as Tom came running toward him. "Take this Magnum and make sure the bad guys are down. I'm OK. I got the bleeding stopped. Go on, now."

Tom took the pistol from Chico and sprinted back to the edge of the wadi. The Mercedes lay on its side in a thin cloud of orange dust, forty feet down. The Russian was crouched behind the shelter of the passenger-side door, trying to steady himself, awkwardly clinging to the window frame. His face was scratched, a smear of blood bubbled from his nose and one lens of his glasses was shattered, but the Glock was still in his hand. He was intent on gaining his balance, but he looked up and saw Tom standing at the rim of the wadi, holding the Magnum in both hands, arms extended, aiming at him.

Their eyes locked again for a moment, closing the circle on that night in Vienna. The front sight of the Magnum followed the Russian's struggle and Tom's finger tightened on the trigger. The crack of the shot was a surprise. The pistol bucked in his hands. The Russian was driven back against the door frame, a bright gusher of blood spurting from his neck. Reflexively, the Russian grabbed the wound with his hand, but the blood continued to pour from between his fingers. He found Tom's eyes for a final second before he collapsed across the door, half in, half out of the car.

Then a searing whoosh of flame enveloped the Mercedes as spilled gasoline caught fire. Tom stepped back from the rim of the wadi, throwing up an arm across his face to shield it from the heat. Peering out from beneath it, he saw the Russian's hair catch fire, then his clothes.

Dazed, Tom watched the bright tongues of flame licking at the dead Russian for a few moments. He studied the scene until the flickers of flame turned to small gray spirals of smoke. The Russian was obviously dead and there was no other movement from within the Mercedes. Aleksandr must have been killed by the crash.

Tom turned away from the wreck at the bottom of the wadi and jogged back to the Rover, checked the still addled Ana, stuffed the transmission in reverse and drove around to where Chico was pushing himself to a standing position.

"What about our chums?" he asked Tom.

"They're down," Tom replied.

"Then let's get the hell out of here before that bunch at the border comes to check on the gunfire. Get us down into that wadi," he said, pointing straight ahead. "We'll run down it a ways before we cross the border. You're gonna have to drive, but I'll show you the way. Go easy getting her over the side. She'll take the slope, just don't ask her to defy gravity."

＊＊＊＊＊＊＊＊＊＊＊

"What about those guys back there?" Chico asked once the Rover was out of sight of the highway.

"I shot one of them. I didn't mean to, but maybe it's just as well. He caught fire when the gasoline went up. When I left, he was smoking and he wasn't moving. Will that pass for dead?"

"What about the other one?"

"I didn't see him. The car was lying on the driver's side. I don't think he could've survived the crash and the fire, though."

"Well, if he did, he's gonna be slowed down some at least," Chico remarked.

"The driver was Aleksandr," Ana said, finally speaking English again. "But who was the other man?"

"A Russian who shot me in Vienna and left me for dead," Tom said. "The one who gave me that scar you're so fascinated with."

"The same guy who shot me shot you in Vienna?" Chico asked.

"It was a long time ago. And besides, it's a long story," Tom said.

****

They followed the wadi east for five, bone-jarring miles before Chico told Tom to turn south. They lost the track entirely then, but the Rover didn't seem to mind. Tom steered them around rock outcroppings and the worst inclines and declines. Thirty minutes later, Chico told him to stop. "You're in Jordan, now," he said. "We'll pick up another track here pretty soon that'll take us into Ramtha. Now that we're across, though, I think everybody could stand a drink. Tom, your lady looks like she could use a couple of aspirin, too. How about that, ma'am?" Chico said, turning back and looking at a weary Ana, sitting forward, bracing herself with both hands holding on to the front seats.

"Yes, my head is hurting," she said. "But what of your shoulder? Do you have bandages?"

"First aid kit behind your seat," Chico told her. "Tom, there's a bottle of Johnny Walker Black in the console under your elbow. Why don't you hand it to me? Then the lady and I'll patch each other up."

Chico took a long pull on the bottle of JW Black and then sloshed some on the gash in his shoulder. "Terrible waste of good whiskey," he said, wincing as the alcohol seared the wound.

Ana retrieved the first aid kit, found aspirin, took four with a large swallow of whiskey and told Chico to come around to the back of the Rover where she could work on his shoulder. He sat on the rear deck, his legs braced against the barren earth, while she swabbed out the wound and bandaged it as if she knew what she were doing.

"That feels better," Chico said. "I don't know if it's your tender touch, ma'am, or this golden elixir, but I think I'll make it to Ramtha. Now let's have a look at you."

Ana offered the left side of her face to Chico and he gently parted the blood-matted hair to expose the crease. "Got all your senses back now?"

"Yes, I think so," she replied.

"You were speaking Armenian to me right after it happened," Tom said.

"You should understand Armenian by now," Ana snapped. "It is a simple language. I learned to speak it as a child."

"OK, then," Chico said. "Let's saddle up. I'd like to get to Amman before dark." Then he noticed Tom's hands shaking. "Wait a minute. You OK, Tom?"

"I don't know," he said. "I feel a little funny all of a sudden."

"Just the 'after-action' shakes."

Tom nodded his head and leaned against the side of the Rover.

"Happens to us all," Chico said. "Just remember, that guy was shooting at us. He was trying to kill you. It's not like you killed him in cold blood."

"I'm not sorry for him." Tom took another pull on the Black Label. Then his teeth began to chatter and he began to shake.

"Sit down, Tom," Chico commanded. "We gotta warm you up." To Ana, he said, "Tom didn't introduce us but he called you Ana. That right?" She nodded. "Well, Ana, there's a compartment under the back floor board with a blanket in it. Get that for us, will you?"

"Don't worry, Tom," Chico told him, wrapping the blanket around him. "Anybody who's not an animal has trouble killing at close range." Tom sat in the driver's seat of the Rover and was quiet for a few minutes, the door wide open, his hands on the wheel, arms outstretched.

"This is all unreal," Tom said to no one, staring at the jumble of rock and scrub brush through the open space where the windshield once was. "A few days ago we were . . . I mean . . . the world was round. But the last seventy-two hours . . ."

Ana reached out to him, her hand going to his shoulder. "Tom, you saved us. He was shooting . . ."

"But it's all so crazy. I don't care if these damned baubles came out of King Tut's mouth, they're not worth killing for. And I haven't run diamonds in more than twenty years. Even Russians don't hold a grudge that long, do they?" He paused for a moment, staring into her eyes. "Was it you he wanted, Ana? That I might be able to understand."

"Tom, you humiliated him once. I think he would have killed you just for that. I am sure now that what Sarkis said is true, that Aleksandr killed Karine and Setta. He did that because of something he wanted from Sarkis. He believed you had it. It is true that you had me also. I do not think Aleksandr still loved me, but maybe he still wanted me. Am I saying it right?"

Tom laid his hand on her cheek. "You're saying it right."

"And the man who was shooting--that is something from long time ago with you and some awful accident that this man and Aleksandr were together. There are many questions, Tom," she said. "Perhaps we will never know the answers."

"I hate to break up this critique of the recent unpleasantness, but I'd like to get to a place where somebody can patch up my shoulder. How you feel now, buddy? Ready to move us on down the road?" Chico asked, seeing that the color had come back to Tom's face and he'd stopped shaking.

"I'm OK now."

Chapter Forty Nine

Amman, Jordan

They arrived in Amman at sundown, dropped Chico at the hospital emergency room to be properly stitched up and checked into the Inter-Continental. While Ana showered, Tom called Raz at the University.

"You're in Amman?" Raz exclaimed. "I only learned this morning that you didn't make the rendezvous in Amsterdam. What are you doing in Amman?"

"We're at the InterCon. Come on over and I'll tell you about it." Tom hung up the receiver as Ana emerged from the shower, swaddled in one of the hotel's thick terry cloth robes, toweling her hair dry. "Raz is bewildered," he said. "Wait 'til he hears the whole story."

Tom couldn't help grinning at the sight of her in the over-sized robe, with the sleeves rolled up and the hem almost touching the floor. "Are you hungry?" he asked.

"Oh, yes," she said.

"Then let's get something sent over right away." With the handset tucked between his cheek and shoulder, he ordered mezze--flat bread, baba ghanoush and koubba--and kofta kebab with a pot of sweet tea, stripping off his clothes and heading for the shower as he talked.

****

"I didn't expect to see you here," Raz said when Tom opened the door. "And Ana. What a wonderful surprise."

"Sit down, Raz. There's still some tea." Raz shook his head and Tom went on. "We've got some bad news."

They took him through the murders of Karine and Setta, the break-in at Ana's apartment, Sarkis' escape into the mountains and their own flight from Yerevan in the stolen Cessna. They told him about the plane crash, their run across Turkey and Syria and the battle at the Jordanian border. Raz listened speechless, mouth agape.

"And that's why we're in Amman instead of Amsterdam," Tom concluded. "And here's your stuff." Tom gave Raz the carnelian seal and the Parthian necklace, still wrapped as Sarkis had wrapped them. Ana gave him the two envelopes sealed with red wax. Raz broke the seals and read the documents while Tom sipped tea and gazed at the flagstone-paved pool area beyond the sliding glass doors of their cabaña.

When Raz looked up from the pages of Sarkis' Armenian scrawl, he said, "I'm not sure I understand all that he has written, but the provenance should make these two pieces quite valuable in the right market. I insist now that you accept a fee. I never imagined it would even be a bother and it turned out to be very, very dangerous."

"No, Raz. A deal's a deal. However, we lost a lot of stuff getting down here, so I won't argue with you about a generous expense allowance," Tom said, grinning. "Mariah, too. She's on her way to close a deal in Morocco and doesn't even have a clean shirt."

"By all means," Raz replied. "Send all the bills to Melikian's. I mean it. For Miss Carroll, too, of course. She was crucial to your escape. Your travel expense, too. And I'll leave some dinars with the cashier here at the hotel for incidentals."

"We also brought Sarkis' coin collection," Ana said.

"I forgot about that," Tom said. "It's over there in Ana's backpack." He got up and retrieved the olive-wood box, splintered, blood-spattered and held together with Russian duct tape.

"It's heavy," Raz said. "This is what you hit the sentry with when you took the airplane? And you carried this all the way?"

"Ana did," Tom said.

"Well, let's see it," Raz said. He made a space on the table among the breakfast dishes and slit the tape with his penknife. Inside they found two cloth-wrapped bundles. One contained an array of coins encased in plastic sleeves and individual two-by-twos--cardboard squares that protect coins between clear plastic seals. "You're the coin man, Tom. What do you think?"

Tom examined the coins carefully before he spoke. "Lot of Tsarist stuff. And Persian. Some of these may be from Central Asia. They'd be rare in the West. I'm sure they're important to Sarkis, anyway."

Raz peeled back the other cloth and exposed the lapis and

alabaster chess men.

"Oh, man," Tom said. "I like coins, but look at those chessmen. What are the dark ones, lapis lazuli? With gold flecks. Magnificent, huh?"

"Yes. Lapis. Alabaster for the white," Raz said. "Wonderful rust veining in the stone. Sarkis showed it to me when I was in Yerevan. He bought it at the vernesazsh for a hundred and fifty dollars. What did he say about the chess set, Ana?"

"Nothing. He only asked that you keep the coins for him."

"Well, the chess set is the perfect souvenir for you, Tom. Sarkis would want you to have it."

"That's a great idea," Tom said, surprised and delighted. "But don't you think you ought to wait until he can okay that?"

"No. You brought the seal and the necklace through and you refuse to take a fee. Sarkis would want me to do it. No more argument. We'll put his coin collection in the safe at Melikian's."

Tom picked up one of the lapis lazuli rooks and examined it closely. Then he compared its mate, lining them up for height and design. "This is incredibly fine hand work. How old do you think they are?" he asked Raz.

"Sarkis told me, but I don't remember now. A hundred years? Perhaps more. They came from Aleppo--like you," Raz said with a short laugh.

Tom frowned, weighing one of the rooks against the other. "Funny," he said. "Same chess piece, same kind of stone, but one's heavier than the other." He turned them over. A circle of new felt covered their bases. He slipped a fingernail under the felt of the heavier one and peeled it back, revealing an inset with a slot.

"Hold on," he said. "What've we got here?" He took a knife from the breakfast table, slipped the blade into the slot and exerted gentle pressure. The inset turned and Tom unscrewed it all the way. In the rook's base lay one of Geghard's seven gold coins.

Tom stared at it for several long moments, still nestled in the hidden cavity of the rook, then held the chess piece out to Raz and Ana. In awed tones, he said, "This is something special."

Raz and Ana bent over the rook and stared at the coin. It was the one that showed men and women holding hands in the center and the

Armenian alphabet around the edge.

"This is gold," Tom said. "Armenian--the letters around the rim--but it's pristine. A proof at least."

Raz took the rook and turned it over, dropping the coin into the palm of his hand. The other side showed Mt. Ararat topped by a cross.

"Don't handle it, Raz," Tom told him. "Gold's resistant to body oils, but we don't know what we've got here. Put it on the table cloth."

Raz dropped the coin as if it had burned his fingers.

"This is ancient hand work," Tom said, bending over the coin on the table. "Shit. This is old. Really old." Tom straightened up and stared at the coin a while longer before he turned back to the chess men.

He examined the bases of each piece. All were covered with fresh felt, but he quickly determined which were the heavy ones. Soon six more gold coins lay side by side on the breakfast table.

"Ana, say again what Sarkis told you that night. Particularly about the coins," Tom said.

Ana paced back and forth in front of the sliding glass doors, one hand to her forehead. "He was . . . how do you say? . . . shocked. And angry, too, but mostly . . . I don't know how to say. Not clear in his thinking. The poor man--his wife had just been killed. Her sister, too. He tried to tell me about the sister. She was paralyzed. He had stolen things from the museum to get drugs from Aleksandr."

Raz interrupted. "I know all about that. I can fill you in later. Concentrate on what he said about the coins."

"This box was the first thing he gave me. I opened the door and he was there. He looked so terrible, I do not think I heard what he said clearly, but that it was his coin collection and something like 'take these to Razmik.' Later, when the men were breaking down my door, he was angry with me because I forgot the box. Then he said in the car something about the box being the most important thing of all. Wait!" she said, her eyes going wide. "There is another envelope." She dashed to the pile of clothes she'd shed the evening before, where she'd left her leather shoulder bag, and began rummaging in it.

With a broad smile of victory, she extracted a long envelope with a red wax seal. "Here," she said, handing it to Raz. "I put it in a different place, but it is like the other two."

Tom and Ana watched eagerly as Raz broke the seal, pulled

several folded sheets from the envelope and began to read. His eyes widened and his face turned pale as he reached the second page. He sat down at the table to finish. With a trembling hand, he gave the pages to Ana. "I can barely understand what he's written. You will have to translate for Tom."

She seized the pages and, struggling to read Sarkis' hurried scrawl, began to translate with growing excitement the story of Palitus, the Sicilian dwarf, the master engraver who created Armenia's first gold coins, his secret room at Geghard and Brother Arteshesh's discovery. It described the stone box and the Persian walnut liner and detailed the obverse and reverse of each coin as it marked a milestone in Armenian history. The letter cited sources at Matenadaran Library to support the authenticity of the coins and a dating between 404 AD and 433 AD. Sarkis noted that the coins predated the gold solidus of Justinian II, minted between 685 AD and 695 AD. Vram Shapur's gold coins were therefore the earliest known example of Christ's portrait on a coin. There was no mention of the dies or the patterns.

Near the end of the second page, she came to Sarkis' discovery of the reason the coins had never been issued--the Roman Emperor, Honorius, had simply forbidden Vram Shapur to mint them. Sarkis didn't try to explain what Honorius had done, but he offered his interpretation of the significance of the coins as the true emblem of Armenian independence--independence from Romans, Persians, Turks and Russians--those who had ruled over them, tried to break the Armenian spirit and even to obliterate them from the earth.

When Ana finished translating, all three of them sat transfixed, unable to speak for several long moments. Finally, Ana broke the silence.

"These coins are what Aleksandr came for," Ana said. "Karine must have told him. Sarkis said they tortured her. We thought he wanted the jewelry, but what he wanted was so much more valuable. And Sarkis did everything he could to protect them. Even leaving his wife without burying her. It is so sad."

Tom's mind raced over the events surrounding the olive wood box, remembering his complaining about bringing it, then breaking it against the hard head of the sentry. Everything in it might have spilled out on the tarmac and who knows what would have happened then.

Not knowing about the treasure it held, would he have carried it from the sinking Cessna in the Batman baraji? Not bloody likely, he thought. But Ana had, even letting it take her to the bottom of that icy lake before she could climb out.

Finally, Raz got up. "These must go into the safe at Melikian's right away. How should I handle them, Tom?" he asked. "I don't want to harm them."

"Cotton's the best. There's more starch in these napkins than I'd like, but I think they'll do. I'd offer you a T-shirt I've only worn for three days, but that seems a tad sacrilegious."

He meant it as a joke, something to ease the tension, but even he couldn't smile at it. Carefully, lovingly, he folded the coins into the heavy cloth napkins and handed them to Raz. "I'd like to see them again before I leave," he said. Raz nodded. "Let me take the chess set, too. I'll have a proper case made for it. The one it came in is a little the worse for wear."

"I'm going to keep that," Tom said. "Bloodstains, duct tape and all. The story's no good without it."

"You still need a new one. I insist."

"What are we going to do about the coins?"

"They've got to go back as soon as possible," Raz said.

Ana looked at Tom. "Is it possible to telephone Armenia from here? I can explain to Minister Manoukian what has happened and ask his advice. Perhaps he will protect Sarkis, too."

"You have his home number, don't you?" Tom asked.

Ana nodded.

"Then place the call. It'll probably be awhile before they can route it, but we might as well get it in the queue. You should probably go over to the reception and get them to help you."

****

"Raz," Tom said when Ana had gone and was occupied with placing the call to Yerevan, "I have another favor to ask. Probably more in Anastas' area, but you can talk to him, can't you?"

"What is it?"

Tom slipped off his money belt, laid it on the table and began teasing out the diamonds from the lining. Raz took one in his fingertips and shook his head. "Are there any more surprises, Tom?" he asked. "Have you also brought a magic lamp with a jinni inside?"

Tom shook his head and said, "That's it. I'd like for Melikians to cash them out for me. I trust you to give me a fair price. I'll let you know where to transfer the funds when I get an account set up offshore. For curiosity's sake, let me know what the value comes to. Just write me a little note with the number on it. Would you do that?"

When Raz left, Tom slouched on the divan, the events of the day finally taking their toll

* * * * * * * * * * * *

"Isn't it wonderful?" Ana said, twirling in the center of the room. "Imagine what Minister Manoukian will say when I tell him. Everything is becoming good again for us."

"The coins are a wonderful find," Tom said. "But why would Manoukian be impressed? The Museum ought to be excited, but the Ministry of Finance?"

"No. It is a sign," she said. "An omen. We will have the loan. I know it. There will be a new Supreme Catholicos. And now we have the coins--they will be the symbol of our true independence, something we have been denied for more than a thousand years."

Tom shrugged. "Maybe so. But if I were you, I wouldn't get my hopes up about Manoukian's reaction."

Ana made a face at him. "You do not understand us," she said and changed the subject. "What hotel is this?" she asked.

"The InterCon. I thought you might like to have a swim and breakfast by the pool. That's why I got the cabaña."

"Ummm. This is wonderful idea. But I have nothing to put on for swimming. In fact," she said with an uncomfortable awareness. "I have no clothes at all. Everything Mariah gave me is now torn and soiled. And the clothes I wore from Yerevan have the blood of the sentry on them."

"I forgot about that. I'll call the concierge and get some stuff sent over, but we're stuck until morning, unless you want to go skinny dipping."

"Skinny dipping? What is that?"

He grinned wickedly. "Au naturel. Dénudé."

Ana put her hand to her mouth to stifle a laugh, her eyes dancing. "Yes," she said. "Why not?"

Energized by the prospect of committing a bit of mischief, Tom sprang from the divan and crossed the room. He pulled aside the drapes and opened the sliding glass doors. He stepped out into the cooling air of the desert evening and made his way to the edge of the flagstone patio. In the soft glow of the underwater lights of the pool he could see no one.

Timidly, Ana had followed him through the door into the night. Now she took his hand and allowed him to draw her forward onto the pool patio.

He turned to her and grinned. "We've got it to ourselves. Come on." He shrugged out of his robe and dropped it on a chaise longue.

She took one long, appraising look at him, and slowly undid the sash of her robe.

He closed the distance between them and took the lapels of her robe in his hands, pulling the robe open and away from her shoulders. He dropped it beside his own with one hand, drew her to him with the other and kissed her.

She kissed him back with warm swollen lips and a darting tongue, then broke away and dove into the pool, leaving him breathless and tumescent. He watched her take several strong overhand strokes, then roll over on her back to wait for him. As soon as he dove in, she turned and raced him to the opposite end of the pool, reaching the darkness beneath the diving board a split second before him.

Hair matted, water beading on their faces, they grinned at each other like two mischievous children. Their eyes locked and they drew together for a watery kiss.

"We are safe now, yes?" she asked when they broke the kiss.

"We're safe."

****

Silently crossing the pool patio toward the cabañas, the figure in the gray jellabah and black and white checked keffiyeh was visible only in silhouette against the muted lights of the hotel lobby. His eyes were fixed on one set of glass doors, faintly limned in the glow of candlelight. As the image drew closer, his heart pumped harder and the muscles in his jaw clamped tighter. So determined was he to reach his objective that he made no effort to hide the limp that had long been an unwelcome challenge to his vanity.

He took comfort in the weight of the Glock 9mm in his right hand, concealed beneath the folds of the jellabah. The Glock felt like a lethal extension of his arm. As he reached the edge of the patio, he moved cautiously to avoid the disturbing any of the chaise longues or the chairs surrounding the umbrella tables. Once clear of them, he stepped deliberately onto the walkway and approached the doors of the cabaña he had been told was theirs.

The sheer curtains were drawn, but not completely. Pressing against the glass door at the jam, he looked into the room. His eyes first found the two candles set amid the china and glassware of the remains of a room service meal. As his eyes adjusted, he scanned the darker recesses of the room. He saw them at the same moment he heard the rhythmic moans and mewling of their passion resonating against the glass. What he saw struck him with paralyzing force. Her head lay just over the edge of the bed, dark hair cascading down the side. The face he knew so well, mouth open, brows tight in the moment of climax, arms and legs wrapped around the man above her.

A tidal wave of anger rose in his chest, burst in his brain and went crashing against his eyelids. He drew back the arm that held the Glock, the powerful arm of retribution, and smashed the painful image before him. Like a mighty hammer, it shattered the glass. For an instant, while a shower of glittering shards and splinters fell before him, he stood in the frame of the door gathering his wrath. Then he threw himself toward the lovers in one headlong rush.

At the sound of the breaking glass, Tom turned his head and saw the robed silhouette of a man in the doorway. Ana screamed and wriggled from beneath him, tumbling onto the floor. In the next moment, the figure came hurtling toward him, an anguished, animal growl bursting from its head. In that split second, the flickering candlelight caught the scar running along the side of the man's face. Avakian.

Instinctively, Tom rolled onto his back, taking the charge with his arms, using Avakian's own momentum to lift and throw him against the wall. The bedsheet tangled in his legs, the echoes of Ana's screams careening about the room, he dove over the side of the bed after Avakian, hands desperately seeking his throat.

His hands found rough cloth and flesh and he caught a faint odor of gasoline just as his eyes were blinded and his eardrums were shattered by an explosion. Tiny particles of blazing gunpowder stung his face. He groped frantically for the gun.

Trapped beneath the bed and the wall, with Tom's weight upon him, Avakian writhed and kicked, knees and elbows flailing.

Tom got his knee into Avakian's belly and his forearm across his throat. He felt the heat and the pressure of the gun fire again and, guided by the muzzle flash, grabbed the wrist that held it. Pushing, twisting with all his might, he pressed the gun toward Avakian's head.

The weapon fired again and Tom felt the searing flame against his side. An urgent signal from some primitive corner of his brain gave him strength for one last push. Using both hands, he drove the gun under Avakian's chin at the same moment he found its trigger and pulled it.

A steaming eruption of blood and brains exploded in Tom's face, blinding him. In one panicky motion, he straightened up and shook his head to clear it. Frantically, he wiped the bloody effluent from his face and eyes. Scrambling, his feet found the floor and he stood up, his naked body smeared with his own blood and Avakian's.

Across the room, Ana crouched on the floor, her eyes wide and wild. He saw her lips moving, but he could understand nothing of what she was saying.

His other senses began to return. Fresh air from the open door wafted to his nostrils the sweet smell of lovemaking mixed with the sharp scent of cordite and the acrid stench of his own fear. He felt a warm trickle running down the seam between his thigh and belly, touched his side and looked down--a dark red ooze. Then the searing pain of the open flesh struck him. Puzzled, he looked to Ana for an explanation.

She sprang up and rushed toward him, the macabre sight of his blood-spattered body making her face a mask of anguish and fear.

He fell just as she reached him.

CHAPTER FIFTY

Amman

The muzzein's call to prayer came to him from a distance, the chanted Arabic sweet and insistent in the morning stillness. He awoke disoriented but immediately aware that his ass was bare against stiff sheets and he was shivering cold. As the space around him came into focus and that special smell assailed his nostrils, he realized he was in a hospital. The blanket they'd given him was threadbare, scarcely more than a sheet. He tried to pull it closer around him, but the movement lit a streak of fire along his side. Shards of memory flashed through his mind--a dark figure hurtling toward him, a flash of light and stinging pellets, half a face blown into bloody pulp.

His heart was pounding and the powerful, rank odor of fear pushed back the sharp aroma of antiseptic. He felt a sudden surge of adrenaline, took a deep breath and tried to settle himself. Deliberately, he slammed the door on the scene and found the call button taped to the railing of his bed.

Presently, the gauzy curtain parted and a nurse in a starched white uniform stood beside him. She was silhouetted against the light from the corridor, her face in shadow. He felt her palm come to rest against his chest in the comfort zone between his shoulder and collar bone, waiting for him to speak.

"I'm cold," he said, liking her touch and the immediate warmth of her hand.

"Of course, sir," he heard a small voice whisper, the 'r's' trilled and aspirated in the Arabic fashion. "I will bring another cover."

She had a nice voice and he was comforted by it, no longer alone. His breathing slowed and he relaxed a little. She returned and spread a warm blanket over him, deftly tucking it around his legs with several firm, flat-handed jabs. Another nurse appeared over her shoulder. "Is that not better?" the second nurse asked in heavily accented English. Out of habit, she gripped his wrist and took his pulse.

He thought she was older because the timbre of her voice

projected authority, but like the first nurse, the light was behind her and he couldn't make out her features.

"Where am I?" he mumbled, frowning, his mind still fuzzy.

"This is the Hospital Ibn Tafail. In Amman. You lost much blood and your wound was contaminated, but you have been cleaned and stitched. Do not worry. You will feel yourself again soon. Would you like water?"

"Please." He realized suddenly how parched his throat was, his lips stiff and cracked, some bitter taste lingering in the back of his throat. Reaching out a hand, she brought a glass from the bedside table and placed a plastic straw in his mouth. "A man is waiting to see you," she intoned, watching him pull on the straw, sipping greedily. She took the straw away to let him speak.

"Who?" Tom croaked.

"He calls himself Melikian." Tom closed his eyes. What the hell had happened? Where was Ana? "Let him in," he told the nurse.

"Only a few minutes," she said, checking the tube on his IV drip and switching on the lamp. Even with the shade turned away, Tom squinted against the light that now revealed the nurse's face. Heavy eyebrows above a hawkish nose and two hard, dark eyes. Her nameplate said Shahin in English and Arabic. She was probably his age.

The nurse moved to the foot of the bed and slowly turned the crank to elevate the backrest so that he could sit up a little. "Be still, please. You must not tear the stitches. I will give you something for the pain and to sleep again," she told him.

Raz's anxious face appeared around the edge of the door. Seeing Tom's eyes open, he surged into the room, drawing a reproving look from Nurse Shahin.

"Tom," he said, ignoring the nurse and pressing against the railing of the gurney. "I just spoke with the doctor. You're going to be fine. Just a scratch, as they say in Hollywood."

"Where's Ana?"

Raz shook her head. "She'll be here soon. There were some difficulties with her papers, but I have a friend at the Ministry of Foreign Affairs and I was able to get him to help. One of your embassy people came also and it has all been sorted out now. My God, Tom. What a mess! Ana was almost hysterical by the time I got there. Fortunately, the hotel knew to call me."

The rustle of a heavily-starched white uniform and the squeak of rubber soled shoes on the tile floor announced the return of Nurse Shahin. She elbowed Raz aside, inserted the needle of a syringe into a shunt on Tom's IV and injected a stream of clear liquid.

"Wait a minute," Tom said to her. "I'm OK. I don't want to be knocked out again."

"Be quiet, please. If you are OK, you would not be here," Shahin scolded. "Do as I say or your intestines will be falling out. Now go to sleep."

His jaw was suddenly too heavy to open, his lips numbing. For a moment, Raz's face swam in his vision before his eyes closed and the drug swept him away.

****

Like a falling feather, he drifted downward. So pleasant. He smiled. Mariah was there beside the boat dock. And Charlie, standing on one ridiculously long leg, was preening his feathers. Mariah waved and skipped toward him, barefoot like a child, her skirt swirling about her.

He saw her framed against the blue sky, the gray-green waters of the lake beyond and the lacy fringe of the giant cypress trees above her. One hand on the balcony railing, the breeze rippling the long flowing robe she wore, teasing a strand of hair.

Then she was in his arms, her breath against his throat, kissing him. Her lips, so velvety, then swelling, hot and insistent. Darkness, floating, a crimson glow, pulsing around them.

Her face snapped into focus again and became Ana's. Those lovely eyes. The water running. The shower. Billowing steam filled the little bathroom. It cleared and then he saw her, bare breasted, brushing her hair. He marveled at her slender fingers and the graceful way they drew the brush through her heavy, dark hair. It swayed and shimmered as she turned her head first one way, then the other.

He put his arms around her and their faces made a smiling portrait in the mirror, his chin on her shoulder, hands cupping her breasts.

"I love you," he said.

"I love you, too," Mariah whispered.

****

He felt her touch and opened his eyes.

She was sitting beside him, holding his hand. The nurse had lowered the railing and Ana's face was only inches away. He smiled.

"Hi, there," he said, feeling stupidly happy, forcing the words from his benumbed lips.

"Hello, Tom," she said. She was smiling, but there was something sad in her eyes that he didn't like.

"Are you OK?" he asked.

She nodded. "You will be, too," she told him. "You were so strong. Aleksandr . . . I cannot believe he would come so far. But he is truly dead now. I was so frightened . . ."

He squeezed her hand and marveled at its warmth. He was cold again. "I spoke to Minister Manoukian this morning," she began. I am to bring the coins home today."

"No," he said. "Not today. Let Raz go. Stay with me."

"I cannot," she said. "The Minister has told me I must come. It is what you call . . . symbol, I think. So much is happening. The Assembly is meeting to make a new Supreme Catholicos. They will show the Roman lance that killed Christ, the lance Jude Thaddeus brought to Armenia--and now the coins have come from the secret room in St. Jude's chapel. It is such a great moment. And the Minister wants me to be part of it." She blushed. "I am very honored by this, Tom."

A void filled his stomach. "And us?" he asked.

"When you return to Armenia. You will come back to help us again and we can talk about . . . well, what can come after for us."

"You can't leave now," he said, struggling to make his brain understand what she was saying. "Come to the lake with me."

"Tom. You must understand. I cannot. My country needs me," she said.

"Your *country?* . . . Ana . . ." he stammered.

"I am Armenian, Tom. I told you."

"Ana," he said, beginning to realize that what he thought there was had never been. "It's peaceful there. No country to save, no

361

killers," he said, frowning, unable to understand why she was leaving.

She shook her head. "I am sorry, Tom. It cannot be time for holiday. The coins have changed everything for us." Furtively, she checked her watch. Her flight was leaving in two hours and Raz was bringing a car for her. He was probably waiting outside the hospital now.

She rose from the chair and bent over him, one hand resting on his cheek. She kissed his mouth softly, tenderly, then kissed his eyes to close them. "I must go now. Please remember what I have told you and try to understand."

She backed toward the door then, one hand raised timidly to her lips. And then she was gone.

He stared at the edge of the door, where he had last seen her, his eyes as dull and cold as a lizard's. Shifting his gaze upward, he watched the blades of the ceiling fan turn slowly and let their lazy motion send him back to sleep.

In his dream, he returned to the lake house and imagined her scent filling every room and her silky voice echoing from the walls. They would make throbbing, sweating, sweet-smelling, passionate love. She'd bathe in his tub, sail in his cove, walk barefoot in his grass--and leave her footprints there for a thousand years.

But even in his dream, he knew that wasn't going to happen.

CHAPTER FIFTY ONE

The Texas Hill Country

Two weeks later, patched up and nearly healed, he made the long, lonely flight back to Texas. Royal Jordanian to London and American Airlines to Dallas. George Smalley picked him up there with a Cessna Centurion and flew him back to the lake.

He dumped his gear in the middle of the floor, showered, got into bed and slept for fourteen hours. When he could finally sleep no more, he splashed cold water on his face, plastered his side with tape to brace it, dressed in Levis and boots, threw on a heavy plaid shirt and his Resistol hat and went to the stables.

There was no one around when he pulled up, so he left a note, saddled Rachel, his favorite mare, and headed for Saddleback Mountain. He told Rachel to take it easy, that he still had stitches. Then he let her have her head, prodding her only when she stopped too long in one place. It was a good homecoming, feeling the coarse hair of her mane and her heavy muscles beneath his legs. The music of the creak of the saddle leather kept time to the hollow clop and scrape of her hooves. Once in awhile, she snuffled as if she were trying to make conversation and he dozed, letting his body sway in the saddle to Rachel's easy motion as she picked her way up the mountain.

An armada of stately white clouds had sailed up from the Gulf on a cool, fresh breeze, dappling the bright blue sky. Yellow blossoms flared from knots of prickly pear cactus.

Rachel slipped on some loose shale and broke his train of thought. He steadied her with his knees, rubbed her neck and muttered encouragement. "Easy, easy, old girl. That's it. You can do it."

As they climbed, he gazed out over the slowly changing vista. Not a house in sight. Just the sky and the clouds and the scrub brush. Gnarled live oaks, some mesquite, huisache and prickly pear.

Around noon, Rachel found her way to an old tank, flush with water from the spring rains, and Tom dismounted. He took off his worn Resistol, mopped the sweat from the inside band with a bandana and swabbed his forehead. A live oak tree offered a spot of shade and he squatted down under its gnarled branches to watch Rachel graze on a patch of new grass.

Three women in his life. Now really only two. Seline's shadow had all but disappeared. She belonged to the past. Ana and Mariah were the two fresh shoots of his future. Ana so exotic, so different from anyone he'd ever known, yet committed to a land-locked, nothing-works throwback of a country where people froze to death in the winter because there was no heat, where they did without electricity and hot water and gasoline and God knows what else? He understood that she wanted to change that, but all the patriotism in the world wasn't going to change the fact that, in the final analysis, the damned country had the slimmest of chances of becoming viable in an unfettered global economy no matter how much money the World Bank poured into it. It was a land populated by thousands of dead Armenians, the victims of Roman conquest and Turkish genocide. He felt only the most distant connection to them while they were vivid and vital to Ana.

An image of Mariah, honey-blond hair and bright blue eyes, appeared and a montage of scenes played languidly across his mind. Their first lunch at the Jefferson Hotel when they silently acknowledged their attraction for one another; the steamy night in the Peruvian Andes when that attraction burst forth; the piquant afternoon in that little café in the harbor at Monastir; drinking the last of the wine before the fire at the lake house; slipping off her clothes and tucking her into bed in Yerevan; her confession of love for him in Republic Square; that desperate embrace at the airport in Aleppo. He smiled. Put together, these were megawatts of electricity rippling through their time together.

Rachel drifted over to him, the reins dangling from her halter. She nudged his shoulder with her great, wet muzzle and he reached up a hand to rub her broad jaw. This old horse seemed to understand after all, he thought, maybe better than he did. He got up and slapped the dust from the seat of his jeans.

"OK, girl," he told her, picking up the reins and fitting his boot into the stirrup. "Let's see if you can get me home before dark. I got to make some phone calls."

CHAPTER FIFTY TWO

Agadir, Morocco

The Air Maroc flight from Casablanca settled down on final approach to the Agadir airport and Mariah felt the butterflies in her stomach begin to beat their wings.

Tom was on that plane.

She'd been waiting for at least thirty minutes, had drained three glasses of fresh orange juice from the snack bar, gone to the ladies' room twice and worn a path in the hard tile outside the arrivals area.

She couldn't be angry with him, but he'd been his typically cryptic self and she didn't know what his showing up in Agadir meant. She'd imagined a dozen things in the week between his phone call and this moment. All he'd said was that he was coming, could she make a hotel reservation for him. 'How many days?' she'd asked, with stupid practicality. Why hadn't she asked 'why are you coming?'

He'd told her a week, given her his flight number and ETA, asked her to meet him at the airport, then said he had to go, they were calling his flight.

It had been two months since they'd parted company in Aleppo-- two months that felt like two years, mainly because she hadn't been able to reach him at the lake house. Just the damned answering machine. Then out of the blue, he'd called, catching her in the shower. She got to the desk to find out that the call had come from the US--Alexandria, Virginia. Finally, the waiting was over. The sonofabitch better be on that airplane. *If he missed it . . . or changed his mind . . . I'll kill him, I swear. No I won't,* she thought. She just wanted to see his leathery old face and his warm brown eyes and watch his lanky, rolling gait bringing him toward her. Maybe something more than that. Oh, damned straight, more than that.

She strained to see the passengers filing off the 737 and then suddenly, there he was in the hatch, at the top of the mobile stairway, aviator sunglasses, khakis and a leather jacket over a button-down blue shirt. He had a briefcase in one hand. Standard equipment, like the rollaway with a laptop riding piggy back that trailed along behind him. The sight of him stopped her heart for a moment and then she let go a long breath, one she thought she must have been holding for a week.

Most of the passengers headed for the baggage claim, but Tom veered away toward the exit. Traveling light. She waved to get his attention. Without a spare hand, he lifted his chin and grinned when he spotted her.

She forced herself not to run, but she met him halfway across the expanse of green and white tile and threw her arms around him. She knew it wasn't good form in an Arab country, but she still planted a wet kiss on his mouth before she let him go.

"You're a good kisser," he said.

"You need a shave," she told him, grinning. "Where'd you come from, sailor?"

"Casablanca," he said, giving her his briefcase and wrapping an arm around her shoulders, letting her steer him toward the bright mid-afternoon sunlight.

"I know that," she said. "I meant before. I've been trying to get hold of you for two months."

"Oh, that," he said. "I went to the lake and turned the phone off. Got some sun, played a lot of golf. Talked to Rachel about things."

"Rachel? Who's Rachel? What things?"

"Rachel's a horse I ride."

She wanted to smash him, but she was so happy to have him beside her and his arm around her that she let him get away with not answering her question. "I'm close to closing this deal. It'll be a very sexy one--a pilot project for a small business microcredit system. There's a bidonville--you know, squatter settlement--just outside of town called Tikiouine and that's where we're proposing to set it up. Some great people to work with. The best, really."

She walked him into the parking lot across from the airport entrance, the heat of a sizzling sun mingling with a fresh ocean breeze.

"You look terrific," he said, changing the subject again. "You're as tan as a camel. I didn't recognize you at first."

"I start early and quit early. The beach is right outside my door, so I swim and catch rays in the afternoon. Here we are," she said, stopping beside a dusty, dented Renault Clio that looked a lot like a horse that had been ridden hard and put up wet.

"Yours?" he asked.

"I bought it cheap," she said. "It's a leftover from the '92 Paris to Dakar Rally. I love it and it isn't pretentious. I'll unload it when I leave."

Tom threw his baggage into the back seat and got in beside her. She put the key in the ignition and rested her cheek on the steering wheel to look at him, a mischievous smile on her face. Then she turned the key and the unmuffled engine roared to life like an elephant in heat. They both burst out laughing.

A short drive brought them to the Tikida Beach Resort hotel and Mariah parked the Renault in a lot down the hill from the main entrance.

"You got a swim suit?" she asked him.

"I've been here before," he said. "I know the ocean is at the doorstep."

"Then dump your stuff and meet me on the beach. OK?"

****

He made one long, muscle-stretching foray into the Atlantic, went back up to the beach and molded the sand into a shape that fit his body. He was lying on his face, dozing in the warm, late afternoon sun, when she came up beside him dripping sea water.

"You should come back in," Mariah said, fluffing her hair with a towel and showering him with water. "It's terrific."

"If you drip on me any more, I won't need to," he grumbled.

She sat down on a beach towel and turned her head toward him. "Want some lotion?" she asked.

He swiveled his head to meet her eyes and grinned, thinking she was quite gorgeous, a nymph fresh from the sea, water dripping from the end of her nose and beading on her shoulders. Her blond hair was matted and spiked in every direction.

"I'm starting to think about a drink and dinner," he said. "What about you?"

"If we hurry, we could go up the coast a little way. I know a rooftop place that has great fish and incredible sunsets. Maybe I can put you in the mood to tell me what happened after Aleppo. All I got from you was that one little note that said the bad guys had been dispatched and told me where to send the bills.”

Tom smiled at her, coming to a sitting position. “Think they might have a good bottle of French wine to go with the fish?”

“I’d bet on it,” she said, getting up and standing between him and the ocean, turning her head sideways to pound water out of her ear. “Come on, let’s go. If we don’t get it together, we’ll miss the sunset.” The light was already turning coppery.

He appraised her frankly, enjoying what he saw

“Did Raz get the bill for that bikini?” he asked. “Or do they call it a mini-kini? It leaves damned little to the imagination.”

She laughed. “I almost lost the top a couple of times out there,” she said, nodding her head to indicate the surf.

“Probably cost a French fortune,” he said.

She grinned. “I’m worth every franc and you know it. Come on, we need to go. Meet you in the lobby in thirty minutes,” she added, heading for the surfside doors of the hotel.

****

The rooftop of *Le Chat d’Espagne* offered a spectacular view of the Atlantic Ocean and Mariah used her influence with the maitre ‘d to get one of the best tables. They ordered the day’s catch from the chalk board and splurged on a hideously expensive bottle of Pouilly Fuissé, asking that it be brought right away.

Mariah began peppering him with questions as soon as the waiter disappeared. “What exactly did you mean when you wrote that the bad guys had been ‘dispatched’? I’ve imagined all sorts of things.”

“Even in your wildest, you’d never guess,” he said. He’d known all along, ever since he decided to come to Morocco, that he’d have to get into this and he’d been over it in his mind a dozen times. The hard facts of it were that he’d killed two men, one almost in cold blood, the other in a bloody melee. He didn’t want Mariah--or anybody else--remembering that about him. He needed to tell it without the gory details, but in a way that satisfied her and put the thing to rest.

He gave her a solemn look and began. “They caught up with

us at the Jordanian border. Just the KGB Major and the Russian. The Mukhabarat wasn't in on it. Good thing. We'd have been pretty badly outnumbered. Anyway, there were some shots fired, but we rammed their car and pushed it over the edge of a pretty deep wadi. That took care of the Russian and, just as I figured, Chico had an 'unofficial' way over the border and we slipped into Amman in fairly good order."

"What about the KGB guy? You said the Russian died in the crash, but . . ."

"We thought we'd taken care of him, too, but it turned out that he followed us into Amman. I guess the Syrian Mukhabarat gave him some help getting across the border and contacts in Amman to run us down. Actually, we were pretty stupid. Once we were in Jordan, we thought we were home free and didn't do anything at all about covering our tracks. We were pretty easy to find, I suppose. The InterCon isn't exactly a low profile place."

"Well, what happened? The KGB guy knocked on your door or what?"

Tom smiled and shook his head slowly. "Uh uh. He crashed through the sliding glass doors. He was pretty determined to have my head, I guess. But it turned out the other way."

"What do you mean, Tom? Damnation, you're the most aggravating man when you don't want to tell a story!" Mariah hissed, fidgeting with frustration.

"He had a gun," Tom said flatly. "It went off a few times. The first one went off right in my ear and I couldn't hear a bloody thing for hours. Anyway, that old adage about not playing with firearms came true for him and he's definitely dead now."

"Was Ana there?" Mariah asked hesitantly, knowing the answer.

Tom nodded. "Yeah, but she's OK."

"What about you?"

"Just a scratch. I'm good as new," he said, inwardly breathing a sigh of relief, thinking he'd managed to slide past the lurid parts of the story.

But Mariah looked at him with suspicion and he waited to see if she would press him. "Why do I get the feeling that you're leaving out some stuff?" she said. Fortunately, Tom thought, the waiter returned at that moment with the Pouilly Fuissé.

The appropriate tasting and toasting rituals were observed before Mariah said, "So Chico Webb showed up and pulled your chestnuts out of the fire. I'm glad about that. He really was your only shot. Peter made some calls, but it doesn't sound like anything came of that."

Relieved that Mariah was letting the gory details of the two killings slide, Tom said, "It was incredibly lucky. Even miraculous. He might not have been in-country. Or just not in the office. Trust me, I do know how close it was."

They gave reverent attention to the setting sun as it began to sink into the ruffled waters of the Atlantic, painting a long streak of cirrus clouds with a spectacular palette of colors that changed moment by moment.

The waiter appeared, poured more wine and lit the candle at their table, shielding it from the sea breeze with a glass chimney.

"The museum guy, what's his name? What happened to him?" Mariah asked.

"Sarkis," Tom prompted. "I don't know. I don't think anybody knows right now. I heard from Raz just before I left the States that they still hadn't found him. That's put the validation of the gold coins and all that on hold. He's not around to defend his authentication and his fellow savants in the coin world are being difficult about signing on." He grunted and shook his head. "All the big hurry to get them back to Armenia was just . . . unnecessary. Even futile."

"Gold coins?" Mariah asked, wide-eyed. "What gold coins?"

"Didn't I tell you about the gold coins?"

"No. You didn't. What's the deal?"

He held her rapt attention for ten minutes elaborating the story of the Sicilian dwarf, the secret room at Geghard Monastery, and the heavy-handed prohibition of their issuance by the Roman Emperor Honorius. That, he concluded, was why the Armenians were viewing the coins as the true emblems of their independence. Then he added, "The coins were what Avakian and my Russian friend were after."

"What a boondoggle," Mariah said. "We didn't have them. Those guys got themselves killed for nothing."

"Actually, we did have the coins. They were in that olive wood box I hit the sentry with. Remember?" Then he told her how he'd almost come home with them, hidden in the bases of Sarkis' fabulous chess men.

Mariah's mouth fell open and she stared at him for a long moment. "You almost left that box at the airport. On the tarmac," she said. "And then when we ditched in the baraji in Turkey. They could have been lost forever."

"Yeah, but Sarkis is no dummy. I've thought about this a lot and I can't believe he'd have let go of those coins if they'd been the only ones. I only saw them that one time and I didn't have a loupe to look at them with, but I swear I remember seeing stress marks--from striking the gold against the dies. They'd been polished into fleur de coins, but still, where the hell are the dies? Wouldn't they have been in that room at Geghard, too? Sarkis will clear all that up when he surfaces, but in the meantime, they're tantalizing questions."

The fish came, head and tail hanging over the ends of the platter, still sizzling in its juices, surrounded by a hearty potpourri of sliced onions, strips of red and green bell peppers, olives and fragrant cilantro. The waiter set a bowl of steamed rice between them and deftly deboned and filleted the fish. He served each of them with a flourish and left them alone.

They ate in silence to give proper respect to the meal and the wine and called for coffee. The evening breeze off the Atlantic freshened, fluttering the candle in its glass chimney. Mariah, in a sleeveless cotton dress, shivered.

"Here," Tom said, passing her the sweater he'd slung around his shoulders, California-style.

She snuggled into it gratefully, then rested her elbows on the table and leaned toward him, gathered her courage and said, "This is one of your most fascinating war stories ever, but so far I haven't heard a whisper, not a hint, not a clue."

Tom knew what she wanted to ask, but perversely, he didn't want to make it easy for her. "About what?" he asked.

"You know," she said. "Ana. Where's it stand?"

Tom shrugged. "She's in Armenia, helping Manoukian save the nation. She was supposed to be the poster girl for the glittering gold coins of Geghard, but that part of her glory hasn't yet been bestowed. From what Raz said, though, she's up to her eyeballs in pushing the loan through. Apparently, she's put together quite a team to liaise with the World Bank people on the feasibility studies. Your gal Katya's in the game, too, along with a bunch of their translator buddies. Levon's got a team of his own putting together the data. They're going to keep feasibility on a fast track."

Unconsciously, Mariah pulled a corner of her lip between her teeth and her eyebrows drew together ever so slightly.

"That's great, but come on, Tommy," she said, pleading a little. "There's got to be something more."

He looked at her, the candlelight shimmering off the angular lines of her face and her impertinent nose, her eyes sparkling. "Rachel helped me sort things out and I'm here, aren't I?"

She covered his hand with hers and squeezed it. "Are you here to say 'hello' or 'goodbye'?"

He raised his eyebrows and gave her half a smile. "I'll show you a little later. They gave me the biggest, most beautiful bed in Morocco. It's not Amsterdam, but I think it may do."

They held each others' eyes for a very long time, their fingers laced across the table, the coffee growing cold. Finally, she said, "There's going to be a moon. I don't swim at night by myself, but if you came with me . . ."

****

Mariah showed up in a dark blue Speedo one-piece suit that told Tom she was serious about swimming. She led him away from the hotel to a stretch of beach where they were unlikely to be disturbed by evening strollers or tourists out for a late-night skinny dip. She spread a blanket on the sand and pulled him toward the water. "Come on," she said. "You barely got wet this afternoon."

They swam out through the darkness until her feet would barely touch. Holding hands, they floated with the easy rhythm of the sea. Laughing, spewing salt water, they let the long combers of the incoming tide crash over them. Finally, she choked on one of the big breakers and Tom dragged her back to the beach.

They flopped down on the blanket and toweled themselves dry. Tom lay back and stared up at the stars, brilliant in the dark of the moon. Mariah sat beside him, a towel draped around her neck.

"Tommy," she said, putting her hand on his belly. Her hand was warm and smooth and as comforting as any touch he could remember for a very long time. Her fingers explored his mid section idly and eventually found the three-inch scar along his side.

"This is new, isn't it?"

"Souvenir from the InterCon in Amman. Trust me, it's a story that can wait. There's one part of the whole story I haven't told, though. I brought some diamonds out of Yerevan and sold them to the Melikians. Call it an inheritance. I just had the funds transferred to Nassau--three hundred and twelve thousand dollars. I've been looking at real estate in Old Town Alexandria. Pretty pricey, but I might be able to swing it. That said, it occurred to me that you ought to be in on the decision, seeing as how I'm going to ask you to spend a good bit of time there."

She tucked her knees under her and looked down at him, the moonlight just beginning to illuminate the features of the face of the man she loved. Slowly, she took his head in both her hands as if it were a chalice and kissed him, lightly at first, then her heart rose, her lips blossomed and she let them speak to him from the depths of her soul, to say that her kiss was a surrender, a commitment and a prayer. When she pulled away, they were quiet for a long time, their hands clasped, listening to the gentle rush of the surf.

At last she broke the silence. "Would you believe I have a bottle of pisco añejo in my room?" she asked, her voice a tender whisper.

He laughed and shook his head. "You don't. Where would you find it? Not here."

"In the duty-free in Paris. It spoke to me in five languages--'buy me, buy me' it said."

"*Pisco añejo.* I guess you remember that's pretty dangerous stuff. Think you're up for that?"

"Don't talk to me about danger after what you put me through in Armenia. And Turkey. And Syria."

"Then let's go crack the seal. I've got a powerful thirst," he said, scrambling to his feet in the loose sand and holding out his hand.

All the former Soviet republics suffered severe dislocations when the Soviet Union collapsed in the early 1990s. Armenia, however, entered this period of economic and political realignment with more than its share of distress. A strong earthquake ravaged the country at the end of 1988 and a flood of Armenian refugees from Nagorno-Karabagh, a province claimed by both Armenia and Azerbaijan, exacerbated human suffering in the country. To make matters worse, Turkey aligned itself with Azerbaijan and closed its borders with Armenia, making commerce with the rest of the world extremely difficult.

An *Armenian Affair* is set in 1995, while the Armenian crisis persisted but after the worst had passed. Although An Armenian Affair is entirely a work of fiction, the conditions of life in Armenia are based on personal observation during two trips to the country in 1995 and on information provided by Armenians living there during that period and the days of extreme national distress following the earthquake and the dissolution of the Soviet Union.

I'm particularly grateful to Steve Anlian and Melik Karapetyan, who gave generously of their time explaining the nuances of the changes then underway in Armenia. Steve and Melik were extremely helpful in supplying maps and other research material unavailable outside Armenia. Richard Aijian trusted me with out-of-print books to facilitate the historical research. Christopher Zakian, Public Relations Officer for the Diocese of the Armenian Church of America, supplied very helpful information on the Armenian Church and Armenia's Christian heritage, as did Fr. Krikor Maksoudian, Director of the Krikor and Clara Zohrab Information Center.

Some of the dramatic scenes in the book involve small planes. Hameed Afzal of Alpha Tango Flying Service in San Antonio was especially helpful in providing the necessary technical details. A number of other pilots offered valuable opinions and points of view-- Beth Neese, Pat O'Quinn, Bob Fodge and Alice Taylor--the sassy lady for whom Alpha Tango is named.

A few stalwarts accepted the challenge of true friendship and
read early drafts of *An Armenian Affair*, which was originally titled The *Courier--Amy, Sam, Howard, Linda, Jeri, Wade and Nuné*. A very special kind of gratitude is due my wife, Jo. She read An Armenian Affair not just once or twice, but many times--and allowed Tom and Ana and Mariah and Aleksandr and Sarkis and Karine and Raz to live in our house during those many months when the first draft was being written, an act of hospitality for which I am deeply grateful.

Fair Oaks Ranch,
September 2013